BAMBOO

A POST-APOCALYPTIC ODYSSEY

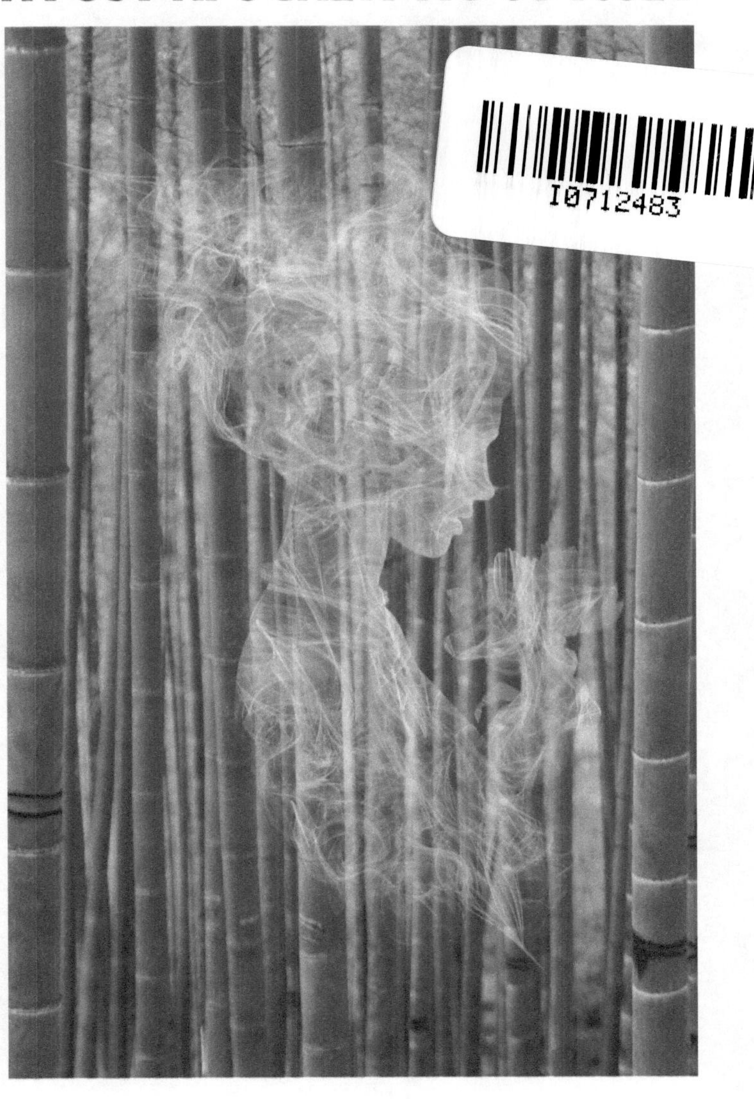

BAMBOO

A POST-APOCALYPTIC ODYSSEY

Exhibit Beta, "Quantum Interpolation of Data Extracted from Non-Dimensional Ephemera"

by

Clark Hilton

Books
Illuminated

Saint Petersburg, Florida

First Edition

Cover and book design by Ann Marie
Chapter art by Csaba X. Kasik from designs by Clark Hilton, © Clark Hilton
Translations of Praguean German to English by Felicia Fairhope
Edited by Shaun Duke, PhD

Publisher's Cataloging-in-Publication
(Provided by Cassidy Cataloguing Services, Inc.).
Names: Hilton, Clark, author.
Title: Bamboo : a post-apocalyptic odyssey / by Clark Hilton.
Description: First edition. | Saint Petersburg, Florida : Books Illuminated, [2023]
Identifiers: ISBN: 979-8-9886020-3-3 (hardback) | 979-8-9886020-4-0 (paperback) | 979-8-9886020-5-7 (ebook) | 979-8-9886020-6-4 (audiobook) | 979-8-9886020-7-1 (graphic novel) | LCCN: 2023921366
Subjects: LCSH: Runaway teenagers--Fiction. | Genetic engineering--Fiction. | Dystopias--Fiction. | Imaginary histories. | Bildungsromans. | Science fiction, American. | Fantasy fiction, American. | Adventure stories. | LCGFT: Apocalyptic fiction. | Science fiction. | Bildungsromans. | Romance fiction. | BISAC: FICTION / Science Fiction / Apocalyptic & Post-Apocalyptic. | FICTION / Science Fiction / Genetic Engineering. | FICTION / Coming of Age. | FICTION / Literary. | FICTION / Romance / Science Fiction. | FICTION / Fantasy / Epic.
Classification: LCC: PS3608.I4653 B36 2023 | DDC: 813/.6—dc23

For permission to use material from the book (other than for review purposes), please contact: permissions@booksilluminated.com.

For bulk purchases for educational use, please contact: bulkbookorders@booksilluminated.com.

Published by Books Illuminated, LLC, Saint Petersburg, Florida www.booksilluminated.com.

DEDICATION:

For Colleen,

sine qua non

"Science fiction writers foresee the inevitable, and although problems and catastrophes may be inevitable, solutions are not."

- Isaac Asimov

"Gilgamesh said to Urshanabi the boatman: 'Urshanabi, this plant is a wonderful plant. New life may be obtained by means of it. I will carry the thorny plant back to my city. I will give some of the plant to the elders there, to share among them, telling them it is called How-the-Old-Man-Once-Again-Becomes-A-Young-Man. And I will take my share of the magic plant, once more to become the one who is youngest and strongest.'"

- The Epic of Gilgamesh

EPIGRAPH:

There is a bamboo grove
around my house.
Several thousands stand together,
forming a placid shade.
Young shoots run wild,
blocking the roads here and there.
Old branches stretch all the way,
cutting across the sky.
Frosty winters have armed them
with a spiritual strength.
Rising mists wrap them
with the veil of profound mystery.
In their healthy beauty
they even rank with pine and oak,
Although they do not vie in grandeur
with peach and plum.
Their trunks are upright
and their knots are far between.
Their hearts are void of stuffing
and their roots sturdy.
Bamboo trees, I admire you
for your honesty and strength.
Be my friends, and stand
about my retreat until eternity.

-Ryōkan Taigu, Sōtō Zen Buddhist hermit/monk
(CE 1758–1831)

A NOTE TO THE READER:

I did not set out to write a novel.

By chance, I had encountered an object of curious construct and peculiar markings: a tiny holographic cube. Though not a scientist myself, I maintain ties with luminaries in a range of disciplines. I'd like to think they revel in my candid views on business and innovation; more likely, they find I am good at keeping a secret. From these genial notables, I assembled a technical team to decrypt and translate the colorful illusion. Techniques and findings are the subject of our paper, "Quantum Interpolation of Data Extracted from Non-Dimensional Ephemera Utilizing Contemporary Narrative Constructs."

Only after I began to collate materials for peer review did I realize the message extracted was not meant for a single recipient. It was a message for the world.

The source medium proved fragile, and a small percentage of data sectors were damaged or lost in processing. Most occurred in the latter parts of the text and are noted as: "STATUS: SECTOR LOST/ DAMAGED," along with a catalog number.

The object's origin remains elusive. The first node translated intimated that its creators were of some unknown future, which seemed to me fantastical. Whether the work of a civilization unborn, a precocious prankster or, equally plausible, a foreign psyop, I cannot be sure.

Some in our sci-tech team were, let's say, shy about methods; with budget and time always far from ideal, I was not one to check the dentition of a gift horse. As I am well short of the education required to verify the specifics of biology and physics depicted, I have breezed over some details in favor of reclaiming the tale's essence from its technological ether. In that imprecision, I beg the reader's indulgence of this unreliable narrator.

Because of the indeterminate origin of the cube, the rigors of translation, and the inclusion of reconstructed text, I am presenting the entire narrative as fiction. You can learn more about my endeavor and the technical team's methodologies from the materials at the end of this book.

Sincerely,
Clark Hilton

Contents

BOOK I: The Anomaly Was Barely Perceptible 1

BOOK II: We Use It for That, Too 15

BOOK III: What's the Unusual Way? 41

BOOK IV: Abrupt Flight from Tyranny 67

BOOK V: Monsters of the Night 81

BOOK VI: The Grasp of a Singularity 101

BOOK VII: A Tomb Made for the Living 115

BOOK VIII: Far Away and Phantom 143

BOOK IX: At One With the Vast Sky 207

BOOK X: A Threat So Unspeakable 259

BOOK XI: You Are Here 279

BOOK XII: A Storm, He Said, Was Coming 325

Postscript

Afterword

Technical Notes

Exhibit Alpha: "Gramercy from the Scions"

Acknowledgements

About

Reading Group Discussion Questions

Reflections and New Findings

More from Books Illuminated

Anathema

BOOK I:

The Anomaly Was Barely Perceptible

It was blind to the comeliness of nature. It knew nothing of art and poetry. It was numb to matters of the heart, deaf to the music of angels. It could not resolve beauty from the massless particles that coursed through its crystalline mind. And the astered tapestry before it was but fodder for its sextant internal.

It glided through the night, tracing lines in the moist ether. It flew invisible patterns parallel and perpendicular. It scribed obscure and lonely arcs on the unbounded obsidian. Its electric eyes scanned, secreting each observation in its manufactured memory.

It was recent to the world; its intellect imperfected. Its dreamless clockwork routed calculations to regions not enfeebled by its incompleteness. Within its spindled body, avionics hummed, pumps circulated hydraulic fluid, and servo motors oscillated at ultrasonic speeds. It was alone in its abstractions, with its fluids and vibrations and pulses of current.

And as the machine of pure reason surveyed its myriad systems, it determined its power stores, taxed by its nocturnal pursuit, verged on exhaustion.

The starred canopy conceded to the insistent glow that carved above from below.

It welcomed the dawn, the gray arrival anticipated with precision. It sensed the great disk rising hot and amber, bejeweling the expanse, and it angled its glassed wings eastward. It soared through the emergent morn, harvesting sustenance from the rays.

Energized, it resumed its quest. Its goal was singular: to sort signal from the noise that now extended to the periphery of its perception — the diamonded surface, liquid and changing, that arched to infinity.

The azure sky and the twinkle of wavelets on the capricious sea were, to it, merely impassive topologies and data points. It sampled the salted air, sifting for the anomalous. It grouped solids and liquids and gasses. It reconciled cones and rhomboids and geometries that altered over time — data stored without understanding, to be analyzed between cycles.

Diurnal currents rose in sultry spirals. The winged automaton rode those gentle updrafts, and from that vantage, it detected an anomaly statistically significant. An object resolved as a lazy amalgam of detritus congregated by wind and wave — castoffs chance-woven into a mat of disparate verdure. The conglomeration undulated, a random swell threatening to tear it asunder. And there amongst the wilting flora — the signature of life.

It tucked its wings, closing on where the mist danced with the faceted surface. A dark form circumnavigated the flotsam with predatory zeal, then plunged to the depths and vanished. This phenomenon it filed and marked for analysis.

It extended its metal talons and hovered for a moment before lighting on a twisted branch that jutted at an agonized angle from the loosely confederated raft. Its inertial sensors now satisfied the debris would support its two-kilogram mass, it rotated its head full compass. Crystal eyes absorbed wavelengths, observed relative motion, and matched same against its library. It catalogued inorganic objects among the organic: a long sleeve, brilliant white, severed at the shoulder; a straw hat with a tricolor band; a cushion in a floral pattern, worn from use.

The breeze ceased, and the facets of the shimmering sea became as glass. Its sharp and aquiline olfactory sensor took in the vapors. Putrescine and cadaverine — the scent of death.

Switching to archival analytics, it mapped anthropometric data to shapes among the dross. Six bipedal bioforms in tangled repose. Five exhibited high superficial reflectivity and a thermal signature equivalent to background. Respiration: negative. These five it cataloged in the "expired" set.

Its electric irises then focused on the sixth. Volume. Length. Surface and core temperatures. Skin: melanin-rich, with low superficial reflectivity, detectable beneath a thin white haze. Short raven locks, frosted with salt. Based on proportional statistics, an adolescent female. Respiration: positive.

It sorted this shape into the "non-expired" set.

She lay prone across the flotsam, her head hanging over the edge of the conglomeration, reflections of the sea glittering her fine features.

Now it hopped down beside her. Chemistry and chromosomes analyzed, attributes recorded — her essence compared to samples on file. A match. Its bronze talons clenched with the excitement of achieving objective, and it chirped.

The girl stirred. Her brine-encrusted eyelids fluttered. She lifted her head and squinted into the brightness. And the electro-mechanical thing observed her, and within its incomplete mind registered the spark of avuncular affection.

Vocalizations unfamiliar fractured its focus. It swiftly surveyed the horizon. An incongruity pierced the mists and the morning. Unapprehensive. Approaching.

And as the metal golem with the glassed feathers took flight, it knew: For the delicate being of raven hair and dark complexion, alone in the jewel sea — a storm was coming.

Gen did not yet know the pain of thirst, or of wounds stinging from salt. That was some days away. For now, hers was the pain of the not quite adult, not quite child — bound in the nervous constraints of zealous parenting.

The front door swished a mechanized goodbye behind her and hermetically sealed out the world from the thatched palm villa she called home. She inhaled the sweetness, glad to be on her own — at least until sundown, when she would again endure the anxious ministrations of her mother and the tedious admonitions of her father.

Hers was simply an errand: ferrying a container from the house to the field. Then she would lug back something vital and precious. As always, this one was the most important thing ever. Mother had arrested Gen's fantastical dream life — where she ruled in a glistening realm of friends and fun — for this sacred chore.

But she was determined to make the most of the day. After all, it was her birthday. Her sixteenth, they had told her. Of the many trailheads, she took the well-worn path to her shortcut.

The girl looked out over the expanse of green and the braided steel cable that cleaved the forest in two, then launched herself onto the zip-line's t-bar. The wire bobbed gently, her feet dangling.

She squeezed the power lever and sped over the verdant canopy — the motor purring electric bliss, its modest solar panel doubling as a shade from the blazing sun. With a smile of exhilaration and the wind tossing her short, curly locks, she held the handles just tight enough to prevent a fall. She didn't want to crush them — Edison had said it was the last good set, cobbled together from spares.

Gen sailed over the treetops across a chasm cut by ancient rains. The wilds in the endless canyon below were familiar, every leaf and rock and creature. Reassuringly predictable.

At this stage of her traverse, Gen's mind strayed to her favored fantasy, riding the zip-line to the gleaming skyscrapers of the big city, meeting new people, making friends her own age. The story's new layer: a handsome youth whose features remained formless — enthralled by her presence.

Mother wouldn't let me go, anyway. Not by myself.

The pulleys click-clacked as she passed a support pole, and the scenery below changed to the colorful groves of bananas, mangoes, and pineapples — a checkerboard of lush fruit trees pocked by conspicuous stands of golden bamboo undulating in the breeze.

It could have been the particular angle of the sun, and only at this hour, on this certain day, in this season of the year. She saw it for a moment, then no more — winding through the bamboo that abutted the pineapple rows and the trees heavy with fruit. In the perfected geometries of organized cultivation, the anomaly was barely perceptible: the ghost of a footpath. It meandered between the crops and beneath the forest canopy and faded into the lush horizon.

1.3

Gen had not yet sailed the forest canopy; had not yet accepted her consequential and petty chore; and had not espied the ancient path. That was some moments away. But monumental discovery comes at the price of awakening — most often, unpleasant.

A chrome-yellow orange tropical sun floated on the azure sky of a van Gogh dream. Froth rolled up sands so white as to glow, tumbling tiny islands of burnt umber seaweed to and fro. The lifeguard tower stood sentry over a crop of beachgoers melted into chaise lounges, its vigilant occupant scanning the shoreline of swimmers splashing in gentle waves. A bowrider sport boat sat beached on the sand.

Reclined on a beach chair was Gen, her mirrored aviator sunglasses perched on her perfect nose, twin suns curved into the lenses, a bead of sweat on her smooth brow. A strap of her one-piece bathing suit had ceded its hold on her shoulder. Her pocket-sized, waterproof notebook lay open on her lap to a page that began with some scholastic note-taking, punctuated by a few lines of a poem, then a fanciful drawing that occupied most of the page — all things proportionate to her interest. The writing instrument lay motionless in her delicate hand. Rustling palms fanned the bouquet of tanning oils that hung in the air — the bliss and the romance of a day at the shore. Impudent narrators intruded upon the sublimity of it all, and in incessant succession. A news anchor spoke:

> "United AgriMundial today announced the distribution of their new high-yield genetically modified corn to farmers worldwide. This enhanced species is insect- and herbicide-resistant, and produces both iodine and ascorbic acid, which will inhibit diseases like scurvy and hypothyroidism. U/A also plans to introduce a variant of soybean, lentils, and sorghum with the same qualitative modifications. Company spokesperson Chase 'Bud' Baardsen has this to tell us."

The image of a nattily dressed businessman occupied the picture-in-picture. With a cheery boardroom smile, Baardsen said:

> "This is a great advancement for the world food supply and world health. The company remains unconcerned about baseless assertions from some so-called authorities that our efforts will result in a monoculture. Because we have ensured that there are enough natural variants stored in the Svalbard Global Seed Vault in Norway, we are assured of expeditious rebound from crop failure should that unlikely event present itself. The company is so confident in the product's safety and the robustness of its contingency plan that United AgriMundial has converted all 28 species of its commercial animal feed to the new genome."

The news anchor filled the screen and toothily began the next article:

> "In other news: Planning a day at the beach? Well, bring your swim fins and a life insurance policy. The Cumbre Vieja stratovolcano on the Island of La Palma is at it again with a new series of eruptions. Nearly one-half of the entire island could collapse into the sea, with the potential of hundred-foot waves crossing the Atlantic, according to a science journal, Geographical Research Letters. Let's hope that more recent numerical

modeling studies are correct and that a massive flank failure like they're predicting is extremely rare. Such events have not occurred within recorded history. That said, there is a house-sized block of coral on Tonga's main island, Tongatapu, that somehow was tossed inland a football field's length, up thirty feet in elevation. They say it's the largest object torn from the seafloor and moved uphill by a tsunami. Still want to work on that tan?"

Had she been awake, Gen would have heard all this. She would have seen the video projected inside her sunglasses: images of the things and ideas encapsulated in the documentaries and newsreels obligated by her schooling. And she would have heard her mother calling to her from the piezo speaker, mingled with the trillion pixels that were the beach, the waves, the gleaming sand.

Had she been awake. But she was not.

Gen's eyes read the world of her REM sleep. She lay on warm sand, soothed by the rhythm of the ocean's waves, among sunbathers and a beached pleasure craft. She rose from her towel and the world bent, twisted, and transformed. Now she explored the contours of a gleaming city. Her ears filled with the sounds of machines and humanity moving all around her and into the subterranean causeways pulsing with the hectic heartbeat of urban life. She gazed skyward from street level into the canyon of soaring structures of concrete and steel and glass and dreams, and bridges across the sky. She strode along the concrete sidewalk past the cafés, bodegas, curio shops, and vendor carts, her joy effervescent as she caught sight of her coevals and compeers now rushing to her, smiles luminous in the brightness — a phalanx of hipsters in colorful shades and bandanas.

"Gen?" a voice said. She beamed at them. A chatter of hellos all around, and giggling. The tribe of five fellow teens — two girls, three boys — collected and swirled around her and one another as they progressed up the walk in their own bubble of consciousness, the world passing as mere scenery. A matched set, filled with the delicious possibility of pairing. The two other girls wore the latest flesh-forward styles, as did Gen; the boys' gear magnified a fresh-faced proto-manliness. Laughter and dance; savory food aromas; the holding of hands; and the feeling that all this would go on forever — as it rightly should — in dreams and otherwise.

"Gen?" another one said. She smiled. They rounded the corner of a marble-clad edifice, breaking into a run toward a vast lawn ringed by a sidewalk with benches, codgers walking dogs, and mothers pushing perambulators. One boy produced a ball, and the six made a game of kicking it among themselves, dodging trees and squirrels and picnic blankets in the lively, busy park.

She emerged from that dream back into the world of the sunny beach. In the distant waters, a singular wave lifted from its brethren, gathering height, its translucent blue blocking the horizon. The monster came ashore, licking up the pleasure boat in its curl. It towered in her mirrored glasses — its roar crescendoed in her ears. The thunderous breaker hurled its imponderable power at the swimmers and sunbathers. It plowed the sand with its colossal hand. Beachgoers abandoned their lounges and umbrellas and lotion and light reading — sprinting inland in screaming terror. She stood frozen, then turned and ran upshore until it lifted her feet from the sand. The massive wall of foaming thunder hammered down, crushing all before it. She floated, helpless, in the turbulence, among the debris and the bodies and the angry waters. A whirlpool caught her in its swirling dominion, sucking her down, the sea closing overhead…

"Gen? Are you studying? Gen!" said Mother's voice.

Startled and stirred, Gen whipped off her eyewear, still projecting their 3-D moving images inside the lenses. She blinked her hazel eyes, trying to wake up, and wiped a drip of saliva from the corner of her mouth. "Um, studying," she muttered, drowsy. "I'm done. Twenty-two lessons on global agricultural economics is enough excitement for one morning."

Gen squinted at the brightness and passed her palm over a sensor. The sun dimmed, and the ocean receded into an organic polymer memory slathered on the walls of the room, its self-configuring coating an amalgam of processor and data containing the knowledge of all that ever was, as curated, edited, and censored by the synthesis of experience and education and injury and the trillions of living cells that comprised Gen's mother.

Gen rose, picking up her little notebook and tossing the video sunglasses onto a side table. She snapped up her towel just as her beach chair collapsed into its carpet of simulated sand, which then retracted into the base of the beach-scene wall mural.

The space thusly returned to its normal state, a living room decorated with kitschy Mid-Century style replica tropical accoutrements. A lamp shaped like a palm tree perched on a table next to an art glass sculpture of a Portuguese man-o'-war jellyfish, its translucent tentacles trailing in delicate crystal threads of purple and blue — a beast best admired in the abstract. The two silvery striped residents of the aquarium navigated a ceramic fisherman and his mermaids in the ruins of their castle keep, a curtain of bubbles as their backdrop, the empty shell of a cone snail nearby. Twin cane bar stools cuddled up to the bamboo posts and thatch awning of a modest tiki bar whose counter hosted the collection of souvenir mugs shaped like Easter Island statues, along with the grass-skirted hula dancer doll, and the teak castanets dangling from a hook gathering dust — whimsical vestiges of the technology-laden compound's former life as a private retreat.

Notebook in hand and still waking up, Gen slung the towel over her shoulder and pierced the rainbow mist that removed lotions, mites, sweat, and simulated sea spray, and sanitized the skin. Surveying her perfected arms and legs, she pondered the pale, misproportioned people frolicking on the white sands of her sunny pixelated sanctuary, their skin ruddy and painful from their day of fun. Gen was the tone of the earth from head to toe, a shade immutable, she supposed, due to the precise daily sun-time prescribed by Mother. She was content with her consistency, as it made choosing the hues of her clothing easier and, importantly, faster, so she could satisfy her mood and still meet the demanding schedule her parents set for her each day. Though the day was special, she knew any abdication of chores or tutelage would be met with stern rebuke.

1.4

Stillness, broken only by the finger-shadows of palm fronds caressing the wall. The Polynesian wicker dresser beside the bedroom door remained perpetually cluttered with girlish trinkets: a small perfume bottle; combs and accessories; tiny molded soaps; an intricate, cast-metal miniature of a towering art deco stepped skyscraper from the Empire State — a smattering of prized possessions, perhaps more suitable for a younger child. The room looked like any teen's, although altogether lacking in the accoutrements of peer connections. Absent were the requisite photographs, sports trophies, science ribbons, souvenirs, and posters of the latest movie and music idols. Missing, too, was a mirror, an attempt by her mother to quell vain impulses out of a disdain for trading on one's looks. There were also concerns that, while Gen appeared to have grown normally (some would say exquisitely), she might develop some asymmetry that would cause the girl undue emotional distress. To date, that concern had proven unfounded.

She had a few of Mother's old books, strangely organic recordings made on wood pulp and glue and dark pigments. She had read them all; admittedly, most were beyond her understanding. *Great Expectations* by Charles Dickens. *Kidnapped!* by Robert Louis Stevenson. *The Trial* and *Metamorphosis* by Franz Kafka. Homer's *Odyssey* and Kahlil Gibran's *The Prophet*. These and a dozen more gathered dust on a high shelf. She was fond of poetry; Emily Dickinson and Edna St. Vincent Millay were her favorites. Yet, try after try, she could not emulate their heart or style. Mother had suggested that she needed to do more living. Gen had objected to that logic, as the two poets she admired had achieved so much, so early.

Showered and quick-dried, Gen swept into her bedchamber, tousling her short raven curls. Not the fussiest of housekeepers, she tossed her beach towel on top of the mound of clothes in a corner. Her notebook landed on the dresser, jostling the menagerie of trinkets. She searched under her bed for her sneaks. She sealed her laces, still half-dreaming of some far off sunny shore.

Adoring eyes gazed up from her small bed, a ring-tailed lemur plush toy nestled in the center of a bouquet of colorful pastel pillows. She picked up the little fellow, stroked his fake fur head, and put him back to bed. It was a gesture some might have interpreted as immature, but Gen's world was without these judgments. In that quiet instant, it crossed her mind that, today being her birthday, her mother might just allow her to deviate from the daily march of chores and permit some particle of fun for the remaining hours.

"Gen?" said Mother as the automatic door swished open. A slight, grandmotherly woman entered with an uneven gait aided by a leg brace. Her long silver hair cascaded over the shoulders of her crisp white lab coat, the ghost of a modern Madame Curie, notably too biologically aged to be the plausible parent of a teenager. Embroidered on the breast of the coat was "Dr. Marie Post, PhD."

"What have you been doing, Gen? I've been calling for you."

"I haven't been doing anything. I got done with my lessons and I took a shower. Do you really need to know everything I do?" Gen donned her favorite floral sun wrap over her swim attire.

"Let's not start that again," said Mother. Her hand wandered into her smock pocket. "Almost forgot why I came in here." She withdrew a stainless steel vial. "I need you to collect a field sample just as soon as you can get there. They'll be waiting for you."

"Right now?"

"Of course, now."

"But I can do what I want after. Right?"

"Ask your father."

"He's not my father!"

Her mother sighed at this chronic refrain.

Gen rose to her feet, knowing she could not avoid the errand. She accepted the vial with an exaggerated delicacy, eliciting a sigh from Mother, and then tucked the precious cargo into a pocket of her wrap.

"Don't lose it on your way back," said Mother. "Don't break it. Or spill it. Or shake it."

"I won't. Gosh, Mother. Can I just go now, please?" said Gen, sliding her personal notebook into another pocket.

"Please do. And I suppose you should have a little fun. It *is* your birthday. Just be back at 18:00 hours. We have a celebration planned."

"We…" she grumbled under her breath, moving past Mother to the door. "By the way, you *do* realize you're missing an earring, don't you?"

Mother fondled the delicate silver owl-dreamcatcher earring dangling from her left earlobe — her right lobe bare.

The bedroom door slid open and Gen slipped out.

She navigated the well-preserved furnishings of the living room toward the entrance, and the automatic front door swished open for her escape.

A masculine voice crackled from the living room's piezo speaker: "This is Father, Gen. Happy birthday. We will expect you at 18:00 hours. Please be careful and return uninjured."

As the front door swished shut after her, she muttered, "You're not my father."

BOOK II:

We Use It for That, Too

The polyhedron levitated patiently in the void. It caressed its confines with a prism of soft light and electric whispers. Beyond its cosmos, walls bare of medal or memento danced mesmerically to the rays. A cot, its bedcover taut. A dresser of flavorless functionality, no particle of sentiment atop. A chair in shadow, draped with a perma-white smock. A room crackling with ozone and loneliness.

The six simu-screens revolved about their axis, shuffling a sequence of encyclopedic recollections, each fading away only to call its successor. It altered its orientation, presenting refreshed facets to its observer, a rainbow projected on Mother's silver tresses.

Her leg went slack, her brace grazing the cot's frame; the metallic scrape voicing her deficiencies. She'd reprimanded herself over the years for choosing the least of the interior cubicles as her quarters; a pretense of personal sacrifice for the sake of the team. She shook off the bitter reminder.

Mother tended the queue of video lessons in Gen's curriculum, the cube diffracting with knowing and memories. A lock of her platinum hair tumbled forward, and she brushed it behind an ear. She hummed a command, speed-viewing the selections as she assembled the content and context she deemed most suitable to educate.

She re-queued the lesson on crops that the girl had napped through, and then loaded a new module — for Gen, a treat — the biology of sloths with toes of three and toes of two.

And there, as welcome as a welt: an interjected module, a deliberate disruption of her curated repertory. She selected the interloping lesson, and an image expanded to fill her view. The furrows in her brow deepened.

An animated globe in brilliant red and blue pirouetted and then settled alongside the toothily grinning visage of an on-camera host. In grand text: "Fair & Truthful with Karl Mucker." It was the sort of personality-driven news magazine that promised naked facts and gave equal time to the verisimilitude of confabulations, conflations, and manipulations.

In the monitor's glow, Mother groaned, a hand on her forehead. She shook her head. "Not this again. Why?!" A familiar rumble of rubber tracks beyond the door turned her attention, but it passed; she was still alone. She returned to the vintage video:

The bow-tied interviewer spewed to the camera. "And we're back. You're watching *Fair and Truthful* and you know me — Karl Mucker. Now we have bioscience genius Doctor Lee van Hauk here to share his news about what he calls the Eos Project, and his promised cure for the disease."

On a barstool at Mucker's high glass-top table sat an olive-complected man in his 30s, handsome and magnetic in professorial glasses and crisp lab smock. In the image's lower third, "Dr. Lee van Hauk, PhD" appeared, along with a string of credentials.

Van Hauk nodded. "Thank you, Karl. A correction — Methuselah isn't a single disease. It's the convergence of numerous agents. A tricky thing to untangle."

Mucker cleared his throat and pressed on. "With him today is Doctor Marie Post, also on the project."

Beside van Hauk squirmed a slim, winsome young woman with tresses the hue of harvest wheat. The on-screen text changed: "Dr. Marie L. Post, PhD, Eos Research Scientist." Her smock was tailored to circumscribe her physique. The single incongruity in her professional attire, handmade jewelry that spoke of borrowed Indigenous designs: bracelets of beads and string, a necklace with a feathered dreamcatcher, and earrings of turquoise and silver. The only caveat to her comeliness: a leg brace that left her restless on the high stool, studio lights glinting off the metal apparatus, betraying her infirmity through the transparent table top.

Mucker dived into his query. "Tell us about your plans. Just how does this cure work?"

Professor van Hauk parried with a brilliant smile on par with his host. "Yes. First, we must find it, which, as Principal Investigator, I will do. I will convene my team at a retreat — that is, a facility — graciously provided by my benefactor, Richard de Neckere, where a world-class research center is being built out as we speak."

"Ah yes, Neckere. The mercurial multi-billionaire." The corners of Mucker's lips curled up in a sugary smirk. "Now, about your colleague here — Doctor Post. Isn't it true that she is a card-carrying member of the medi-skeptic group OVA, the Odic Vitalist Association? Looking to inject some anti-science, pardon the pun? Not saying it's a bad thing. You can't deny that society's trust in science is on the wane. How will her affiliation with this group influence the research?"

Van Hauk opened his mouth, then astutely hesitated. Post's eyes darted from Mucker to her boss as the camera centered on her face.

Mother knew what came next. She hummed a command to speed through the unpleasantness:

"nonoIonlyattendedmaybeoneortworallieswellmaybehalfadozenthatwasaI neededtodomyownresearchopenmindednessisthekeytonewdiscoveriesane xplorationofalternativesislikehealthyrightIdonthaveanyregretsIwasyoungt hatswhatIbelievedthenthingshavechangedandIvelearnedalotanywaythatw asallpriortomycontractingpolioandIbearthescarsasyoucansee—"

Mother slowed the speed to normal:

"…I've long since renewed my adherence to conventional medicine."

"No atheists in foxholes, eh?" said Mucker, his gaze set on van Hauk. "We've had your university associate, Doctor Grumman, on this show many times. He won't be joining you?"

Van Hauk cleared his throat. "Grumman is a good man. He'll be holding things together for the next six months while I head Eos."

"Speaking of the university, some are saying this 'retreat' is your escape from the controversy over your most recent divorce and the persistent misconduct with coeds. There was even a poetry contest to describe your, um, behavior." Mucker consulted his notes. "Here we go. 'There was an old prof named van Hauk, Who drew dirty things in black chalk, The Nobel for biology, And so keen in morphology, Watching the girls like a hawk.'"

Van Hauk folded his arms, then put his hands back in his lap and squared his shoulders. "Look. Those charcoal nudes had no prurient intent. I've always had an interest in art, and I could draw before I could walk." His voice raised an octave.

"Just one more example of lesser minds attempting to tear down their betters. And hardly a stellar example of prose. We're here to talk about my science, aren't we?"

"Yes, but the public needs a complete picture of—"

"Let me tell you," said Van Hauk, painting on his most glistening smile, "about my first science project, when I was just a boy. An accidental one, really, and the catalyst for my entry into the profession. I was in the woods, and I came upon a group of kids gathered around a log. The focus of attention I could not make out, as I was in need of new glasses. Well, the other boys all of a sudden jumped back."

Mother commanded the recording to speed ahead — the video galloped:

"onlythenIunderstoodtheexercisecanafrogmaintainitsphysicalintegrityoro therwiseenduretheeffectsofafirecrackerplacedinthemostconvenientorifice theanswerofcoursewasthatitcouldnotandmyproximitytothesubjectoftheh ypothesisledtoacertainspecificenlightenmentintwopartsoneeviliseternala ndtwofrogscannotmakefastgetawaysnowIwascoveredwithorgansandappe ndagesoftheunluckyamphibianbutIwassofascinatedbytheuniquenessandsp ecificityofeachlittlepartthatItooktothereassemblyofthempiecebypieceuntil aroughapproximationofthisonceelivingcreatureappearedonmomskitchenta bleandsothisbaptisminblood—"

Mother commanded the presentation to resume its natural pace:

"…if you will, sparked my interest in biology, which, of course, translated well to biochemistry, resulting in a Nobel Prize." Van Hauk crossed his legs and leaned back, satisfied.

The interviewer's nose scrunched up, then he composed himself. "Quite a tale. I understand that the university abruptly concluded its collaboration with some of the big players in the biotech industry — steered, as they are, by flagless stockholders and not by pure medical advancement. Some say you've gotten quite wealthy. Are you leaving the university? What can you tell us about that?"

"Research requires backing. That's all there is to it," said van Hauk. "Whether it comes from a strapped governmental entity or the ample pockets of the private sector is less important than getting those results. The key is to drive the research forward most efficiently."

"So, during your sabbatical from the university, you headed up the uncertified floating labs at the behest of the 'krypto-kids,' as they're called — the ultra high net worth longevity club. And you cashed in a tidy sum in untraceable currency. Reports say the problem started there."

"That's not how it happened," van Hauk barked, then composed himself. "There were problems, yes, but their team had no discipline. They put someone else in charge and I resigned in protest. I was no longer there at the time of the unfortunate events. And when it was over, the crypto-currency I was paid with collapsed. It's entirely worthless."

"All the more reason for a fresh dupe. Isn't it true that this Eos thing is just a way to dodge blame and quietly mop up the mess?"

"I will not honor that question with an answer. This interview is over," said van Hauk, pulling the mini-microphone from his smock.

"That's not a yes or no, Doctor van Hauk," Mucker called after his receding form.

The empty seat conspicuous between — Mucker and Dr. Post shifted uncomfortably. Mucker put a finger to his earpiece, then flashed his veneers to someone off-camera.

"Well, then. Doctor Post. May I call you Marie?"

The young woman nodded with a stiff, thin-lipped smile at the intrusive familiarity.

"Marie, what's your role with this Eos retreat, and do you think, as Professor Bird does, that it'll be so easy to brew up a cure?"

"*Doctor van Hauk* and I have a plan of action that will speed the project. I will head up day-to-day lab operations, directing our team, and compiling my article notes for publication."

"Fair enough. Can you tell us a bit about yourself, Marie? What brought *you*... to bio-science?" He tipped his head to the left.

You. As a woman, she thought. The younger version of Mother withered at the question, so often danced out in these miserable interviews, and the useless cycle of responses that drained her credibility. She struggled to call up her canned answer. "Well, I—"

"Don't be shy, Marie. We're listening. Any hilarious childhood incidents you'd like to share?"

"Well, I was born… I mean, of course I was born… and raised in the Northwest, and my entire family is scientists, physicians, and academics, so bio-science became my alchemy." Her hand unconsciously toyed with her dreamcatcher pendant, the scratching picked up by her lavalier mic.

Mucker gestured toward his chest with a tiny wave, and Marie lowered her fidgeting hand from the jewelry.

"Science has always been, to me, as close as we come to true magic," she said. "Of course, my parents wouldn't fund my college program if I studied sorcery, so I chose biochemistry and molecular biology." She paused, hoping it would sound hilarious or profound. A pithy note to wind up the grueling interchange.

The interviewer tipped his head to the right, spaniel-like, retaining his stiff smile.

She continued, spilling to fill the pause. "I developed a talent for RNA splicing, which led to several roles at international food and drug giants. Prominent, uh… pharma companies…"

Post prattled about trivial career milestones and personal minutiae. Mucker, needing to fill the time — and not one to stop a perfectly good train wreck — let her exhaust her lungs.

"Eventually, I returned to academia," said Post. "I've always wanted to break barriers in science. Bring more ancient viewpoints into the present environment. Sometimes conventional medicine doesn't have all the answers."

The interviewer continued prodding and poking, tipping his head to one side, then the other, as if listening. Post filled in gaps and dug herself into holes for three more grueling minutes. When she realized she'd digressed into a tale about a pet cat, she stopped mid-sentence. "Should I go ahead and talk about the Eos Project now? I—"

"That's all the time we have. Thanks so much for coming, Misses Poke."

Dr. Post's jaw undulated with unspoken corrections as Mucker spun toward his close-up.

"Next week, we'll hear from an expert in how your gut can make better decisions than you can, how the spirit world influences your finances, and the latest wave of cures that come right from your medicine cabinet at home, or hey — maybe even from your vet. Till next time, I'm Karl Mucker."

The video ended, the grinning announcer now a still-life of plastic sentiment and big teeth. Mother dismissed the image and returned to the curriculum, the offending presentation having elbowed to the head of the queue. She sighed.

The blue lightning of a rekindled memory flooded her mind, the beguiling face of a young man of unfinished destiny, and a last stand against the dying of the world. In the waning days of that absolute reality, the chaos spawned by unreason eclipsed the disaster's inescapable magnitude. Apathy and anger overwrote scientific proscriptions. Vanity had wrought catastrophe. Greed and insolence had washed it into the waters and all had drunk with vigor. The bones of nations already fragile were crushed under a mass of inequity and intentional misinformation, the infected passing the catalyst through solids, liquids, and the air.

The tumult and kismet had quirked her own path. She had volunteered to care for the afflicted. If not for the remonstrating rabble that blocked her ingress to the overburdened clinic that day, she too might have succumbed.

Following the Eos Project press junket, she had been in the news almost daily, and the eccentricities of her likeness and her distinctive limp made for a toothsome target. Recognized in streets and shops, she secreted in a colleague's flat. She had lost touch with home and family and could only suppose their circumstances.

In these last and desperate hours she had acquiesced to a rendezvous with a young intern, likewise sans connections, for a carnal expression meant as defiance of destiny. His truancy was dismaying; she wondered if another more comely provided his balm, or if the disease had brutally preempted their appointment. She feared it some cosmic-level joke, and that she, in her sufferings and wounds self-inflicted and celibacy unintended, was the punchline. The romantic rebuff heightened the appeal of the esteemed professor's invitation to participate in Eos.

And through it all, she knew it was van Hauk's inadvertent contribution that had set this final course. An ironic reversal of fortune for those elites who sought immortality at any price; they had left open a door and the fomenters of our collective folly stole in.

Revisiting the mortifying interrogation had propelled her from the present to her would-be paramour and his untold fate. Would it not have been better to die, embraced in the superficialities of love, than to endure humanity's inglorious curtain?

"Marie!" Father's electric voice chimed in over the piezo speaker. "I have queued a new module into the lesson plan. The 'Fair & Truthful' interview. It details the period not long before our team embarked on our scientific research, which I think will be informative. And a counterbalance to the other materials."

"No, no. We talked about that one already. It's too negative. You'll just upset her. Honestly, Gen is simply not ready for such things."

"You are exhibiting unwarranted self-consciousness. You're projecting your emotions onto the subject. She must learn to think on her own. The material is appropriate for a sixteen-year-old."

"Well, you can say that, but she's just not developmentally—"

"We have little time left to lay the groundwork, as you know. You persist in feeding her crop reports and zoo animals and home movies. Two days ago, you agreed to introduce new stimuli that included the history of our work here. Without exposure to these facts, her education will be incomplete. I am in the chemicals repository. If you need assistance, you can find me here." A pop from the speaker, then silence.

Mother deleted the offending interview.

The looming shape of the landing spot heralded the end of Gen's glide above of the canyon. As the gentle thrill of the zip-line waned, she felt a growing anticipation: spending a little time with Edison. Gen leapt from the t-bar to the landing deck with the ease of a trapeze artist returning to her aerial platform. *I'll ask him where that path goes.* She checked her pockets for her notepad and Mother's sample vial; reassured as to their presence and integrity, she ambled down a familiar trail.

••·—•··

Edison peeled the yellow skin and savored the product of his toil. He leaned against the banana plant, contented for the moment, bearded cheeks pumping on the pulp. A bit slipped past his lips and plopped onto his faded floral print tropical shirt, the bulge of his belly thwarting gravity's inexorable pull to the Earth. He plucked the masticated morsel from the confluence of button and fabric and returned it to his enthusiastic maw, enjoying a moment of solitude and the shade of broad leaves. Wild gray hair poked from beneath his floppy straw hat, which bore a wide band of white, blue, and red; the colors, he often said, of a long-forgotten banner.

Edison was aged. He was rotund. And by every outward indication, he was happy.

The hand slammed through the trunk of the banana plant at chest height, just missing Edison's ample abdomen. He did not move. He did not flinch. The moist and slender hand withdrew with a sucking sound as the gash closed behind it.

"You're late," said Edison.

"Maybe a little," said Gen, wiping the sap of the banana plant on a corner of her wrap.

"Let me see."

Gen presented her hand.

"Good. No swelling. Pain?"

Gen shook her head.

"Never forget. Always tuck your thumb in."

"I know. Because it can break off."

Edison tucked his thumb into his palm. "That goes for knife hand strike, ridge hand strike, or straight punch." His thick, gnarled hand instinctively flowed through practiced forms in quick succession, the snaps of air stirring a banana leaf without contact. "The thumb is the 'Achilles' Heel' of the hand."

"And pull my toes back. And kick with only the ball of the foot. Or the edge. Or heel. Or, umm, the top part."

"The instep."

"Can I ask you something?"

"Sure."

"Why do I need to know this?"

"To protect yourself."

"From what?"

Edison took one more bite and tossed the rest of the banana, and then felt along the fresh wound in the plant's trunk, now sealing itself with sticky sap.

"I hope I didn't kill it," Gen said.

"Don't imagine so. Plants are amazing survivors. They can't run away, so they figured out how to heal quickly from just about any kind of attack."

"A plant, running." Gen giggled. "You try, Edison. Do that one." She pointed to a neighboring banana plant, its trunk unblemished.

"Oh, a human… most human beings, even with intensive training, would have a tough time doing that. I couldn't, even when I was in tournament shape. What I mean to say, young one, is that what you have is special. It is not to be used in anger. Or for power or revenge. Remember to use it only when you absolutely must, and with the greatest humility."

"I don't understand—"

A delta-shaped shadow undulated over Gen, Edison, and the banana the old man had tossed on the path, the strips of peel splayed like outstretched wings. Gen looked skyward and shaded her eyes. For an instant, it eclipsed the sun, then it was gone.

"What was that?" she asked.

"I'll show you later."

"Almost forgot. Here. This is for your sample." She produced the vial from her pocket.

"Gonna need a bigger one than that. I just had two cups of tea," Edison said with a chuckle.

"What?" said Gen, genuinely confused.

"Never mind."

The pair moved up the trail past meticulously plowed and weeded furrows of green bamboo plants standing straight and strong and tall — each the diameter of a man's thigh, soaring into the sky. A symphonic rendition of Vivaldi's *Spring* played softly from an outdoor speaker.

Six workers in pristine white hazmat suits groomed the base of each bamboo culm, cleared each of debris, and adjusted the drip irrigation, working the plantation like farm hands.

Edison swept his hand out toward the forest of bamboo. "I remember when I planted these from seed. The culmination of a life's work."

The nimble brown girl and her stocky grayed elder followed the trail of crooked stone pavers to his workshop, the industrial structure nearly consumed by a tapestry of vines, blending it with its verdant surrounds and nearly overwhelming the solar collectors on the roof. A windmill at its peak turned lazily from a tall stalk.

Edison tugged a huge mat of greenery from the black panels, tendrils and leaves fluttering to the ground. Then he opened the shop door.

A furious flapping of wings and the whine of gyros buzzed Gen's head. She ducked. "Edison?!"

"Sorry about that," he said with a grin. "Come on in."

Gen followed with some trepidation. "Wow. It looks all new in here." She gazed here and there.

"Yep. You'd never know there'd been a fire."

Inside, it was as clean and white as any laboratory. The same springtime symphony continued from the field and filled the room, emanating from a tiny player next to an intercom on Edison's work table. A menagerie of metallized tanks and delicate pipes angled between inscrutable pumps and motors, tubes spiraling from one to the next. Steam rose from the phalanx of metal hoppers, kettles, and drying kilns. Glass vials of liquids and powders perched on the counter, labels all laser-etched, all as she remembered.

She surveilled the lab's restored appointments from tiles to rafters, a new reality belying her recollections. Here and there, intimations of inferno, where gray ash sullied surfaces either resistant to remediation or impractical to replace. And here and there loitered stools of incongruous rattan liberated from an unknown venue, their lacquer scorched, though manifestly functional.

Positioned at the premises' peak, amongst the patchwork of repair, a late addition: a small flap swinging from mismatched hinges, the doll-sized door situated where no thing could crawl up to it nor down from it. A long peg extended beneath and perpendicular, the protuberance inscrutable.

At a more anthropomorphic altitude, a shelf spanned the breadth of the lab's short side, stacks of aged tomes hodgepodged upon it. Their decayed covers lent an earthy essence to the scent of ozone and sanitized steel. A selection of classic literature and poetry, made curious by their residence betwixt manuals solely scientific. Shelly. Atwood. Eliot. Ballard. Teasdale. Books in exile, banished to this alchemical Elba — deemed by Mother too disruptive to risk their sequester in the main house, within easy reach of an unformed mind. Books familiar; Edison having read to Gen from these dangerous pages in surreptitious and avuncular tones. His voice would waft through the lab, a cloud of ideas Gen scarcely comprehended, though she adored the meter of the verse and she knew the words were important.

To Gen, this place of patience and affection *was* Edison. Surely he had a house somewhere in Eos, she supposed, although she had never seen it. Her eyes fell upon a cot of canvas and bamboo tucked under a table. *Maybe he never leaves this room.* Relegated to a lonely corner was Edison's bamboo desk, its wicker weavings frayed, credenza freshly singed. There exalted his vintage equipment: a rusting transmitter, its analog meters asleep. Affixed to its side were the last spare parts he had — survivors clinging to a shipwreck. Beside it, a microphone, an electrical modernist art piece cast from material long gone brittle. Black cables snaked outside to the metal rod that reached skyward beyond the roofline. Alone at night, if atmospheric conditions were favorable, Edison would power the machine and speak to the microphone. "Fat Man to Carrington" was his mantra, repeating words and numbers for hours, calling to a colleague on the other side of the world who would not answer. Once, Gen had run a late-night errand for her mother. She had found Edison at the radio, its dials alive with power, its glass eyes aglow. He seemed to be laughing, his rotund chest heaving uncontrollably. She touched his shoulder. He could not respond, the woven desktop damp with tears.

Gen perused a tidy arrangement of framed certificates, freshly mounted on the wall just above the radio set. Among various foreign-sounding words, each featured a name. "Edison Bell. That's you."

"Yep," Edison replied. "Finally found a place to hang 'em up." He pointed to each, in turn. "Bachelors, masters, doctorate. Triple major in chemistry, horticulture, and electronics."

"Mother has one, too," said Gen. "What do they mean?"

Edison chuckled. "They mean I was overeducated and underemployed. That's why I came to Eos. There were three vacant job openings." He caught Gen's puzzled gaze. "Anyway, I'm here now."

Gen's eyes danced across Edison's perpetually bustling work bench. Nested among electronic miscellanea: PC boards, microchips, a claw foot with pneumatic talons, and a bronze wing peppered with photovoltaics. Something gazed back at her — a spherical electronic eye. It blinked. "Looks like a bird."

"It is," said Edison. "Well, those are spares. You briefly met the proof of concept."

"What does it do?"

"Bird stuff."

Gen stroked the finely crafted feathers of the wing, inexplicably the work of Edison's plump and gnarled hands.

"Ever tell you about my dog? How I fixed his leg?" Edison said. "I took some chips from an old phone, formed some scrap aluminum, and added a few parts I found at a garage sale. Anyway, I thought to myself, why not build a whole new animal?"

"If you fixed your dog's leg, why not fix Mother's?"

Edison chuckled. "Well, um… Let's say she wouldn't sit still for anything like that." The old man turned off the music and then leaned into the intercom. "Cut me a sample from row three, culm five, node eight. About 100 grams should do it."

Gen picked up the little music player, turning it over in her hand. "You must really like this music."

"Kind of tired of it, actually. But it helps the bamboo grow. At least I'd like to think so."

"Now you sound like Mother with her 'oneness' stuff."

"Something like that. Plants and animals are pretty much the same thing, you know. Humans share about fifty percent of our DNA with trees, almost that much with cabbage," he said. "You don't have anything against cabbage, do you, Gen?"

She giggled. "Well, no." Her fingers explored the arcane contrivance with its petite speaker and volume control.

"It's piezoelectric. Let me show you." With his pinkie nail, Edison flipped out a miniature handle, then cranked it in tiny circles. He turned it back on and handed it to her, the sound of strings and woodwinds filling the room.

She rotated the handle a few times, then returned the player to the worktable, where it resumed belting forth its symphony into the intercom.

A side door opened, admitting a hazmat-suited worker into the decontamination stall. Mist enveloped him, then disbursed. He opened the glass inner door and presented his sample case to Edison. "Here you go. Celebrate later?" he said, then stopped short, oddly hesitant. "Oh. Hello Gen."

"Hi Dr. Wellesley," Gen replied, recognizing him through the visor of his helmet, a shock of gray hair hanging in his eyes. The man nodded and took off through the decontamination stall.

"Let's get this processed," said Edison. He brought the sample case to a table, slipped on rubber gloves, then snapped up a pair of tongs and loaded the bamboo stalk section into a chamber on one of the mysterious machines. He uncapped the metal vial that Gen had brought, mounted it in a receptacle on the machine and then pressed a series of buttons. A monitor flashed a cryptic readout as it pulverized and processed the plant matter. "Your mother's going to be really happy. If that's possible."

Gen snickered, then thought about it. "How come?"

"This proves we've controlled programmed cell death," said Edison with a gleam in his eye. "It's been a long time coming. This species of bamboo flowers every 130 years, and we've stopped it from going to seed and dying. This entire field would have been brown and dry."

"Programmed cell death? That sounds bad."

"It can be good. The human body uses it to kill off defective cells. Most animals and plants have a pre-programmed time when cells in their body die. Bamboo, of course, is curious because the entire species dies simultaneously, no matter where they are in the world. Makes it a great test subject."

Having completed its processing, the machine ended its readout and dispensed the material into the vial. Edison gently capped it. He wiped the exterior of imagined crumbs and presented it to Gen.

"Don't I need gloves?" she asked.

"Nah. As long as you keep the stopper on, you won't contaminate it."

Gen nodded, a little offended. "Okay." She slipped the vial back into a pocket of her wrap.

Edison leaned into the intercom. "Everyone. Come on inside and wish Gen a happy birthday."

"How did you know?"

"How could I forget?" He set out an assortment of laboratory glassware: beakers, flasks, and graduated cylinders. He grabbed a beaker, moved to a spigot that protruded from the rotund copper barrel of another contraption, and turned the tap.

"Another sample?" asked Gen.

"Yep, this one's for me," he said, downing the vaporous yellow liquid, huffing, then wiping his lips.

"What's that?"

"Bamboo liquor. Fermented from the surplus of our experiments. Waste not..."

"Can I try it?"

"You're not old enough. Besides, you wouldn't like it."

Gen frowned.

Edison relented. He selected a small test tube from his supply rack, then dribbled-in a finger of the stuff. "Don't tell your mom." He handed her the vessel with a wink.

She sniffed it. Sweet. She sipped — coughed, choked, spat, exhaled fumes — her throat afire with the high-octane concoction. She stomped her feet and grimaced. "Tastes like cleaning fluid!"

"We use it for that, too. You were warned." Edison chuckled. "It's flammable. Take my word for it." He glanced up.

Gen followed his eyes to a charred corner of the workshop ceiling, above the still.

With a whoosh, the six white-suited workers shuffled into the workshop through the decontamination chamber door. Edison turned up the volume a little on the music player's symphonic selection.

The first, Rhodes, flipped off his headgear and took up a beaker. "Hit me," he said, and Edison obliged. The other five doffed their hoods as well, each gray-haired and impeccably groomed — all PhDs, as their embroidered names affirmed. Three men, Cornell, Wellesley, and Tufts, and two women, Laurel and Ivy. Each took one of the varied vessels, an ounce or so of the liquor swirling at the bottom.

"To programmed cell death," said Tufts.

"To programmed cell death," said the others in unison as they raised their glassware.

"Long may it live," said Wellesley, touching his vessel to each of theirs with a clink.

Rhodes, having quickly drained his glass, pushed his way back to the nozzle and refilled.

"Take it easy, Rhodes," said Cornell.

Rhodes knocked back the beverage, and drew another from the stainless steel tap, glaring a challenge at Cornell.

"Happy birthday, Gen," offered Laurel, lifting her glass a tad. The others halfheartedly chimed in and then downed their drinks.

Gen realized Rhodes was staring at her; she took a step back toward Edison.

"We haven't heard anything different for years and years. What I'd give to hear some new music," shouted Rhodes. He traded his glass for the music player. "How about some Beatles or Rolling Stones?" He held out his left hand, twiddling his gloved fingers, using the music player to make tiny picking strokes at his belt line with his right hand; he bobbed his head and hummed the Beatles' "Birthday."

Gen didn't know what to make of the man's kinetic spasms.

"Knock it off, Rhodes," said Wellesley.

Rhodes picked up his glass, drained it, and refilled. "You know something? There was once a full bar in the main house. Every type of brandy, rye, and scotch, and two-dozen after-dinner liqueurs. There was Kahlúa, and Irish Cream, and fancy drinks in pineapples and coconuts, with little paper umbrellas…"

Edison glanced at Ivy and shook his head — his eyes begging for her aid.

"Now is not the best time for this discussion," said Ivy, her brow furrowed.

"And there was a pool, before her father turned it into a cistern," said Rhodes, pointing a pinkie at Gen, "And there were girls by the pool…"

"We can reminisce another time," said Edison, attempting to disarm him of the loaded beaker, but Rhodes retreated to the still and rearmed.

"Before he effed everything up and took the world with him," said Rhodes as he downed another drink.

"Shut up. There wasn't much left by then, anyway," said Tufts.

"There was always hope," said Edison.

Gen searched Edison's face, puzzled by a history she'd never heard.

"Such a genius. He couldn't even check his fuel tanks before he took off," said Rhodes.

"Just let it go," said Edison.

"Maker of monsters," said Rhodes.

Ivy whispered to Gen, "He gets this way when he has a nip. Don't mind him."

Rhodes spun to Ivy. "Mind your business. I'm just drinking this fine bamboo liquor. That's all I'm doing. I'm not saying anything. I'm not saying anything at all." Rhodes pointed at the girl. "She's an aberration. That's all I'm saying."

Gen took another step backward, hoping to make herself a smaller target.

Laurel, wistful, chimed in. "I kind of liked it better when there were cities and… And we could have proper parties. Things like that."

Rhodes tossed the music player on the floor and crushed it underfoot. The tune stopped with a crunch.

Upset and confused, Gen burst outside.

2.3

Edison found Gen crouched between the culms, the mighty stalks towering above her, many times the height of her home. The girl was poking the soil with a twig. She rose, but didn't face him.

"He's mean. They're all mean to me," Gen said, tears brimming.

"They're just exhausted, Gen. We've been at this for a very long time."

"He broke your music player. Aren't you mad?"

"I think they're mostly tired of me dwelling in the past."

"I don't understand," Gen said. "And what did he mean about rocks and bugs?"

"Stones and Beatles. Those were names of popular… never mind."

"But why does he hate me?"

"Apologies, Gen. Everyone just had a little too much to drink." He put his arm affectionately around her shoulder and gave her a squeeze.

She hugged him back, and then let him lead her from the bamboo field. Gen saw a shadow of something stretching its wings. She turned and looked at the apex of the workshop roof, an owl-like creature perched there. The afternoon sun glinted off its bronze feathers. "It's watching us."

"Ah, that's what I was going to show you," said Edison, grateful for the distraction. "That's Hoyl. My avian automaton. The rats think it's an owl. Keeps 'em out of the crops."

Gen offered her arm and made a kissing sound to beckon it to her.

"Careful. Talons," warned Edison.

Hoyl's heart spun up with a high-speed whir. It spread its wings, which oscillated more like a hummingbird's than an owl's. The bird-shaped machine lifted off and hovered. Then it flew in a wide arc, deftly avoiding the palms and stalks of bamboo encroaching on the little clearing. Hoyl looked down with its sensor eyes, diligently scanning, calculating speed and distance, factoring in the light breeze. Bird-like, but cold; metallic; pure objective. Hoyl descended toward Gen's outstretched arm, making a few fine adjustments. Calibrating. Its steel talons opened. As its claws closed around her forearm, Gen gasped, but held still. Blood pooled around the indents in her arm. The owl's head rotated 180 degrees, and it looked directly into Gen's eyes — curious, though innocently indifferent to her pain.

"Why's it staring at me?" she asked, cringing.

"It's imprinting on you, getting to know who you are. That way, it will know you're not prey. You're family now. Of course, it's not quite all programmed. I want to add speech and some other functions."

"Imprinting? You mean like a baby chicken? I don't want any stupid robot thinking I'm its mother."

Edison's smile faded.

Gen realized she'd hurt her friend's feelings. "I mean, it's nice, though. I like the feathers. Photovoltaic?"

Edison nodded. "Hoyl. Time to go to work." The automaton swiveled its head toward Edison, chirped once, spread its metal wings, and took to the air.

Gen watched it rise above the palms. She grabbed her arm, bleeding from where the bird's talons pierced her flesh.

The metal creature dived into the bamboo rows and pounced on an unsuspecting something.

Edison pulled a kerchief from his pocket and wiped the blood from her arm. "Sorry. It needs some fine tuning. I need to teach it not to clamp down so hard."

Gen held her arm in the sunlight. Her punctures stopped bleeding. After a few seconds, they began closing. Edison watched, transfixed.

"Edison, silly, what are you staring at?"

"Always fascinating. That might not last forever, Gen. Better learn how to be careful."

"You worry too much." She grinned and shook her head.

"I *promised* your mother and father that I'd always watch over you, that's all," Edison replied tenderly.

"He's not my father!" she retorted, then realized he wasn't teasing her.

By the time Edison looked again, Gen's wounds had healed, the redness diminishing by the second.

A swish above their heads signaled that Hoyl was sweeping the furrows. The pair's eyes followed the feathered machine as it swooped on a brushy corner of the field, then arced into the sky.

From the workshop, a crash — Edison and Gen turned. When laughter bubbled from within the shed, Edison sighed. "I'll clean that up later."

Gen idly slipped her hand into her wrap pocket, finding the vial there. "I guess I'd better go back," she said, turning toward the forest. She stopped and turned around.

"Edison?"

"Yep?"

"I saw something. When I was up on the zip-line. There's a path running through the bamboo stands and into the forest. That way." She pointed. "I never noticed it before. Where does it go?"

"Well, heck. That's just the old 'Welcome Trail' from way back when Eos was a resort. That's where they used to bring people up."

"People came here? From the city?" asked Gen, wide-eyed.

"I suppose…" His eyes took to a horizon only he could see.

She waited for an answer that she knew would never come. Adults were prone to incomplete explanations.

"Tell your mother and father congratulations."

"He's not my father…" she said, turning again to leave.

Hoyl glided overhead, wings humming with electric precision. It tallied its instrumentation, adjusted gyros, and tickled the ground with its photonic altimeter. It intercepted Gen's path, positioning itself eye-to-eye with the girl in retrograde hover, agile as a hummingbird. Hoyl measured her core and surface temperatures and heat reflectivity. It quantified surface chroma and albedo and then stored her exterior dimensions and geometries in its permanent memory. It metered pupil dilation versus emotional response, recorded reflex rates, and voice-matched to its library.

Gen stuck her tongue out at it.

It followed her for a moment, then circled back to Edison, landing on his shoulder.

"Good boy," said Edison. The bird's steel talons pierced Edison's tropical shirt, leaving the printed white hibiscus petals pocked with blood. Edison winced. "Reduce talon pressure, please." He put a finger inside his collar to feel the wound. He looked at the blood on his fingertip and said, "Hoyl. Sample." A slot on the bird's breast opened, exposing a small slide surrounded with circuitry. He pressed the bloody digit on the slide. The slot withdrew into the mechanism. "A promise is a *promise.*" He hailed Gen. "Head straight back, would you?"

Gen waved without turning around.

And then, as if an afterthought, Edison called out, "Happy birthday." Gen would go her own way in her own time. Good for her, he thought. Little acts of rebellion, once in a while, were healthy. She was turning out to be like a typical teen. He wondered if she had somehow intuited her place in this world.

He watched her recede; the bamboo occulting her now in their stoic prolificacy. He considered how much she was like that bamboo: straight, strong, and resilient to forces of man and nature. And he wondered what adventures might await her. Edison doffed his straw hat and looked up into the glass-clear azure sky. He wetted a finger and thrust it into the air, as if to read the weather.

He knew: For Gen, a storm was coming.

2.4

The forest was rife with delightful distractions, and Gen was in a mood to experience them all before the day's chapter closed. Edison's results, the birthday activities — these things could wait. The waning daylight would not.

She could predict the annual ritual. They would pretend she was having fun, even though she wasn't. They would fixate on her as they often did. Scrutinize her like one of their lab experiments, as if her height and weight, pH, oxygen levels, and other general chemistries were more important than her happiness. They simply didn't understand her at all.

Gen pushed through a stand of bamboo into the lush underbrush, then broke into a run, stepping skillfully between plants and tree roots. Pushed herself to run harder. Grabbed an overhanging tree limb, startling a ring-tailed lemur as she swung herself over a mud puddle where a pair of large tortoises cooled themselves. Charged up to a boulder as tall as she was, leapt on top, then hopped down the other side — part ape, part gazelle. A green snake lunged. She dodged it without flinching.

She sprinted upslope to the mount's round peak, an outcrop of gray basalt burnished by the winds. She doffed her sun wrap, her notepad and the item for Mother still safe in a pocket, then set her footwear atop. Gen poised on the precipice, and with a most subtle flex of muscle, leapt high into space. She arced away from the imposing crag, toward the great pool of green-blue far below that anticipated the young Aphrodite's return. As the lithe missile pierced the surface, a flock of pink flamingos took flight.

The girl glided to the depths, suspended in the womb-warmth of her other mother. A constellation of silver bubbles danced in her wake, and small fish followed, mistaking the sparkling beads for their shoal. A shadow passed overhead; Edison's mechanical bird, perhaps. She languidly returned to the surface, more afterthought than need.

Not Hoyl; instead, the familiar buzz of her parents' hovering drone, propellers stirring an indentation into the water.

"Gen, come back home immediately," came her mother's voice from its tinny speaker.

"We are waiting," her father's voice chimed in.

Gen splashed water up at the loitering sentinel. "Spies!" she barked back, only half kidding.

2.5

The calm evening sky offered a pink-blue sunset that pained Gen to bid goodbye. She headed up a narrow path her feet knew well. Mother had taken her here when she was small, and she had come here many times by herself. The rock she always tripped over. The soft spot with the mud. The vines and roots encroaching. She remembered that time when... She couldn't quite resolve the details. Her memories composed the outer edges of a jigsaw puzzle; they did not add up to a greater whole. Footnotes on events, but not the events. Shorthand for a childhood not quite remembered, yet so close in time that recalling it brought frustration. *Maybe that's how it's supposed to be, now that I'm almost a woman.* One's self, shedding its skin to emerge into the adult form, leaving behind the ghostly remains of the juvenile — the polyp of a jellyfish, the chrysalis of a butterfly, the husk of a locust, the brown and shriveled blossom dropping to the forest floor. Memories turning to dust, favoring the future.

She tried hard to remember all the other birthdays, but beyond the most recent few, there were no recollections. Her childhood was there, and yet somehow it wasn't.

Her toe dragged on something hard, jutting up from the leafy ground. She turned around to see what had tripped her. A paver lay tilted and exposed from a recent rain. She pushed aside a branch. She was at the crossroads of a leaf-covered but obvious path, perpendicular to her accustomed route. In the small clearing a few yards beyond, she could see a bench like others she'd seen here and there around Eos, except this one was weathered and ancient. Seedlings sprouted from the leaf mulch accumulated on the seat, cleared on one end for a recent, solitary visitor.

The trail continued into the woods. It moved in the same direction as the path that she glimpsed from the zip-line — the one that Edison hinted was for people from the city. *This would be fun to explore.* With the sun waning, her investigation would have to wait for another day.

She snapped a thin branch to mark the trailhead.

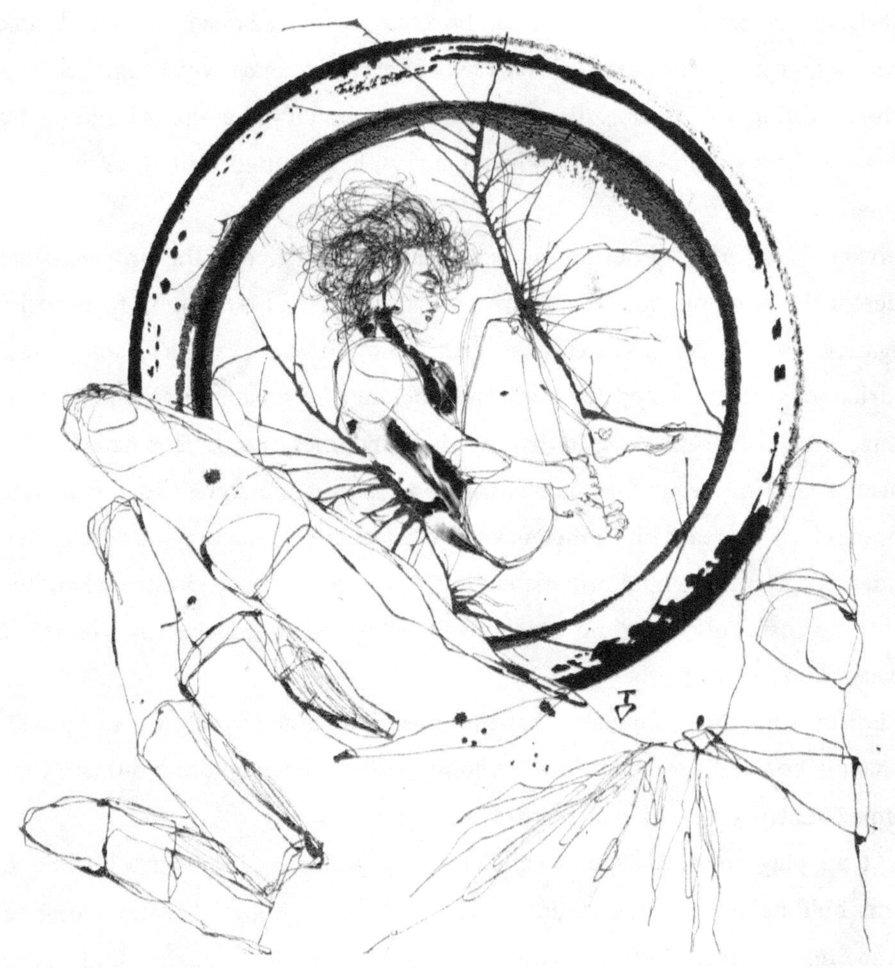

BOOK III:

What's the Unusual Way?

Dread weighed down Gen's feet as she reached the clearing not far from her home. A feeding flock of scarlet ibises loped out of her way, then resumed their search for grubs. The pesky drone buzzed on ahead, shooing the ibises to flight.

The thatch roof of her home came into view. The house had originated many years prior as a private retreat. Its designers had skinned its bones in natural materials to resemble an idealized bamboo hut, as if the famed architect Frank Lloyd Wright had gone green. Grass reeds and palm fronds wove together in a warm rendition of informal living, a perfected imitation of homebuilding by natives of some tropical land, reimagined with trappings suited to wealthy travelers.

Atop a long pole sprouting incongruously from the roof, the propeller-like blades of the windmill rotated dispirited in the near-still air, failing to meet its obligation to the home's electrical grid. The gleaming, black photovoltaic quadrilaterals perched atop the roof and pocking the greater surrounds would capture enough energy to exceed their needs many times over. Edison had proudly informed Gen on several occasions that one of his ancestors had invented a compound to increase the efficiency of the panels. In theory, he'd said, the augmented invention could provide endless power for residences everywhere for little to no cost. This was of no concern to Gen, her life untouched by worries of scarcity from any quarter.

Edison sometimes lamented that the invention came too late for the world, not having gone into production when most needed. "Back before mountain tops became countries," he'd kidded, but did not explain.

At his play on words, Gen's childish imagination would conjure kings and queens holding court in the clouds, each peak its own imperial realm, closer to heaven than humankind could have imagined in their quaint and facile philosophies. At the sight of the lazy windmill and Edison's proud panels, this whimsical notion again formed in her consciousness. It did not entertain her today, though, filled with apprehension as she was.

The parental doppelgänger returned to its cupola on the roof, the drone's propellers seeming to mock her as it glided into its little garage, evicting a pair of green parrots inspecting the ephemeral vacancy. The drone wiped its glass eye, then settled into its charger to await the next time she stayed away too long.

3.2

Gen hesitated just beyond the purview of the sensor eye that granted or forbade entry, half-dreading whatever birthday silliness her parents would make her endure, half-expecting a scolding for missing the appointment, just like on her birthday previous. They always served up some sort of dessert — typically pineapple cake, admittedly her favorite — but then they insisted she extinguish, in one breath, tiny candles that increased in number with each cycle. She wondered if it was supposed to be fun or merely one more of the many physical and intellectual tests they imposed on her. On any other day, her parents never emitted expressions of joy and certainly never sang; on her birthday they would greet her with delight, then sing her the same silly song, one with her name in it, which she had presumed they made up just for her.

She stepped forward. The eye scanned, quantified, compared to the profile library, and admitted the girl.

The cloying aroma of baked pineapple hung heavily in the dim, empty house. For a fleeting moment, she imagined Mother popping out of the hallway with festive tidings. Before her on the dining table was an abandoned spread — a celebration halted midpoint. A platter hosted a cake topped with several candles melted and snuffed out, one slice already gone, and two more candles with goo on the bottom beside the sticky cake server. One clean plate, empty, a fork beside. On all the birthdays she could recall, they had greeted her with smiles and levity and lit candles and a chorus of, "Surprise!" She felt the heart-sink of Mother's disapproval over something only mothers would disapprove.

Lost amid Gen's thoughts and the ambient whirs, hums, bubbles, and drones, a rhythmic, squeaking rumble tracked across the floor, approaching her from behind. A shadow followed up her back until it towered over her.

"You are late. We started without you," said her father.

Gen jumped. She spun around, fists up, thumbs tucked as Edison had instructed. "Don't sneak up on me like that."

"Do not be late again," said her father, his voice crackling with electronic noise.

"And stop bossing me. You're not my father."

"I'm as much of a father as you've ever had."

Ignoring his unsolicited rejoinder, she was already heading toward the alcohol-suffused sanctuary of her mother.

3.3

Gen dragged an anchor of apprehension down the hall to Mother's lab. Another ultrasonic beam sensed her, scanned her, scanned her again as if unsure, and then the thick glass door reluctantly disappeared into a wall, the surge of sterilized air a last protestation to her ingress. She postponed the inevitable collision over her tardiness by orbiting at a prudent radius from the maternal singularity.

In the lab's illuminated epicenter, the electron microscope and DNA sequencer occupied an exalted locus, disused dust covers neatly folded beside. Mother labored over the scope's ocular lens, twisting the coarse and fine adjustments, idly tucking a strand of long, white hair behind her ear.

The essence of a physician's office saturated the perfectly conditioned air, free of dust, bacteria, viruses, and indiscipline. Though the lab was stark and white and stainless steel, it was Gen's second home. Small animal cages, empty for as long as she could remember, filled another wall; the scent of rodents just detectible over the disinfectants and chemicals bubbling away on the long tabletops. Paraphernalia common to laboratories peppered every surface: pipettes, scales, centrifuges, Bunsen burners, freezers, hot plates, coolers, stirrers, water baths, beakers, and test tubes. A metal hood and chimney stood ready to usher chemical gases outside. An autoclave on a chromium cart sterilized the tools of this trade.

Heat rippled from the steel skin of a commercial medical waste incinerator, outsized bolts holding it fast to a thick concrete platform. The "pot belly stove," as Mother called it, exhausted the discards of her pursuits up the lab's flue.

The hydroponic garden was aglow with soft hues of blue and red. It dominated a windowless wall, parallel canals of enriched fluid circulating amongst the roots of eager seedlings, reaching for the artificial sunlight. The metal fixtures buzzed sympathetically with the thrum of pumps, autoclaves, transformers, and deep freeze compressors.

In the lone window hung a hoop woven with a delicate, threaded web, feathers suspended from the lower half of the circle: a dreamcatcher installed by Mother. For a few moments each day, the sun would paint the delicate and organic spirit-shadow against the technological realm.

A faint glow emanated from a handmade shrine across the room, a polished specimen of lapis lazuli stone at its center, a lit candle before it, hyacinth blossom offerings at its feet. Gen surreptitiously picked up a blossom, absorbed its sweet scent, then placed it back on the shrine. If not for the present tension, the teen would have chided Mother for her decidedly unscientific penchant for magic and myth; her faith in kismet, fortuity, the great consciousness, and in the stars. Now was not the time.

"I see you. Give me just a couple minutes," said Mother, her eyes affixed to the microscope's eyepiece. She paused to note observations in her journal and returned to the ocular lens.

Gen hung back and peered into the little Pyrex window of a tabletop oven, baking away, its exhaust fan humming. Inside, something glowed white-hot.

"Use the UV goggles," Mother scolded.

The reproach quashed Gen's interest in the goings-on in the oven. She then entered the dark section of the lab. White light, her mother had claimed, was toxic to the ongoing experiment there. The glass-fronted steel lockers, each perhaps large enough to accommodate a pair of shoes, formed a grid, the dimensions of a residential window. She always liked the sound of the little lockers opening and closing as her parents tended to whatever resided there, sealing so solidly and confidently. She peered into one, her eyes adjusting to the near darkness. An apparatus in miniature — a Ferris wheel — slowly rotated glass vials bathed in the softest cyan, plastic tubes pulsing nutrient to each, a small fan dispersing conditioned air over the experiment's platform. Each vial on the wheel contained a single specimen of biological tissue the size of a cotton swab's tip, cylindrical like the punch her mother used to sample crops. Gen subconsciously felt along the row of annular keloids on her upper arm, which roughly matched the dimensions of the specimens in the revolving vials. The flesh tumbled in their nutrient seas, the languidly turning wheel the prime mover of their mechanical galaxy, each luminescing under the lockers' tiny LEDs.

Gen turned to a bed of small plants. She caressed the fuzzy soft leaves, her fingers tickled by the unfurling buds, alternating rows beaming blues and reds. Under the blue light, her hand luminesced blue. Under the red, her hand, like the plants, shone pale gray. She could almost feel the spectral change from row to luminous row. She stopped at a blue row, regarding her hand glowing bright as Earth's Moon. *Pretty.*

On the steel table next to Mother's microscope, Gen noticed a saucer that bore a last bite of cake, a dirty fork beside.

"The cake's good. You should try it," said Mother, eyes still focused on her microcosmos. Her journal, usually guarded jealously, lay open beside her.

Gen edged closer and looked over her mother's shoulder at the carefully drawn doodle of a beaded necklace with a pendant in the center, followed by a scientific dissertation:

> The center pendant is the key for the series of locked genome data maps to the perfected genomes contained in the repository. The repository serves as a sentinel for the entirety. The repository is self-sufficient and does not undergo senescence.

> The genome maps are encapsulated in discreet sub-nano chambers, representing approximately 8.7 million species: Animalia, Plantae, Fungi, Chromista, Protozoa, Bacteria, Archaea, and Viruses. Each is housed in a platinum-gold matrix of our own design, fused with an indestructible titanium-porcelain cladding, white in color, resistant to UV radiation and the elements. The wire binding the chambers is a high temperature composite with a nominal tensile strength of 200 gigapascals, with a self-fusing clasp.

The key is of a similar construct, albeit several magnitudes in mass larger, which refers to and is cross-referenced to the Integrated Taxonomic Information System (I.T.I.S.) from the Smithsonian National Museum of Natural History, the Kyoto Encyclopedia of Genes and Genomes (K.E.G.G.), Kyoto University, under the Japanese Human Genome Program, and the National Center for Biotechnology Information (N.C.B.I.), part of the United States National Library of Medicine (N.L.M.), a branch of the former National Institutes of Health (N.I.H.)."

Detecting Gen's prying eyes, Mother flipped the journal closed. "Anything from Edison?"

Thus deprived of snooping, Gen retrieved the vial with Edison's carefully prepared sample from the pocket of her wrap. Mother took the vial, held it to the light to ensure its integrity given its circuitous travels, jiggled it next to her ear, looked again, inserted it into a receptacle on one of the many machines, then pressed a few worn, backlit buttons to initiate analysis.

Gen had hoped the success of her expedition would brighten her mother's mood; that her safekeeping of the precious product of the scientists' infinite toil would be rewarded. She watched for her mother to at least glance up at her from the microscope. "Edison said you'd be happy to get it. So—"

"I already had the answer. Nice to get a confirmation, though."

Gen searched for something else to say. "It snuck up on me again."

Mother sighed. "Don't say 'it.' He's your father."

"He's not my father!"

"He's the father you've got."

"Still…" Gen picked up the fork and took the last bite of cake.

"Be nice. We have something for you." Mother donned the UV goggles and peered into the window of the tabletop oven. "I suppose it's providence that we finished it on your birthday." She set the oven to a cool-down cycle, fingers of frost crossing the window, and soon the whole glass crystallized with ice.

"Finished what?"

"You'll see." The equipment pinged behind Mother, having completed its redundant analysis of Edison's sample. Mother pointed to the scale. Gen stepped aboard and cast her gaze across the room while Mother journaled her weight, 33.41 kilograms, on a hand-drawn chart.

Through the shelves, Gen espied the robotic lab assistant as it quietly rumbled in.

Mother patted the seat of a stool, and Gen hopped on as the blood pressure cuff made its way past her elbow and Mother tightened the flap. Gen felt the growing tightness, then just when she thought her head would pop, the pressure released.

Mother scribbled in the journal, then quickly wiped Gen's fingertip with an alcohol-moistened cotton ball, lanced it, wiped off the first bead of blood, then smeared the next droplet onto a waiting slide, which she whisked into the microscope.

"Nominal, nominal, and nominal. Good," said Mother, now somehow scribbling in the journal without taking her eyes away from the microscope.

The Lee II opened the oven. On a carved granite necklace bust hung a string of ceramic stones the size of pearls, a pendant at its center, each still slightly warm. The robot removed the string of jewels with its hydraulically actuated hand. "We have decided that you are ready for this now," reported Lee II.

"Happy birthday, dear," said Mother, at last turning away from her work.

Gen took the necklace from the robot's hand — a finely crafted string of synthesized puka shells, strangely iridescent, culminating in a deep blue, veined lapis lazuli stone pendant bearing a bas-relief of a lemur. She recognized the ultramarine stone as her mother's favorite, its larger cousin holding the place of honor in Mother's curious little shrine in the lab.

"A lemur. I love it! So cute, Mother. Thank you," said Gen.

Mother nodded toward Lee II. "Thank your father."

Gen reluctantly turned to the robot's audio input mic. "Thanks... *Lee.*"

The Lee II's voice processors analyzed the content and tone of the girl's response. Then the column of hydraulics, pneumatics, springs, wires, levers, chips, sensors, and hinges, topped with a holographic image of Dr. Lee van Hauk's head, smiled back.

"Be sure you really like it before you put it on," said Mother.

"Why?" asked Gen, wrapping the puka shell choker around her delicate neck, its clasp closing with a sharp click. The necklace was stunning, but she supposed that such a gift came with caveats. She surmised perhaps she would now have to do more chores in the lab or double up on her studies. These details she would negotiate later. She touched the intricate gift around her neck. "Sorry about being late, Mother."

"My fault," said Mother, glaring at Lee II. "You should learn to be on time, though. So, what's your birthday wish?"

The robot's 3-D holographic face smiled, its voice circuits choosing a cheery tone. "You're sixteen today, Gen. You can have anything you want. Anything at all."

Gen paused and looked around the room, thinking hard. She thought about the most exciting thing she had ever seen in her lessons, the most intriguing things she had explored in Eos. "I want to see the big city!"

"Define 'see the big city,'" said Lee II.

"You know, the place Mother and Edison and everyone else came from. The one in all the videos with all the people… and boys! I want to ride an escalator. I want to take a taxi. I want to eat food from a cart. I want to go there and see it. And meet people."

"The city?" asked Mother. "It's so crowded, people everywhere, pushing and shoving. You'd simply be stressed by the rigors of competing in a very competitive world. Sharing your existence with the noises and neuroses of the city."

"How would you know? Either of you. You haven't been there in years," said Gen.

"We have everything we need right here," said Mother.

"She is right. You have everything you need. Food. Friends. Things to do and all the time in the world to do them," said Lee II.

"Why can't I see it, at least? Are you afraid I would tell everyone your secrets?" asked Gen, testing them.

"We have no secrets here, Gen," said Lee II.

"All you *have* are secrets," said Gen. "There's a whole world out there. I've heard about it. People. And parties. And what my father did to the pool, apparently. And you never even told me about any of it."

Lee II blinked, scanning his crystal memory.

"That's what Eos is all about. Shutting out the world. Turning our backs on it," said Mother. "At least for a while."

"It has kept us all from harm. From disease. From war. You have never had to look into the face of poverty or prejudice. We have been isolated, yes, but we think of Eos as asylum, security, and survival," said Lee II.

"We left behind the world so that we could save the world," said Mother.

"And now we have. At least theoretically," said Lee II, touching Gen's necklace with his clasper.

Gen pulled back. "How? How did you save the world? Save the world from what?"

"From itself," said the robot.

Gen's head was spinning.

Mother explained. "It's much more than a necklace, Gen. I think of it as a trinity. The shells are the lock, and the pendant is the key, which opens the door."

"Door? What door? What are you talking about?" said Gen.

"The door is the future of the world. The door to the repository for all the data sets cataloged in the locks," said Lee II. "It is the culmination of all of our research and toil."

"You mean, all these years of slaving in a lab, and all you made was this necklace? No wonder you don't want to go to the city. They'll think you're crazy. *I* think you're crazy!" said Gen, exasperated.

Lee II swiveled toward Mother. "You need to explain this more clearly, Marie. I seem to lack the required emotional subroutine."

"You see, Gen," said Mother, "it's your destiny."

"It is the most important thing on this earth," said Lee II. "The most important thing."

"Then *you* wear it!" Gen felt around the back for a clasp; there was none. She tried to lift the choker over her head, but could not, its circumference just loose enough to allow her to swallow.

"And it functions only if *you* wear it, Gen," said Lee II.

"Why?"

"Remember the electrochemical cell clock you used to play with?" said Mother.

"The potato-powered clock?"

"It's something like that," said Mother.

"I'm a clock?"

"Technically, no. Your biochemistry powers the mechanism," said Lee II.

Gen's jaw went slack.

Lee II continued. "As your mother indicated, it is more than a necklace."

"We think it's time you understood where you come from. You are our daughter because we made you," said Mother.

"We...?" Gen looked at Lee II, her brow furrowed. "Mothers make babies. Besides, Dr. van Hauk was my real father."

"And I'm sort of... your adoptive mother."

Gen had long known that she lacked her mother's sky-blue eyes and straight, golden hair, favoring her purported father's cocoa complexion.

"I'm adopted. Is that it? All this time, and you didn't tell me?"

A bit flustered, Mother picked up her journal, then set it down again. "You were... conceived, but not in the usual way," she said, easing into the sensitive talk she'd rehearsed in her mind but hadn't dared utter until now.

"What's the *unusual* way?" Gen quizzed the two conspirators. "In vitro? I already know all that stuff."

Lee II and Mother exchanged a look.

"What?" asked Gen.

"Gen, what I mean is that you're our daughter, no matter how you got here," said Mother.

Lee II said, "It was actually quite fascinating from a scientific standpoint—"

Mother gave the robot a cross look and shook her head.

"We planned to explain everything when you were ready," said Mother.

Gen looked at the pair, searching for what they might be suggesting.

"You must explain now," said the robot to Mother, detecting an adrenaline spike in Gen.

"Gen, listen," Mother said. "We wanted to mend the world. Really, what most parents attempt to accomplish by procreating is just that, even if they don't realize it. Most parents see their offspring as the repository for their hopes and dreams for the future, continuing on after their own biological systems fail. In biology, natural systems combine for the most likely benefit of the progeny, giving them the best tools to survive, to repel adversity, and to function productively for the longest period — in effect, to influence the environment for the greatest duration, for the greatest good."

Lee II added, "This is an efficient utilization and application of legacy. To project virtuous intent into the future. Certainly, there are benefits to combining the best traits of a species via the conventional fusion of X and Y. This is accepted science. We have taken this principle another step. A fusion, if you will, of Plantae and Animalia."

Gen's brow furrowed.

Mother said, "Animals and plants have their own, and often not dissimilar, solutions. What we've birthed in our little lab is a synthesis of best practices in the animal and plant kingdoms. What we needed was that repository, so to speak, for delivering virtue and integrity into an unforeseeable future. That was our hope for you. So you see, Gen, we wanted to mend the world." Mother searched the girl's face for a sign of comprehension, but found none.

"But what did you do, exactly?" asked Gen.

Her mother resumed the long-prepared speech, hoping it would come out right. "We knew we would need someone to carry on our legacy. But we were childless, you see. It was beautiful, really. We wanted to… to create… you. So, we took cells and cultivated them, just like a little seed in a garden. We tried and tried, and then, lo and behold, there you were, a precious little dot of life. Then you grew and grew until you were born." Mother paused her storybook tale of Gen's creation and looked into the girl's eyes, once again hoping for a glimmer of understanding.

"Genetically, you have more in common with an avocado than with your mother," added the robot. Mother glared at him.

"What?!" Gen collapsed onto the stool, stunned, the bite of pineapple cake suddenly wanting out. "How was I born?"

Her parents were silent.

"*When* was I born?!" She searched their faces. "*Was* I born? Hatched? Boiled up in a beaker?"

Lee II flashed a stern look. "Gen, that is not important. You must calm down. Understand that you are destined for greater things. Science needs you." He paused, then added, "You are making too much of this."

Gen broke into tears. "I'm not a girl. I'm not even human!"

"But you are, Gen." Mother consoled her, putting a hand on her shoulder. "Human cells grown from a hair follicle from your biological father and blended with the best that the human genome has to offer."

"And thirteen RNA ingredients from plants, which provided your superior strength and healing abilities," Lee II said.

"You're actually superior to most other humans," Mother said. "Maybe all others."

"Given the limitations of our equipment, we improvised, converting the protein synthesizer from meat protein to plant protein," Lee II said.

Gen blurted, "The protein synthesizer? You mean the one in the kitchen?" This particular bit of news certainly did not soothe Gen; it fueled the knot burning in her belly and started her young head swirling. "You're lying! Why didn't uncle Edison tell me, or his helpers? Or were they in on your little secret, too?!"

"Wellesley, Cornell, and the others all came here to Eos to enable the science first and foremost, Gen. Especially Dr. Bell," the robot replied in a matter-of-fact tone. "Of course they were cognizant of our work. If not for their contributions, you would not be here today."

Mother glanced at Lee II, then added, "We all wanted to observe how you would develop if left to do so naturally. Without interference."

This was exactly the kind of clinical talk that repulsed Gen, and this time, they were talking about *her* in the same way that they talked about the cultures in their petri dishes. Angry tears welled in Gen's eyes, furious at her parents and the other scientists, too, for keeping this revelation from her — especially Edison.

"If you're just making babies in a lab, how come there aren't any others? Do I have a brother? A sister?"

"Sisters," said Lee II.

"How many?"

Mother dodged Gen's gaze and began tidying several test tubes in a rack.

"How many sisters?" Gen said, turning to the robot.

"Twenty-three," Lee II replied with robotic candor. "Defective."

"What do you mean? Where are they?"

The robot looked toward the medical waste incinerator, purring away in its white-hotness.

"You killed them!" With the back of her hand, Gen swept a rack of empty test tubes, crashing them to the floor. "You're monsters. Both of you!" She grabbed a centrifuge and threw it hard, the missile disappearing through a wall without resistance. Mother grabbed her journal and two specimen racks and ushered them out of harm's way.

"Stop her, Marie," said Lee II.

"Gen, stop it," said Mother.

Gen gripped the hulking incinerator barehanded, ignoring its searing heat. With a physical power mismatched to her diminutive frame, she ripped the furnace from its moorings, steel bolts popping, and tossed it aside with a crash. The hot exhaust pipe belched flames. The smell of burning flesh stung her nostrils. The girl looked at her palms — charred and oozing.

Mother backed against a far wall as the robot retreated into a safe corner. The hungry flames climbed the walls. The glass incubator doors cracked. Plants in the hydroponic garden wilted.

Gen stood, aghast, unable to comprehend the destruction she, herself, had wrought.

Lee II extended his telescopic arm and pulled the fire suppression switch that glowed like a cherry in the smoke and the ash. Red lights flashed, and the sprinklers sent out their quenching carousels — destroying the products of intellect, of ambition, of time, and of love.

Gen fled the lab, her tears drowned in the doleful rain.

3.4

Gen lay facedown on the bed, her head buried in the pillow, soaking it in her fury. *They shouldn't have lied to me. But I didn't mean to ruin the whole lab. Not really.* Everything around her was a fiction. Her parents were not her parents. Her friends were not her friends — just colluders in the conspiracy orbiting her. Worse, she was not a person. Just a manufactured thing — a proof of concept. An organism in a petri dish to be prodded and examined, stained, and smeared on a slide.

Her hair smelled of smoke and sorrow. The blisters, still fresh on her stinging fingertips, stirred a cryptic craving for daylight. The sun had long arced away from Gen's anguish, relinquishing its eminence for another day.

This wasn't the first time she had acted out in anger, but she knew that this time she'd done substantial damage. They would forgive her like always, and things would go back the way they used to be. But how could they, now that they had revealed their secrets about her? And what about the others — her sisters? Was she equally disposable — the contents of a beaker to be washed out, or a defective specimen to be annihilated in a kiln of white-hot flame?

The rhythmic beeps of the fire alarm ceased, and the house quieted. She rose from her pillow and opened her eyes, soaked in trepidation. Was she a failed experiment? Were these her last moments on this earth? She could no longer blink. She could no longer think. She waited for the moment that would usher her end.

Mother called softly from outside Gen's closed bedroom door. "Your father and I understand that you're unhappy. You're feeling rebellious. Do you think that pleases us, Gen?"

"I don't care."

"Gen, it's okay. It's all been a shock to you. But you need to accept this. You're very special. The most special thing in the world."

"They said I'm an aberration. A monster!"

"Nobody said that."

"Yes, they did. Edison's friends."

"I'm sure they didn't mean that."

"Go away, you liar!" Gen pushed her face into her pillow.

The door slid open with a gentle swish, and Mother hobbled inside, one large smock pocket weighed down with her journal. She regarded Gen's slender form curled upon the bed, and sighed. Mother's hair was wet from the sprinklers, and she kneaded her ancient mane with a towel. She leaned against Gen's dresser to steady herself and wiped her leg brace dry.

"I owe you an explanation." Mother draped the towel over her shoulder and reached into her lab coat pocket for her journal, its well-worn brown cover bulging with scratch paper and article clippings stuffed between the pages. It was bound shut with a stretch band that barely contained it all. "This represents everything that we did here. Originally, I thought this would be for a paper that I wanted to publish someday." Mother sighed. "C'est la vie."

Gen looked up from her pillow, regarded her mother and the journal, groaned, and turned away. "A paper? I can't believe you!"

"Gen, please listen. You're mentioned in here. Some of it might be a bit over your head. Think of it as a… a family history," Mother said. She removed the band and opened the book, scanning for a benign place to begin.

"Leave me alone!" Gen said, tossing a ruffled pink pillow at her.

"Gen. You must learn to control your impulses. It's just not socially acceptable."

Gen's sobbing began anew, angry and sad at the same time. "Socially acceptable? Who cares?! I'm never gonna meet anybody, anyway. You've made me a monster. An isolated, ignorant, lonely monster."

Mother closed the journal. "Gen, I'm sorry you feel that way. Your lessons were intended to acclimate you to your future purpose, not give you unfulfillable fantasies — and that's my fault. Your father was probably right. But I wanted to shelter you from all the negativity in the world, to see it at its best. I didn't want to expose you to these uncomfortable ideas."

"Uncomfortable ideas? You mean, like, I was cooked up in a lab? I'm not a real person? And by the way, Gen, everybody knew but you? Stuff like that?!" said the girl.

"We wanted… I wanted… for you to grow up as a normal girl, and maybe, in sparing your feelings, I made things worse. Anyway, it's not what you think. It's much better. It's wonderful, actually. Gen, here's my journal. You can read anything in there. No more secrets." She placed her journal on the end of the bed.

"Were you sparing my feelings or just preserving your experiment?" Gen asked pointedly.

"We'll talk in the morning, dear." The door slid shut behind Mother, leaving only the scent of the ruined lab and broken dreams.

Gen sat on the edge of her bed and picked up the journal. She fanned the pages: a dizzying array of data tables, formulas, doodles, hypotheses, processes, fanciful speculations, trials, and errors. She stopped at a random entry:

> … therefore, plant stem cells are described as totipotent cells. Substituting for the instruction to generate roots and stems, the undifferentiated stem cells normally found in the meristematic tissues have been trained to build and regenerate mammalian organs and tissues…

Turning the page, she read a bit more:

> … repairing or in some cases completely replacing them, thus ensuring a self-regenerating subject that can sustain typically lethal injury or infection and repair itself for an indefinite period.

> Due to this self-regenerating mechanism, some defected subjects are proving difficult to destroy. Recommend instituting a security alarm system on all Rodentia subject cages.

Her brow furrowed. Her lips quivered.

She threw the journal across the room, then melted back into her bed. The pages fluttered down, cold as snow.

3.5

The outdoor security light beyond her bedroom window escalated its influence, and soon the familiar silhouettes of swaying palms danced across her bedroom wall.

How strange it all seemed to her now. Everyone she had ever known had been keeping a secret — that secret — from her. The teen's thoughts wandered through her childhood in search of happier moments. She remembered all of it — and none of it. Her memories were as mists on the sea. She and her parents on a picnic — her father, a living man. Playing on a crowded beach. Edison tinkering on machines, his beard as black as coal. Her mind whirled. Which were her lived memories, and which were inventions?

She watched as the hypnotic sway of the shadows played across the wall, the trunks and fronds miming an imagined colloquy between two scientists debating the results of their experiments. She brought the covers up to her neck, then she pulled the sheet over her head, puffing through it like an anxious child.

Beyond her door, out in the hallway, voices drummed a muted argument. Gen flopped the covers off of her face. The murmurs rose and resolved into words.

"What will we do?"

"Everything has changed now… never be the same."

"You should have told her…"

"… putting your emotional needs above science…"

"It was your responsibility…"

Gen listened hard, the silent shadows on the wall fighting in the breeze.

"You can't…"

"…defective…"

"We never should have…"

"…terminate."

The disquieting murmurings fell silent, then footsteps and the rumble of tracks receded down the hallway. Gen vowed to stay awake, eyes fixed on the door, ready to flee if a needle was brought. Overcome with exhaustion from the day's ordeal, she could not sustain the watch. Her eyes fluttered, then closed, the plush toy lemur tucked under her chin, her whisper-pillow gently lulling her with truths that used to be.

The pillow softly spoke of things and ideas, and spun electric myths from facts and fictions. It molded the world into puzzle pieces that feigned a fit and cast histories like spells into convenient realities that told the girl who she was and how to be. The misty vibrations charmed her mind with conjured remembrances, detected and assuaged fears, and rewarded obedience with encouragement — and her neurons, thus stimulated, synthesized bridges between what was and what was not. The pillow murmured softly-softly through this night, as on those nights before, and for all the sleeping girl's time since her emergence on this Earth.

Pressurized air meandered through the electrostatic grid and wrested through molecular filters of exotic fibers and carbon; its soft murmurs cooled to the optimum temperature and humidity. Bacteria and viruses were removed, as were traces of gases, allergens, and respiratory droplets. The vent directed the perfected atmosphere around the room in subtle vortices, tickling the nano-coated walls, discouraging errant particles from any thought of adherence. A curl of Gen's fine hair danced on her forehead as she slept under the watchful button eyes of her plush toy lemur in the little girl's room full of pink memories she could not quite remember. In the balm of this perfected womb, dreams came quickly.

A sound that only she could hear beckoned her, and Gen sat up in her bed. Her toes touched the tiles, and she glided to the bedroom door, which opened in anticipation with a soft hiss. The living room was librarian silent save for the aquarium's bubbling purr and the hum of the transformer that pumped her semi-sentient guardian paternal with sufficient potential to complete his daily tasks.

Gen drifted across the room, a spectral form in moonlight, her gossamer nightgown flowing.

She came to her mother's lab. The ultrasonic beam of the lab door admitted her with its familiar hesitancy, the glass door disappearing into the wall as a puff of sterilized air teased a lock of her hair.

The lab was pristine white and polished steel; the floor, dry, the incinerator sitting atop its pedestal as if no altercation had occurred. All was as it had been.

Gen was attracted to the dark section of the lab that protected the grid of glass and steel lockers from the toxic white light. The lockers were so intriguing, so solidly built, and she felt herself drawn to one in particular. She peered into the soft glow of its interior. The miniature Ferris wheel rotated the glass vials as LEDs bathed them in soft blue, plastic tubes pulsed nutrient, and fans circulated perfectly tempered air. Each vial held a tissue specimen, cylindrical, about the size of the row of annular keloids on her upper arm. The bits of flesh tumbled in their seas of nutrient, the wheel rotating languidly as the specimens spontaneously luminesced in their vials.

Gen opened the locker, retrieving the menagerie in miniature, the wheel ceasing its rotation as it was separated from its power. She brought the platform to a worktable beside the binocular microscope and gingerly extracted a vial from its harness, leaving the nutrient tubes attached. She positioned the vial on the stage plate, turned on the bottom lamp, and manipulated the coarse and fine adjustments until all was in focus.

The sample was very much alive, tiny heart beating franticly, yolk sac following in time. Anchoring it to the top of the vial was a fine webwork of capillaries acting as a synthetic placenta. For a second or two, she thought she heard it making the feeding sound of an infant tumbling in its lonely mechanical womb.

Then she found herself looking up into the cold cycloptic lens of the microscope, one specimen among many, bound to a petri dish, its sticky agar and a net of pulsating vessels holding her hostage. She struggled against the restraints. The incinerator door opened; flames roared. She tumbled into the inferno.

The clinging agar softened into downy quilts, and Gen was back in her bed, Dr. van Hauk's concerned countenance close to hers, the man looking as he had in the photographs. He examined her features intently, her mother nearby.

"It's alright dear. You'll be fine," said Mother.

"But Mother. The Ferris wheel. The babies. They were crying."

"It was all a silly dream. Go back to sleep, dear. You'll need your rest. Tomorrow is your birthday."

Gen's eyes snapped open. She was again alone in her dark bedroom; the smoke smell now faint. *It was a dream. Wasn't it? Was it?* Gen stared at the ceiling and imagined what her last day on this Earth might be like. She would wake at the prescribed time. She would open the shades of her little room, and the sun would stream in, burning away the brooding of yesterday. She would shower and dress and make her way to the kitchen table where she would break the fast, contemplate her lessons and chores, and think about all the things she would never do with the friends she would never have. There would be a little prick on her arm, like the round punch samples her mother would take from her arm while she slept, when she wasn't really asleep, and when Mother would take the sample into her lab and look at it in her microscope in her clinical and loveless way, test and make notes, and then deposit the tissue in the incinerator where the flames would convert it to ash and gas, and footnotes in a journal — without ever knowing that Gen had followed her and saw those things she was never meant to see. This time the little prick on her arm would be poison, she was sure, and she would collapse on her quilt, dead, and her father — not her father — would carry her to the lab, placing her corporeal body in the heartless kiln to be reduced to ash and gas and one more footnote in a tattered journal.

Gen threw off the covers and leapt up.

Gen's mind raced with the insomnia-fueled rapid fire of her newest, greatest fears. She rubbed her arms, trying to extinguish the nightmare of the incinerator's flames licking at her limbs.

Are they going to poison me? Do they think I'm defective like the others? The sisters — how old were they? How did they die? What was wrong with them? Am I even a real human being or just a thing? I'm not a thing! I'm a person! Why did they lie to me? Edison. Edison knew, and he lied, too! They called me an aberration. A monster! I didn't mean to start the fire! Maybe it wasn't so bad. Or maybe it was. All they did in there was make this stupid necklace I can't take off. And they made me, so they say. This can't be true. Maybe this is some kind of test — to see how I deal with this kind of stress. This is how lab animals feel, being poked and prodded. But why? Whatever it is, it's unfair. Completely unfair.

Gen looked around her little room. *I have to get out of here.*

She tossed her bright green knapsack on the bed, unbuttoned the flap, and stretched out the drawstring opening. Out rolled her brushed metal water bottle, its filter cap connected by her hand-braided tether. She put it back inside. She reminded herself to refill it before she left.

One by one, she stuffed the sack with her little-girl personal effects. A jeweled perfume bottle made for smaller hands. A little coconut soap in the shape of a clam. A pewter miniature of a skyscraper. A monarch butterfly barrette. Beaded bangles and earrings. A toothbrush fashioned from bamboo. A tin of the natural toothpaste her mother had concocted. A pink, wide-toothed comb for her curly hair. Her thoughts raced again. *They cooked me up in the lab! In the protein synthesizer from the kitchen? With what? Plant AND animal DNA? The necklace wasn't made for me. They made me for the necklace!*

Gen tried to refocus. *What do I really need?* She flung open a dresser drawer with a thunk. She stopped still, listening, watching the automatic door for movement. Vowing to keep quiet, she pulled out a sports bra, gym shorts, and a sky-blue T-shirt imprinted with a family of puffy clouds. She eased the drawer shut and stepped back; her heel crunching something underfoot. She froze, glancing again at the door. She lifted her foot and reached down. A page from her mother's journal. Gen looked around the room at the debris field, Mother's fevered thoughts scattered across her floor.

She slipped the clothes in the pack. She knelt on the floor to gather the oddments of her mother's overworked mind, putting the pages and scraps back together, taking a few liberties with the proper order. Then she wrapped it in its stretch band and parked it on the edge of the dresser.

She retrieved the beaded moccasins from under her bed and slipped them in the knapsack, too. She regarded her collection of books. Fragile paper bundles harboring tales of love, loss, virtue, and adventure. They would weigh down the sack, and she had read them all, anyway.

She opened the bottom drawer to a jumble of girlish prized possessions: a few toys, a shiny stone, a decidedly human-shaped root she'd discovered in the forest, and the handicrafts children concoct and parents post proudly in the kitchen. Souvenirs sans recollections. *Did I make these things, or did they tell me I made them?*

She picked up the memprint album — digital documentation of her purported past. She flipped through the mosaic of her life, its pico-capacitors humming in colors, hinting at motion. Mother in an uncharacteristic tropical smock dress. Gen, looking much as now but with a bow in her then longish and voluminous curly hair. The flesh and blood man that they said was her father, from the early days, posing next to his blue and white seaplane. Gen as a toddler on Edison's knee, tugging his silvered beard, the pair delighting in a weathered tome. A grove with rows of date palms, guava, and papaya. Edison's helpers tending the sun-drenched bamboo stands. In a setting of perfected domesticity, Gen's face, younger, lit from below by a dozen tiny candles, a corner of the robot's holographic head intruding on the scene. *My birthday. Were they just trying to manufacture one more memory?*

She dragged a fingertip over her family entire: Mother and herself on a freshly enameled bench, a cathedral of forest framing them in jades and tans — unremembered. And there, in the colors and the electric serenity, confirmation:

With her lips, or with her eyes, Mother never smiled. She would take the memprint album, if only to sort the disharmony of truth and fabrication.

Gen scanned her room. Large button eyes gazed up into hers, begging to come along. Careful not to stir the tiny bell around its neck, she gently tucked the plush toy lemur into the knapsack, patted its little head, tugged the drawstring gently, and blanketed it with the flap.

Gen turned to go — she saw Mother's journal on the edge of her dresser. She opened the pack and shoved the journal deep into the bottom, and then made sure the lemur was comfortably situated, its little head at the top as if it required oxygen. She closed the pack and looked at her room one last time. *I won't be back.* She sighed and stepped to the bedroom door. It slid open, and she peered out. The house was dark and dormant, save for the chorus of electronic devices. The door slid closed after her. She padded down the hallway.

On the dining table, the cake lay just as her mother had left it. Another saccharine story; a pretense dropped when inconvenient. Its sugared scent soured her stomach.

The thing that claimed to be her father was in sleep cycle atop its dock in the living room — the monotonous bubbling of the aquarium and the whir of air ducts almost soothingly hypnotic. She passed the dusty Tiki bar with its evanesced spirits and fearsome-faced mugs. She crept quietly to the front door, the purr of the room interrupted by the swooshing pneumatics as she slipped out.

Her heart pounded, fearful and thrilled. *My life is just beginning.*

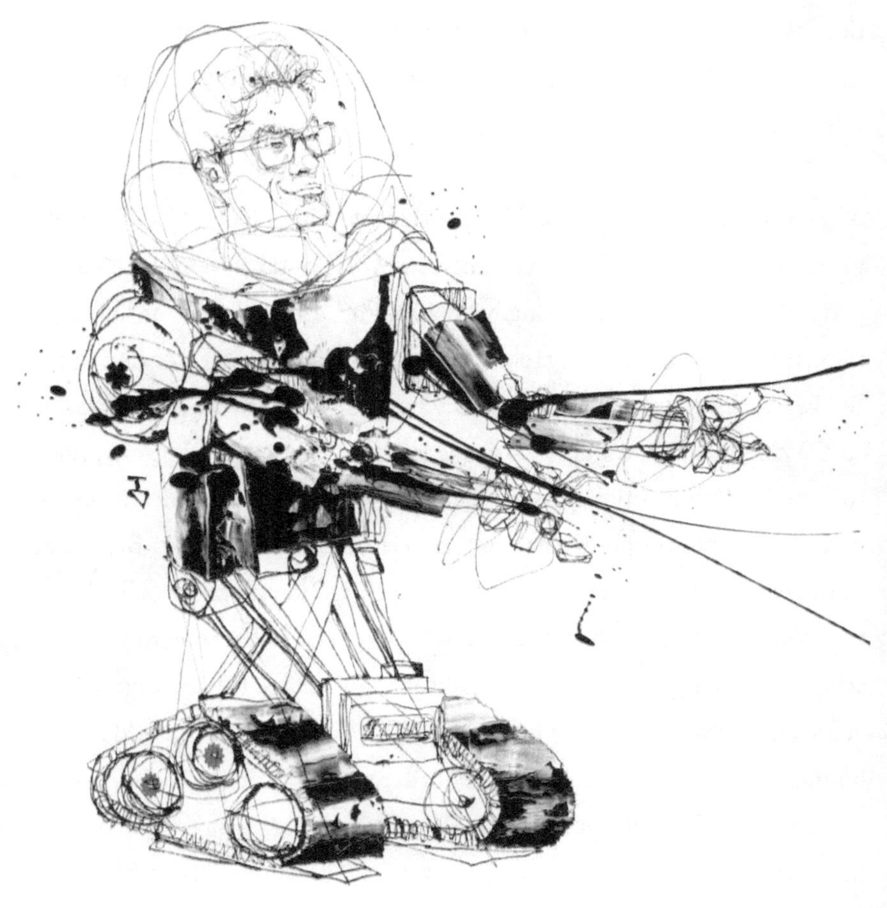

BOOK IV:

Abrupt Flight from Tyranny

They had done it.

This was the solution; they would save all of humanity from the disaster. In a clean white lab, clustered around a large monitor reverberating with charts and diagrams and the ephemera of their trade, three scientists, all in their 30s, combed each glorious, hope-filled fact with their eyes. Dr. Lee van Hauk, PhD, head of the research project, had seated himself center, flanked by Dr. Marie Post, PhD and Dr. Edison Bell, PhD. Beside Dr. Bell hummed the custom circuitry of one of his creations: a squat, robotic automaton on treads dubbed "Lee II" by van Hauk, which seemed to look on with similar, if simulated, interest.

The three scientists were equal in letters, yet stratified by influence and force of personality. Dr. van Hauk, Nobel-Prize-winning biochemist, enjoyed a tenured professorship at an esteemed university. He'd taken a sabbatical to head a privately-funded genetic longevity hacking project, one of a confluence of unfortunate events that triggered the Methuselah disaster, his hope being to find the key to reversing said disaster. Dr. Post sought to avert disasters of a different sort: a career that had stalled with the fading of her youthful beauty, relegating her to lusterless lab positions that precluded professional recognition, and a dalliance with fringe philosophies that left her lame and alone. Dr. Bell, arguably the most educated of the trio, held sheepskins in chemistry, horticulture, and electromechanics, but had found a safe paycheck in the exacting but overlooked science of water purification for medical applications. He had eagerly accepted Dr. van Hauk's offer to exercise his polymathic skills. The three could be described as bombastic, wispy, and affable, in that order.

Van Hauk's mind was on fire. The formulation that they had just validated included a key solution — the perfection of the cure. This morsel of existential consequence, memorialized only within his voluminous mind. Each of the team had already received a dose of this final version and was, at least in theory, living proof. To van Hauk, this represented the salvation, redemption, and restoration of his career. Naturally, it had the added boon of helping mankind. Immediate broad implementation was necessary, he announced. Post and Bell concurred with the obvious, although they remained uneasy because van Hauk guarded the key to the innovation so closely that he was the sole keeper of it. Only van Hauk knew.

Van Hauk asserted it was imperative that he inform his counterparts at the university. He quickly made a copy of the essential files, the robot's screen registering same. The threesome debated as to the proper authority to contact, but van Hauk put his foot down with a literal stomp. Professor Grumman would believe them, he told the others; Grumman was not like the rest, and van Hauk had a longstanding collegial acquaintance with the man. Grumman could be trusted.

Excited to make the announcement, van Hauk turned to his personal device and collected himself in front of its lens. The connection was unreliable, an increasingly common issue. He growled blame at Bell and then tried an audio-only call. Voice communications failed, too; even the Sat-Com could not raise a signal. Van Hauk scolded Bell to get the damned communications fixed; he was tired of excuses.

Post elected herself to assist Bell, hoping to deescalate the tension.

With the pair busied thusly, van Hauk slipped a portable drive out of the robot's data hub, stashed it in a zippered portfolio he'd fished from a drawer, then slipped in a hasty selection of papers he thought would bolster his claim of authorship.

Ever the engineer, Bell checked connections as Post repeatedly tried the communication. Post whispered to Bell that the man seemed ready to lay sole claim to their communal work. Then the pair noticed the vacant drive port on the robot's output banks and the hiss of the automatic door. Van Hauk was gone.

•••─•─◄•••

Almost manic, and with the portfolio tucked under his arm, van Hauk took an impromptu shortcut through the verdant landscape down a narrow, unkempt path. He deserved recognition; he was a PhD, tenured faculty, a published academic author, and a sought-after speaker according to the back cover of the self-published book ghostwritten in his name. Behind every great man was a staff that cleared the path for the prime mover, and he was that prime mover. He did the real work. And he needed this. He had earned it. It was not his fault that the scientific community could be blockheaded, unable to accept radical new ideas; true progress often came at a price. With this solution, the mistakes that had inadvertently caused the current trouble would be wiped away. In a world where science had come to be regarded with suspicion and derision, his work would restore public trust — and clear his name.

Menacing grunts and the thrum of hoof-falls rushed at him from the underbrush. A sounder of wild boar. He picked up the pace to get ahead of the irascible guests. How stupid to bring the boars here in the first place, he mused. A sharp cut to his ankle, straight through his good trousers, sent him limping away as fast as he could move, expletives in his wake.

Van Hauk made it to the clearing, only to find the boat dock partially submerged. The water was now a foot higher than the last time he had seen it, just two months before. He sloshed toward the seaplane, leaving a trail of blood, adrenaline forbidding him to feel the sting of the salt water. Tuskers still in pursuit, the pompous professor threw off the mooring line and jumped into the aircraft. As he mounted the pilot's seat, van Hauk chuckled to himself with smug relief that the salvation of the world was almost preempted by 220 pounds of bacon. Buckling his seatbelt, he briefly bemoaned becoming a vegetarian.

Van Hauk performed all the preflight checks he could remember, hands shaking with the kind of excitement most common to the rush of getting away with something. Battery. Fuel. Mixture. Throttle. He jammed the key in and turned it, then switched on the alternator. The engine objected, then with a few bangs and a cough of gray smoke, came to life.

Just as the plane eased away from the dock, Dr. Bell jogged breathlessly into view from the main path toting his mechanic's tool case, frantically waving his corny straw hat. Van Hauk willed his eyes forward and pushed on the throttles. The pontoons slapped the waves until the craft and its insolent pilot were aloft.

A buffeting breeze bullied the aircraft, flustering the flyer, but the trouble soon subsided, and his concern was supplanted by a sudden regret at not bringing his shaving kit. When the matter with Grumman was settled, they would resume their old ritual at their most favored pub — the mahogany tavern that smelled of ferment and the fruity body spray of coeds. He was too long dry, and besides, the damned staff had failed to stock sufficient stores of his preferred aperitifs and digestifs at the research center.

As the plane finally gained altitude, the engine's steady hum sputtered and cut out, the main fuel tank spent. He cursed the fuel gauge. Seeing that tank 2 was half-full, van Hauk switched over. No good. Air in the line, he concluded. He switched again between the two tanks. No luck. The combination of a sufficient decrease in airspeed and an increase in angle of attack resulted in an unrecoverable reduction of lift. The controls became sluggish in his hands, the stick shaking as the plane went into a stall. The contemporary Icarus calculated possibilities and trajectories and found none appealing. The physics were immutable. Velocity increased, control surfaces became unresponsive, and even van Hauk's stratospheric ego could not keep the little seaplane aloft.

The animals in the forest grew silent just before impact.

4.2

Long before Gen's debut as a being, the Eos project, for all its vaunted and exuberant beginnings, had sputtered to a halt. Due to an unfortunate and rapid attrition among the ranks at the research facility, Dr. van Hauk found his brilliance staunched by the slowed pace of work. Not one to tolerate the nonoptimal service of his ambitions, he conscripted Dr. Bell to convert his tinkering side project — a robot — into a data portal and lab assistant. Bell obliged, augmenting the capabilities of the machine to handle the repetitive tasks so often visited upon laboratories.

Bell presented his upgraded creation, "Edison Junior," to van Hauk, who promptly re-dubbed it "Lee II."

Van Hauk wanted more; he wanted to grace the robot with a copy of his own genius, all the technological mastery, experience, and know-how. With this enhancement, van Hauk would at last be able to work shoulder to shoulder with an equal. Dr. Bell developed a method to transfer in the needed set of data gleaned from van Hauk's notes and recitations, and equipped the robot with a form of extended cognition — its synthetic neurons distributed throughout its chassis, anthropomorphically divergent from divine inspiration. Van Hauk meticulously recorded his own voice prints into the robot, hour upon hour, incessantly speaking, which he would have done anyway — a habit that might have accounted for his extended bachelorhood. Soon, the machine was operating side by side with van Hauk, even toiling alone into the night until its batteries reached their designated recharge cycle.

When the team's research work culminated in the sought-after solution, they were briefly ecstatic. The professor's air disaster left the others to carry on, now sans both communication and transportation. Van Hauk — or more correctly, what remained of him — became a valuable source for tissues of the brain and other organs. An erstwhile unused microfluidic Organ Chip that Dr. Bell had previously installed in the robot was then imbued with the intellect of the man, the voluminous, luminescent data set cleansed of its originator's less convivial emotional quirks. The transfer and transformation were complete, save for the narcissistic spark that fueled his brilliance. The lab assistant automaton, thus augmented, stood in for the late head researcher, this successor being comparatively inoffensive in demeanor and therefore congenial as a coworker.

Van Hauk had been a genius. He was also an asshole. Now he was neither.

•··•·•

Some time passed. The thing that was the professor was sleeping and did not know for how long, and it did not matter. The holographic head was in power-saving mode, eyes closed in electronic sleep, dimmed to the faintest outline; metal torso collapsed atop the base, which roosted astride the charger unit. Its familiar scent was in the air; not of toil and the wisdom of years, or a masculine cologne, or even liniment for aging knees, but of ozone and plastic, of the chips waiting to come to life again at the prescribed time. Efficient. Distant. A set of instructions to be executed.

Data sped from memory via the dock to the laboratory computer system, which had survived the recent incendiary incident. Sensors monitored fluid level and pressures. Defragmentation and error correction were ongoing. Gyros spun a test run that would assure vertical upon engaging movement. Inertial inputs from each extremity were assessed. Humidity was adjusted within the confines of its frame. An active air circulation system and one of the passive variety ensured that core temperatures were optimal. Olfactory: check. Optical: check. Chemical tasters: check. Touch: check. Audio: check. Collision avoidance: check. Mapping:

on. New instructions: on. Upon reaching a full charge from its dock, it would activate.

The Lee II — the amalgamated knowledge, experience, and remembrances of Dr. Lee van Hauk — opened its hologram eyes. It yawned with a pixeled maw of perfected dentition extracted from archive photos captured in news reports early in his departed namesake's career, tempered by the desire of its architect to rid the earth forever of the contemptuous smile the man had been quick to beam during debate over even the smallest detail. It understood compliance and duty and cycles and objectives. It suppressed ambition, desire, cravings, emotion, and petty jealousies. A man reduced to metal and plastic, hydraulic actuators, rubber treads, and electric current. Where it retained semblances of humanity, its systems attempted to squelch the impulses to maximize efficiency. Nevertheless, it felt something beyond its programming that approached a paternal affection for Gen — an instinct that even it, with its networks and sensors and electric mind, could not completely comprehend.

It cycled through the scheduled pre-dawn survey of the building's sensors, one anomaly apparent: The front door had opened and closed one time during the night. It initiated its facility surveillance sequence and turned on the lights.

4.3

Gen's familiar path transformed in the moonlight as the ink of shadow metamorphosed friendly landmarks into fiendish postures. Branches clawed at her, the forest bent on impeding her escape. The sickly-sweet, oppressive fragrance of night-flowering plants singed her throat. She would do well to rid herself of this place. It was unhealthy, fraught with peril. She feared that, by some means and at a time not of her choosing, she would be absorbed into a hypothesis or reduced to a footnote in another of her mother's never-published papers.

The broken edge of a tilted paver scraped Gen's shoe down one side. Realizing where she was, she searched for the branch she'd snapped. The fresh sap confirmed her previous discovery of the hidden trailhead. She was glad she had thought to mark it; from this direction, and in the darkness, it was even more difficult to see.

She pushed aside the dense branches and beheld the weathered bench on its carpet of leaf litter and mossy pavers. Vines had knitted together, encircling the bench as curtains adorn an opulent living room, the Moon's light filtering through the intricate weave. *A secret garden.* A private place to collect one's thoughts and, perhaps, to dream. She wished she had discovered it before it was left to nature. Still, it was beautiful in its desolation. A tiny patch of heaven bathed in gray beams and silence.

She perceived a delicate shadow cast on the ground. Suspended beyond her reach, a weathered dreamcatcher dangled from a limb, its hoop a wilted oval, its feathers and beads draped in moss. A tired totem drained of dreams. *Mother.* She sat on the bench in the spot cleared of leaves, and cradled her head in her hands. *What if I was wrong?*

An urgent electronic pulse cut through the humid air from the direction of the house — a sound unfamiliar to her. She jumped up. *That's weird. Wait. Maybe that's the alarm Mother said they sounded whenever a lab animal escaped. Back when they had lab animals...?* She huffed in frustration. "So I'm the lab animal. Fine."

She looked back toward the main path. *Maybe they're already tracking me.* The branches had closed over the opening, obscuring the entrance in dense flora. *I won't go back. I won't.*

She turned around and marched across the moss-covered pavers. A few steps beyond the bench, her foot landed on something hard and flat among the leaf litter. She knelt and brushed it off with her palm. A brown metal sign, rusted at the edges, featured a simple silhouette of a man walking, an arrow pointing left, and a designation: "Eos Guest Pavilion 8 KM." Her heart leapt. *This must be it. The path people took to enter Eos. People from the city.*

Freedom beckoned. She sprinted down the leafy trail, the persistent beep diminishing with each stride.

4.4

Leaves and branches stroked Gen's bare arms and legs. Brushy boxwood chased along the path, its placement cultivated, ceremonial, processional as it arced around boulders and ancient tree trunks. *The trees are fatter than Edison's belly.* Gen chuckled. She wondered what he would think of her abrupt flight from tyranny and his unintentional role in showing her the way. Edison always praised her independence; surely she was not just another specimen to him.

A knot of guilt grew in her gut over ruining the lab and leaving them all behind. She tried to blank her mind, filling it with the dappled early morning sunshine. The air was sweet with the earth and the flowers. *What a good day to start my life.*

The path narrowed further and the tangle of vines and fat roots had taken over in the years since its last use. A flat stone randomly jutted from the black soil — a paver like the ones that led to her front door. The trail faded into a leafy hollow, barely wide enough for her to pass. An echo of the passage and of the people who had once trod upon it.

The track widened and then vanished into a small clearing. Before her was a low, muddy spot, with grass and woodland beyond. *Am I lost?* She pressed straight ahead across the marsh, ankle-deep in muck, eventually finding solid ground where the path took up again. There was a whisper of an old walkway: three broad, shallow stair steps and the decayed remnants of a handrail, its wood gray and twisted. A metal post tilted into the path, bereft of signage, its purpose long forgotten.

•• •—••• ••

Hours had passed, and Gen had seen no hint of the big city. The walk had exhausted her, and she was paying for her lack of sleep. She came upon a peculiar palm tree. The base was bent by wind and weather, almost parallel to the ground; the upper trunk curved skyward with the renewed enthusiasm of a survivor, its broad umbrella of fronds inviting her to recline in its woody embrace.

She put her knapsack in her lap, took out the water flask, and shook it. Her mental note to refill it had evaporated in her haste to escape. She dribbled the few drops on her outstretched tongue and resolved to find a pond or puddle so she could run some water through the filtration cap. She stowed the empty vessel in her pack, then rummaged in the recesses and dredged a piece of candy, a confection her mother often conjured from scant supplies.

Cradled by the tree, she thought this moment might inspire a bit of poetry. She popped the sweet in her mouth and drew her little notebook from a pocket. She flipped to a page where she'd begun a poem and slid the stylus from its holder. Gen gazed to the clouds and recited aloud from a Teasdale poem Edison had read her. Though he had seemed deeply moved, its subtleties eluded her; its meaning a frustration. She used it now as a template for her own effort, counting its beats on her fingers:

> There will come soft rains and the smell of the ground,
> And swallows circling with their shimmering sound;
>
> And frogs in the pools singing at night,
> And wild plum-trees in tremulous white;
>
> Robins will wear their feathery fire
> Whistling their whims on a low fence-wire...

Gen tapped her writing instrument on her lip, eyes following her notations:

> This bright morning I am going to see my friends,
> They are young like me and number five,
> And we dance and then sing,
> And...

Defends, trends, mends. Alive, arrive, hive. Bring, ding... king? How many syllables? And what would these young friends do, exactly? Hovering the tip over the paper, she grappled with rhythm and rhyme to reaffirm her reverie. No pretty prose apparent, her creative well as dry as her flask. A doodle of a lemur reclined at the bottom of the page. She traced its delicate lines, then pocketed the little notebook.

She plucked her plush pet from the pack, cupped it in her hands, and softly consulted her collaborator. "What rhymes with 'friends'?" The tiny bell on its neck tinkled.

Finding the toy's contribution more comforting than creative, she stroked the stuffed lemur's fuzzy forehead and tenderly tucked it back inside. Then she noticed Mother's journal jammed in the bottom, a disheveled mess.

She set out to collate the jumbled sheaves. Her mother's chronology by moon phase unhelpful, Gen matched threads of thought by the shifts from cursive to block and back, in a spectrum of felts, ballpoints, and greasy leads that recorded the fits and starts of the project's untidy continuum. The lined leaves documented the genesis, epochs, and initiatives of research — starting, ending, then unending. The dense and fevered hand, growing steadily unsteady.

Nestled against the frayed cover, she found a folded sheet affixed to the first page by a rusted clip. She slipped the yellowed paper from the clip and unfurled it. A typewritten note — the words of someone she had never known, apologizing to his friends:

TRANSCRIPTION OF THE FINAL REPORT BY DR. H. YORK, PHD.

Dearest colleagues. I am voice recording this, as I've quite lost fine motor control. Typing or writing has become an exercise in futility. By now, you have discovered the rather conspicuous evidence of my deception. That I am infinitesimally older chronologically than what my curriculum vitae and my identity chip would presuppose. This negligence was not meant to be malicious.

Forgive me, but had I disclosed the actuality of my dotage to this team, I could not guarantee a place among you, those held in my highest esteem, in our humble mission of saving the world. You see, I was adopted as a schoolboy, and the agency justified their slight underreporting of my age as, let's say, an exercise in marketing. I was aware even then of this particular erratum, but kept silent on the matter to assure rapid assimilation into a loving home.

As we had shown, the myelin sheath erosion as well as the epidermal lesions are the primary prodromes of the event. The pain, so far, has been manageable and is not presently evident, owing to the damage to peripheral nerves. Everyone is a bit different. I have been lucid until now, although I am perceiving those often reported sensory phenomena. Flashes of color and hearing tones that are most assuredly a fanfare for my dynamic conclusion—

Gen stopped reading, puzzling over its meaning. Adopted. Lies. Saving the world. *Why did Mother keep this? Did she know the man?* She folded the mysterious missive and slipped it back under the clip.

Satisfied at her effort, she flipped through her crude restoration. It flopped open to a recent entry, and there lay Mother's missing dreamcatcher earring, perhaps an impromptu bookmark. Gen held it up and looked at its delicate details, then returned it to its place in the book. She closed the worn cover, bound it in its band, and then slipped the tidied journal into her sack.

She felt the weight of weariness. For now, any secrets she could sift from the cryptic entries would have to wait. She settled herself in the crook of the tree, and then shut her eyes.

Gen dreamt of things that could have been but never were. In her crib with her favorite toy. A mother and father, loving and supportive of her. A school with classmates her own age. A fantasy past. She awoke incensed at the illogic of it all. How odd and cold and abnormal her life had been.

The sun's rays no longer overcame the density of the foliage, and the forest grew dim. She threw on her knapsack and chased the daylight, now fast on the wane.

At length, the teen happened upon a uniform wall of greenery half again her height, crossing perpendicular to her path. The barrier was dense with vines that wrestled rival plants for their day in the sun, including the occasional orchid. She plucked a blossom and perched it behind her ear. *There must be some way around this.*

She looked left and right for the edges of the obstacle; it continued unbroken as far as she could see, dissolving into the infinite forest.

4.5

Gen probed the verdant wall. She tore at the vines, pulling them from a scaffold lost to time. Within the vegetation was a chain-link fence, rust overtaking the zinc galvanization engineered to preserve it from the elements. *Why had they built this? To keep their precious little experiment from escaping?!*

She glimpsed something whitish protruding from underneath — the broken edge of a paver promising the path continued on the other side. She tugged her pack's shoulder straps tight, then scrambled over the barrier.

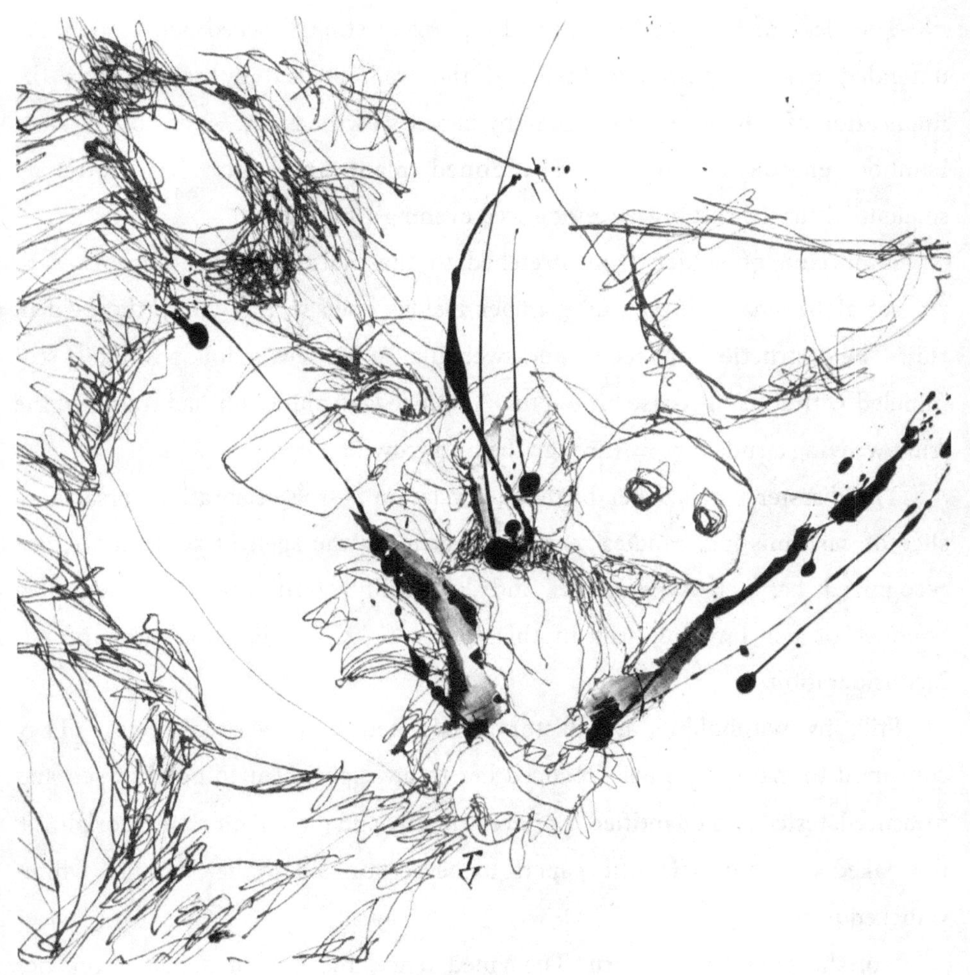

BOOK V:

Monsters of the Night

Gen deftly dismounted on the other side, pleased at overcoming the artificial obstacle. Now beyond the brushy barrier, she resumed the path. As unkempt as the trail had been before the fence, the forest on the far side was denser, and the canopy of trees coveted the fading light. She wound along the disused pathway, each jag and jog a new mystery.

The clash of heavy sweetness and a pungent stink shocked her nostrils. An untended field of pineapple breached the trail, pocked by sage palms; the implication of cultivation overridden by nature's own desires. Stands of yellowed bamboo encroached on the abandoned plantation's borders, clattering sequentially as the soft breeze announced evening's approach.

A horizon of golden fruit stretched to the plot's irregular margins, each perfect globe smashed, the pulpy amber insides open to the world, the field in ruin. The destruction was recent and sweeping. At her feet, a dollop of moist scat mingled with tufts of coarse brown fur. A four-legged plunderer had trampled the fruit, weaving a rude furrow through the overgrown pinery.

The disaster recalled her birthday revelation — the celebration forsaken, a slice of cake missing, candles melted. Even under the spell of adolescence, she recognized her self-centeredness and her willful tardiness. Each despoiled bouquet of her favorite fruit in this lonely field, a commemoration of her inconsideration.

Still, by withholding her history from her, they were dishonest. They conspired to manipulate her. Reduced her to an experiment to be observed and measured, tested and quantified. Her every bodily and mental quirk memorialized, the naked object of scientific papers to be scrutinized by her parents' white-smocked peers.

No, she would not return. The vined fence, the line of demarcation: her personal Rubicon. A mirror reflecting a life imagined, not lived — to be stepped through and shattered. Something good and sweet had been thrashed, plowed under, excreted upon, and left behind, and it was she herself, by her abdication, who had crushed the fruits of their egos.

A wave of anger flooded her, pouring sudden tears down her flushed cheeks. Her mouth went dry, her throat tightened.

A few steps away, a spigot peeked from a weatherworn pump house; wood grayed and twisted, screws reduced to stains, solely a recollection of what had been. *Water!* She crouched beside it, wiped her tears, then fished out her flask and held it beneath the tap. She turned the rusted knob. Burping sulfur smell and obsolescence, it spat black goo onto her hand and into the flask, then sputtered a vile farewell and gave no more. She recoiled, then twisted the faucet's wheel closed.

Ferns at the field's perimeter rustled with a thing of calculated vigilance. The teen froze and listened, unable to pinpoint the source. She shook the filth from her flask, stashed it in her knapsack, and moved on.

••·•—◆••

Gen continued toward what promised to be a break in the dense flora, where she hoped to get her bearings in the near-darkness. The rising Moon winked through the swaying treetops, hinting at a hospitable geometry. The peak of a roof. A wall, tilted acute. A sign leaned forlorn against the structure, its message all but erased by the elements: *Welcome.*

Edison did say people came here long ago. People from the city. She realized the clearing was consumed by the collapsed remnants of a thatched pavilion, the skeleton of its mossy, mushroom-pocked roof topping the rotten heap. Vines laced through the mangled pieces. A palm sprouted from its center. Flattened corpses of barstools peeked from beneath. Wheels of an upended electric cart breached the tall grass. The path took up again on the far side and stole away into the brush. Gen resumed her trek, grappling for the meaning of Edison's tossed off riposte. A rhythmic roar pulsed from the forest ahead, whispering of unknown adventure as that auspicious word caromed in her head: *People!*

The thicket began to thin and a gentle breeze carried a disharmony of algae and rot. The forest gave way to a patch of gray sand littered with pebbles, shells, coral, seaweed, and driftwood. Movement among the stones resolved into fiddler crabs, brandishing their largest claws for love and war, then bravely retreating to burrows as the girl neared. Living creatures she had seen only in her lessons.

Ropes of foam met her at the water's edge. The Moon marched whitecaps from an endless horizon.

A zephyr softly teased her hair with an epiphany — the place she called home was a lie.

Gen's eyes welled with tears of rage and betrayal. Her knapsack slipped from her shoulders to a fingertip, then to the sand. She reached down into the pack and dug out the memprint album. Shaking, she chucked the album as hard as she could. It splashed, floated for a moment, then sank.

She snatched up the sack and retreated from the water. A wrinkled leaf fluttered to the sand, lines on both sides crowded with doodles and speculations, more ink than page.

She sat on a palm log, dropped the pack between her feet, and wept into her hands.

When the edge of her anger had dulled, she uncovered her eyes. Then she spotted it: On the bottom of the knapsack, a small round object emanated a faint glow. *They're tracking me!* She grabbed the pack and tugged the beacon. She felt and picked at its edges, trying to figure out how it was attached. It held fast, Gen nearly ripping the canvas.

A grunt! Gen turned, scanning the dark forest. Something crashed through the underbrush like a ship's bow, charging straight at her. She took off running along the water's edge into the moonlit night, her feet pounding the narrowing strip of sand, ferns and fronds whipping her side. Then she stopped. *The stupid knapsack!* Her clothes, Mother's journal, her little plush friend. She could not leave them behind. The tides would rise and steal the pack, the lemur's button eyes pleading, her prized possessions succumbing to the drowning sea.

She looked back just as something unseen and powerful tossed the knapsack high in the air. She froze. A single red eye glowed. A flash of ivory. The thing snorted. Fear drained the guilt and sentiment from her. She turned and ran.

•• ⁃⬤•

Adrenaline propelling her forward, the teen continued to walk the pebbly strand by the light of the Moon, amid the pulse of waves and pops of seaweed bladders underfoot. Gen would keep the ocean to her right; that way, she would not backtrack. There was no cityscape in sight, but she thought surely she would reach it if she kept going.

In her lessons, the big city lay to the north. She turned her gaze to the starry canopy, bemoaning her sloth in studying its nightly progression. Somewhere in its expanse lay the map to her salvation, illegible.

She longed to curl up under the brush to sleep, but the threat of ambush by the forest creature kept her moving through the early hours.

5.3

Wrested anew from its horizon, the sun found Gen progressing along the shore. She brought a palm-full of ocean water to her lips. The brine burned her throat, and she spat it out. She had no food or drink for her trek and regretted eschewing the birthday cake to spite her mother. She scanned the margins of the forest for color, hoping to spot the familiar fruit they grew on the farm. Mango, papaya, guava, pineapple — she'd even settle for those sour wild berries that Edison had so often weeded out of his fields.

A rustling in the treetops just beyond. A conspiracy of lemurs traversed the canopy, chittering calls of camaraderie. *I'm like you now. Free. No more arbitrary rules or schedules or chores. No more lessons for the sake of lessons. No more lies.*

An enormous purple blossom bent into her path like an offering, its stem ringed with hand after hand of bananas. Stomach grumbling, she surveyed them — all unripe. Recalling Edison's tutelage on finding natural water sources, she tipped one of the enormous leaves and sipped the moisture that trickled down its midrib.

Banana spider! Gen tumbled back, falling on her behind. The creature perched on a green-yellow phallus, raised its front legs, and hopped forward to defend its territory. Satisfied with its valorous display, it retreated between the fingers of fruit.

Gen picked herself up and brushed off her shorts. A dragon's hiss. Gen froze. Amid a colony of prickly pear cactus, an ancient mountain moved. It hissed another warning, then resumed munching the juicy red fruit and flowers of the spiny plant, its shell and beak impervious to the needles. *Just a giant tortoise.*

She chuckled to herself. "Hello, old fellow."

She edged closer, letting the tortoise grow accustomed to her presence. "Hope you don't mind sharing." Careful not to prick her fingers, she plucked a ripe fruit. She scrubbed the thorny areoles against a coral outcrop, bashed the hard bulb, then peeled it. The flavor reminded her of watermelons. The nectar ran down her chin, and even before she finished the first, she plucked one more. She rubbed off its thorns, then cracked it open and ate it. This wild place might offer everything she needed for her journey, which would end, and only truly begin, at the gates of the big city.

Gen trekked throughout the morning, searching the horizon for the great metropolis. *It's probably just around the next bend.*

5.4

Above the sea wrack, she spotted a curious object near the forest's margin. She moved closer to investigate. At her feet lay a curved square-oval. Aluminum, corroded paper-thin in spots; a constellation of tiny holes pocking its surface. She wrestled it from the tangle of roots that clutched it from the waves and then flipped it over. The side that had been protected by its entombment was enameled bright white and sky blue, and fitted with a recessed handle. *A small door? How did it get here?*

Dappled sunlight revealed its genesis. Shoved nose-first into the thick greenery was the wreckage of a small craft, sunk into the turf nearly to its weathered belly. A tree limb threaded into one side window and out the other. It shared the design and color scheme of her treasure, though the colors of the craft were muted by exposure. A hazy blue stripe began at the crumpled nose and continued along its flank to an opening in the shape of the little door, ending at a faded number on the tail. A pontoon, detached and half-buried in sand, echoed the blanched blue motif.

The wings splayed like a bird that had expired mid-flight. Its propellers, bent at impossible angles. Parts and pieces of great achievement, now a disassociated heap, a curtain of vines holding back the puzzle from washing out to sea.

Gen slid her hand across the wing, its rivets crude and imperfect against the airfoil so carefully formed. She moved to the other side. The craft's passenger door was ajar, hanging from rusting hinges. She peered inside. Four seats, the rear two ripped from the floor, jagged scraps of metal erupting from them. One seat was somewhat intact, vestiges of upholstery still loosely draped upon its frame. She climbed aboard and sat on it; before her was a bent wheel jutting from a crumbling dashboard.

Cracks spider-webbed the windshield. She attempted to turn the control wheel; it would not budge. She studied the gauges, frozen at an inconvenient moment. *Sometime in an unknown past, people used this to go to faraway places.* She tried to imagine where. Up in the sky. Unfathomably far. *Somewhere...* Then she recalled stories whispered, half-finished. *This is a plane. My father's.*

The jumble of uncomfortable thoughts wearied her mind, and she was overcome with exhaustion. She yawned, slipped off her shoes, and curled up in the pilot's seat. Soon she was fast asleep. Dreams came quickly.

Gen stepped out of her hot mist shower, toweling her hair, and sat in a passenger seat behind the pilot, the plane aloft. She looked out the window at a puffy cloud in the infinite azure sky. The aircraft was clean and new. She could just see the dark curls atop the aviator's head. Was it her father? She climbed into the front passenger seat for a closer look. His face turned to her and smiled; then suddenly Lee II was at the controls, preprogrammed smile beaming as it held the wheel in its grabbers. The floatplane pitched forward, the robot pilot calmly presiding as they accelerated toward the earth. She braced herself against the dashboard as mangrove branches and palms flew past the windows, thumping and banging. She screamed as the plane rammed into a palm tree with a thunderous blow. The nose crumpled. The windscreen blew in, crystal shards casting random rainbows. Metal shredded, peeled back. The cabin contorted in agony. Ragged edges tore at her skin.

A sharp pain jolted Gen awake. A blue land crab the size of her hand had embedded its larger claw in her big toe. She pulled it away, but the claw remained — indifferent to the eviction. She tossed the creature out of the plane's window onto the sand, then attended to the twitching nipper, still sawing a cutlet from her toe.

A blue swarm of clacking, clashing claws — dozens of its kind attacked the dropped crab. Pinching it. Crushing it. Ripping it apart. Ravenous. Forcing chunks of the quivering flesh of their unlucky kin into their multi-part maws.

Gen grimaced as she extracted the disembodied pincer from her flesh. She cast it out — then saw the crazed consortium below, engulfing their own. At the gruesome sight of the rent crustacean, she heaved the prickly pear pulp onto the seaplane's wounded wing. "Cannibals!"

She wiped her chin, then returned her attention to her injured digit. It stung, and the claw had broken the skin, but she eased her shoes back on. She jumped down to the sand. The concussion of her heels signaled a dinner bell to the writhing horde. *Vibration. They're attracted to it.* She hopped onto a coral rock, narrowly escaping the wave of pincers.

The girl leapt from outcrop to outcrop, and soon she was beyond the carnivorous crustaceans' sphere of interest. She took up her trek along the shore, keeping turf to her left, surf to her right.

The buzz of ten-thousand hornets rose from behind. Urgent. Relentless. Rushing fast up the beach, stirring plumes of sand and dried seaweed. A drone. Scanning the narrow shoreline. Hunting her.

Gen shielded her eyes from the whirling sand as she ducked into the tall brush and curled up tight. She held her breath, hoping to prevent detection. The unmanned craft shooed a flock of terns from the shore as it zigzagged, surveilling an invisible grid. The drone hovered at the plane wreck. Then it traced a matrix directly over her head. Movement in the treetops called the drone's attention to a leaping lemur and her baby. Then it whirred out of sight.

She exhaled. *Good.* She had evaded its nosy sensors. Her relief turned to irritation — no one had bothered to search for her in person; not even Edison.

She rose from her grassy hiding place, shading her eyes from the glare — and there, sprouting from a gentle rise, jagged geometries that spoke of a distant skyline.

5.6

The slope was overgrown with low brush. Sand peeked between succulents and grasses; a blooming hyacinth marked one corner. She had wildly misjudged the distance and proportions. At her feet, a dozen or so sarsen stones jutted from the soil like rows of crooked teeth, stained with algae, lichen, and moss, under the dappled shade of surrounding trees. Several of them stood on end; a few were tilted or flat on the ground. A lonely little hill untended for ages.

Carved into each slab were a letter and a name, unfamiliar. *Who were they?* Gen realized that these markers were improvised from the pavers used on the trail. In her video lessons she'd seen places with stones arranged this way, although with precise and ornate carvings, and surrounded by the weeping kin of someone departed. *Graves.*

The paver closest to her was tipped forward, nearly flat to the soil. She got her fingertips underneath and righted it, then knocked off a clinging clump. Scratched onto its dirty face: "L. VAN HAUK." *My father.*

5.7

So he was real. Gen plucked a hyacinth blossom and placed it atop the van Hauk stone, as she'd seen in her videos. The gesture gave her no relief from the strange, dark feeling. *That airplane. What a terrible way to die.* What was the man like, she wondered. She suspected he bore no resemblance to the robot that claimed his name. And how much of him — the real van Hauk — was a part of her?

Sharp, strange sounds in the distance. Bellowing vocalizations of impressive intensity. Gen caught sight of a pod of creatures bunched together on a coral outcrop offshore; she thought they might be seals. She watched as they jostled for position, space a scarce resource on the teeming islet.

She imagined the barks, growls, roars, and moans as the friendly chatter of playful teenagers. Their heads seemed outsized, unlike what she remembered from her tutorials. Proportioned like human babies. *They're so cute.* It lifted her mood and fed her yen to meet people her age, to fall in love, to experience firsthand the faraway city. She felt the pull to join in the reverie. Answering the siren calls, she kicked off her shoes and waded into the sea. *Maybe I can pet one. Make friends.*

She was barely halfway to the rock, the waters chest high, when she saw the flash of fangs. One beast sank its teeth into another, grabbing it by its neck and shaking it to death. Blood ran down the white coral. Gen stopped — horrified. The brutes' calls morphed into a mix of distress and aggression as the fighting spread from one to the next. Soon it was an all-out turf brawl. As the mob's growling intensified, she covered her ears. One creature looked her way, then slipped into the water, speeding toward her. Gen unfroze and retreated, battling the current. She reached land, snatched her sneaks, and bolted up the beach.

5.8

Gen had continued along the narrow strand between the forest and the sea, the formidable foliage insistent on shading the sliver of beach. How long she had been walking, she couldn't tell. Mother had encouraged her to stay in the sunshine — something about thermal calories. It made little sense at the time, but now her hunger was overwhelming.

She scanned the local flora, dominated by vivid but unfamiliar plants. She was unsure what might be edible, and as Edison had told her, some fruits were forbidden for ample reason; they were poisonous.

A flock of mockingbirds circled overhead, and then, in a dis-unified swarm, lit on a tree heavy with fruit. She thought it a good sign and stopped beside the spontaneous aviary of scrappy, talkative songbirds. Every limb and twig was occupied by its own fowl. She bent a branch down for a closer look. The fruit was a dark purple; here and there, the blossoms that remained were spikes of creamy white.

She plucked one of the tiny oval plums, unleashing a squawking protest. The flesh felt soft, and had the disinfectant essence of Edison's special elixir. Her doubting lips lingered. She saw a bird tearing into a plum, and assuaged by that validation, she scrunched her nose and took a bite. Its skin was thin and its astringency puckered her face and curled her tongue. She discarded the pit, then plucked another, and another, as she appeased her appetite.

The birds quieted. They began weaving and bobbing in a behavior unbecoming to birds, losing their footing, some dropping to the sand, others flying away in odd loops and dives. They were hopelessly intoxicated. She leaned against the straight, light gray trunk, enjoying her respite and watching the fowl frolic at her feet.

An ant detoured across her elbow and she watched it continue down the tree, rejoining the trail of its kin extending from canopy to roots, a six-legged caravan transporting their bounty home.

"Home," she whispered. The word had lost its meaning now, under the shade of the tree and the influence of the sun-fermented fruit. The few birds not yet giddily responding to gravity flittered clumsily from branch to branch, consuming all they could of the aromatic offering.

The teen was happy and sad and mad and happy again, in the same colorful instant. Rainbows made music, and the mockingbirds danced as clowns in the sand. She laughed at their teetering; their ecstasy and intemperance.

The sun commanded its amaranthine beams to trickle through the branches and the leaves, and between the fruit not yet fallen. Gen felt its gentle rays waltz across her skin. A dissonant chirp intervened. She looked into the canopy and spotted a lone bird perched high above, framed by prisms and fluctuating facets.

It was large. It was indifferent to its supposed peers. It did not partake in the revelry. Its stoic owl eyes focused, triangulated, and observed the delinquencies. Its capacitors sung with a surge of current. It compared and rectified and tested assumptions. It clenched its steel talons around the branch and stretched its photovoltaic wings to meet the sun.

Hoyl...? Gen's eyelids grew heavy, and she could no longer resist the effects of the sweet purple flesh.

5.9

When Gen opened her eyes again, her head ached and felt heavy. Despite this new discomfort, she stood up, resolved to make the most of what remained of the day. She walked along the water's edge. Her thoughts churned as the sea. *I miss Edison and Mother. I miss my bed and my room. Maybe I should go back.* But that way lay the garden of stones, forsaken. She pondered the dreadful permanence of death, only nominally cheated by her father, his shadow-self embodied in her mother's robotic assistant. She considered the infinite coast before her; the purgatorial repetition of it. *Is this what it's like to be dead?*

Something caught her eye — glinting emerald from within a mound of desiccated seaweed on the beach above the waterline. Sand flies buzzed the mound to near opacity. She approached the secreting jewel and drew back its blanket of brown stalks and fronds. The odor singed her nostrils and sent a shockwave from nose to toes. Flies exploded upward and were drawn down again, as if magnetically. Therein was the focus of the insects' intense interest: the liquefied entrails of some creature, any scaffolding that could have contributed to easy identification of genus and species now lost to the heat and scavengers.

Beneath was a cylinder of translucent green. Barnacled and scuffed white around the edges. *A bottle.* She had seen them in her videos, vessels dedicated to the dispensing of drinks. This one with feminine curves and made from glass like the beakers and flasks of Mother's laboratory. With a twig, she prodded it away from the stinking mass, then rinsed it in a tide pool.

The top had been sealed with some type of plastic, a bastion for a natural cork jammed in its neck. Gen held the container up to the sky. Inside was neither beverage nor brine, but a sheet of paper tied round with a ribbon. She located a coral rock, and with a flick, freed it from its prison. She unfurled the ruled scroll, exposing its intimacies at last to the world. Its tottering hand recalled her own first forays in penmanship. The formalities regarding the date of encapsulation and the sender's identification had long since faded from the juvenile dispatch, but there was enough to set her wanderlust afire:

Biscayne Elementary School, grade 5. We are studying ocean currents, and have dropped 33 messages into the ocean, one for each student in our class. If you find this message, please let us know where and when so we can plot this on our map.

Gen leapt into the air and screamed in joy. There were young people. Like her. In a real school. Friends doing things together, just as she always imagined.

5.10

With the little missive neatly folded, tucked inside her notebook, and slipped in her back pocket, Gen resumed her trek, her homesickness abated. Excited by the communication — from the city, she assumed — she became so tightly wrapped in her own thoughts that she was not completely aware of the stretch of beach fading to near nothingness. The sand narrowed to a jagged expanse of coral, the forest grasses almost meeting the water. The teen navigated the obstacle course of sharp stones and seaweed, wondering if her shoes could sustain. *How long until I reach the city?*

A sandy streamlet meandered in from the sea to a low spot at the forest's edge. Gen's eyes traced the lazy tannin trickle to the darkness of a bog, its muddy bottom sucking away the light. And above, in the canopy of mangroves, a glint of white — a boat held aloft in the wave of greenery, as a dream. She advanced as best she could through the scrub until she could no longer penetrate the mud and the tangle of mangrove roots. On the craft's stern, she could see a small metal fan, its blades battered and bent like the shriveled petals of a pansy, mounted to a shaft that disappeared inside the hull. Along its side, gold flecks offered the remnants of a script on the edge of perception: *The Beagle.* Its decrepit condition aside, it recalled to Gen the pleasure boat perpetually anchored in her indoor beach scene back home. *Maybe that's how the people came here from the city.*

As she pondered the craft's odd elevation, the grasses next to her rustled. A feral piglet snuffled among the roots and the debris washed in by the tides. *So cute!* She bent and picked it up. The baby squealed and snapped at her fingers, and Gen stood bolt upright. Just as she released it, she saw four more piglets rooting nearby. She hoped they were more interested in finding food than nipping her; she stepped back. They grunted, stood their ground, and sniffed and squinted at the stranger in their midst. Saliva dripped from their jowls and their bone-white milk teeth.

She had heard stories of beasts in the forest, but had never encountered one during her trivial traverses around Eos. Perhaps the crashing waves and the relentless din of her thoughts drowned the animals' earlier warnings. Now, a chorus of frenetic grunts surrounded her, resounding in the humidity. She was still too close to the juveniles, and they were now too ready to charge. She had trespassed on a family of wild boars!

Something fast approached, a wave of green and yellow scrub giving way to heavy hoof falls and angry grunts. By the time she was aware of the dominant boar, it was almost upon her. It was three times the mass of a man, with triangular tusks that jutted from its jaw at an oblique angle. Its breath was hot, and the beast smelled far worse than the bog.

She sidestepped its sharp and flashing ivories, but not before a flick of its head sent a tusk into her thigh just above the knee. She gasped.

The tusker turned. It glared at her with one red, hate-filled eye — the other scarred over, lost to another of its irritable species, no doubt. She realized how she had evaded a more serious gashing: the boar's monocular vision. The murderous cyclops popped its jaw and slobbered foam. It pawed at the earth, hackles raised. *Was this one-eyed boar the same monster that charged me that first night on the beach?*

Beyond the first breakers was a rocky outcrop, its base swallowed by foaming waters. If she could make it there, the beasts would be denied their retributions.

She broke for the safety of the sea. The cyclops led the charge, followed into battle by the sow and her young. Gen slogged through the waters, now over her thighs, blood trailing from her wound. The boars bounded into the surf after her.

The wild porcine family paddled out toward her rock sanctuary, snorting with ire. Just as suddenly, they retreated, thrashing madly to reach the shore, leaving her to her rocky refuge. Gen noticed the squeakers numbered one fewer. She scanned the water. Waves foaming pink. No sign of the straggler.

She recalled a picture of a bronze statue; a little mermaid on a rock in a faraway harbor, chased there, she surmised now, by some murderous swine. Until the brutes moved off of the strand, she would make herself comfortable inside a smooth depression in the rock. The boar and sow stomped the sand while their brood rutted and squealed.

Was that metal fence a cage to keep me in, or to keep these beasts out? She thought about her parents, such as they were, and their desire to protect her from harm and sadness, even if their efforts were misguided and aggravating. Her mind raced between anger at their constraints on her and revelation at the motives behind their overprotectiveness. And suddenly Gen missed them: Mother with her dreamcatchers and white lab smocks, and Lee II, her metal and plastic father figure with his ribbed treads and ozone scent. She missed Edison's kind laugh the most; and she could even forgive his cranky assistants their resentments.

A wave crashed, showering salt spray on the unnerved girl. When the hateful animals lost interest, she would wade back to the beach. For now, her sanctuary from the beasts and the breakers was this rock island, little more than a boulder. Surveying the options within her geography, she considered a leap up to a coral peninsula connected to shore, but decided not to chance the challenging chasm. Open ocean represented two other points of the compass. Incensed swine sentineled the remaining alternative, and she had underestimated their attention spans.

She identified a distinct, bumpy ring above the waterline as sun-dry barnacles — sustained by sea spray, she surmised. Moments later, she noted a disturbing change. The water climbed the coral peninsula and her place of safety with surprising swiftness, the sea creatures now well below the waves. *This must be a tide, like in my lessons. Caused by the contest of sun and moon.* As the waters rose, the coral cliff funneled the waves into an alcove, the outflow meeting the inflow in a violent conspiracy — the water swirling counterclockwise, a depression in its center opening toward the seabed.

The natural confluence created a whorl of salt and foam that hissed danger and death — hypnotic and horrible in its power, ripping at the coral cliffs. It made an awful sucking sound as the seabed met the sky, and she could see its sandy bottom. A bit of driftwood merged with the swirling lip, cartwheeled, and vanished into the maelstrom. She crabbed to the peak of the rock and tucked herself tight and waited.

In time, the tide went slack; the whorl ceased its protestations, and the gurgling pit collapsed upon itself. The water bore nary a ripple. Gen realized the sounder had made a quiet retreat, leaving the beach pocked with their scat and frenzied hoofprints.

The tumult subsided; safe to dive in and swim for shore. The distance was short, maybe five times her height. She took off her shoes and threw them hard onto the spit of sand, out of reach of the sea.

Something appeared in the water. Something dark and powerful. Something unknown. Waiting. Calculating. Now it slipped between her rocky perch and the shore. In sunset's fading light, she craned her neck to see what exactly was passing beneath. An eye assessed her, and then it was gone. It was too quick, the water too deep. She could not make out its form. This leviathan, she knew, was why the swine had fled; terrifying, even to the ferocious boars. Swimming to shore was out of the question. She would have to wait until the tide receded again, taking the mysterious sea beast with it.

She would use the lull to rest and recharge. She wondered what time it was; then she realized such a construct didn't matter; she would rise and set with the sun from now on, free of her parents' contrived limitations.

She cast her gaze to the horizon for the presaged city skyline. She remembered being told that great cities never slept; surely its million lights would become apparent. Soon enough, the sky had filled with the stars and the Moon; the metropolis, conspicuously truant.

Gen watched distant daggers of white-hot lightning reach down to the sea, majestic and silent. A green-white finger traced a long arc over the ceiling of the Earth, heading toward the purple horizon. The celestial matter entered the bosom of the atmosphere from its infinities, where it warmed and glowed — for the first time and its last — before evanescing. *A meteorite. Beautiful.* It reminded her of Mother's tutelage, a melding of science and of myth. Her mother used ancient legends as mnemonics to recall abstruse abstractions otherwise disremembered in the interminable housekeeping of her expansively cluttered mind. Waxing especially unscientific one day, Mother had told her that these "shooting stars" portended the imminent arrival of a companion. In this moment, Gen let herself be warmed by that prophecy. Finally, a friend in her friendless world.

She contemplated her tidal exile — perched upon the rock jutting from the waves, safe from beasts of land and sea, if only for the moment. She checked her injury from the angry boar's tusk, still oozing. *It will heal when I get some sun.* She tore off the hem of her shorts and tied it around the wound. She would stay here above the crash of the waves and certain death all around her. She would wait until dawn.

She tucked herself into the hollow in the rock, out of sight of the monsters of the night.

5.11

For a while, the waters ran smooth and deep. Soon the violence returned, the whorl began again, and after a time the sea retreated, leaving no sign of any adversary, alive or otherwise.

When the dawn came, all that remained was an open stretch of soggy sand between her rock and the shore. Gen climbed down and made her way back to her shoes, awaiting her in the wrack above the waterline.

Carrying the bottle's invitation in her pocket and the portent of the shooting star in her heart, she set out on her journey anew, following the endless horizon of sand and shells. She'd seen no cities or people yet, but she knew the only way was forward, her future somewhere ahead. Right now, she was hungry.

The skies grew overcast, and cool droplets kissed her bare arms and legs. She always liked this kind of shower, a gentle respite from the day's heat.

The rain rose to a roar. Round, angry drops stung her skin, chasing her under the cover of a tree that stood alone in a clearing, other vegetation bowing in deference. She sheltered beneath the canopy of leaves and yellow petals glistening with milky sap. Small green apples mingled with the flowers.

"Perfect." She picked one from a low branch. It smelled sweet. It tasted sweet, too.

Savoring the fruit, she thought herself Eve in that first garden. Among the leaf litter that ringed the insular tree was the fur of an animal, no doubt munching on the fallen fruit. She moved the compost with her toe to relieve the critter of its hiding place. It was a rodent. It was dead. She grabbed a fallen branch and raked the dry leaves at her feet. Other small creatures emerged; birds and reptiles and small mammals — all dead. A boar piglet, its teeth embedded in a shriveled fruit as a cloud of flies sang its last rites.

The rain drummed the forest canopy, rivulets mixing with the tree's milky sap from the topmost branches, conveying it to the leaves below, then to those below those, the many tributaries flowing in white streams to the ground.

Her hand started to itch, then burn. She dropped the branch. Her lips tingled, and she spat out the remnants of the little apple. The sweet taste turned bitter. The bitterness became a great pain in her esophagus. She clutched her tightening throat.

The girl looked up past the yellowish flowers and the greenish fruit to the tallest branches, the white tree juices falling upon her face, arms, and legs. Then she realized: This arboreal aberration was, of course, a manchineel tree — a toxic species, as Edison had warned. *The Little Apple of Death!* She turned away — too late.

The sticky white poison burned her lips and skin. She could feel her flesh blistering, hear it crackling. Her face felt on fire. Now in her eyes — blinded! Throat too tight to scream, she ran out into the storm, wiping the caustic resin from her face and arms — only the sound of the waves to tell her she must be back on the beach.

She collapsed on the sand, moaning in pain, eyes stinging and swollen shut. Pink blisters rose from her flesh, leaking fluids from every bit of exposed skin. She lay on her back, blind, raw, panting, pummeled by pounding rain.

BOOK VI:

The Grasp of a Singularity

Gen lay still on the sand, eyes white, skin raw, as the rain ministered to her ravaged flesh and hushed her sobs. Distracting herself from the distress, she focused on recalling a lesson on botany and one of Edison's tall tales. *Hippomane mancinella*, family *Euphorbiaceae*. Edison had painted the manchineel as a wickedly sadistic local tree, with tempting but evil fruit. He'd even claimed that its deadly milky sap had tipped the poisoned arrow that felled an ancient explorer. *Little apples of death, for sure.*

The clouds had cried themselves dry. She sat up to take inventory. Her skin, still pinkish and hot, had begun to heal, regaining its natural olive color beneath hazy epidermis. She had never felt more glad of this restorative power as the auxin worked its way through her wounded cells, abetted now by the sun's rays.

Gen rubbed her eyelids, then hesitantly opened her eyes. The burning blindness had diminished to scratchy lids and a hazy clarity, casting prismatic artifacts that danced through her damaged corneas. Blues and reds and yellows and bright streaks, a rainbow consuming the entire periphery. The pattern, though entertaining, panicked her; she might have finally done permanent damage to herself.

The eyes are the last to heal. Edison had offered those words when she'd been injured in an accident in Mother's lab. The hydrogen generator colluding with just enough oxygen. The explosion propelling Gen through the bio-safe doors. Shards of glass tearing at her face and body. Her eyes, he told her, would heal slowly owing to certain deficits of circulation in the cornea, a natural limiting of the flow of nutrients to ensure clarity of vision. That was the only time she saw Mother cry. She'd thought it a mother's angst for her child's welfare; reflecting on it, Gen wondered if Mother merely wept for the integrity of her sentient experiment.

She rubbed her face, dislodging a sheet of skin; she held it to the sky. Through her optical fog, she perceived a perfect negative of her visage, even the imperfections, dotted with the freckles and minor asymmetries she knew. Gen's sloughed flesh peppered the sand around her, and when she stood, an outline of her body remained. The makeshift bandage over the boar tusk gash slipped down to her ankle, the blood dry, the wound rosy, but closed. The sand beneath her feet was bright and crystalline, the outcrops of coral bone-white and dry save for a few rainwater-filled depressions. Sunlight, usually her friend, now heightened the glare. Though her vision was diminished, possibly permanently so, she obligated herself to resume her wanderings.

Through the opacity of her poison-damaged eyes, she navigated the thin strip of shoreline. She shied from the forest's margins and the shallows, not wanting to risk another encounter with the boars or the dark underwater form she'd seen near the maelstrom. She proceeded with circumspection and measured steps. A mistake during her convalescence might be unrecoverable.

The shadows lengthened. The beach grew rocky, and the tide rolled in, the sand sequestered beneath the lapping waves. She could detect a jagged silhouette in the distance, stretching from the forest to the sea. *The city?* She rubbed the last curled flecks of dead skin from her arms and picked up her pace, stumbling over the uneven strand.

As the promised skyline loomed larger, it lost any suggestion of geometric form. No skyscrapers or spires. No bridge crossing a great expanse. It was not a city — only a natural ridge jutting from the shore, bisecting the beach perpendicular to the surf. Her hopefulness and peculiar visual impairment had conspired in this illusion, and she dropped to her knees, crushed with disappointment.

She inhaled deeply, collecting her thoughts. *No drones combing the beach since yesterday — or was that the day before?* Her so-called parents, and everyone else at Eos for that matter, must have lost interest in her. Just an experiment that did not confirm hypothesis.

She took account of her travels and the beginnings of this odyssey — the excitement of going somewhere new, free of the shackles of deception, free to make new friends. The imponderable length of sand behind her seemed a timeline of the universe going back into a distant past that, like her own, was unknowable. The only certainty was that she aspired to conquer the rocky obstacle before her, and she hoped its summit would give lay to the land and solidify her itinerary.

She stared up at the obstruction, which was more than thrice her height. It was steep and black and unwelcoming to her passage. She ran her palm over the face of the dark crag. The rock was porous and alternately smooth and razor sharp.

"Ow!" She looked at her hand, abraded, the first thin rivulets of blood emerging. *Lava rock.* A tongue of ancient volcanic glass, birthed eons ago from some fissure now hidden deep in the forest. The flow had crossed the beach and, hissing in protest, dived beneath the waves.

Resolved to overcome the imposition, Gen leapt upon a boulder. It was slick with algae but skirted with barnacles, their vacant shells serving as purchase for her sodden footwear. She balanced there for a moment, considered an efficient path to the crest, and jammed her hand into a vertical crevice above her head. She made a fist, locking solid against slippage, and pulled her body up to a ledge where she found a tentative toehold. She persisted, handhold to handhold and ledge to ledge, finally cresting the narrow plateau.

The apex achieved, she scanned the horizon through the gossamer gloss of her tangle with the manchineel tree. A ribbon of sand stretched endlessly before her. The tide and the waves advanced against it, and she could just discern random sections of the shoreline being subsumed by the sea foam. Her head drooped; her shoulders slumped. *No city.* The waves beat heavily upon the barrier; the spray rising high into the air, raining upon her, a stinging baptism of brine.

Sunlight traced an ominous curtain of green-black clouds at sea, swirling and angry. The sun relinquished its domain and she could feel the air turn cool as the breeze stiffened. A frond snapped off a palm and swept past. Even in the cocoon of her former life, she knew this sky warned of danger ahead and she would have to locate some sort of shelter. She had a twinge of regret at being so far from home, but there would be no time to backtrack now, as it would take days, and the deluge was imminent.

Thunder rumbled across Poseidon's expanse. The sliver of strand below was still dry, seaweed and driftwood just beyond the reach of the tides. She jumped down to the beach, slipped, and tumbled face-first onto the sand.

Irked but unharmed, at least she was on the other side and could determine the best prospect for refuge. She brushed the sand from her face, the last vestiges of her ocular injuries falling away. Her vision had cleared of the prisms and fog that had plagued her.

Just beyond her nose, a tiny snail made its way past a bit of coral, and Gen took in the subtle patterns and hues in its conical shell. She watched as it slipped over the edge of an elongated impression in an undisturbed section of the sand. Jubilant, she pushed herself up for a better look.

Yes, she was sure. A human footprint.

6.2

Gen's heart pounded. She stood to get a better look — other impressions in the sand, leading down the narrowing beach now consumed by the rising tide, then leading back up to the edge of the forest. The shooting star was indeed the portent of friendship, just as Mother had said. *People! From the city. A girl, or maybe a boy.*

Her mind raced to recall a lesson Edison had endeavored to teach her — repeatedly shaking her right hand, smiling, and instructing her to recite a special greeting. She practiced under her breath, brushing the sand from her arms and legs, heedless of the liberal deposit in her hair. "Hello, my name is Gen. What's your name?"

She followed the footprints up the beach toward the edge of the forest, her own foot falling inside one of the indentations. She stopped and looked. It was the same size as her own. *Maybe someone my age?* Beside it, a slip of paper lay pinched between two pieces of coral. *Another message, just like the one in the bottle!* She picked it up, its ink faded by the sun and the rains.

"Hello!" she called into the expanse. Only the nervous mew of a mother lemur amid the rustling of the forest.

Lightning flashed, highlighting several palm fronds scattered on the sand. A gust flipped over one elephantine leaf. Underneath, a knapsack much like her own, plastered with sand. Her hopes rose, and she cast her gaze toward the forest, then across the beach. *They'll be coming back for it.* "Hello?" She tucked the note in her pocket.

Another blue bolt from above. An object, contorted and metallic, glinted in the sand two paces away. The once bottle-shaped thing, its lid on a hand-braided tether, was crushed — bearing a multitude of punctures from powerful canines.

A crevasse opened in her consciousness, and she tumbled in. *Incredible. Impossible.* Pressure building between her furrowed brows, she sat on a weathered palm log, considering the pieces, then sorting the puzzle, and then confronting an improbability. *It can't be.* That was her flask. That was her knapsack. And the footprints — they were hers.

She had kept the water to her right, the land to her left, so that she would be certain not to double back. The linear path had, nevertheless, circled upon itself. "Eos is an island?!"

For all her peregrinations, she had gotten nowhere, drawn back as an unlucky planet in the grasp of a singularity. The footprints, the shooting star — illusions. She was alone.

She knelt beside her knapsack, its tracker still pulsing. Tears welling in her eyes, she picked and tugged at the blinking tattletale, but as before, it would not relent, the beacon fused to the fabric. Her mother, if nothing else, was thorough. The knapsack moved. She stopped tugging. The drawstring was loose. She opened the pack. Atop the mementos and personal effects, a baby ring-tailed lemur gazed up, clinging to Gen's plush toy lemur doll. She stroked the creature's tiny head with her thumb. "You poor little thing."

A crash of leaves and branches overhead. The mother lemur came sweeping down from a limb, landing right next to Gen and the infant primate. Her baby abandoned the doll and latched onto its real mother, little arms wrapped around her neck. The mother lemur touched Gen's outstretched hand as if to say, "thank you," then bounded back to the tree line with her wide-eyed tyke and disappeared into the canopy.

Mother. She wondered if her own mother might be worried about her at this very moment. Maybe she had been wrong; her parents seemed to care about her safety, and surely were not plotting to get rid of her. Her feelings on filial piety were at odds. She understood, now, why they had claimed that going to the big city was impossible. Still, she begrudged them their silence about the true nature of Eos and its hostile perimeter. Worse, they had lied to her about herself. Contemplating her cherished childhood toy, the one she refused to leave behind — she could not recall any memories of playing with it.

The girl returned to the palm log she'd sat upon when she first arrived to this stretch of sand a few days ago, and opened the knapsack between her knees. Atop her possessions were a couple of stray pages from Mother's journal, the focus of the baby primate's childlike curiosity. She pulled the topmost one from the pack.

Tiny bite marks marred the first few lines of the entry. She studied the words of her mother, intense script and block strokes that chiseled truth from adversity.

Day 2.

Everyone settled in now. Lights up, heads down. Step 1, know thine enemy (see handout).

Pattern seems consistent, though poor communication among health agencies make reliable data scarce. Origin hard to pin down. Multiple vectors possible: food, fomites, aerosolized agent, close physical contact (kissing/sex), O.T.C. fruit/veg supplements. Or nature furiously saving itself, using our frailties against us.

Symptoms at onset remain curious. Not typical viral expression. Gene shuffling detected with exponentially accelerated rates of mutation. Presenting as reversed chronological age, most pronounced in midlife and older. Smoothing of features, rubescent lips, abated lentigo. Rhodes christened it "charmedema." Patients initially report more energy, self confidence, and a craving for social engagement.

Then it all goes to Gehenna. Approx. 3 days after onset, eczema-like patches, bullous lesions, fatigue. Some recover, mostly children/young adults. The rest suffer aggressive necrosis of flesh, connective tissue, and bone. Mature patients tend to die within hours of their first or second bout. Death by acute simultaneous cell structure collapse is activated by two cytokines, triggering PANoptosis (Pyroptosis, Apoptosis, Necroptosis). Z-DNA binding protein is crucial for the activation of these pathways, and there is suggested an additional, unidentified pathway to accelerated cell death. Anecdotally, some survivors experience exceptional wellness, then rebound and die soon after. One clinic attempted to quarantine the afflicted. Unfortunately, those patients were set free by misguided mobs.

Mortality statistics underreported. Settled on approx. 39% dead worldwide in first wave.

How to develop a single cure for a condition with many potential causes & sketchy data?

Given manufacture/logistics logjam and public resistance to all things science, how to deliver the correction?

"Wait a minute…" Gen slipped the found missive from her pocket, smoothed it, and held it against the journal page. A match. She groaned. Not a greeting from schoolchildren. It was another page of Mother's journal. She read the sun-faded ink.

Day 1.

I arrived last night with Lee and a chatty engineer named Edison. My first stint leading research — my stomach churned the whole flight. The advance team seemed glad to see us. I'm relieved to find two colleagues among the group.

Today we officially begin the Eos Project. Eos, Greek goddess of the dawn, to represent what we hope will be a new beginning for us all. Disassemble the agent(s) and discover how to beat it. The lab is more than we could have asked for. High-end equipment and an impressive supply stockpile. Our host, more than gracious.

I dread today's team meeting, our first. Everyone will want to revisit personal concerns, bemoan public sentiment, and basically lick their wounds. After our meeting I will need to assign stations. Then inventory the pharma vault. Can't be too careful.

I should start at the beginning. How this happened. That part is a little obscure, as it seems to have emerged from many corners. As it stands, the world has split — believers in the rigors and results of science, and those who have turned their backs on us. One suspected source — extra-medical self-experimentation by wealthy longevity proponents. They were looking to cure aging and defy death. Even virtuous goals, when pursued by the un-virtuous, create a rogue wave that is bound to birth disaster. Others blame elements in our common environment — water, air, crops — that intermixed into a deadly brew. Rumor circulated that those over 40 had manufactured the disease. "Hack attacks" — the diseased, mostly young adults, coughed or spat on the elderly and the foreign-looking. Some mobbed and murdered. Clinics breached/ burned. So we needed to mount this vital research away from violence and safe from disruption of delicate processes.

All of us were required to test negative, and just in case, be under age 40. We are sequestered at the facility to reduce exposure. No family or "plus-1" allowed. I report directly to the Principal Investigator, Dr. Lee van Hauk. Brilliant. Difficult. It's going to be a long 6 months.

I am excited to co-lead this project. The most important work any of us will ever participate in. Our task is impossible: to mend the world.

The palms bowed to the changing winds, and Gen looked up from her reading. *Mend the world?* In the distance, emergency sirens blared.

6.3

Startled birds took to the air. The sirens wailed their long rising moans. Gen knew what it meant. A storm of significant magnitude was approaching. At such times, all in Eos would enter the rudimentary compartment they called "the shelter" to wait for the storm to pass. She was already due for an uncomfortable conversation about her temper and her flight; it would be unbearable in claustrophobic quarters among the rusting cots, musty blankets, and tasteless dried food.

Her ears popped. A magnificent gust blew in from the sea and tore at the beach, peppering Gen with sand and shells. Black clouds swirled above the treetops. She shook the sand from her knapsack, secured the top, slipped the straps on her shoulders and tugged them tight.

Edison, always full of advice about situations she thought she'd never be in, had warned her to seek shelter on higher ground if she found herself too far from home when a storm came. She headed back up the same trail she had descended some days ago, hoping to wait out the weather under a tree.

The first wave caught her by surprise, lifting her off her feet and tossing her up the path. As the deluge returned home with equal violence, she gripped a vine and held on tight, lest she be pulled into the surf. Gen stood up, half surprised and half insulted by the inundation. She would not wait for another demonstration of the power of the sea; she ran, the storm sirens wailing and urgent in the distance.

She climbed over the vine-covered fence she'd conquered in her escape. *Back to my cage.* It meant admitting defeat, but she vowed this sorry condition would be short-lived. Gen would strike out on her own again when the weather cleared, even if only to live somewhere else on this… island.

She heard the squeal of tree trunks relenting to incredible power. She took too long to discern the roar of rushing water from the din of the storm. The second wave bowled down the fence and licked at her heels.

Above the rising wind and the blaring sirens — a familiar voice.

"Gen! Gen, over here! This way!" Edison emerged from the underbrush, moving quite a bit faster than his bulk would suggest. She rushed toward him. He wrapped her in his big bear hug, then he grabbed her forearm and practically dragged her up the trail. "Your parents are worried sick!" he yelled over the chaos.

She yanked her arm away. "You knew all along and you didn't tell me!" Lightning cracked — she cowered, and he latched onto her hand.

"Knew what!?"

"We're on an island!"

"Yes. An island. Of course." He ushered her along a scruffy path that she had not traveled before. "This way. Shortcut."

In a few moments, they were in a clearing at the edge of the carefully cultivated columns of bamboo. A gust moaned through the bending culms. The sky roiled. Rain pelted her head so hard it hurt.

Gen and Edison joined Wellesley, Laurel, Tufts, and Rhodes; the scientists queued on the zip-line platform, lab coats pulled over their heads for protection. Rhodes stood next in line to make the crossing. The trickle in the ravine, which Gen had easily stepped over so many times before, was now a river.

"Ivy and Cornell made it," said Wellesley over the din. "The t-bar is on its way back."

The braided steel cable writhed in the wind. Gen looked down into the ravine. In a minute, it had grown into a raging torrent, the water thick with mud. Uprooted trees floated by. Boulders rolled downstream. She wondered if a passing branch would tangle in the line as the water level climbed, and Edison's eyes told her he was thinking the same.

The zip-line motor screamed as it braked to a stop. Rhodes grabbed the t-bar and without hesitation swung the handles over to Gen. "Destiny calls," said Rhodes.

She looked up at the man who had once called her a monster, with new understanding of his toil, and that of the others, to make the world right again. She hugged him tight.

"When you get to the house," shouted Edison over the thunder, "go right to the shelter." He looked at the rush of water climbing the sides of the ravine.

"What about you? What about everybody else?" asked Gen.

"We'll follow."

Gen gripped the handles. "Why didn't you tell me?"

"Tell you what?"

"How I was born."

"What does it matter?" answered Edison. "We all love you. No matter what."

The electric motor whined as Gen launched across the expanse, squinting through the onslaught of wind and stinging rain, the jungle rushing by.

"Gen! Please forgive me!" Edison shouted into the wind.

She glanced behind her, Edison's concerned visage shrinking into the jungle as he clutched his straw hat to his head. Gen clung to the t-bar, wind-whipped foliage stinging her face, arms, and legs.

Time slowed, every second a minute. Rain pounded. The ravine's banks eroded to rocks and thick roots. The other side of the chasm fast approached, and she raised her legs to clear the raging rapids. A shard of lightning sliced across the sky and found the zip-line's main support. A screech of metal — the cable went slack, and she felt herself flying, untethered. She squeezed her eyes shut and reached out to absorb the force. She crashed into the muddy wall of the ravine, a cascade of rubble cruelly raining upon her. Stunned by the impact, Gen strained to stay conscious and hold on. Another bolt illuminated the tangle of tree roots and teenaged limbs dangling from the scarp.

"Edison!"

Her friend stood helpless on the platform with the others, separated from his charge by a raging cataract now threatening to overcome its modest banks. The ground trembled around Gen; the deluge rising to the rim. Soaked with fear, slipping on roots and mud, she lifted herself up over the edge. She looked back at the huddled group on the platform, the severed zip-line whipping above.

"Get to the shelter!" yelled Edison from the now submerging platform. "We'll find another way. Go!!"

Gen turned toward the house. She could just make out a tiny light from the family compound. Hope.

She picked up her pace, dodging the palm fronds that whipped her face and legs in the torrential downpour. Merging tributaries, running blood-red from leaf litter tannins, cascaded into the narrow path. She sprinted through the mayhem, throwing rooster tails of dark water from her heels.

The roar of pelting rain and falling trees drowned the siren's moan. The wind turbine atop her house spun at breakneck speed, straining to face into the erratic, angry gale.

She felt the water rise over her ankles. She pushed on; the beacon getting closer. Salvation. "Mother!"

A wave rushed through the forest and knocked her down. Caught in a maelstrom of foam and debris, she grasped a sago palm, its leaf blades cutting her hands. "Mother!"

A roller penetrated the woodland, catching trees in its curl. It brought its apocalyptic wrath upon the compound, crushing both house and lab into straw and tears, drowning the weather siren's final protestations. Another wave followed — bigger by a factor of two. It towered, angry white and green, and erased all before it.

"Mother!!"

Crack! A huge coconut palm toppled toward her. Gen steeled herself for impact and oblivion.

BOOK VII:

A Tomb Made for the Living

Nothingness. Then a rhythm emerged from the void: the beats of Gen's own heart. The percussion crescendoed, and she roused. She lingered darkly beyond the threshold of rational thought, adrift in a cocoon of insensibility that benumbed wounds both deep and superficial. She had floated in the arms of an unknown mother — for seconds or eternity, she could not know — and slowly it came to her that she was alive.

Her eyelids fluttered. She squinted in the blazing sunlight, one eye cemented shut. Her tongue lolled from thirst; her lips, parched, her cheeks and hair veiled in a haze of gossamer white, the lapis pendant of her puka necklace dangling.

She was lying prone. Her head hung over the edge of a platform of sticks and straw, just above silvered reflections on placid water.

She reached into the pool and brought her dripping hand to her face and wiped her eyes. It stung but eased the knife edges of the crusted brine. She tasted it and winced.

A crystalline ghost in a puka necklace stared back from the mirror surface, framed in a mass of amber algae suspended in its domain.

A ripple set her reedy mattress into a gentle roll. She raised on an elbow. The pool expanded to the periphery of her vision. She blinked hard. This was not a pool, but the open ocean.

From the depths came a horrible creature — all floppy flesh and spines, much like the seaweed itself. It gave a fearsome croak and lunged at her, mouth agape, as if to swallow her whole.

Gen's scream caught in her scorched throat. She thrust out her hands in defense, capturing the beast before it could strike.

The "monster" was merely an ornate, frog-like sargassum fish about the size of a plum. It croaked another warning, the best the tiny creature could.

"Sorry, little guy. You gave me a scare," she mumbled, surprised by her own raw, scratchy voice. She let the plucky hitchhiker down onto its raft of seaweed. It burrowed into the yellow-brown mass and disappeared.

She tried to roll onto her back, but her knapsack, still strapped on her shoulders, got in the way. She sat up. Now she could see that she was on a lonely raft, too — an accretion of detritus collected by the currents — bamboo reeds, palm fronds, seaweed, the back of a rattan chair, and shattered sections of palm trunks. A worn straw hat with a distinctive blue, white, and red band clung to a clump of sargassum weed. "Edison?" she heard herself say, in the weakest of whispers.

The girl struggled to stand, the soft and ephemeral surface of the raft shifting under her weight. The smell of decay stung her nostrils. Kelp flies buzzed in clouds. Gen's head was buzzing, as well. Dizzy; nauseous. She rubbed her eyes and looked around. She attempted to make sense of the images now searing her soul. Mixed with the flotsam were several bloated human corpses with deep lacerations caked in blood, some with their eyes popped from their sockets. Crabs clattering over the ballooning bellies. Scraps of white garments, blindingly luminescent in the sun. Familiar sandals, and Edison's tropical flowered shirt.

Her weight pushed apart the loose confederation of flora beneath her. The raft gave way under her feet and she fell into a nightmare of lifeless bodies and splinters of palm logs, floating free. She vanished below the floating graveyard — then surfaced, frantic, coughing, treading water, bobbing in the debris. Gen tried to scream, but her tumescent tongue would not cooperate.

Then she heard it. It was unmistakable. The sound of taunting laughter.

7.2

Gen spun around, unable to pinpoint the source of the laughter. Instead, she saw a set of teeth — somewhere between the serrated maw of a shark and the huge canines of a lion — feasting on human flesh liberated from the floating refuge. Bodies bobbed, then disappeared into the depths. An orgy of tearing flesh and crushing bone, punctuated by bellowing roars. She had heard those calls before from the brawling brutes just offshore at Eos.

She struggled to keep her head above water, reaching for any debris that could still be buoyant. But the raft had dispersed; sunk beneath the waves, or carried away by the current. Now, she was alone in the vastness of the ocean — yet not alone.

The last corpse was pulled below. A moment of stillness — then twin nostrils broke the surface, exhaled a geyser of mucus, and sniffed the air.

She could see the bow wave of another beast heading for her — a mountain of water on the move. Terrified, she turned and swam as hard as she could.

A disk of fine netting spun out across the sea, its hand line trailing from the swivel horn at its center. The cast net's lead weights pulled its hem down, veiling

Gen from head to toe, pinning her arms at her sides. She wriggled piteously against the restraint.

A bulge of water advanced on her. She screamed. The net's line went taut, and she was snatched away from her pursuer. The monster surfaced: onyx predator eyes on a huge snakelike head, a shred of clothing caught on blood-crimson fangs.

Gen felt herself tugged along, fast then slow — tantalizing the predator's appetite, but keeping her feet just beyond the mammalian jaws. She gulped for air — her nose and mouth filled with water.

"Pull!" said a gravelly voice.

The net was a chum bag, the girl merely bait for trolling a larger quarry — a deadly game. With a flick of its flippers, the animal gained on the netted catch. A pair of jaws surfaced, baring diamond teeth.

"Pull, stupid!" the man yelled again.

"Whadda ya think we're doin', Bilge?!" said another.

A hard tug on the hand line — the jaws snapped shut, denied their prize. A spear jabbed at the water, missing the creature. Gnarled hands lifted the girl over the port gunwale of the fishing craft, tossing her in the boat like a soggy rag doll, atop salvaged jetsam and flopping fish. She coughed up water. Her breast heaved with her first full breaths. She lay crumpled and in shock, shivering from abject fear.

"Caught quite a minnow," said Bilge.

And so they had.

7.3

The shapes of three men intruded on the blinding sun above Gen's head.

"What is it?" asked Reef, scratching his scruffy, short cropped blond locks.

"A mermaid?" said Bilge.

"A selkie," said Lobster with a goading giggle.

The trawling trio stood panting in their craft, a beat-up, flat-bottom aluminum jon boat about as long as all three men laid end to end. It was vessel enough for fishing the open sea solely because it was what they had.

The three were disheveled, dirty, and pungent, with beard stubble and crudely chopped short hair. Bilge and Lobster had survived into their 30s, though their gaunt, weathered faces and ample scars painted them as refugees from a famine. Reef, about a decade younger, was short and wiry, with a ruddy complexion and a halo of wild hair bleached from the sun. Three hobos in a boat.

The girl lay across the middle of the craft, the net's swivel horn perched atop her head, the hand line trailing, her whole body cocooned by a spiderweb of translucent strands of plastic monofilament. The fishing net's gauze-like weave glistened in the sunlight, lead weights along its edge, holding the net fast to their unconventional catch.

"Is it dead?" asked Reef, nudging the bundle with a toe.

Bilge grabbed the cast net's weighted edge and lifted it off the teen's limp, sunburned, and saltwater-sore-riddled form. The men leaned in to satisfy their curiosity. Around the throat of the motionless girl, the puka shell choker glinted in the sun.

"Well, looky here, pearls or some such," said Lobster, flashing a devilish grin. He slipped his fingers under Gen's choker and tugged at the prize.

Startled, Gen popped her eyes open — reflex sent her foot into Lobster's groin with unprecedented velocity. He sailed skyward in an impressive arc, arms and legs flailing, nearly leaving behind his grimy digits in the necklace's tight loop. He smacked the ocean's surface two boat lengths away with an inelegant splash.

Reef and Bilge retreated to the bow. They stared at Lobster's vacant cap, bobbing on the surface, no sign of the man.

A long moment passed — Lobster's head burst from the brine, wide eyed, gulping air. Fueled as much by anger as fear, he kicked and pinwheeled his arms against the swell, desperate to propel himself back to the craft.

Bilge gathered a rope and flung its knotted end toward Lobster's thrashing hands.

"Grab it!" Reef yelled.

Lobster's bloody fingers grazed the rope knot as he went under.

Reef took up an oar and paddled for the spot where the man had vanished. A bulge of water from something unseen accelerated toward the disturbance.

"It's after him!" Bilge gathered the rope, scanning for a glimpse of his mate.

A gnarled and bleeding hand latched onto the boat's wood-plank transom. Bilge clambered over Reef, the fish, and the selkie, then grabbed Lobster's wrist and lifted him in.

The sea beast, foiled in its pursuit of an easy meal, bumped the little boat from beneath in protest, rocking it violently. Lobster heaved a lungful of water and coughed. He sat up, then pulled his cap from his shirt and fitted it on his dripping head.

"You kicked me block 'n tackle!" Lobster rose and threw the net back over the girl, then roped her from toes to nose to ensure compliance. Adding injury to the insult, he realized he'd cut his fingers on the necklace wire. He pulled the bandana from his throat and dressed his bloody paw. He gathered up the whimpering bundle and hefted her to the stern. "She-devil."

"It's coming back!" said Reef.

The bulge of angry water charged the boat. It grazed the craft's keel with its massive body. The vessel rocked, and the men crouched to keep her from tipping. They searched the water on all sides.

Lobster took up an axe and raised it over his shoulder. "It's a big one. Get the gaff!"

Reef grabbed the long gaff pole and stood ready, aiming its barbed spearhead toward the water. "Look sharp, Bilge. You point and I'll stick it."

Bilge leaned over the starboard side. He looked over the port side, then the bow. "Where'd it go?"

A shadow swept over them, about the size and shape of a small owl. Bilge looked up. The shimmering acrobatic avian soared high, disappearing into a speck as the fisher leaned out over the gunwale, straining to see.

Gen struggled to look beyond the tight mesh of the net. "Hoyl?" she whispered.

Bilge never saw the creature that leapt from the waves — at least not from the outside. His beheaded body sat down, as if to take a rest, then tipped over onto the deck, pouring its life onto Gen's feet.

At the savage sight, Gen blacked out.

7.4

For a moment, the two remaining seafaring souls stood silent over their decapitated compatriot — Bilge's body lying atop their meager catch, beside their improbable castaway, in their tiny boat, on the deep and indifferent sea.

Then Lobster burst into hysterical laughter.

The man seemed to have lost all sense, and Reef judged this as dangerously inappropriate, given the precarious positioning of their puny shallow-draft boat on a vast ocean rife with killers. Among the younger fisher's calculations: Lobster's greater mass, experience in matters of close conflict, and sensitivity to subtle movements that might jeopardize his personal integrity. Reef raised his gig pole, careful that a shadow not signal his elder of his intent to render him inert.

Detecting the younger's shifting weight, Lobster ceased his manic revelry and put hand to blade. Reef simultaneously reassessed his own survival prospects and Lobster's further potential contribution: rowing the great expanse homeward. The younger elected to stow the gig pole below the gunwale so that it, and he himself, could be of service another day.

Fins, tails, and snapping maws churned the crimsoned water. Being practical men foremost, each tucked away his sentiment and took up a rod, casting in opposing directions into the trembling, red confliction. Lobster checked over his shoulder for a distant landmark to get his bearings. He regarded the selkie, slumped in his net. Their return to shore could wait.

Each man reeled in a smallish, sore-pocked grouper, then cast again. Soon, the water calmed, the blood no longer entertaining the schools of silvery scavengers. Reef looked at the haul, disappointing despite their efforts.

Lobster regarded the sea, reluctant to give up its bounty. "The fishes be gettin' bored." He considered Bilge's headless body, lying where it fell. "Waste not, want not." He smirked and grabbed their friend's remains, preparing to deboard the decedent. "Goodbye, old chum!"

Reef quickly laid his hands on Bilge's boots.

Lobster's fishing knife flashed from its holster. "Not your size."

Reef heeded the elder's counsel and retracted his fingers from the footwear.

Lobster claimed his prize from the dead man's feet. "I commit his body to the sea." He hefted the carcass over the side and lamented, "Lucky devil."

The water again swirled in a violent, red orgy of life and death.

7.5

The two seafarers took up their gear and cast again. A heavy silence hovered between them as each focused on his menial task. The pair did not share any grief over their departed fellow; sentiment was not the way of these simple gentlemen. Neither would ever come to terms with the absurdly grizzly event, the shock now folded into a neat black box and put away. These two merely shared the requirement of a boat, and the intent of bringing home a catch sufficient to quell the usual grousing that the dinner was too meager. Each man took up a station; the stronger in the bow, the weaker to the stern. Reef gambled that Lobster's covetous mood had passed and put a hand toward the footwear.

"You want them fingers?" Lobster's knife appeared point-down atop Reef's outstretched paw.

Reef withdrew, eyes wide, shoulders narrow.

A solid six hundred heartbeats passed as the pair continued the current chore, their accord being one of silence. Two men inside a craft, each alone on his own plane.

Gen stirred in the net, its fibers confining and uncomfortable against her sun-toasted skin.

The younger man regarded the girl, by his estimate, not quite an adult, but more than a child. A tender thought arose in the sinewy fisher, one far from the salt spray and toil. Being youthful and unconstructed of mind, he could not hold out any longer. If he solicited Lobster's opinion, perhaps his elder might feel vindicated, respected, even appreciated, and let go the hostility, if not the boots. Reef glanced over his shoulder at his preoccupied compatriot presiding over his tackle and line. Then he turned to his own half of the ocean, cleared his throat to break the silence, and brought himself to ask the man what he knew of love.

Lobster sighed. He glanced at his calloused hand, more accustomed to the gashes and slashes of seafaring than to the caressing of a lover's cheek.

Reef, now too aware of the size of their vessel and its dearth of places of safety, backed against the gunwale and awaited storm or sermon, and steeled himself for the barrage of words or fists or both.

Lobster doffed his cap and a greasy curl fell to his eyes. He brought up the salt from his gullet and spat a whitened dollop mindlessly onto the rusted deck. He collected his thoughts and spoke, more to the sea than to his anxious shipmate.

He warned that a wise man turns his back on all affections;
that love is shallow and short-lived.
When it calls someone to its embrace, to turn away.
The moments of bliss, he opined, were few;
the torment, emergent, would be assured for eternity.
The truth of love, as he saw it, was that it lies;
that love consumes all and gives back nothing;
and that love has no desire except to beget issue,
and to continue the circle of suffering.

At this, Reef felt sick. He hesitated to continue, but given that the man had volunteered his insight, he challenged him again, asking about the fisher's thoughts on marriage.

Lobster shaded his eyes from the glare of the mirror sea. He swept back his wayward curl and donned his cap.

He told the young man that as all were born apart,
so they should remain apart.
To make no bonds.
To let there be a great wave between each other.
To stand near, but not together,
as the pillars of a shared abode are frail and fleeting.

The younger man, invoking his paternal inclinations, pressed his inquisition — albeit in a smaller voice — regarding Lobster's predisposition against children.

Lobster drew a thick breath from the thick air.

He offered that one's children may or may not be one's children.
They are the result of animal instinct unrestrained;
therefore, they do not belong to the parents, supposed or otherwise.
They belong to themselves and to the future that may never come.
Youth has no yesterdays, and few tomorrows;
and one may not dwell with them in either domain.

Shocked and unsettled, Reef searched his mind for a topic less inciting, and asked the weathered mariner for his thoughts on charity and giving. The answer came slowly, as if Lobster was recovering from insult.

He ordered the younger man to give nothing of his possessions;
for he had little that should not be guarded for his use tomorrow.
He questioned the good of the fisher's net cast by the hands of another;
or the catch in the maw of the other.
There was, he declared, neither sustenance nor satisfaction in that.

Lobster punctuated his proclamation with an alimentary expulsion, which momentarily ballooned his britches and startled their passenger.

The short, sharp sound roused Gen from her semi-sentient state. She lay stifled in the net; weak, seasick, and praying for a breeze. She forced open her salt-swollen eyelids. Through the narrow slits and sun streaked haze, she witnessed teacher and student silhouetted against the blue-white heavens, locked in their corrupted philosophizing. She shivered with fever. She retched, dry and unproductive, the sound calling the pair's attention away from their exchange.

Lobster took a breath, about to add to his dour reflections, but lost his thread.

Reef adjusted his derrière atop a coil of anchor line, then again stoked the seaman's fire with a more palatable theme, eating and drinking.

Lobster licked his crusted lips, as if nostalgic for a past meal.

He granted people do not survive on air.
And so long as there is rain, people would drink.
All was there for the taking.

He picked up a gaff, swiping the sharp point over Reef's head as he spoke.

They killed the fishes, and they ate the fishes;
and then they were consumed by the fishes.
Tit for tat.

Reef contemplated the toil of their day and wondered aloud about work.

Lobster stowed the gaff with a quick and reckless flick of his wrist, the sharp end impacting the aft close to Gen's head, the man seemingly unconcerned at nearly impaling the young catch. The girl was almost too weak to blink her swollen and blistered lids.

Lobster continued, now speaking of work.

Support of the flesh was a curse written on every brow;
that work merely kept people from hating life;
that life was darkness;
that it bided time;
that was all.

Dispirited by Lobster's bitter response, Reef pressed him on joy and sorrow.

Lobster grinned.

He exclaimed that there was joy in other's sorrows.
Laughter arose from the tears of another;
how else could it be?
The deeper the sorrow in others, the more joy one can attain.
When joyous people looked deep into their hearts,
they would see that, in truth,
they were delighting in that which brought others despair.
Sorrow and joy were inseparable;
without one there could not be the other, he declared.

Gen was affronted, less by the malodor of the unwashed interlocutors than by the cynicism of their dialectic. She found the dialogue's pattern familiar, though its content, false. Inverted. Twisted to mean something else. The benevolent and pure made malicious and obscene. A vandal obliterating an artwork. She tried to remember the source; perhaps a book of prose poetry that Edison had read to her.

Casting a glance at their castaway, then considering the capriciousness of the elements and the common dependency of mortals upon shelter, Reef tested the straggly scholar on houses and places to live.

Lobster gathered a tattered net together, examining a fresh tear.

He explained one guards all one has behind fastened doors.
More than that, a house holds one's secrets and shelters one's longings;
a house is a tomb made for the living.

Reef reluctantly concurred. He cast his mind about for a new topic. He regarded the waning integrity of his own garb, smiled, and asked Lobster to talk of clothing.

The elder adjusted his rope belt and proclaimed that clothes concealed much of the ugliness and stench of one's being.
Garments were a welcome harness and chain;
a shield against the judgmental eyes of others.

Reef conceded Lobster's point on attire, asserting its further utility against burns from the sun. He asked what he knew about buying and selling; barter and trade.

Lobster grunted and cast his line again.

He said to Reef that the earth barely yielded her fruit;
however, a man shall not want if he knows how to fill his pockets.
In exchanging the gifts of the earth, he said, a person shall never find abundance or satisfaction, unless the exchange is born of greed and contempt, and leaves others in hunger.

When toilers of the sea like themselves meet the weavers and the potters in the marketplace, they should place their thumb firmly on the scales so that value is not weighed against value.

He warned to suffer not the barren-handed to take part in one's transactions, who would sell their words in exchange for one's labor.

He told Reef to say to such men that they should come along to the sea and cast their own nets;

for the land and the sea shall be as un-bountiful to them even as to the fishermen.

Fixed on the red smears on the little boat's deck, Reef thought to remind Lobster that such was the unfortunate Bilge's reward. Hoping to avoid Lobster's long blade and short temper, he refrained, tilting the talk toward crime and punishment.

Lobster, relishing his own contrarian stance, reminded his self-inflicted student that though much of him was a man, more was animal.

There was enough of him that was man to know crime and punishment.

And there was enough animal in the man to embrace transgression and ignore most any consequence.

There is cause and effect, and the trick of it all was to do more causing than effecting.

There was, he said, no difference between the wrongdoer and the righteous.

Both were the same.

Both were to blame.

The murderer should blame the victim.

The unfaithful husband should condemn his wife.

The roots of good and evil were forever intertwined.

His counsel on the matter:

Screw unto others before they screwed unto him.

Reef played along, out of fear and fascination, asking the buccaneer what he made of laws.

Lobster laughed, saying that those who wrote the laws wrote them for others to obey;
that laws were made for breaking.
The only law was that there was no law.

Reef had to agree. He angled another bait in front of Lobster. Freedom.

And Lobster said that he had seen others worship their own freedom,
even as they humbled themselves before the tyrant.
That freedom was slavery, as some ancient sage had said.

Lobster did not believe a scintilla of what he, himself, had uttered. He raised a foot onto the gunwale and gazed over the sea.
Curious if the man ruled with head or heart, Reef beckoned him to speak of reason and passion.

Continuing his unwitting corruption of the ancient prose poem, Lobster declared that there was a battlefield upon which reason and judgment waged war against passion and appetite.
Reason and passion were the rudder and sails of the seafaring soul.
If either sails or rudder were broken, one could but toss and drift, or else be held at a standstill mid-seas.
Reason, ruling on its own, was a constraining force;
and passion, unattended, was a flame that burned to its own destruction.
That was their current state — both constrained and heading toward destruction.

Reef's thoughts turned to those he cared for, should he one day not return from the sea. He asked Lobster about pain.

Lobster regarded his own gnarled hands; the patchwork of scars from hooks and knives and razor-toothed fish.

He told Reef to keep busy, and he would not mind the pain.
Lobster paused, realizing now that Reef's worry was the pain of loss.
Then he scolded that much of Reef's pain was self-chosen, so he should keep his suffering silent.

Reef asked if by "silent," Lobster meant for him to turn inward, to pursue self-knowledge.

Lobster shook his head, and said that Reef already knew the secrets of the days and nights and, in the sleep of death, what dreams may come.
He warned Reef not to seek the depths of his knowledge;
for the self was a turbulent sea, as boundless as it was meaningless.

Reef felt flattened, every hope crushed. He wondered aloud if there was value in teaching.

Lobster was relentless. He said that no one can reveal to a person the wisdom he already possesses, and if Reef were indeed wise, his knowledge should not be lent to another.

Finding that selfish, Reef asked about the value of friendship.

Lobster wiped his face with his blood-clotted rag and glared. Reef recognized there would be no need to explore that subject further with the friendless man; instead, he asked his elder for his words on speaking and talking.

Lobster railed that most spoke to hear their own voices and flapped their lips merely to keep themselves entertained.

He urged the young man to speak when spoken to, and then only reluctantly, as his words would be used against him.

The silence of aloneness was a blessing to one's ears and well-being.

Reef absorbed the sage, if dispiriting, counsel. He then asked about time.

Lobster advised that time, like the young man, is measured, not immeasurable; he urged him to embrace the past with longing and the future with disdain.

The men's eyes followed a disturbance in the water as it circumnavigated their little boat.

Reef concurred that their time was measured; he asked of good and evil. He could almost hear Lobster's greasy gears grinding into motion.

Lobster said he could speak of the evil in him, but not of the good.
One is evil even in sleep.
When one strives for gain one is a root choking earth's breast.
A person is evil in countless ways,
and they are not good when they are not evil.
The nature of good is illusion.
The nature of evil is the nature of all things.

Troubled by Lobster's words, Reef asked what he knew of prayer.

Lobster seemed to take a dark delight in Reef's query and said that people pray in their distress and in their need.
They pour their darkness into the ether and weep.
They ask, and they shall not receive.
They beg for the good of others and they shall not be lifted.
For they have entered the temple invisible, and pray in words unheard to ears imagined.

Lobster slipped his knife from its holster and stroked the blade in languid circles on the gunwale. Reef watched, uneasy, but persisted in his inquisition, owing to inertia and self-preservation. As long as he could keep his elder occupied, he thought he would be safe. So he inquired anew what he made of pleasure — how to distinguish the good in pleasure from the bad. Lobster's knife gleamed in the sun. He slipped it back into the fraying holster.

He rolled the word around in his head —
pleasure — a wrong committed in drunkenness.
Pleasure is not freedom;
seeking pleasure only brings rebuke.
One can dig for treasure but would find only a root.
Forget pleasure to forget regret.
Shun all pleasures so they are not stored in the recesses of one's being.

Lobster turned aft toward the rotted net, the lolling nymph entangled within. Aiming to distract Lobster from the imperiled stranger, Reef catechized him on beauty.

Lobster broke his hungering gaze and turned back to Reef.

The man answered that beauty is a thing of might and dread.
Like a tempest, she shakes the earth beneath and the sky above and drives waves to engulf.
That was what the aggrieved and injured said, and that was what he said, too.

Gathering that Lobster saw divinity in this earth-rattling force, Reef asked his thoughts on religion.

Lobster huffed.
There was no solver of riddles, he proclaimed.

People may look to the heavens but would not see him walking on clouds, outstretching his arms in lightning and descending in rain.

They are alone, Lobster explained, and they always have been.

Reef inquired on death.

Lobster turned and glared daggers. Reef flinched — his pole clattered from his hands into the boat. An avian shadow rippled between them. The pair followed it across the sky.

With that, Lobster continued, less caustic, reflecting on the truer words of the teachings he knew.

The owl, whose night-bound eyes were blind unto the day,
could not unveil the mystery of light.
People would seek the secret of death, he told him;
they would not find it unless they sought it in the heart of life.
Life and death were one, as the sewer and the sea were one.
To die was to stand naked in the wind and to melt into the sun;
and to cease breathing was to free the breath from its restless tides.
Only when one drinks from the river of silence, he warned,
shall one indeed sing.

Reef thought for a moment. He considered the words, and then the man — and the man's keen knife so close at hand. He nodded and responded that all that he said was good and true.

Despite her delirium, Gen had silently absorbed the exchange, dovetailing it to a written work she knew well. "That's not right. You've… you've got it all upside down." She faded again from the exhausting farcicality and the heat.

Gen lay torpid, bound by net and rope in the blood-smeared hull, head propped on a box of tackle. Sunburned. Lips parched. Her damp clothes steaming in a relentless sun.

In the bottom of the craft, their piscine quarry had supplanted the body of the decapitated angler. Tit for tat. The catch was modest, both qualitatively and quantitatively.

Soon, the sea lapped against the sides of the aluminum boat, the rhythm rousing Gen back to awareness. She instinctively licked her lips, her tongue dry and swollen. The odor of humanity singed her nostrils — a bouquet of sweat, body oil, and clothes rancid from gutted fish. Primitive. Unbathed. Foul.

She felt the boat pitch and roll as Lobster pulled a fleshy mass over the gunwale, its tentacles flailing — a huge squid. Swift as an apex predator, he stabbed it through one of its enormous eyes. The animal's life drained away. He pulled the suckers from his forearm, raw, red rings pocking his skin.

"I'll do it," offered Reef.

Lobster nodded. With a flick of his own knife, Reef slit its mantle.

"Mind the ink sac," warned Lobster just as Reef nicked said sac, the dark purple spraying his face.

Lobster laughed. "Don't waste it." He grabbed the sac, cut it free of its owner, and squeezed the last drops of the dark viscous fluid into his mouth, some of it running down his dirty chin.

Gen grimaced and turned away.

A few bits of business remained for the anglers, having followed the sea's adventures to their logical and inevitable conclusions.

Was the discourse between the older man and the younger man classically Platonic?

More or less, with the greater application of their amity attributed to the latter, the magnificence of their aquatic vocation demanding a certain congeniality and cooperation — given the confines of their vessel, the capriciousness of their chosen venue, and the flailing of fish and knives occupying the greater and lesser of their days.

And how did they signal their single commonality?

In excretory palliation. First, rising together on the starboard, in demonstration of, and as members of, the eternal brotherhood; then opposed, the latter and lighter migrating to port with a certain obvious supplication to the former, along with a respect for their craft's tentative buoyancy, exacerbated by the acute list credited to the greater mass of the former.

And why did they depart?

Given that the amber streams were opposite and equidistant, and unified in force if not volume, and owing to Newton, a name resonant to neither, there was little change in the trajectory of the inconsequential craft. Only the micturic penumbra precipitated by a wayward zephyr gave rise to remembrances of, longing for, and anxious consideration of, their point of embarkation. And after apologies appurtenant and befitting men of the sea — that is to say, none — they reclaimed their rotting tackle from the depths.

7.7

The breeze swelled, and the pair instinctively looked to the skies, reading the roil of clouds that confirmed it was time to return to shore.

Reef took up an oar. "The sea wants us home."

"What with that selkie aboard, the fishin's ruined anyway," said Lobster as he tossed his mate the oar's twin. He took the measure of his catch, his crew, and his castaway, then settled in on the bow.

Reef mounted the oar locks in their sockets. His sunbaked arms dipped the blades into the implacable sea, and the jon boat lurched forward.

The young oarsman was unlike anyone Gen knew from Eos. She took in the contours of this unfamiliar face; he was gaunt and his hair was light, but not gray. He resembled the carefree youths in her video lessons, although weathered and filthy. Their eyes met, and he turned away.

The craft's pulsing movement at the urging of the oars unsettled Gen. She strained to peer over the gunwale. She saw the boat's gentle ripples as it made slow progress across the misty sea. Her muzzy mind imagined this was the boat of myth and legend, the one that ferried souls to the underworld.

Lobster glanced back at the girl-shaped lump inside the net, taking up the stern of his boat. It was the end of a long, hard day at sea. They had embarked as three and would return as three, although the loss and gain seemed, to the sailor, hardly equivalent.

Shapes rose on the horizon, a jagged white mosaic against the bluest of skies. Despite the bright sun, a halo of fog rolled up and over the tops of the strange structures.

The distant geometries reminded Gen of the headstones she'd seen. Then she wondered if they could be buildings — her heart leapt. *A city?* This could be merely a trick of the eye, or perhaps she was dead or dreaming — her heart sank. Real or illusion, the vision was luminous in the late day's sun.

A giant devil ray breached the surface some distance off the port side. The creature hovered, as if reconsidering its trajectory, before returning to its natural abode with a slap of its flat fins.

7.8

Hoyl soared Icarus-high, an inconsequential speck against the postmeridian sun. The bird, not a bird, banked and rolled, orienting its crystalline wings to gather the most power in the least time. Gyros twisted within its metallic breast. Its solid state sextant sighted the horizon and noted changes in angles and elevation. It rose on the currents, and in another moment, it was gone.

Silent and spent, Lobster and Reef threaded through the mists and uncertainties, guided by guts and providence, and a fortuitous following sea. The fishers navigated their malodorous and macabre vessel through mats of seaweed and blooms of algal foam.

The craft rocked and lurched along. Gen drifted in and out of consciousness in her monofilament cocoon, her head bumping against the transom in time to every pull of the oars. Bubbles of green-brown foam overtopped the hull and caught in her hair. The oozing globules crackled and popped and insulted her nose, and in her torpor, and confined as she was, she could not brush the fizzing foam away.

The sound of seagulls and breaking waves. The boat glided past a sad, algae-stained high-dive board that hovered inches from the water's surface, a remnant of a once splendorous resort oasis. Ghosts of lounge chairs and parasols peppered the pool's sandy bottom.

Towering above Gen was what seemed to her the life-sized incarnation of her prized pewter miniature. A once-magnificent hotel, shedding chips of faded pink paint in the blazing heat, its lower floors inundated by the sea. A grand lady of an era unknown. The tallest structure she had ever seen in real life. The parapets and setbacks, curvaceous. Windows ornate as an artist's frame. She raised her head, trying to fathom the opulence. *Not a mirage. The city.*

Pairs of curious eyes peered from windows on the upper floors. Deep set. Dark circles. Sunken cheeks. Slack faces. Intrigued, or perhaps troubled, by the oddly human-shaped bundle tangled inside the men's cast net. Gen tried to focus. To stay awake. She saw men behind the broken panes. She saw women and children. Bedraggled. She supposed they were searching for one of their own. One who embarked at daybreak and did not return at day's end. Would they mourn and rend garments? Would they console or lay blame? Exultation and despair cartwheeled through Gen's mind. Exultation at the discovery of the city so long occult from her. Despair over the horrific fate of the fisher. Her wounds ached, the salt burning into her open sores. She wanted her mother. Her eyes rolled back, and she lost consciousness.

Wavelets crossed the submerged poolside deck, dashed onto the rear of the hotel, and drew back to the sea. Reef guided the little boat to a section of the structure just above the waterline, sprouting an outcrop of rusting industrial kitchen ducts. Lobster jumped from the bow, landing with the grace of an acrobat, and vanished over a ledge. Reef spun the tie-rope around a rusted vent pipe with aplomb, securing their vessel against the tides.

From a high window, a little girl in rags smiled and waved. Reef raised a hand in acknowledgement, glanced to see if Lobster was watching, and returned to his chores with haste.

Lobster reappeared with a surfboard. It was longer than he was tall, and green with algae. The jagged, semicircular chomp taken from its nose declared both the might of the biter and the ultimate disposition of the board's erstwhile owner. He eased into the water and floated the surfboard alongside the boat. "Help me get her on," he said. "And leave her in the net. Don't want no trouble."

"How about the boots?"

"Keep 'em."

"What about the catch?"

"Got bigger fish to fry." Lobster laughed a hearty sailor's laugh.

7.9

The harsh sun and sea spray dropped off into a musty canyon of darkness. Gen opened her eyes with a start. She struggled to move, but found herself still wrapped in the weighted fishing net. She was floating again. This time on a narrow board. It was unsteady, and any action threatened to topple her from her wobbly perch. She realized she was being pulled along feet first, the older fisher leading by the board's leash, up to his waist in gray water. The stink in his wake stung her nose, and the space melded the odors of mildew and the shore of her recent peregrination. The passenger and her ferryman had entered a terraced hall of considerable expanse, inundated with sea water. A chandelier hung from its apex, akimbo, its crystals black with mold.

She peered between the monofilament webbing that bound her. A parade of Romanesque marble statues and mirrored walls, all stained green with algae. A palace more befitting Poseidon.

A long desk ran the length of a wall, the level of the water reaching for its thick marble top, and there, alone, waited the rusted remnants of a call bell, long silent. Behind the desk was a checkerboard of small compartments bedecked with numerals, green with oxidation.

Gen reached back into the plethora of video lessons to which she had been subjected: Art. Architecture. Culture. Work. Leisure. This was a hotel. But dilapidated. Rotting. The check-in counter awaiting guests who would never come.

A mezzanine hovered above, a floor between floors bounded by a rail and open to the lobby. At its edge, dirty children in rags cast their fishing lines into the lobby waters below.

Gen was the singular participant in the processional, save for the uncombed porter of her makeshift stretcher. All eyes were upon her. *So many eyes.* She imagined herself, again, as a specimen under her mother's microscope. A foreign body on a slide.

As Lobster pushed past the waterlogged check-in desk, he brushed aside the spider web of fishing lines. The waifs cursed him foully; the smallest of them spat into the water, igniting a ripple of children's giggles. Their elder looked up and glared, and the juveniles scattered.

Lobster pulled the bier along like purgatory's gondolier, on a heading to a broad, curved ramp rising from the waters to the mezzanine.

"Who are you?" Gen asked. Her voice echoed off the water and walls.

"Nunya."

"What?"

"Nunya business."

"What…? Where am I?"

"Hell."

"Where are you taking me?"

"To meet the Devil," said Lobster.

A wave crashed against the hotel's side, cascading through a long-shattered plate-glass window, pouring thousands of gallons into the sodden lobby. It caught the surfboard broadside, flipping Gen into the brine, the weights of the net pulling her below.

Lobster fished out the flailing bundle and threw her over his shoulder. She coughed up an ocean. She wanted desperately to break free; run away. The net was too tight around her to allow struggle, and she was too exhausted and frightened to move, anyway.

The last of the curious waifs darted for the shadows as Lobster crested the top of the ramp and entered the grand mezzanine with his netted bounty. Gen's head was inconveniently close to the filthy fisher and his fetid clothes, the fragrance rousing her like smelling salts.

The mezzanine lounge was at one time opulent, the stale elegance of plaster crown moldings and foil wallpaper clinging purely out of habit. The sad husk of an intricately carved mahogany wet bar, grime-covered and forgotten. A grand piano, collapsed under the weight of time and sea air in a heap of splinters and black lacquer, its ivories the teeth of an extinct leviathan.

Faded, framed photographs of persons unknowable, perfected in their complexions, bedecked the walls — their subjects posed in strange garb both stiff and inappropriate for most occasions. Some held small golden sculptures of an idealized man. Beyond, a vibrant fresco offered a sailless African dhow, steam boiler proudly puffing its way into maritime and cultural history. On the dhow's deck, a man in a sweaty shirt and cap hunched over the boat's steam engine while a slim, fine-featured woman in a long white dress and broad bonnet reclined under a shade at the stern.

Lobster proceeded past the decayed diorama undistracted, moving straight toward a door, next to it a rusty sign: "Stairs." He was strong, but weary from the long day's watery work. He chose the shortcut. He moved toward the pair of stainless steel doors, two buttons beside, one with an upward arrow, the other downward.

His dirty finger pressed the up-arrow button. With a deep rumble, the mechanism shuddered to life. After a moment, a sour chime, and the metal doors slid open to offer conveyance. The doors slid shut behind them and the little box darkened to the unreliable lumens of its emergency light.

Gen didn't quite understand this tiny room with its steel doors. Through the net, she could see a panel of buttons; two at the bottom were hand-marked "flooded." She detected a faint, scratchy, rhythmic sound; perhaps music.

Lobster chose the topmost button, marked "P." The elevator thumped hard, jerked, then carried them skyward. She felt the strange weight of her first elevator ride as the tired machinery lugged its payload. Her ears popped. When the car reached its destination and bobbed to a stop, her stomach didn't. She heaved a schooner of salt water.

Then the metallic maw opened to disgorge its riders. Lobster's heavy footfalls broke the silence of the top floor's unlit hallway as he transited the constellation of fallen paint chips dotting the midnight blue carpet.

Gen could just make out numbered doors on either side. Something fluttered past her throbbing head. Bat or bird, it was too dim to tell. Her stomach churned and her heart raced.

Lobster arrived with his prize at the last door at the far end of the hallway. Beside it, a tarnished brass placard read: "Bridal Suite."

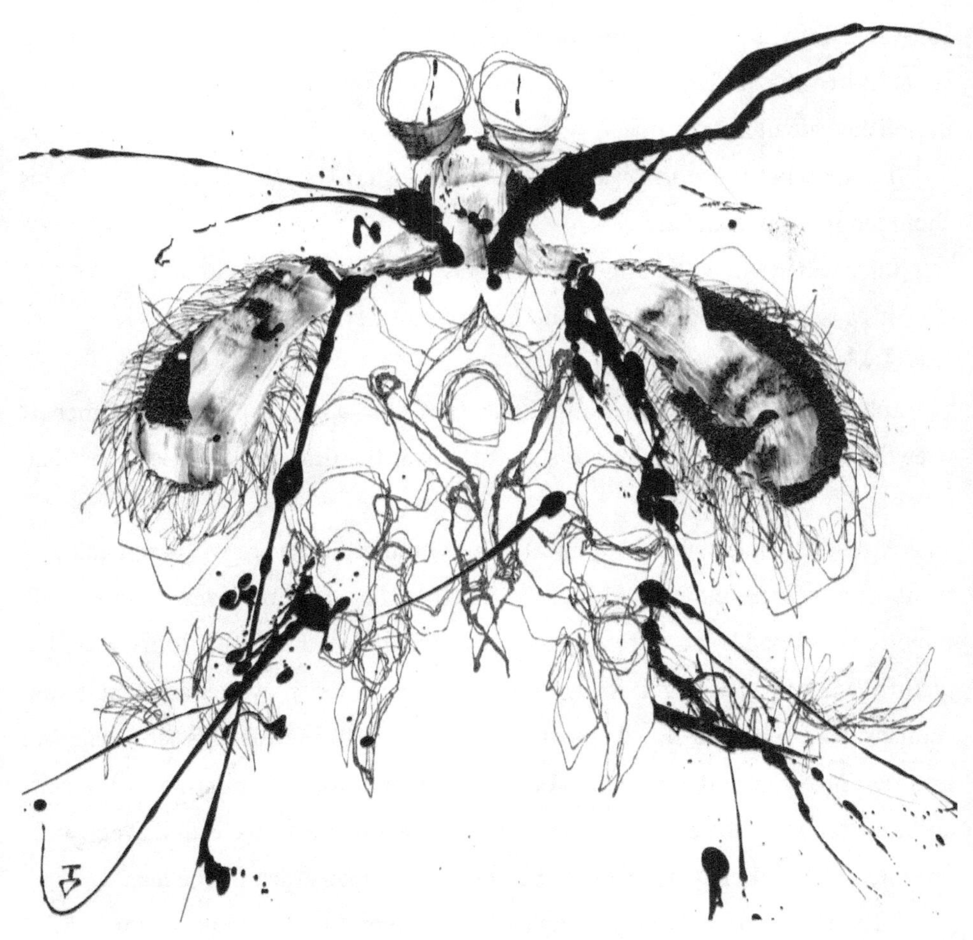

BOOK VIII:

Far Away and Phantom

Lobster rolled his head, neck stiff from surveying sea and sky. He knocked. And waited. He doffed his cap and, with equal parts hubris and haste, smoothed his grimy hair with his palm. He knocked again. "Room service!"

From beyond the door came a commanding male voice: "Enter."

A deadbolt clattered, and the wedding suite's door swung open. There stood Saltwater Taffy, in crudely crayoned lipstick, bursting out of her skimpy top and short skirt. She flashed a wry half-smile at Lobster, impeding entry with her unpolished albeit ample appeal.

"Looky what the storm washed in," said Lobster. He shifted the parcel on his shoulder and started inside.

Taffy halted him with a finger to his chest. "Don't bring that in here!"

"It's a selkie." Lobster winked and pushed past her.

"A what?" said Taffy.

Lobster dumped the bundle that was Gen onto a gaudy pink satin armchair near the entrance. The girl let out a groan. It was the first dry land Gen's feet had touched for days.

"A selkie. A mermaid. A mythical half-human sea creature with the head and trunk of a woman and the tail of a fish," said Luddy. The man was standing, tall, imperious, framed by the afternoon sun overwhelming the suite's floor-to-ceiling picture window. His rigid form was unified in a crisp white dress suit and similarly snowy button-down shirt and shoes, the only contrast, his sable hair and opaque, mirrored aviator sunglasses. The garments were as pristine as the self-cleaning miracle fabric smocks Gen's mother wore. He was clean shaven, well-groomed and strikingly handsome, the only flaw a small crack in one lens.

Taffy tried to peer into the many folds of netting. "It stinks. Like rotten fish."

"She. And she'll clean up nice," said Lobster.

"So, why's she tied up? She bite?" said Taffy, with a laugh.

"She's feisty. Took three of us to get her into those ropes."

"Lobster. Unbind her, please," said Luddy.

The fisherman huffed and shook his head; he certainly wasn't eager to untie her after the blows she had dealt him on the boat. "You stay still, she-devil." He steeled himself and approached Gen haltingly, untying the rope that bound the net to her. He grabbed the net by the hem and the yoke of the cast line, and then lifted, unveiling the girl like a bride. The monofilament crosshatched her raw skin. She whimpered, then blinked and looked around her, wide-eyed and shaking.

"Like I said. She'll clean up real nice." The lead weights of the cast net clattered softly as the fisher carefully folded it to stow.

Despite the filth and the scars of her trek, the ingénue was a natural beauty.

"Not much to her," scoffed Taffy.

"Where are you from?" asked the tall man, folding his arms, the distressed girl's image reflecting in his mirrored lenses.

Gen's eyes darted around the room, accosted by colors and shapes unfamiliar. The bridal suite was at once palatial and lascivious. A place that had seen many brides demand romance and many grooms fall short. Gaudy crimson carpet, gold vein antiqued mirrors, and peeling gold-tone chrome. Faded hearts-and-doves wallpaper in black, maroon, pink, and gold curled away from a high corner. The living quarters were apartment-like, with a seating area. Just beyond, the heart-shaped nuptial bed, its pink satin duvet aged and faded, a matching sunken spa tub completing the tableau. A crystal pitcher and glass waited on a room service cart, sparkling and cool. Lending an incongruous gravitas to the frivolous decor: an ornate burled walnut executive desk and a bookshelf crowded with dusty tomes.

"She ain't never seen a place this fancy," said Taffy.

"Do you know where you are?" Luddy asked the girl.

Gen's gaze absorbed the multicolored light glowing through a stained glass window as overbearing as the room's occupants, its massive scope befitting a Gothic cathedral. A beach scene like the one in her home tanning suite, but amended. Frozen within its ostentatious carved frame, newlyweds leaned into their first married kiss beneath a bough of palms as the full moon rose in a cyan sky, its glow reflected in the ocean's sparkling water. A pleasure boat, beached on the sand. A lifeguard tower in all its playful pastel beauty, its tanned sentinel surveying breakers and beach through dark glasses.

Gen opened her mouth but produced only a dry cough.

"Water," Luddy commanded.

Taffy begrudgingly took his cue, disappearing into the bathroom.

Moving with the stiffness of a man much older, Luddy seated himself in a chair behind the desk. He leaned forward. "Bayside or oceanside?"

"Ocean," Lobster reported.

"And the compass?"

"Dunno. Maybe southeast. Probably out there a while on account o' the shape o' da bodies keepin' her company," said Lobster. "The biters got 'em. Almost got her, too." Lobster chuckled, omitting the details.

Luddy settled back in his chair and rubbed his chin.

Taffy returned with a murky glassful. "Here you go, sweetie."

"Fresh water, please," said Luddy. "In a clean glass."

As she turned around, she stuck out her tongue at him. Lobster smirked. Taffy retrieved the pitcher from the service cart, filling a tumbler along the way. As she passed, Lobster grabbed at the glass. Taffy swept it out of reach.

"Just lookin' to slake me drought," said the fisher.

"Nuh-uh, get your own."

"It's the only clean water in the whole damn place."

Gen licked her lips; they were parched, sunburned, blistered. She took the glass from Taffy and gulped it down. The water detoured to her windpipe, and she coughed. "I want to go home."

Lobster and Taffy looked at each other and chuckled.

"It speaks!" said Taffy. She bent close to Gen's face, peering at her features. "Pretty." She huffed.

Gen pulled back. "Get away from me!"

"Told you she's feisty," said Lobster.

Luddy leaned in. "Taffy…" he warned.

"Don't look so feisty to me," Taffy said, snatching the glass back from the girl.

Gen noticed an abstract geometric symbol tattooed on Taffy's forearm. She recalled such marks on Lobster and the other fishermen. She wondered what it meant, remembering a video lesson on tribal rituals.

"What's that green thing on her back?" Taffy said.

"Some kinda sea bag," said Lobster, wrestling the knapsack off Gen's shoulders.

"Hey! That's mine!" Gen tried to stand.

Taffy cracked Gen on the temple with the water pitcher. The girl slumped to the floor with a thud, a deep gash on her forehead. She was out cold. Blood seeped from the wound.

"Taffy! You fool!" Luddy rose from his chair.

Taffy turned away and scowled. Lobster dropped the knapsack.

"Put her on the bed," ordered Luddy.

Lobster took Gen's arms, and Taffy grabbed her feet. They flopped her on the bridal bed, the girl landing in Taffy's own nocturnal indentation. Taffy groaned at the trespass.

The bedchamber's ornamentation rivaled the rest of the suite, with crystal lamps and the same red, pink, and black befitting this onetime stage for Olympic lovemaking. The spa tub, empty, awaited its next adventure.

Lobster tossed Gen's knapsack on the night table. The tracker was dark, its winking call for help forever muted.

Gen's puka necklace caught Taffy's eye. "Ooh. I'll take that."

Lobster grabbed her wrist. "Ya' don't wanna touch that." He showed her his hand, wrapped in the blood-stained bandana.

Taffy jerked her hand free, then turned her attention to the damp knapsack bulging with Gen's seawater-soaked personal possessions. She tossed out the soggy, stuffed toy lemur, the bell around its neck tinkling as it hit the floor. Then out came a few hair clips, the wide-toothed comb, a mushy bar of soap, the cast pewter skyscraper miniature, moccasins, and a spare top. Taffy held Gen's girlish shorts to her own ample hips, modeling them for Lobster. He smirked. She tossed the shorts on the carpet. Then she spotted something glinting in the bottom of the pack: the tiny bejeweled perfume bottle. Taffy snapped it up, opened the top, and sniffed. "Nice," she said, securing the lid, then tucking it into her bosom.

Lobster took his turn, jamming in his hand and pulling out Gen's mother's journal. "Some kinda book," he said, sniffing its leather cover, then tossing it on the floor with Gen's other accoutrements, where it landed with a thump.

Taffy looked down at the soggy tome. Her face went stony. The interloper on her bed could speak — and could read, too.

"Pick that up. All of it. Whatever it is. I do not want things underfoot," said Luddy. The accused conspirators obliged, shoving the scattered articles back in the sack, topping it with the stuffed toy.

"Except the book. Hand it to me, please," said Luddy.

Lobster obliged, fishing the journal from the depths of the sack and placing it in the tall man's outstretched hand. Taffy scowled at the cowed mariner.

"Now, leave!" ordered Luddy, impatiently.

"You heard him. Out," Taffy said.

"Both of you," said Luddy.

"Right," said Lobster, taking an open-mouthed Taffy by her elbow. She dropped the stranger's satchel to the floor.

"But Luddy…!" whined Taffy.

Lobster herded Taffy out of the suite, she trotting in her heels to keep up. The door closed behind the ejected pair, and the latch slid home.

Luddy made his way to a wall, opened the lid on a brass horn, and spoke into the tube. "Send up a meal tray. For two. Right away, please. With a fresh pitcher. Thank you."

A tinny voice echoed a quick confirmation.

Luddy parked the journal on his desktop, then moved across the carpeted expanse with measured steps and sat down at the unconscious girl's bedside. He took her face in his hands, reading her fine features, then feeling the bump on her brow where Taffy had struck her. He drew a handkerchief from his pocket and dabbed off the moist blood. It seemed to him as though the wound had already closed. He was only half-surprised. "What sort of thing are you, I wonder."

8.2

The drowned journal lay open upon Luddy's desk, drying in a light breeze afforded by open jalousies. Pages curled in the sun; the inked hypotheses, formulas, and findings running in desiccated rivulets of black and blue. Luddy rose from his desk chair and stood before the picture window, a sentinel of stiff vigilance. The panorama encompassed the wild sea and a tranquil bay. Carcasses of skyscrapers pocked the bayside waters, sunbeams streaming through their carbon steel bones. City-sized ocean liners lay abandoned, half-submerged, some in impossible angles of repose, the once outlandishly luxurious leviathans rusting in their Valhalla. Beyond, a rainbow heralded the end of a distant monsoon.

The tall man put a hand to the windowpane and felt its warmth. He let the sun caress his face. He touched his wristwatch, its missing crystal allowing his fingertips to address the hands directly. The meal tray would arrive soon. The "SoBes," as they called themselves, heeded the circadian mandates of sunrise and sunset, paying little notice to their sovereign's anachronistic references to precise hours and minutes. He gave his watch a few shakes to stimulate its self-winding mechanism.

A timid knock on the door.

"Enter," said Luddy, the ocean rollers reflected in his mirrored lenses.

The door swung open, and a cart rolled in, bedecked with a long, white tablecloth, hosting a fresh water pitcher and a silver serving platter under a silver dome. Tending it was a gaunt, petite, servile woman, pin-up braids framing a careworn face, her tattered maid's uniform bearing a name tag: "Marina."

"By the bed," he instructed.

When Marina noticed the teenaged girl lying unconscious on the satin duvet, she averted her eyes, then pushed the cart next to the bed and turned back to him. "Anything else, sir?"

The sound of the sea. The tall man at the window. A room full of emptiness. A breeze rustled the journal's pages. Marina slipped out of the bridal suite, closing the door behind her.

Luddy shuffled toward the cart, reaching out until the silver dome's handle met his hand. He lifted it and extracted one of the seaweed-wrapped fish morsels. He popped it in his mouth whole. As he chewed, he sat down on the edge of the bed beside the senseless teen. His toe brushed the edge of the pack, still on the floor. He shook his head, then picked it up and set it on the bed beside its owner. Luddy had not yet the opportunity to question the girl about her origins. He did not even know her name. He listened as her shallow breaths grew less labored.

He stood and turned his attention to the heart-shaped tub. He twisted the brass faucet knobs. The cascade filled the suite with a tranquil white noise.

•• — •• ••

Within the strongest beams of the sun resided a glass shelf, repurposed as a garden. It housed a multi-colored menagerie of potted plants among a greater number of vacated vessels. Luddy picked up a mister and sprayed each specimen in turn. Droplets collected on his white jacket's sleeve, beaded, and dripped off. He focused his attention on two identical aloe veras in clay pots, both a bit larger than a man's fist. He wiped each leaf of the succulents with a fingertip, removing bits of dust. "I see the twins are doing well," he said, half to his verdant friends and half to himself, and he returned the mister to the shelf.

Luddy considered his guest. The materials she had brought with her, and their import. The effect of her presence on the delicate civil equilibrium he had labored to establish. He heard the water running into the tub and, sufficiently stimulated, moved briskly to the powder room.

The service cart's tablecloth stirred. A girl of about six emerged from beneath, elfin, a child of lack, her hair in golden braids neatly wound around the crown of her head. She stared at the teen with curious eyes. Touched Gen's cropped raven curls. Tried to pry open a sunburned lid with her little fingers. No response.

Keeping one eye on Gen, the child opened the flap of the green sack and was greeted by the stuffed toy lemur, peeking its fuzzy head out of the top. The waif smiled in wide-eyed delight. She grabbed the toy. The tiny bell around its neck tinkled.

At the familiar sound, Gen roused. "Hey, that's mine!!"

8.3

The little girl flung the hotel room door open and darted out with her prize. Gen gave chase. The sound of the running water masked the fracas and footfalls, and the girls were long gone before Luddy emerged from his restroom respite.

Gen sprinted down the hallway after the tiny toy thief, her steps booming as loud as her pulse. Scruffy heads with slack jaws peeked out of rooms as the pair zoomed past.

The child looked behind and squealed, Gen's toy still gripped in her hand as she disappeared around a corner. The little girl raced down a dark hallway, a disorienting juxtaposition of light and shadow. Here and there, tarnished silver-domed room service trays lay on the floor next to the numbered doors, abandoned by guests. The waif tripped on a tray, fell, and dropped the stuffed lemur. The silver dome clanged against a wall. She snatched up the plaything and scrambled away, disappearing around another corner.

Gen pursued the commotion. She dashed down the hall, vaulting a minefield of tray covers without breaking stride. She came to a "T" at the end of the passage, listened for a moment, then took off, following the faint footfalls.

The mini-fugitive tried a door — locked. Another. No luck.

Gen rounded the next corner in time to espy the petite pilferer ducking behind a door marked "Maid Service Employees Only." She bolted up the hallway — tried the knob — locked. She pounded. "Hey! Give it back! Open up!" Infuriated, she gathered the tips of her fingers together, tucked in her thumb, and thrust her hand clean through the door. A tiny shriek satisfied Gen that the culprit was cornered. She reached inside, ripped off the knob, and shoved the door inward, nearly knocking it off its hinges.

The shelves of the windowless closet were filled with frayed white towels, not more than rags, and empty containers still outgassing chlorinated solvents and lavender. A headless mop handle stood in a corner, tucked into a rolling bucket. On the far wall was a square metal opening marked "Laundry."

The tyke clutched the plush doll and edged backward.

Gen held out her hand. "Give it back!"

The child cowered and pressed the plaything to her chest.

Gen hesitated. Before her was a very young girl who had taken a nearly worthless object — and yet Gen was on the verge of violence. The teen's shoulders slumped. She felt her cheeks get warm, ashamed. "I'm… I'm—"

"You're a selfish little turd!"

Gen stood gobsmacked by the child's colorful rebuke.

The waif tossed the toy into the metal maw, then darted past Gen into the dim hall and disappeared.

Gen lunged into the opening after her doll — she found herself tumbling head-first down a chute, catching her stuffed animal on the way. A blur of smooth galvanized steel walls raced past, giving her hands and feet no purchase. She managed to flip herself right side up. The duct sloped left and she banged her butt, the toy popping from her grasp. Falling. The chute straightened. Her palms and soles squealed on steel. An abrupt turn — Gen's shoulder slammed hard. The smell of stagnant water and air suddenly cool. A glimpse of light ahead — she landed with a splash!

8.4

Gen opened her eyes in water dark with tannin and rust, stirring with sea life. Something wrapped around her: black, torsional, with elastic limbs, a smooth head, and a single, enormous eye. Gripped by the thing's appendages, she struggled against its thrashings until both finally popped to the surface. Brown water spouted from its snorkel.

She looked at it — it looked at her — both screamed.

"I told you kids not to come down here. You're scaring off the…" said the man encased in a too-small black rubber suit, as he slid his squoval swimming mask and snorkel up to his forehead. His eyes now combed her unfamiliar features. "Who… What… Where'd you come from?" A pitiful little fish wriggled on his three-prong spear.

Gen broke free from the frogman's grasp and pointed up into the laundry chute's square opening in the ceiling, its discharge door dangling open. He huffed, then released the neck flap on his wetsuit. He looked at the soaking wet girl, and up at the chute, then threw his head back and laughed.

Flustered, Gen turned around in the waist-high water. "What is this place?" She snatched her plush toy as it floated by.

"Fishin' hole. *My* fishin' hole, actually." He worked the puny catch off of his barbed trident and put it in a pouch. "You must be the new one. I'm called Jetty."

Brow furrowed, Gen only glanced at the diver, her focus on how to escape the odd underground pool and its odder occupant. Rusted shelves, empty. Water, trickling down a wall. Towering metal boxes lined the room's perimeter, flooded halfway up their cyclopic glass portals. The white enameled cubes seemed to float as silken clouds in a tannin sky. A concrete room, illuminated by a row of small, high, algae-stained basement window panes, leaking, the ocean determined to enter. A puffer fish peered in, inflated its spiny body, and darted away. "Nothing to say?" The frogman slipped his mask and snorkel back on and sunk below the brown surface.

Now alone with the echoes of sloshing water, Gen espied a sign on the far wall — a figure climbing a zigzag. Yellow and black slip-hazard stripes ribboned on the pool's surface. Flaked red paint denoted: "EXIT." *A staircase?*

The water swelled with the passions of pursuit, the darting dance of predator and prey. A splash. The frogman surfaced, a flat fish the diameter of his hand flopping on the tips of his trident. He parked his mask atop his forehead and spat his snorkel. "Fishin's bad. Somethin's getting at 'em before I can," he complained. "Gave each other a plenty good scare, didn't we?" he said, as a strange look of relief moved across his face. The water warmed and ambered, and Gen stepped back, disgusted.

Something moved under the surface. The man turned, a cat espying his mouse. Jetty jabbed at the water like a madman until he speared his quarry. He drew up his gig. Flailing at him in its death throes was a colorful, lobster-like arthropod about the length of his arm, its dagger legs reaching out to draw the diver close, rainbow eyes trained on its captor.

"Mantis shrimp," said Jetty. Distracted with his audience of one, he paid no heed to the twin hammer appendages aside the animal's mouthparts as they locked into position. "Just a baby."

Gen clutched her sopping toy as she hugged the periphery, edging toward the exit.

The creature's crustaceous weaponry shot out, the rock-hard hammers smashing the glass on Jetty's dive mask. He yowled.

She looked back at the man in horror, then thrust herself from the water and raced past the zig zag sign and up the basement stairs.

8.5

Taffy perched on the edge of Luddy's desk, legs crossed, turning the leaves of the journal from the girl's sack. Those pages not still damp were now warped as rollers on the sea, and the scientist's scrawl sailed the peaks and troughs of her logic. Taffy came upon a folded sheet clipped to the first page. She slipped the paper from the clip and unfolded it. "Weird."

"What's weird?" asked Luddy, as he felt the plump leaves of a succulent in his window garden.

"It's just a piece of paper with stuff printed on it. I mean, it's not handwriting."

"Clearly a message that the journal's owner thought valuable. Continue."

She read aloud from the yellowed sheet. "Transcription of the final report by Dr. H. York, PhD. Dearest colleagues. I am voice recording this, as I've quite lost fine motor control. Typing or writing… an exercise in futility… evidence of my deception… older chronologically… Forgive me… Something. Something. That's funny, Luddy. He talks big like you."

"Please continue."

Taffy sighed. "…the myelin sheath erosion…. epidermal lesions… prodromes… lucid until now… flashes of color and hearing tones… And then something about 'my dynamic conclusion.' What's that mean?"

"Try not to summarize, please."

She sighed, then resumed. "My deepest apologies for my outburst last night. I realized I would not be available to complete our important work. The cursed sores had appeared, and I was incapable of hiding the inevitability from you, my dear friends."

Luddy turned his head. "Sores?"

"Yeah, cursed sores."

"Please continue."

Taffy traced the lines with a fingernail. "Like the unfortunate Gregor Samsa in Kafka's sad tale, my metamorphosis had begun." She chuckled. "Kafka."

"Most likely not ours," said Luddy. "Is there more?"

Taffy found her place. "The discord I initiated table-side was for your benefit, you see. A minor deceit, so I might sequester myself here in my quarters. Of course, in my natural absentmindedness, I neglected to bring a tarpaulin to my abode. More aptly, my morgue. You'll see that I have draped my bedsheets on the sofa as my funerary shroud. The configuration of the improvised bier should afford easy disposal. I gambled we would find the cure before my clock rang midnight — and I lost. I realized that Batch A2-9029-C was unsuccessful when I felt the first lesion appear. By the way, the time from paresthesia — those first tingles — to presentation, and serous drainage, was startlingly short. A nearly insufficient period to intellectually process. I am, even at the lateness of the hour, simultaneously horrified and fascinated by the syndrome." Taffy shook her head. "Luddy, I don't understand some of these words."

"Keep reading."

She frowned and pressed on. "It is indeed the most egalitarian of diseases. We had found it permeated all strata of society. Classes, races, economic groups. As it turns out, we humans had more in common than we had supposed. Our ability to acquire disease and transmit it to others. Our shared facility for unlimited suffering. The disease itself was malign in its manifestation. Graphically evident when certain of our numbers were reduced spontaneously to odiferous organic puddles. To our detriment, we widely ignored the phenomenon at first, just as we deemed hantavirus and other hemorrhagic contagions an issue afflicting faraway lands. Blamed them on poor sanitation or ignorance or racial inferiorities. Cultural bias being a primary tool in the efficacy of plagues. We lost time navigating those biases. A mistake. A very costly one.

"I rescind my reportage that the process is painless. I am just now paralyzed. Without doubt, the blood-brain barrier has been compromised, the pain centers stimulated. Chills. Extreme nausea. Booming cephalalgia. The pressure. The bell tolls for me. It has been my pleasure. No, honor, to work with you all. This is the final entry of Doctor Hamnet York, PhD. I trust you will continue the research and hit upon the optimal and equitable solution. Godspeed, Team Eos. Oh, my G—" Taffy flipped the paper over, but there was no more. "Huh. That's all there is to it."

"Uncanny. He appeared to be observing his own death." Luddy turned a plant in the window garden, exposing neglected leaves to the sun. "Please continue. Something from the handwritten passages."

She tucked the missive under its clip and returned to scanning the journal entries, but then bookmarked a page with a finger. "Why not tell Lobster to round up some men and go catch the girl?"

"She's tired. She's hungry. There is no place for her to go," said Luddy. "Continue."

Taffy returned to her saved passage. "In these test subjects, we have isolated the Hayflick limit on cell replication imposed by the shortening of telomeres with each division, thus controlling mitoses and the apoptosis process. The research was inspired by the resetting of epigenetic clocks in gregarious bamboo species, e.g., Bambusa Vulgaris." Taffy sighed. "This book isn't very good. It's just gibberish."

"Is it?" said Luddy. He picked up one of his twin aloe vera plants and felt the tumescent leaves.

"I think you like those plants more than you like me."

Luddy stifled a smile. "Did you know that the aloe vera photosynthesizes during the day, but to reduce evaporation in arid conditions, it exchanges gasses only at night? That means it collects carbon dioxide only at night."

Taffy huffed.

Luddy plucked an imperfect leaf from the base of the aloe. "I need you to do something for me. Listen to my instructions, and follow them exactly."

Taffy entered a hotel room, a potted aloe plant in her hand, Gen's knapsack strapped over her shoulder. The decorative theme of this cramped cubicle could generously be called "simple," its sparse utility rendering it unappealing to the other residents — hence its availability. A small, sagging bed with two flat pillows, a plain dresser, and a chair. A mirror above the dresser; cracked diagonally, only a shard remaining. Wrinkled wallpaper. Stains blotting the ceiling. And a charred mark above an electrical socket, memorializing an incident of undetermined vintage.

Taffy tossed the teen's sack atop the dresser and made her way to the window. She pulled the cord on the withered drapes. They parted, unleashing billows of dust. She grimaced and coughed as she tucked the plant into a patch of sun at the corner of the sill. She tugged at the window handle. It would not budge — the pane painted shut.

Taffy chuckled a little at the thought of the teen tolerating the humble hovel — but there was a time when she herself would have thought this sorry room as sumptuous as Luddy's suite. She eyed the air vent near the ceiling, directly above the headboard. She stepped onto the freshly made bed and removed the vent cover.

STATUS: SECTOR LOST 01:08:005;14 (See Technical Notes)

Marina pushed her housekeeper's cart through the dark halls until she came to the room at the end. She eased the cart over next to the door and entered.

Taffy spun around, her hands frozen on the opened knapsack.

"Oh. Miss Taffy. I was just bringing the towels," said Marina.

Taffy let go of the knapsack and huffed. "Well… I was just bringing a little gift from Luddy." Then she waltzed out.

Marina nodded deferentially after the tall man's woman. Hung the towels in the cramped bath. Smoothed out the bedspread. Fished a pillow from a shelf on her cart to replace the one missing. She ran a finger across the tattoo on her wrist;

an intricate rune, uncompleted. She wiped her beaded brow, then held her hand up to the vent. No air. But she hoped their guest would not mind.

8.6

Shivering as much from fright as the dampness of her clothes, Gen peered down a long hallway as dark and dank, she thought, as those that once held casks of Amontillado.

The walls were plain, scarred with the ghosts of wooden forms that had once held-fast fresh concrete, and bereft of the ornamentation she'd seen elsewhere in the hotel. Chunks were missing from the bone-white walls; a puzzle with pieces lost. Along the cracks and seams were crystalline niter ridges as sharp as quartz, evidence of years of seawater intrusion. Next to her, a sign on a metal door read: "Staff Stairs."

The crude passage angled downward to a flooded grating that bisected its path, gurgling and burping gray fluid. Pipes and ducts serpentined the length of the ceiling, paralleled by a string of tiny lightbulbs hung without care, their reflections shimmering on the slick surface. Beyond, the hall angled up toward an unknown end.

She warily proceeded down the hall amid drips, echoes, and murmurings through rusting ductwork. A canvas-sided laundry cart, missing a wheel, rested on its side. Now she knew where she'd seen the metal boxes before. Their geometric shapes meshed with memories of a day of surreptitious explorations of a forgotten facility at Eos. She had wandered the unfrequented viscera into the ghost of a once bustling workroom lined with elephantine equipment, the shelves tidy and stocked as if laundresses would reemerge from a hazy past and resume their chores. An old commercial laundry from a linen-scented era, encapsulated. But the strange, subterranean caisson she had just fled looked pillaged, and pummeled by decay and inundation.

A crash! Gen turned around. A chunk of concrete had spalled from the ceiling, smacking the floor where she was standing moments before.

At the midpoint, she hopped over the flooded grate, nearly losing her balance on the slippery surface. She wrung out her watery companion as she ascended the slope of the tunnel. She mounted a low concrete platform that accommodated a pair of metal doors with familiar up and down buttons. Opposite, a single door seemed more promising. She pushed it open, her nostrils assaulted by the stench of things not long dead.

The pipes that serpentined the hallway here twisted illogically along the ceiling, then disappeared into the walls. A string of tiny colored bulbs illuminated a room furnished in peculiar geometries fashioned from sheet steel that had long ago lost its luster, a thick mix of corrosion and grease reaching to the floor.

Massive metal counters bisected the room and lined the periphery. Three sinks in a row, each large enough to bathe in. Cabinets rising to the brown stained ceiling, some with doors hanging. Condensation covering the walls. Empty steel racks. Utensils on hooks. An oven, its door ajar, smoldering with embers of driftwood. The stainless steel counters reminded Gen of her mother's lab — but sans scientific equipment and the alcohol-infused clean lab smell. Instead, there was a scattering of cooking implements better suited to giants.

This place. It's a kitchen.

Evidence of fresh butchery, the source of the reek, bedecked the flat surfaces. An empty skin of a green iguana. A fish head. A pile of bloody feathers.

Just above the floor, a dirty gray high-water mark traced across the walls and equipment, memorializing a flood. Decades of traffic had eroded the concrete floor, the stone aggregate exposed here and there, the patchwork almost artistic. A couple of porcelain floor drains, crazed and veined with rust, sat open, their cast iron grates pushed aside as if something below had elected to be something above.

A glass-front display cooler hummed. Gen put her hand to the misty door. It was cool, not cold. She tried to resolve the curious forms within. She drew closer. A huge saucer eye stared back. Stored inside: a pair of crimson carcasses, suckered appendages dangling — the mangled squid that Lobster and Reef had caught, alongside another of the same, half of its tentacles severed at the hilt. She shuddered at Lobster's sadistic blinding of the beast, and the fishermen's strange fascination with its ink sac — Lobster cutting it out and consuming its dark liquid as if eating the heart of a lion.

Something wet and wiry whipped past her ankle. She gasped as the thing scampered past her, into a drain. Repulsed, she darted across the kitchen and through a pair of swinging doors.

••·—•·•

Sunbeams penetrated a wall of fractured floor-to-ceiling windows through years of grime. Gen recalled the cursory lesson by Lee II on window washing, when he clasped a squeegee in his mechanical hand, made a graceless stroke across the glass, and then, as if frustrated, dropped the tool and rolled back into the lab.

Large round tables ringed by chairs dotted the expanse. The bulk of the folding tables, the round and the rectangular, reclined against a wall beside a rack of chairs, reminiscing.

She scanned every synapse and landed on the video lesson about social eating: dapper, well-mannered diners feasting from plates mounded with exotic foods; the hum of clinking utensils and soft tunes and cheerful chatter. And now she perceived the persistent sounds permeating the vast volume of this structure. The entire building seemed to ooze with it. She realized she had heard it first in the moving metal box — some form of music. Soft. Muddy. Scratchy. Void of warmth and passion. The same tune, unceasing. Insipid.

The clatter of kitchen utensils. She peeked back through the kitchen door's portal. Bony vagabonds now crowded the tables, knives flashing in the dim light. Suddenly, a face looked back. Gen sprinted across the banquet room and slipped out a door.

8.7

The heavy and ornate double door clicked closed behind her and Gen found herself on a broad platform — a strange place, yet familiar. Across the chasm, the fresco mural of the funny old boat, the dilapidated bar, and the snaggletoothed ruins of the piano. She cast her gaze beyond a rail; below, the flooded lobby. All things she'd seen through the gossamer net and her indisposition. Nearby, she expected, would be the metal box in which the fisherman had conveyed her, with the black buttons, emetic music, and stink. The box whose quaking left her queasy.

A mechanical rumble called her attention to the far end of the mezzanine and the steel doors. Above them, in the row of small circles marked B, L, M, 1 through 11, and P — the "M" flickered on. As the disquieting compartment clunked to a stop, a discordant ding.

Gen froze, not knowing who or what it might disgorge — the gruff and grungy fisher, or perhaps his repellent associates. The metal maw slid open. Vacant. She exhaled. After a moment, the doors slid shut. She was alone, and that was good. She saw a door marked "Stairs" and jogged to it, her wet shoes squishing with each step. She grasped the handle and slipped inside.

She stood there, listening, swallowed by uncertainty and gloom. She wiggled her toes in her soggy shoes. *Am I leaving a trail?* Her eyes adjusted. She was at the base of a dark stairwell. She climbed the stairs and stopped at a landing, exiting to a forever hallway of windowless doors, uniform and anonymous save for numbers on little plaques. A sliver of daylight emitted from a distant opening. *A way out?* She moved toward the portal.

She peered in. It was a large, empty, disused hotel room with its door long since commandeered, a floor-to-ceiling gap in one wall leaving the space open to the sky. Beyond, the remainder of a broken balcony, a corner gone, along with part of the rail. Despite the yawning openness, this was a dead end.

The door behind her creaked. She gasped.

"Oh! You're here. I was just getting your room ready." A thin woman stood half-hidden behind the door. On her lapel, a name tag: "Marina."

"What?" said Gen.

"Your room." Marina smiled and held the door for the drenched girl to enter. "Mister Luddy says it's yours. Says you may stay here as long as you like. Says you may go any time you please."

"Luddy?"

"The man in white. Upstairs." Marina cast her gaze up to a place beyond this ceiling, the next, and the next.

Gen surmised she meant the icy man in the obscenely opulent suite.

"I don't want to stay. I want to go home. Now."

"Home? Where's that?" asked Marina.

Gen surveyed her mental map, realizing she had no bearing. "I'm not exactly sure."

"Well, dear, why don't you just come in and rest a little bit? Then you can make up your mind," said Marina.

Gen peeked in. Her knapsack was on the dresser, flap open. "Hey! That's mine." She swept in and grabbed the sack, then turned to leave, the plush lemur in her other hand still moist from her tumble into the inundated laundry.

"Oh, that's a real doll! I haven't seen one in so long. My daughter would love that," said Marina.

Gen looked at the little lemur toy — the impetus for her absurd adventure.

"Here. We'll put it in the sun to dry," said the housekeeper, her gaunt hand gently reaching for the toy.

Gen pulled it close, but then cautiously relented.

Marina wrung the plaything out as she crossed the room. She placed it in the warm sun on the windowsill and straightened out its ringed tail and poised its doll eyes to take in the view. Her tender treatment of the toy dissolved Gen's distrust.

Gen scanned the room. A small window on the far wall. A door to a small bathroom. Spartan furnishings.

"You'll want to keep the door locked while you're in," Marina said. Then she flipped the knob for the deadbolt back and forth to demonstrate. It clacked solidly.

"Let me know if you need anything," she said, pointing to her name tag. "I'm called Marina. Welcome to Deco."

By the time Gen thought to say her own name, the maid had already closed the door behind, the cart's wheels squeaking away.

Gen locked the deadbolt. She turned the handle to test the action, and the deadbolt released. She locked it again.

She sighed and turned to assess the accommodations; despite Marina's preparation, they were humble and sparse. The room smelled of mildew and neglect. Dingy walls. A peeling ceiling, old paint curled like leaves in autumn. The bedding, little more than tatters. Opposite the bed was an armless wood frame chair, its maroon cushion flat and cracked; above the plain wooden dresser, a fraction of a mirror, tenuous in its frame. Bedraggled curtains bedecked the small window, their art deco pattern faded and stained.

Gen wiped the perspiration from her neck, her puka pendant stuck to her skin. She moved to the window and tugged at the window frame — she thought if she tried any harder, it might break. She nearly knocked the potted succulent off the sill. From the bathroom, she retrieved a drizzle of brownish water in a cup and gave the plant a drink.

This room. This building. These people. All rotten. Gen considered her own home, ordered and genial by comparison, regardless of the well-used furnishings and the scuffs where her mechanical father had cut corners in his navigations. Her present abode was considerably cramped compared to her girly quarters at home; and infinitely inferior to that strange swank suite somewhere above. She would not sit down in the repellent room. She would consider the present quandary temporary, an inconvenience to be tolerated until she could find her way back home.

Gen peered through the hazy window to the horizon. She was, it seemed, at substantial elevation, maybe three or four times the height of her house. Beyond stood a mass of tangled iron I-beams that once supported an even taller structure, its base surrounded by unsettled waters.

The sight somehow called to mind her dazzling dimensional simulations of city skyscrapers — looking down through a massive glass on the pulsing metropolis. But something was wrong. This place had grown, lived, and reached the end of its life cycle — a stand of dead stalks. Gen's addled mind filled with fragments of swirling senselessness.

Her knapsack, weather-swept and idle on the vacant beach;
The housekeeping closet door, slammed shut by the toy thief;
The ancient tortoise showing her the succulent treat;

Jetty's skewered and dying mantis shrimp, a fading rainbow;

Rising from the pond, her parents' drone ushering her home;

Tumbling down the long metal shaft after her stuffed animal;

Forest underbrush along the slim path, tickling her thighs;

Lobster thrusting a knife into the captured squid's orbit;

Rows of crooked pavers, the last bearing her father's name;

Fog rolling up and over the illusion of the crystal city;

Fruity sweetness and the scent of alcohol with Mother's last bite of cake;

The lizard husk, curled and drying on the steel counter;

An event preserved in a memprint, not truly remembered;

The steel mouth sliding open, revealing the dark, mobile box with black buttons;

An electronic eye winking at her from Edison's workbench.

Mother...? Gen burst into a torrent of tears she could not explain. She threw herself on the bed and sobbed violently. Exhausting the last bits of her energy, she closed her eyes — a cacophony of memories fond and conflicted and far away and phantom.

8.8

The tiny jellyfish rose and fell in its cosmos, perimeters defined by the five glass plates of the algae-tinged aquarium — the lid, a thin sheet of scrap steel, tossed on the shelf above by one of the careless kitchen staff.

The jelly was the size of a sewing thimble. It had one black dot for an eye — stupid, unblinking. It pulsed with a certain regularity, then halted for a moment as if confirming that it was, in fact, a jellyfish in a glass plate cosmos. Its bell was clear as crystal. It trailed four transparent threads covered with stinging cells, and if not for its black-dot eye, it would have been, for practical purposes, invisible. To the fish, the cyclopean creature was certainly undetectable, evidenced by their twisted remains peppering the bottom of its abode. To the cooks, the skull and crossbones crudely drawn in the tank's grime sufficed to ward off fools and daredevils.

A rat scurried across the chopping table. Its comrades rummaged through a bucket of fish tails and entrails bustling with flies. Another poked its head from a floor drain to assess opportunities.

The cooks scaled, slit bellies, and separated gill from head. They prepared the fish and seaweed and divided it into portions more or less equal. One paused mid-fillet to flick a brazen rodent off the table with his blade. The cook returned to his chore, the rat to his expeditions.

A boy of about four pushed a step stool to the counter just beneath the aquarium. He climbed the little treads with his little legs until his little head was even with the rim of the tank. His little eyes scanned the waters with curiosity. He sensed a *something* that was not there, yet was. He edged his hand up over the aquarium's rim.

"Get that kid outta here!" said a man, whisking the squealing tot off the stool. "Almost put his hands right into the poison."

"Why don't you keep a lid on that damn thing," said a woman.

"Not just yet," the man grumbled.

He lifted a ladle from the rack and squinted into the green-tinged tank, first from the top and then from the side. The compact cube of living gelatin was only visible by the distortion of the surrounding water — the way the light lensed around its box-shaped bell. He scooped it up, pushing the ladle in a figure-eight pattern to capture as great a length of the tentacles as possible. He raised it from the water and held it up to get a better look. Hanging over the lip of the ladle were the thinnest of threads, glistening with silvery venom. "That's the last one."

"Until Bilge gets back with more," said the woman.

"He's not coming back. I'll collect 'em myself tomorrow. Too many rats."

The man retrieved the lid from the upper shelf and slid it over the aquarium. He weighed it down with a dirty dinner plate. He found a chipped bowl, dried bits of a former meal stuck in the bottom, and deposited the ladle's watery contents. He could barely detect the eye of the wee beastie, and imagined it would glare at him if it could. He moved the grate away from the floor drain with his toe, revealing a porcelain trough pocked with pelleted droppings. He set the bowl down and nudged it closer, stopping just as it threatened to tip in.

The aroma of refuse and water lured a furry prospect up from the drain. Its whiskers found the bowl. It sniffed and, satisfied, took a drink. The creature pawed at the submerged scraps. It did not perceive the pinpoint of black staring back from the broth. The rodent convulsed. It shuddered. Lacerated by swords unseen. It writhed in pain. A blinded eye swelled from its socket. And soon the maligned scavenger was dead.

8.9

Gen awoke to the sound of footfalls, squeaking wheels, and whispers. *Where am I? What is this horrible room? Is this a dream?*

Three gentle knocks on her door. "Miss Gen?"

Gen sat up. *Not a dream.* She caught her reflection in the triangular remnant of the clouded dresser mirror. Her features seemed to have an odd texture and grayness. She had grown up with few opportunities to study her own visage and had not been concerned with appearance. Seeing herself just now, she wondered if perhaps this was why her mother had not allowed a looking glass in her room.

Another knock. "Miss Gen?"

She extricated herself from the bed, remembering the emaciated woman, Marina. "Go away."

The door unlocked with a clack and swung open. "It's okay," said Marina. "I have the master key."

A service cart squeaked its way in, Marina propelling it from the aft end. "I left you a towel in the bath. Oh, if you're looking for your things, I put them in the dresser." Suddenly, the small room filled with a rancid reek. "Mister Luddy said to bring you this. We chipped in from our share."

The cart bore a plate with pieces of unidentified beige flesh wrapped in dried seaweed. Orbiting flies alighted on the feast. Marina gave them a perfunctory wave. The flies scattered, regrouped, and settled again — an unappealing condiment for the off-putting repast.

"Coral?" Marina called behind her. "Coral, get in here!"

"No!" came a tiny, stubborn voice from the hallway.

"Right now!" Marina barked. Her sudden sternness startled Gen.

The little girl peeked into the room. Gen scowled, instantly recognizing the scamp from the laundry closet incident.

"I told you about my daughter, remember? This is Coral." Coral hid behind her mother, clinging to the skirt of her uniform.

"We've met," said Gen, flatly.

Coral stuck her tongue out at Gen, then ducked back behind.

"You're looking a little better," said Marina.

"No, she's not. She looks weird," came the little voice.

"Quiet, Coral," warned Marina. She smiled at Gen. "You'll want to eat. You slept two days."

"Two days…" She had not eaten since before the storm struck Eos. *How long ago was that?* She had never in her life felt quite this hungry. Suddenly compelled, she went to the window, threw open the curtains, pressed her face to the glass, and received the sun's benediction.

Marina gently took Gen's elbow and guided her back to the cart. "You must eat."

The teen waved the persistent flies away, picked up one of the grotty fish rolls and sniffed warily, wincing at the acrid odor. Her eyes teared. Catching Marina's encouraging smile, Gen forced the whole disgusting delicacy in her mouth and choked it down.

"Good?" asked Marina.

Gen chewed the raw bite and swallowed, hoping for the aftertaste to abate. It did not. "That's terrible. Can I have something else?"

"There's nothing else," said Marina, a bit hurt.

A man's voice cut in, "We have plenty of cake." Lobster poked his head into the open doorway.

Gen recoiled. *Was that disgusting brute eavesdropping all this time?*

"Shut up, Lobster," said Marina, almost pleading.

"Why don't you tell 'er about our special cake? Very special cake."

"Not around the child," said Marina, cupping her hands over Coral's ears.

Lobster chuckled, "Why not? She'll find out soon enough." He grabbed Marina's wrist and twisted, revealing the cryptic, two-dimensional grid tattooed there, along with a similar cypher on his own wrist. Gen recalled the same curious designs on Reef and Taffy.

"Yours is a comin' any day now," taunted Lobster, as he held onto the maid's wrist.

"Let go of me!" Marina wrested her arm from Lobster's grip. "Come, Coral. Let's go." She hurried out with her tyke in tow.

Lobster lingered. "You don't look the least bit weird… for two-day-old catch." He left the room with a deep bow, closing the door after, his laugh trailing down the hallway.

Gen twisted the deadbolt. The mean remarks spurred a new emotion: self-consciousness. Her fingers assayed the curve of her face. She returned to the dresser mirror and crouched before the shard remaining. She wiped the haze from the looking glass and examined her ragged reflection. She was a canvas of peeling skin; a cruel impersonation of the ceiling's curling paint. She must have been at sea for a long while. *Awful.*

She rubbed her cheeks, forehead, nose, and chin, shedding imperfections until her complexion was fresh and radiant. She brushed dry flakes from her arms and legs. The ghastly sunburn, plum-sized blisters, puffy eyelids, and saltwater sores had healed.

The air hung heavy with the rancid redolence of things long dead. Gen picked up her plush toy lemur from its sunny ledge. Nearly dry, its faux fur was now rough and crispy. She brought it to her nose; musty, but not particularly putrid. She cradled it and fluffed its coat, a melancholy rendition of Madonna and child, then put it back on its resting place. Sniffing the air, she isolated the annoying aroma: the lingering odor of the foul fish.

Gen gazed out of the window, queasy from the queer cuisine. An olfactory memory flashed: Deep among the tall bamboo, a ring-tailed lemur mother and baby lay on the forest floor in a deathbed of leaves, rotting in the glinting sunlight, the warmth magnifying the reek. The mother had made a leap of faith — and faith had failed. The creature and its offspring had fallen to the ground from the high canopy, her back broken, the baby clinging, left to suckle its last before succumbing to nature.

The succulent plant on her windowsill, thriving when she first saw it, was now yellowed and shriveled. She held it up and perused its desiccated contours: curious and sad and beyond help.

Gen tugged at the window again. Stubbornly stuck. She ran her fingertip along its border — long ago painted shut and melded into the decay that was this place. She looked beyond the dirty pane to the endless plane of breakers. *Did I come from that direction?* The watery horizon was barren of evidence of Eos. No landmark. *Surely it's out there. Somewhere.* Her mother would be worried about her. Calling for her. Mother would look in Edison's lab. She would walk between the towering culms of bamboo. She might even see Gen's tracks on the beach and wonder if she was still alive.

From the window, Gen imagined her route to this strange place, the actual trek an obscurity. Below her, the ghostly outline of a pool, its bottom now an artificial reef of mangled lounge chairs and skeletons of umbrellas, an algae-stained plank hovering above it. Various levels of the hotel complex revealed themselves from this vantage, some submersed, others reaching upward for one last breath. Industrial air vents dotted one shelf of the structure. A surfboard with a chunk missing lay wedged between two of the rusting steel conduits.

A more distant structure paralleled the waters: a seawall, noncommittally appearing and retreating under the waves. Lobster's jon boat levitated from a harness rigged to a thick, curved pipe that sprouted from a cubical base. The craft swayed with the ocean breeze.

Gen placed the lemur toy atop the dresser, then opened the top drawer and retrieved her knapsack. Moving with purpose, she set out a little blouse — one of many that her mother had sewn for her — along with her other clothes, mementos, and girlish accessories. She swept her hand inside the drawer, hunting down a stray. Retrieving her moccasins from under the bed, she packed her sack, saving the lemur for last.

She snuggled her plush plaything into the top of the knapsack, pulled the drawstring tight and buttoned the flap. She slipped a strap over her shoulder, ready for a departure without goodbyes.

8.10

As she moved toward the stairs, Gen felt her back pocket, the little notebook safely tucked there. She tugged the shoulder straps tight — the pack felt light. *Mother's journal!* She raced back to her room.

At the dresser, Gen dropped to her knees. The second drawer was empty. The bottom drawer was stuck. She heaved on it — the drawer relented. She fell backward on her butt. A jingle of metal on glass announced a cylindrical object rolling to the front. A small jar, its faded label depicting a dimpled berry. Inside, a folded page and a brass key. *Kind of like Marina's key that opened all the hotel doors.* She twisted off the rusty lid and unfurled the coarse, brittle, yellowed paper. Along with dense black print was a black and white photographic depiction of a man and woman in a small, whimsical boat, a sailless dhow with a boiler in its midsection — a craft christened the "African Queen." She slid the drawer out as far as it would go. Confirmed — no journal. She returned the jar to its obscurity and slammed the drawer. The culprit surfaced in her consciousness. *The tall man!*

●● ●—●● ●●

A murmur emanated from the bridal suite; two individuals, maybe three. Then the stilted cadence of a female voice reading aloud. Gen knocked. The voice ceased mid-utterance.

"Where's my journal?" Gen called. She listened, then knocked again, harder. She tried the handle — locked. "Fine. I'm leaving!"

●● ●—●● ●●

Gen waded through the flotsam and septic stench of the submerged lobby, tightening the straps on her knapsack as she passed the tumbledown doors to the sea. She treaded the bottom, walking on a path until her feet lost purchase and her head went under. *Okay, that must be the pool.* She swam to the low rooftop with the ductwork, then lifted herself over the lip. She stood up.

Shielding her eyes from the sun's glare, Gen gazed across the ocean, hoping to spot a landmark from this better vantage. Only the languid roll of waves from the horizon's edge. *Of course. The curvature of the earth. Eos might be just beyond.*

She spotted the fisher's sorry vessel and her face lit up. It was suspended in the breeze by the arced metal arm on the concrete base she'd seen, affixed to the seawall. A boat davit, craning Lobster's craft away from the water. She made her way onto the wall. The base cube was one of a pair. Four rusted bolts jutted from the crown of the other cube; whatever was once mounted there had been claimed by the sea.

Gen pushed on the curved arm, swinging Lobster's boat out over the water. It hung mid-air from the rusting cable, dancing like an insane marionette. She grasped the gunwale to steady it. *How do I lower it?* The cable was wound tight around a spindle. *A winch.* She tugged on a handle and the boat dipped a bit. She hand-cranked the watercraft down. As it met the sea, a wave caught it broadside and tossed it into the air, slamming Gen full force, knocking her off her feet. She rebounded and tried to corral the boat, but the waves would not relent. She jumped inside and grappled with loosening the harness — the boat flipped — she hit the water. The oars bobbed in the unruly currents, one bopping her on the chin.

Gen trudged back to the hotel, drenched and defeated.

••·-•◆•·••

The service bell rang on the check-in desk, relentless. A boy pumped the once-chrome button, the water to his chest and nearly to the desk's fractured marble surface, the juvenile tormenter challenging Gen with his eyes. The dissonant din rang through her bones. She covered her ears. The horrors of the past few days melded with the maddening sound, and she gave into her impulses.

She lunged for the boy, but he was already beneath the opaque water before her outstretched fingers could find his throat. A moist glob plopped on her arm. She looked to the platform above, into the dirty faces of three waifs forming their lips into cannons for their second spittle volley, their legs and arms jutting from banister and balustrade. Rage propelled her onto the desk, and she leapt for the mezzanine railing as the kids scattered, subsumed by stairways and vanished down halls. She stood on the mezzanine, alone. She put her face in her hands and sobbed.

When she finally composed herself, Gen looked around the empty mezzanine with its wrecked piano and bar. She recognized the hand-painted mural she'd seen first through the cast net, and again when she'd been lost in the building. The mural depicted an old open boat with a man aboard and a woman sitting in the stern under a canvas awning, an onyx cylinder midpoint, chugging black smoke. The man sported a white cap and a stubble of beard. The woman wore a long white dress and matching bonnet of a vintage, unfamiliar. Letters across the boat's gunwale spelled out, "AFRICAN QUEEN." *Just like that old photo in the jar.*

Gen noticed something curious about the mural. It was textured; the paint seeming to have soaked into its medium. She had learned about paintings of this type in her videos. This was a fresco, a process of applying paint to fresh plaster to imbue an uncommon luminosity and depth, the art an integral part of the wall. Theoretically, a fresco could last many hundreds of years.

Gen ran her fingertips over the surface. She could almost feel the rivets in the iron boat, the pattern of the woman's tattered parasol. A perfectly round chunk of plaster, a finger-width thick, answered to the pressure of her fingertips, and fell intact onto the floor. Myriad tiny fibers jutted from its bone-white edges. She was about to fit the wayward piece back in when she espied, inside the niche, a brass lock with a keyhole — like on the door of her mother's mysterious, off-limits chamber. Gen felt along the fresco's uneven surface, finding a faint imperfection — a crack, fine and straight, at a right angle to the floor and parallel to its twin an arm's length away. A secret door, concealed in lime and sand and paint, in prescient fear of discovery. Hidden by an artist unknown for a time inestimable. She aligned the plug to match the artwork and pushed it back into its socket, burnishing its edge with her thumb — then retreated, hoping to avoid blame for the damage.

Defeated, Gen climbed the stairs to her floor and her assigned room. She closed the door behind her and turned the deadbolt against the disappointment and embarrassment and failure. She stood by herself without answers, without friends, without family. She slipped off her knapsack and drew out the toy — wet again. She placed him in the window to dry, his beaded eyes focused on a home he, too, longed to see again. She stared out her small window at the little boat that had bested her.

A soft whistling sound disrupted her lament. She listened at the door. She checked the bathroom sink. Then she noticed the vent register high on the wall above her bed. *Why didn't I see that before?* She stepped up on the bed for a closer look. The register was ajar. She pried it off and reached in, pulling out the obstruction: a pillow covered with gray dust, the style of the pillowcase matching the ones on her bed. At once, air flowed in, dancing through her hair. It was not refrigerated, filtered air like in her own bedroom back home, but at least it was ventilation. *No wonder this room's so stuffy.* She tossed the filthy pillow in a corner and fitted the register back in its frame.

Two timid knocks at her door.

8.11

"I don't know why you want it back now. It's dead," said Taffy, as she handed the little pot with the shriveled aloe to Luddy.

He placed it on the window shelf beside its vibrant and green twin, then ran his fingertips over the two plants. "What do you know about gas?" he asked.

Lobster chuckled.

"A gas is, like, in the air," said Taffy.

"I know I got plenty to go around," said Lobster.

"I shall take that under advisement," said Luddy.

Taffy groaned.

An uncomfortable silence. Luddy turned his head as if to listen.

"I best be goin'," said Lobster. He closed the door behind him.

Luddy continued. "Yes, like the air. Air is composed of a number of gasses. Oxygen, carbon dioxide, nitrogen and some others I can't recall. Maybe argon…" He collected his thoughts for a moment. "Animals use oxygen to turn food into energy, and they exhale carbon dioxide. Plants do the opposite. They absorb carbon dioxide and output oxygen. Without oxygen, animals die. Without carbon dioxide, plants die."

"So? The plant died. What are you getting at?" said Taffy.

"This plant is unique. Recall that I said it intakes carbon dioxide only at night. That's the only time it breathes. This plant suffocated from lack of carbon dioxide. It did this in a sealed room with an animal that exhales, or should exhale, lots of carbon dioxide."

"I don't understand."

"I don't quite understand it myself. But our new guest, I think, is special."

8.12

Two knocks on the door, more urgent. Gen peeked out.

"Wanna go to a party?" said Coral with a guileless smile, then whispered, "it's a burst-day."

Gen looked down at the waif. She started to decline, but then her stomach growled. "Will there be cake?"

"I guess."

•• ·—•—●•• •

Coral led Gen by the hand through labyrinthine passages, the tot deftly navigating a narrow course inscrutable to all but children. They emerged near the banquet room, Gen still a little boggled by the maze. A klatch of SoBes in festive handmade hats was filing into the room through the main door. Gen headed toward it.

Coral tugged her away. "Not there. That's for grown-ups. Over here is for kids." Taking care to stay out of sight of the partygoers, she tugged the teen toward a side door, slipped in behind a statue and crouched, pulling Gen down with her. "We're not s'posed to look."

The two girls giggled. Conspiracy was new territory for Gen. Breaking the rules, she realized, was more exciting with an accomplice. Gen glanced around for Coral's untamed contemporaries. None appeared. Fine by her.

Gen peeked from behind the statue. The room had changed since she had last seen it. Tables had been unfurled and focused on a single point, a lone chair with a folded tarpaulin resting upon the seat. The room's mustiness was losing its battle with the fresh funk of fish. Against the far wall, a rectangular table displayed a paltry buffet of bite-sized, sargassum-wrapped seafood — with a bit of space for a centerpiece yet to arrive.

Merriment and laughter. The revelers converged on the spread, each snatching a plate from a stack and parking a few tidbits on it as they moved down the line and back to their tables.

A pair of SoBes in waiter whites waddled in — between them a brownish, tiered stack of cylinders with ornate filigree. The partiers parted to make way for the confection. The two servers lifted it into place amid the buffet. A flake of its ancient frosting shell fell away, and one waiter quickly worked it back in. It seemed to Gen that this "cake" was not for eating, and had not been for a very long time.

Gen glanced up, recognizing their hiding place as an algae-stained replica of the famous Venus Rising, her own hand braced on the goddess's slimy buttock. She pulled away. Coral tittered.

Lobster loped in and sat at a front row table. He turned and proclaimed to no one in particular. "Don't nobody go in the basement till it dries up some. There be biters."

The two servers unfurled the tarp, stained at its center, and draped it over the chair. Then they took pains to extend its corners out to cover the widest possible area. The remaining SoBes left the buffet with their meager hors d'oeuvres, filtering into place at the surrounding tables.

"Where be the guest of honor?" said Lobster.

"That's me!" said a raspy voice from just beyond the room. In hobbled an emaciated man, naked save for a cloth diaper and an eccentric hat in the likeness of a grouper, its open mouth facing front and the tail behind. The man was covered with oozing sores. One of his eyes was injured and swollen shut, and his limbs bore the added insult of a recent tangle with an outsized crustacean. His revealed discomfort was palpable to all in attendance.

Gen realized the man was Jetty, the gig-fisher she had tussled with in the laundry. "I met him," she whispered to Coral.

Jetty shuffled to the chair to light applause and seated himself.

"Happy *burst* day, Jetty," said the group in unison.

"I guess," said Jetty with a nervous laugh and a wince.

Gen snickered over their juvenile confusion of the word "burst" for "birth." In any case, she thought, it would be awful to be the focus of such a gathering while in such a pitiable physical state.

Marina approached the celebrant with a kit in a rolled cloth, then knelt beside his chair. Gen surmised that the woman was about to draw the man's blood — her own mother's cyclical ritual to assess Gen's vitality. Marina unfurled her bundle, then presented her handmade steel and bone implements to the crowd. She uncorked her bottle and swirled its purple-black contents for all to see. Jetty reluctantly held out his arm, revealing a boxy tattoo in the shape of a two-dimensional grid, incomplete. Marina tap-tap-tapped a last line into the design.

"Best hurry up," someone mocked. Marina turned, then sighed and continued her work, completing the geometry. She collected her tools and left him. Jetty's eyes welled with tears, not for the pain of the needle, but for a milestone reached.

Gen wondered if they would ask Jetty to make a wish; she thought his best bet was to wish for his skin to heal.

Jetty looked askance at the others, then closed his eyes. Indeed, his lips formed a silent wish. Then he opened his eyes and smiled like a man who believed he had beaten fate. He looked at his tattoo — now a finished work.

A couple of SoBes chanted softly, "Pop. Pop. Pop."

The voices rose, then hushed at Lobster's dark glare.

Jetty sat still for a moment. Then his face spread into a broad grin. "See? Nothin'. Told ya it weren't today." Then his features flashed painful — panicked. His flesh reddened and oozed a bloody sheen. His wounds darkened, the islands of festering flesh merging into a single continent of putrefaction. His throat bulged, and from deep within came gurgling. He shuddered, his nostrils two fonts of black fluid. Squeezed his eyes shut, ichor oozing from under his lids. His limbs went limp — a dropped puppet.

Lobster snatched the fish hat from Jetty's head. The unfortunate's body slumped, then fell to pieces, liquefying onto the impatient tarp, the denuded bones effervescing to fatty foam; the diaper now a sopping rag of reddish-pink and ocher, an excremental reek overtaking the gangrenous dank.

Coral screamed and darted away. All eyes turned toward the unclad sculpture and the dark-skinned stranger, her mouth open in horror.

"Rude," muttered a SoBe.

Taffy turned, too, and a corner of her lip curled in a smirk.

A moment, then a choreographed flurry. The two SoBe servers bussed the funereal tarp as the others took to the buffet to pick at the last bits, the scent of death hanging in the sticky air.

Gen backed into the shadows and heaved up acrid chunks.

8.13

Voided of the view and the victuals, Gen rushed out from behind her sculpted hiding place, through the crowd, horrified and repulsed.

"Who *are* you people?!" said Gen, brushing past Taffy.

"Why don't you ask Kafka?" Taffy snipped, pointing past her. "On the roof. Right up those stairs."

Gen didn't look back, feet pounding, propelling herself away.

"All the way at the end of the hall," Taffy chirped to Gen's retreating form.

Wiping vomit from her lips, Gen flew past the guest rooms. Here and there, dirty waifs peeked out from their dioramas of despair. "What's wrong with *her?*" said one boy to another.

A narrow door loomed: "Roof Access Employees Only." Marks of hammer and lever attested to prior attempts at intrusion. Gen peered into the cracked, wired-glass portal, revealing darkness beyond. She turned the knob and shouldered the door — the rusted hinges would not yield even a particle of arc. Then she cocked her leg in the manner Edison had instructed. At full extension, the kick displaced the door from its oxidized frame, slamming on the wall behind. Beyond, a column of stairs rose into the gloom.

The slap of tide water below echoed in the tubular stairwell, faint reflections dancing up the walls, a rain of decayed stucco twirling in the moldering air. The stairwell was plain and cramped. It seemed to Gen a passage for a long-gone servant stratum who crept invisibly between the walls and in the basements. Phantoms unseen and unheard by the paying guest class.

Gen climbed to the next landing. The iron banister, utilitarian in the best of times, was twisted into a hazard of corroded tubes and spikes. She abandoned the rail and felt her way along the wall. Chipped paint nipped at her fingertips and burrowed under her nails. She passed another landing, then another. Above her, the structure twirled into darkness. She pressed on to the next floor, and the next, in the dimness. Rebar jutted like spears from the decaying steps. Landings trembled, seemingly supported solely by force of habit.

Gen tripped, fell to her knees — the impact reverberating through the bones of the cavernous column. She could hear the sharp twang of concrete spalling. A large chunk fell from above, nearly striking her. The meteor propagated an avalanche that rippled to the waterlogged lower floors with a distant splash.

She froze, her heart pounding, measuring the merits of a downward retreat. Below, a metallic bang, then darkness. Now she could resolve a sliver of sun high above.

Gen compelled herself to continue her ascent. *Almost to the top.* She got on her hands and knees and moved tread to tread, testing for inconsistencies in the masonry. Missing sections had been patched haphazardly with found wood, the replacements themselves now exhausted. She felt a jab in her palm — a splinter. She dug at it with her thumb, then gave up and reached for the step closest.

Gen's fingers slid into a soft mass. She brought her hand to her nose and recognized the pungent scent from the aviary back home. *Guano.* She was, at once, overcome with nostalgia and disgust. She shook the repellent glop from her fingertips, then wiped the remainder on a step. She stopped and listened. From somewhere beyond came the soft flapping of wings. The sound grew as she continued to ascend; the structure shuddering with each harrowed step. *That woman! It's her fault I'm in here!*

The sound of metal on metal. Gen looked up to the source. "Hello?" She could see now that the illumination above traced the perimeters of a hatch, partially dislodged as if some angry giant had peeled it up, then flopped it back in place. She took more care now, as the higher steps had borne exposure to the elements.

The light was better here, owing to the rough treatment of the hatch. She navigated a crumbled ledge with aplomb and stepped across a gap within sight of the last landing. A hundred chirping bats took wing — their perch, the vestiges of fire sprinkler pipes that clung by a single sorry bracket. She hugged the wall, watching them fill the stairwell from top to bottom. The next several steps were gone, leaving a huge gap between where she was and where she wanted to be.

Anger overtook fear. Gen planted her feet and leapt to the landing. It tilted under her weight, rebar snapping, chunks of concrete falling to the floors far below, and then she found herself in midair, reaching upward, flailing, bats surrounding her in a frenzy of wings. Her hand fell upon a section of rusty railing. Her fingers closed tight around it. She dangled there, concrete ricocheting off the walls and tumbling into the gray abyss. In an instant, the railing came loose and Gen was suspended somewhere between heaven and hell. She screamed. Time slowed. A blinding whiteness enveloped her.

A hand grabbed her wrist, hoisting her like a rag doll up through the hatch. Gen shaded her eyes from the overwhelming sunlight, the welcome sensation of a solid surface beneath her feet. Her eyes adjusted, and a face resolved from the ether. Gen gasped.

He was a youth of about eighteen; handsome, with wild charcoal hair and the shadow of fine stubble common to adolescence. His eyes widened with an intensity to which Gen was unaccustomed, and he spoke: "The Messiah arrives only after he is no longer required. He comes on the day after his arrival. Not on the last day, but on the very last."

And with that, he was gone.

8.14

Shaken by her narrow escape from calamity, Gen scanned the confusions of the roofscape for the strange young man. A bewildering topography bereft of humanity. "Hello?" she called. Only the disharmony of unfamiliar sounds in the wind, and wet footprints, fading.

Her hands and knees were bloody. She tucked herself into a corner of a parapet. She pulled the wood shard from her palm, her wounds stitching together in the sunlight. From this vantage, she could see a convoluted collection of flat roofs at varied levels, unified by a castle-like rampart that suggested a rambling medieval estate, infinite sky beyond.

Before her was a chaos of abandoned custodial projects, some contemporary, others from an unknown past. Cylinders of a rolled roofing material lay strewn across the expanse, flattened by years of sun and storm. A brigade of big tar buckets rested on their sides, the black, blobbed contents rigidified mid-flow. A large-bristle brush protruded from one such spill, imprisoned in an obsidian delta of resin. Shallow ponds of petrified pastel paint inhabited scattered cans. Unidentifiable metal parts littered the surface, some in piles, others orphaned in the asphalt desert. A broom, the handle broken. A mason's trowel embedded in a cone of solidified mortar. A rotten squeegee atop dirty rags. Skeletonized small animals and a clump of feathers that had once been a wing.

A room-sized aluminum box with silvery fins and tubes occupied the center of the rooftop, expelling warm air. She wondered if it was part of the ventilation system. Its metal carcass was abuzz with belligerent wasps, a fair warning of their squatters' rights.

An assortment of windmills improvised from found items pocked the roof. A sextet of the smallest sprung from the perimeter. Two more, each about the size of a box fan, appointed the corners — all gimbaled like weathervanes, twisting into the humid and fickle currents. Mounted on a tripod was a two-bladed version of impressive diameter, its prime mover an aircraft propeller stoically tracking the prevailing breeze of the blue expanse, its rotating vanes languidly tapping nature's power. A few desiccated carcasses of sea birds had collected at its base, casualties of the insolent blades trespassing on their flight path.

The rotors beat the air with symphonic regularity. Worn bearings moaned. Generators turned. The entire power plant an amalgam of salvaged items and electromechanical improvisation. Wild black vines of electrical cables, their countless splices bandaged but not healed, snaked toward a central mechanical room camouflaged to match the building's stuccoed façade. The unperfected system, Gen speculated, supported those in the ruined floors below. She recalled Edison's preference for solar panels, having found the windmills of Eos fickle.

Beyond the forest of equipment, the cluttered rooftop held layers for her eyes to explore; she could scarcely take it all in. She rose from her place of safety and looked over a ledge. Among the wedding cake tiers of elevations that comprised the building, she noticed a low platform, the lowest elevation on the structure. It covered an abandoned, inundated wing. Water lapped at its edges. Here and there, a tiled surface lay exposed, hinting that the rooftop had once seen more formal gatherings — a terrace patio. Enough of its art déco design remained that Gen could identify the same daring geometry that carried through the hotel's interior. A section of the patio was reserved for tending large, soft batches of drying sargassum seaweed, a lone woman laboring over one of the mats, carefully arranging strands of the desiccating algae. A broad metal frame mounted on an adjacent wall had, in better times, borne a canvas shade — now ragged fishing nets stretched its expanse to dry. Gen supposed that the nearly submerged terrace served the SoBes as a dock, a workspace, maybe a place of gathering.

A squeal of hinges called her attention back to the medley of shapes. Riding the waves of wrinkled asphalt was a singular door to a room barely wide enough to accommodate it. A sign on its rusted skin depicted a man walking down steps. *Stairs. I hope they're better than the ones I climbed up.* Her sneaks smacked the sticky tar as she crossed the roasting rooftop. She opened the door and peered in — a small landing introduced sturdy concrete treads, blackness beyond. "Hello?" Her voice echoed in the shaft. She closed the door and continued the search for her youthful savior.

An enormous barrel on a scaffold dominated a corner. Wooden slats, grayed by ages in the sun, bore vestiges of an undignified depiction — a child and a playful animal, its meaning lost on those living in this soaked oasis of sunken dreams. Metal ladder rungs led to the rim. A maze of handmade gutters directed rainwater to the tank from the few points above. Between the slats, water oozed into mossy pools, devolving into rivulets that cascaded black and green down the aged hotel's flank.

Then, from the corner of her eye: a shadow, moving fast.

8.15

Gen scanned the jumble of hardware that pocked the rooftop, hoping for a glimpse of the young man. An umbra flowed across a rampart, then stopped, as if watching. "Who's there?" she called. The phantom slipped away. "Come out! Why are you hiding?"

A slosh, then a splat over the water tower's lip onto the hot rooftop. The youth's voice came from somewhere above: "Hiding places are countless. Escape is only one. Possibilities of escape, of course, are as many as hiding places."

"What…?" Gen called toward the tank. "Are you the one who pulled me up from the stairs?"

"A stair not worn down by footsteps is, from its own viewpoint, only a dull thing formed of wood," said the voice amid the sloshing.

Gen detected an oddly familiar literary cadence in his cryptic communication. "Um, I don't know what that means, but thanks for saving me," she said. "That woman. Taffy? She told me to come up here. To see you. I've got to get home. Right away."

The voice intoned again, "From a certain point, there is no longer any turning back. That is the point that must be reached."

She climbed the leaky tower's rungs and peered over the rim. Inside, a set of ragged clothes lay wadded on a rotting wooden ledge. Floating in the algae-tinged water was the youth, naked. She averted her eyes. "Uh… like I said, I've got to go home."

The boy spat a fountain and treaded water. "The only proper approach is to learn to accept existing conditions."

"Okay, fine," she retorted. Fed up with the cagey boy, she dismounted the great wooden barrel and headed toward the stair house, navigating the vines of electrical wires that meandered the rotting roofing.

The boy followed, tugging his pants and shirt on in an awkward ballet. He stepped in front of her, stopping her short. Her hands formed into fists — the offensive posture startling the boy. He deflected, explaining the door was to be used as an exit only. "One becomes more distant, the more one hesitates before the door," he said.

Gen still had no idea what he was talking about, but she had never met anyone her own age, and couldn't help but stare at the stranger. He was approaching adulthood yet, in some dimensions, his development had fallen short. She took in his handsome face and the scattered pubescent beard — not a wrinkle on his brow. The only dissent from his boyish beauty: pinkish scars on each cheek flowing from the corners of his lips toward his temples, muted by his youthful stubble. Now she saw the complexity of a life of hardship just behind his thin smile. Compassion washed over her and she relaxed her fists. "I'm Gen. Are you Kafka?"

"I may have arrived late, but I'm here now," Kafka said, putting his hands on her shoulders.

"You ran away. Why?"

"What I have to do, I can do only alone."

She buried her head in her hands, and the weight of all that had happened erupted into a cascade of tears. "I saw a man… dissolve. In front of everyone. It was horrible. What's wrong with these people? Can't you tell me?"

"One lies as little as possible only by lying as little as possible. Not by having the least possible chance to do so."

Gen sobbed. The youth smiled and wiped away her tears with the hem of his shirt. He shifted to plainspoken language to confirm that he was called Kafka. He was born in this place, which was called Deco. The people called themselves the SoBes. Gen already knew about Deco and the SoBes, but she let his expounding confidence wash over her as she fell into his dark eyes.

He took her hand and turned her palm upward, an eyebrow raising at the girl's clean forearm, absent any inscription. His own mark was now visible on his upturned wrist — the beginnings of an inked grid resembling those she had seen on the others. He indicated that it was a method to keep track of their days. That he had ceased the practice, finding the tattoos a useless ritual — the onset of the sores foretelling the day and time of expiration with fair accuracy. He let her hand fall gently to her side. As to the matter of the graphic demise of the man, Jetty, the boy explained that it was merely his time, as would come to each, some day when their forty cycles had been lived. Certain of the SoBes had turned the natural phenomenon into a celebration, he told her; something to which they could look forward. He found such ceremonies a pastime of fools. "The meaning of life is that it stops."

"You mean everybody here just…?"

He chuckled, then realized the guilelessness of her question.

The sea breeze picked up, and the windmills turned, blades spinning apace. The wind whipped through Kafka's clothes, billowing them around his stringy frame. He offered his hand to Gen and brought her to the side of the building farthest from the sea.

Gen gasped — at once shocked and in awe of the beauty in this desolation. A gray bay extended to another horizon, interrupted by islands of drowning rubble gasping for air just above the waves. The ragged skyline of once eminent architecture had become salt-encrusted steel cadavers — a narrow strip of semi-submerged buildings in advanced states of disrepair, most reduced to forlorn piles. They reached upward from their moist and moldering graves, denying their mortality even in their inexorable decay. The wind whistled through their bones like an aeolian harp, the mournful notes drifting across the expanse. The sun illuminated the superstructures from what seemed innumerable angles, projecting a tangled prism into the sultry air. Mid-bay, a ship, almost as long as the skyscrapers were tall, lay aground and half-submerged, long retired from service. Closer still, palm stumps jutted finger-like from the muddy shoals, petrified, arthritic, their barnacled trunks draped with rotting sea grass, topped with an icing of guano. The structure she stood atop seemed the only one habitable.

The hotel lay with the ocean on one side and, on the obverse, a canal broad as an avenue, with a sweeping bay beyond. The canal was deep enough that even from her high angle, she could not see the bottom. Alleys of flowing water joined the sea with the canal, forming eddies and swirls of foam within a rectilinear geometry of city blocks. The opposing side of the canal was appointed with an array of squat structures of more recent vintage than the hotel, now ghosts gleaming in the sun — others still standing, their bottommost floors (and Gen supposed their hidden entranceways) submerged in delicate swirls of red and green algae. From her digi-lessons, she surmised these were likely shops and services that once catered to the city's dwellers.

On either side of the hotel were tall piles of dissolving concrete and stairways suspended in mid-air, memorials to things once thought eternal. Here and there, detritus gathered in the eddies formed at the confluence of deluged streets and the sea.

She wondered if this was this the city of her desire. Her brow furrowed.

Kafka expounded that multitudes of people had lived in the constructions long ago, that storms tore away the towers' deceitful skins, that rain and salt spray found their frailties, and that their metal frames would someday rust down to the waterline. The youth seemed almost pleased at the thought. Windmills squeaked to a stop in unison as the air became still. The waters quieted, neither wave nor ripple in sight.

Gen puzzled at how he could know these things; it seemed that he had received an education, though very different from her own. "All those people in the buildings. What happened to them?"

Kafka nodded to the foot of the hotel below. Dozens of SoBes emerged, a choreography of filth-covered, two-legged fire ants scrambling down exterior walls and crumbling steps and rusting steel ladders. They converged where the water licked at their partially submerged and rotting concrete home. The SoBes urgently plucked driftwood from the waterline and from every nook where a log or branch or other floating flotsam had found provisional mooring.

"What are they doing?" asked Gen.

Kafka explained the SoBes were a tribe of fishermen and gatherers, scholars of wave and tide. Presently, the tide was slack and would remain so for only a short while, and here demonstrated were the means of supplying firewood to the kitchen stoves, materials that could be fashioned into tools, the occasional edible offerings from the sea, and other articles that might sustain their meager subsistence. "Better to have, and not need, than to need, and not have," he said.

Eternal plastics in various forms were common in the mix and certain exotics revealed neither time nor place of origin, Kafka explained. Chunks of volcanic pumice stone fortuitously floated in with regularity, the abrasive useful for sharpening of knives, removal of hair, and debridement of wounds. The ocean currents carried gifts from both near and far to their doorstep — all for the taking, in trade for the SoBes' stoop labor. "But they're not in an easy position. To to think they are would be unjust," said Kafka. "If you have food in your mouth you have solved all questions for the time being."

Kafka pivoted back to mundane vernacular, and opined that, to parents, children are merely furnishings or fashion or objects which, for a short while, satiate social pressure. Once grown, they are perceived as just another competitor for scarce resources and then summarily ejected from that sphere of affection. Families, he said, were constructed for perpetuating pain, and were quite successful at fulfilling that function.

She wanted to deny everything the boy uttered — an indictment, too, of her own fragile delusion of blissful domesticity.

Kafka ducked behind one of the obscure structures and returned with a small spyglass better suited as a souvenir or a child's toy. He swept his hand over the vista of want and told the girl that the wretched below were, for but an instant, the recipients of adoration. He extended the collapsible tube and offered it to Gen. She placed the wide end to her eye. He smiled and gently turned it around for her. She squinted through the foggy, scratched plastic lens, aiming at the foraging rabble. Now, she could see their rags of clothing, the oozing wounds, the missing digits, and the sunken cheeks of hunger.

Kafka inquired about Gen's origins and how she came to be among the SoBes. Gen lowered the spyglass, and obliged the best she could, recounting her running away, and the storm, and the strange boat ride, and of her overwhelming guilt, and the imperative to find her way back home.

When the girl had stopped to take a breath, Kafka said, "My guiding principle is this: Guilt is never to be doubted."

She looked deeply into Kafka's eyes, so rapt by the presence of the young man, his affront went undetected.

He continued, "How can anyone delight in the world unless they flee to it for refuge?" Then Kafka kissed Gen on the forehead.

Electricity sped to Gen's toes, then back up again. *It happened.* She wasn't quite sure how to respond. *What do I do now?* Aflutter, she turned back to the canal, raising the spyglass to continue her scan, hands shaking.

The lens came to rest on a SoBe, separated from the gatherers by some distance as he perched on an outcrop of ruins near the water's edge. He artfully threw his cast net. The silent net spun in the air, piercing the surface of the water with barely a ripple. In spite of the surrounds, a serene scene. Gen thought of Edison's teachings about the dignity of work. Another image formed in Gen's mind from a book that her mechanical father had recited to her from the banks of his emotionless memory. Captain Ahab's last encounter with the great white whale, Moby Dick: Ahab, tangled in the twisted hemp lines of his harpoon, bound to the beast — the fates of the two forever intertwined. And then flashed the moment she, herself, was ensnared by the fisher's net.

The castnetter gathered up his weighted web and plucked out a few sardines. He collected the net to cast again. Gen glimpsed what looked like the stern of a boat — a canoe, she thought — as it slipped by just beyond the castnetter's view. It seemed to her to be made of translucent film stretched over a frame, strange markings here and there like those glyphs inked on his bedraggled brethren. A flash of sunlight on metal blinded her. She lowered the scope and blinked, and wiped the lens on her shirt hem. A splash. She peered through the eyepiece again — both castnetter and boat were gone, only waves on the water. "What was that?"

The youth abruptly took Gen's elbow and suggested they find a shaded place to sit.

8.16

Gen and Kafka sat tucked in the shade of the stair house, her head resting on his shoulder. The girl had grown up reading poetry and prose on the topics of love and life and beauty and truth. Somehow those abstract lessons withered, and then sprouted anew with a palpable organic sensuality as they poured from the lips of the handsome youth.

The boy spoke of his authors and philosophies, of passion and reason, and of the import and pointlessness of it all. He spoke with clever persuasion of things Gen might have contested, save for the magnetic oration. His young male voice so unfamiliar, yet comforting, as he sat ankles crossed, tapping the edges of his footwear together to punctuate each point, light sports shoe against dark boot. The affectation of his mismatched shoes spoke to her of the same youthful rebellion that welled within her.

Despite herself, she felt her eyelids grow heavy. Waves crashed against the seawall, pulsing through the hotel's foundations in a gentle heartbeat. The setting sun embraced her cheek, separating her from her travails, and soon, the torment of her recent days was overruled by sleep.

Cradled in the arms of this strange boy and Morpheus, Gen was conveyed upon the mists of memories that never were; the music of the windmills' rotating blades a discordant accompaniment to her journey.

·· ·—●··

Gen again was striding down the sidewalk in a gleaming city roaring with bustling crowds and machinery, deep in a valley of breathtaking skyscrapers of glass and steel. Her ubiquitous klatch of young compeers coalesced around her. The sweet tones of a violin — one youth tithed the busker's open case with a coin. They continued together along the walkway toward their common destination — a place of merriment that she never seemed to get to, the perpetual poetics of her non-arrival. Their chatter was lilting and happy, though she could not make out words. She was the center of their universe, as they were the nucleus of hers. Something in a shop window caught her eye: a mannequin fortuitously mirroring Gen's form, cocoa skin tone, and hair color, modeling a two-piece pink bathing suit with matching thong sandals. She went inside and promptly exited with a shopping bag, then carried on with her waiting friends. Gen glanced up at a billboard perched high on a pole: an advertisement for a cologne with a name she could not pronounce, a bare-chested young man presenting a sapphire crystal bottle, his face resembling Kafka's. She smiled. One of her male companions gave her a jealous glance, and she kissed his forehead. Light and shadow played across her face as she passed beneath a row of blossoming Japanese cherry trees. Pink petals danced on a breeze as warbling wrens took wing.

·· ·—●··

A rusting windmill turned to the sea to greet the new day, its blades cutting the humid air with a squeaking, rhythmic regularity. Waves of light and shadow wandered across Gen's slumberous features in synchronicity to the dutiful mill's languid rotations — Cleopatra fanned by her servant.

"King tide!" a cook yelled as he ran for the kitchen door, hopping over the rats boiling up through the porcelain floor drain. At the first spits and gurgles erupting from that drain, the others dropped their utensils and abandoned their chores, scurrying past panicked rodents and each other in a scramble to safety. The last to leave stopped to press his mouth to the brass speaking tube on the kitchen wall and he cried out, "King tide, sir. King tide!"

•• •—•—••• ••

Luddy stood with his hand on his window, absorbing the early morning's warmth and noting a disquieting vibration. At the cry from the brass tube's twin by his desk, he calmly opened a drawer and removed a bright orange case, snapped the latches and folded it open to a thick-barreled pistol accompanied by several cartridges of matching caliber, empty slots revealing the flare gun's not-infrequent use. Luddy loaded and locked, made his way to a slider, and stepped onto the open balcony. The bulge of angry ocean beckoned at the hotel's back door. He grasped the rail, then aimed at the sky and squeezed the trigger, his warning flare bisecting the bluest of skies with smoke and fire.

•• •—•—•• ••

The bang thumped through Gen's chest. She snapped awake. Just beyond the hotel rampart, she saw the projectile spewing hot orange flame as it rose to apogee. She rubbed her eyes and rose from her resting spot next to the stair house. She was alone. "Kafka?" Squinting into the morning sun and wiping saliva from her cheek, she called again. "Hello?" She tried the stairway door — locked. Surprised, she tried it once more. "Huh…"

She felt the hotel rumble. She ran to the ledge and looked to the sea, an overwhelming froth of conflicted currents, mutually agreed only in that they were on a fast heading to shore.

•• •—•—•• ••

The angry tide surged into the lobby, tumbling scales and fins and shards and shells and SoBes grappling for handholds against the sweeping current. An eddy drew a child below the surface in a bloody swirl. The waters overwhelmed the check-in desk and ascended the ramp, eyeing the black lacquer of the crumbled piano and the worm-eaten mahogany bar.

Reef rushed Marina and Coral to the mezzanine elevator and pressed "up," other SoBes collecting behind them. The door opened, disgorging ankle-deep seawater, and he crowded his family in, along with ten other passengers. Reef selected the next floor up, and the door closed. The car rose, sluggish with riders and water. It reached its destination with an anemic ding and lurched to a stop. The doors parted, spilling pungent sea-foam into the hall along with Marina, Coral, and Reef.

A little boy inside the elevator car pushed a button — "flooded" scratched into the metal bezel beside it. "No!" Alarmed adults panic-pressed the higher numbers. Reef tried to intercept the door, but it closed on the riders' stricken faces. He pounded the call button in the hall as the elevator descended to the inundation. The bell two floors down intoned dully. Screams from below. The hydraulics strained. The car grumbled as it rose once again and stopped on Reef's floor.

The door opened, delivering its contents with a gush that nearly knocked him off his feet. Body parts in a bloody sea. A man crawled from the car but did not get far — yanked back by the ankles. A moan in agony, a snap, and silence. Clicks from within the metal box. A compound eye peeked out from the elevator doorframe, face to face with the fisher. A rainbow of prismatic perfection.

"Mantis!" yelled Reef, rushing his wife and child away.

From the elevator unfurled a man-sized mantis shrimp, fresh from the slaughter. It rose on its finned tail and stalked them down the hall.

Guest room doors slammed shut ahead of the fleeing trio. At the far end, a service stairway door — the only way out. Reef pushed. No good. He looked through the little reinforced window. The stairway had collapsed against the door, enormous slabs of concrete chocking it from behind.

A room service tray clattered against a wall. Reef turned — the monster advancing. The creature's tri-pupiled eyes homed in on Reef, now shielding his wife and daughter with his own body, their backs to the blocked exit. Rainbow colors flashed with excitement, crab-like legs clacking in anticipation of another kill.

"Don't look," Reef said.

Coral screamed.

•• ·•——••••

Gen heard a child's high-pitched shriek coming from the roof hatch. She threw open the metal cover, unleashing a river of bats. She looked down into the ragged maw. Little remained of the risers and treads, and the handrail dangled from a single bolt. In a flash, she intuited the trajectories required to avoid injury during descent. The teen leapt to the first crumbling landing and spidered her way down. Concrete spalled from the ceiling and walls as she hastened toward the source of the scream.

•• ·•——••••

"Push!" said Reef, shoulder to the door, torso twisted to stare the beast in its otherworldly eyes.

"I am!" said Marina, palms pressed so hard they turned white. Coral, whimpering in terror, kicked and banged with her little fists.

Through the glass, Marina saw Gen land in the stairwell. "Help us!" Marina screamed.

Gen threw aside the rubble, the concrete light in her hands.

The creature cocked its chitin-hard hammers — Reef ducked, and it shattered the window just beyond his head.

Gen yanked the door open and Reef pushed wife and child into the stairwell. The two fell into Gen's arms. The creature's claws pierced Reef's ribcage. Gen saw the decision in his eyes. She reached for him, but he pulled the door shut.

The mantis triggered its twin bludgeons, snuffing Reef with a horrible snap and a spray of crimson.

Gen knelt with Marina and Coral in the tears and the blood.

In the hall, Lobster gathered up his net for the cast of a lifetime. "Do that to my best ship's mate, will ya? Ya devil!"

The animal turned, Reef's severed arm in its mandibles. It flashed a rainbow warning, eyes ranging and focusing on its next victim. Lobster pitched his net and trapped the mantis in a veil of knots and rope, the man-sized shrimp's many legs weaving it into greater entanglement. Lobster backed away. The mantis clattered forward. Lobster tossed the net's hand line into the elevator, reached inside, pushed a floor button, then let the doors close. The mantis advanced, then came to the end of its rope. The car rose, sucking in the rope like a strand of spaghetti, the rising elevator whisking the netted mantis to the door. The net tightened, crushing the neon-eyed terror, and its rainbow orbs went gray.

"Eats for a week!" exclaimed Lobster.

Marina and Coral wept in the stairwell, Gen comforting them. A shadow from above. Gen saw Lobster peer in through the bloodied portal and turn away. Gen emerged into the hall. A blanket covered what remained of Reef. She gingerly guided the new widow and child around the carnage.

An almost omnipotent voice grated through the lethargic air ducts: "Who's gonna feed 'em now?"

The guest room doors opened as the parade of sorrow passed, and then, after a moment of furtive rumination, closed without a sound.

8.18

The flash of torchlight on metal. The cleaver hung mid-air as if contemplating forces and vectors. It floated weightless, with silvery impatience for the fulfillment of its unified purpose, the blade accelerating now, only coming to rest once cartilage and tendons and muscle and bone were riven — metamorphosis from what once was a living being to what was now meat.

The butcher lowered each portion of the being-that-was into the brine, and then raised it to dry. It would be lowered and raised many times until the coat of salt was thick and sparkling, protective against rot, and as ghost-white as its butcher.

The day's catch was good, and the castnetter's boots fit his butcher's white feet just right.

8.19

The ocean drained from the hotel, seeking its level. Thin rivulets flowed from the guest rooms and the halls and the stairwells, carrying with them little rafts of debris. The streams and their castaways converged into a cataract that cascaded over the seawall in a pitiable and fetid falls.

The SoBes busied themselves with cleaning what they could with what they had — which was little — and the bodies of adult and child were laid upon an exposed outcrop of crumbling concrete to await the birds and the return of the sea.

The zenith of the tide had been both bane and benefactor. Inside the walls of the drowned resort, fins and tails beat the smothering air. The impromptu catch, stranded on sodden carpets and in silted corners, was harvested eagerly and conveyed to the kitchen.

•• ––•• •

Gen accompanied the shaken mother and daughter to their room and left them to their grief. A dreadful thought darkened her mind. Something might have happened to the young man from the rooftop, too. She had not seen him since the sea ushered in its wrath. As she made her way back to her own joyless quarters, she inquired after the youth by name — his whereabouts and itineraries. None would answer. Not a single SoBe would meet her gaze, as if concealing some shared secret from her.

Gen's thoughts remained with the mesmerizing youth. *Is he the one? Was I destined to come here?* The strange feeling, so new, somehow felt so right. Her skin tingled.

She passed a door that seemed, on the X and Y, to correspond to the stair house on the rooftop. Under orders of her restless heart, she turned back.

The door had four screw holes within the specter of a sign long absent. It opened freely, unencumbered by rust or rubble. The faint scent of urine greeted her. From her vantage, it seemed the stair treads and risers were intact, so different from her earlier, treacherous ascent. Gen surmised this was owing to the weathertightness of this stairway's rooftop shelter. A thick rope hung from the balustrade above, its looped end oscillating in the slightest arc. Perhaps children were using it as a swing, she thought. She climbed up the innumerable steps, justifying the intrusion on the young man's turf. *I'm just checking on his safety.*

As she had reckoned, she emerged from the stair house onto the windmill-pocked rooftop. She considered her return, and chocked the door with the broken handle of a tool, unknown. The sun was blinding white, its rays amplified by the myriad facets and verticalities of the summit's rambling façade. All was silent. Untenanted.

"Kafka?" Even the windmills stood mute sentry. "Hello?"

Recalling the blush-worthy water tower incident, Gen called. "Kafka, are you in there?" She mounted the ladder nearly to the top, consciously avoiding a look over the edge. "Kafka?" She dared to peek. Only her own reflection in the green water. Something fluttered and landed on the far edge of the barrel. It spread its bronze wings, charging its photovoltaics with a soothing hum. "Hoyl!"

The feathered robot dug its metal talons into the rotting wood. "Hoyl. Find Edison." It did not move. "Hoyl. Go find Edison. Go. Go!" She shooed it until it chirped at her, then fluttered its wings and took to the sky. "Stupid bird."

Gen dismounted the water tower and peered over the parapet, thinking she might search for the strange youth among the complication of sagging terraces.

Below, the turbulent waters receded slowly from the base of the hotel. A faint breeze seemed to inhale from the oceanside. The most recently greased of the windmills answered to that delicate breath, turning away from the sea. She watched the ponded waters draining from the terrace patio just above the sloshing of the confused tides, stranding islands of seaweed and tangles of driftwood.

Several SoBes stood in ankle-deep water atop the tile mosaic as they attended to a hulking cylindrical object that had crashed into their drying rack and wrapped itself in their nets. Gen supposed it had washed onto the elevated courtyard, a refugee from the violent tide.

She watched as the SoBes worked their tangled nets from the object, pulling the webwork from protrusions and barnacles and limpets pocking the beached intruder. There revealed: a colossus in stucco cement, thrice the length of a man, a headdress of dead oysters accumulated in its voyages. The thing bore the fierce features of a primitive idol, sporting a contemptuous grin befitting the devil. Yet this was a modern imitation, a gash revealing its inner self of fiberglass and chicken wire. The visage reminded Gen of her mother's favorite kitsch mugs and the video lessons about the Easter Island Mo'ai and Polynesian Tiki — massive stone and wood carvings of spiritual significance, worshiped by their human creators as bringers of protection, fertility, plentiful crops, or calm seas.

Gen could make out embossed letters down its side: "LUAU." She sounded out the name, "Looo owww." She chuckled at the word's peculiar tonal quality and supposed that the original purpose of the totem was commercial art — the treasure perhaps part of a restaurant sign long ago swept from its moorings. It must have meandered through canals and inlets and bays for ages before coming to rest within the SoBes' reach.

One woman grabbed a handful of seaweed and wiped off a glob of algal slime from the idol's sculpted face. Two great shimmering eyes, a mosaic of pearlescent abalone shells, glared from deep-set sockets. Gen gasped. Some of the SoBes fell back on their butts. Others, terror-stricken, sought solace in one another's arms.

•• ••• ••

The waters accelerated their retreat — a rebound against the recent surge. Within moments, the inverse was manifest. The sea drew back far beyond its natural repose to a new extreme, baring a great expanse of sandy seabed. The susurration of waves had waned to a whisper. Shallow pools dotted the moonscape of sand and mud. A scatter of fish flopped helplessly against gravity and the stifling air.

Gen turned to the bay and the semi-submerged structures across the canal. Horizontal bands of green and orange and blue, each perhaps half Gen's height, lay exposed on the remnants of a wall. The stratigraphy of algal and bacterial stains, a sad rainbow chronicling humanity's fall from grace. The curtain of some forgotten history had been pulled back with the water's ebb, revealing walkways raised to thwart seasonal inundation, and fortifications bolstered against perennial submersion, then amended again and again, reacting to the ocean's inexorable rise. Engineering of solutions had given over to architectural improvisations, to desperations, to panic, then finally to abandonment — a record in sophisticated ramparts of reinforced concrete, beneath bulwarks of brick and mortar, rising to a loose confederation of rubble at the apex.

It seemed to Gen a lesson in archaeology and folly — the layers of excavations revealing the secret story of a civilization's rise and fall. Ages revealed in a sequence, the depth of one artifact in relation to another, and another. Slime-coated and broken sidewalks. A row of abandoned cars reduced to bouquets of sponges and barnacles. Streets of mud and sand; storefronts devolved to dim caves. Oyster-encrusted street signs stood as memorials to those times when, Gen imagined, good friends once traipsed happily from boutique to restaurant to club, only to repeat the unvirtuous cycle a few hours later. Friends she would never know.

Only now did she gather the nature and totality of this place. It was a city, yet a city no more. She had come too late; the glistening, convivial metropolis of her longing was extinct by eons. A tear streamed down her cheek. She sobbed.

Gen's self-absorbed sorrow was arrested by the movement of the group on the patio terrace, as they abandoned the found idol and its haunting eyes for the anomalous transformation on the ocean side.

She wiped her tears. The toe-tingles of Kafka's forehead kiss had waned, and she felt a sinking abandonment setting in. Did she crave more than a kiss on the forehead? Did she want to slap him for leaving her to wake up all alone? Perhaps a bit of both. *Maybe he's outside with the others by now.* Gen headed for the stair house.

• • – • – ◆ • •

The plush toy lemur's innocent button eyes gazed out the window at a world it could not comprehend. It was lifted from its home on the sill, its furry head stroked as the window retreated away.

The lemur was plunged again into brown water, this time in a stained porcelain bowl. Its eyes looked up into an unfamiliar and unloving face, whose reddened lips curled in a sarcastic smile.

Its eyes made a final plea for clemency as a handle was pushed. A maelstrom began to devour it, and its head spun into darkness with a final glug.

• • – • – ◆ • •

The retreat of the tide had taken the memory of the slaughter with it, those moments of terror supplanted by the scent of opportunity. The SoBes gathered on the newborn beach with rusty buckets and dull plastic containers of every size and shape. The motley mob descended on the sopping plain, fetching fish and mollusks from the ooze. They pounced upon the floundering delicacies — a horrible sort of karmic justice — forgetting instantly and forever their fellows lost in the watery invasion.

• • – • – ◆ • •

Gen made her way down the soggy carpet of the mezzanine ramp to the lobby. Seaweed and sandy mud formed dunes that rose along the walls and piled against the check-in desk. Despite the newly deposited oceanic debris, the lobby now appeared expansive in the absence of the natural level of the sea, its rotting smell freshly oppressive. Near the open doorway at the far end of the lobby, she espied the gruff mariner, grunting as he tugged and rocked his jon boat to free it from its precarious position jammed among the flotsam. *Him again.* She circled behind him, intending to slip out a window frame that had lost most of its tinted pane.

"You'd best scrape up some grub for your charges," said Lobster, fixed on his task.

She froze, straddling the window frame. "What do you mean, 'my charges'?"

"The woman and the girl." He tossed a rusted pail over his shoulder. She snatched the missile mid-air.

"If you don't feed 'em, the others'll tear you apart," he said, working his craft back and forth.

"What? Why?!"

"Cuz them's the rules."

She turned to go, then sighed. "Have you seen Kafka?"

Pausing his toil, he shook his head more at the querist than the query.

Gen huffed at the filthy fisher. Pail in hand, she lifted her other leg over the sill in continuance of her intended trajectory. She passed the pool, now a shallow revealing its captive wrecked outdoor furnishings and listless algae blooms. She came to the edge of the slimy seawall and looked out over the expanse of freshly exposed beach, dotted with stooped SoBes.

A conspiracy of the sun and the moon had drawn back the waters to reveal a desert of sand pocked with the castoffs of generations — pier pilings, hardware rusted beyond identification, flaccid jellies with purple tentacles in spaghetti piles, and an assortment of plastics immortal. The seabed was naked to the burning rays of midday. Surprised by their abrupt eviction, crabs scuttled about in search of an unoccupied tide pool. The SoBes followed the sea's retreat, waifs and vagabonds alike, armed with a bucket or sack, chasing down the choicest gilled morsels stranded on the sand. Most moved with brisk purpose, frantically filling their containers with fish and passing them along in a harvest brigade. Some worked solo, fingers combing the sand for whatever could be found.

Gen jumped down onto the newly minted beach. She hesitated, then picked up a motionless minnow by its tail and plopped it in her bucket. She scanned the odoriferous moonscape for another easy target.

"Better hurry up," said a SoBe over his shoulder to her as he two-handedly loaded the inverted dome of a silver serving tray, black with tarnish.

When he'd turned away, she stuck out her tongue. From her spot on the sand she looked back toward the seawall — exposed to its full height, its resident barnacles and oysters closed tight against their sudden reversal of fortune. She surveyed the collection of scrawny scavengers scattered across the sand. *My charges?* She bristled at the notion that the young fisher's death conveyed responsibility for his wife and child to her shoulders. She fought with herself and decided that she would do it this once — just to silence the surly sailor.

She raised up to scan the horizon of frantic foragers, and she wondered if her wild-haired hero might be among them.

8.20

The thing that did not belong peeked from the sand, sheltered by the seawall's short shadow. It had evaded discovery by the scavenging horde — the slow work of gravity and the agitation of the currents having ensconced it below the sea floor. The erosive effect of the recent surge had exposed a particle of its mass — now perceptible, but only to the sharp-eyed, only on this singular day, and then only from one opportune angle.

As it happened, a lone SoBe gentleman, dimpled champagne bucket of dying fish in hand, had moved downbeach from his brethren foraging in the sun, and into the shade of the seawall. He bent to adjust the tatters of his footwear, and from that particular perspective glimpsed an uncommon object of pale blue. He initiated his investigation. The blue color was enameled onto sheets of formed aluminum. The method and materials meant nothing to him except that they were unique in his experience. He tested the emergent element with his toe. Hollow. He burrowed around it with a driftwood stick, then furrowed its muddy encasement with his heel, but found the trenching technique lacking.

He moved to the far side — an area that, in his estimation, would offer the greatest purchase. He yanked upward until the tendons in his scrawny arms and legs and pencil-thin neck threatened to snap. He was a man of modest vitality, as was common to his ilk, and the partially buried structure could not reasonably be expected to yield. He dumped his catch and repurposed the champagne bucket to unbury his treasure.

Within a few enthusiastic minutes of excavation, the thing that had resisted revelation emerged. Its sky-hued metal served as a sort of roof, curious in its absence of shelled adherents. It topped a framework of fiberglass and timber painted white, the wood well-preserved in the low oxygen environment of the muck, remarkably pristine considering its possible length of immersion. It was nearly upright, though tipped on its side. A hollow had formed by the convergence of the roof and a short bench and the paneled sides. The cavity was dark and concealing, owing to its position occulted from the sun.

He dropped to his hands and knees for a better look. A single eye peered back from the blackness. He rose, debating whether to call over his compatriots to share in the bounty. And in that moment of deliberation, an elephantine translucent proboscis slid out from the obscurity. It sniffed at his heel. A quick, flaccid hydraulic sound, and the poison harpoon skewered him above the ankle, piercing the other leg through the calf for good measure. The blinding pain short-circuited the SoBe's brain just long enough for the venom to paralyze his diaphragm and for the fleshy mouth to draw him in up to his knees. As soon as he was engulfed to the shoulders, the responsible party revealed itself — a cone snail of immense size, its shell the color of bile, its distended stomach bulging with its prize. The sated culprit slinked off with its catch to meet the distant surf, a trail of mucus glistening behind.

Upshore from the incident and absorbed in their chores, the others of the gentleman's tribe were spared the spectacle.

A woman stooping over a tattered canvas bag of fish raised and looked out to where the sand met the far and transient horizon of the sea. Her mate was no longer at her side, although a vanishing trail of his drowning footprints pointed to the farthest point of the hotel's naked seawall. She had cautioned him on his unbounded curiosity. Like all of her tribe, she had foreseen this tragedy — in the night, in her tortured sleep — but would do nothing, could do nothing, to forestall its occurrence. Whether the guests of this forsaken resort were seers, or simply had a limited scope of possible outcomes, they could not discern. The visions always drew down darkly on their prospects and concluded with little ambiguity — that their lives, though wanting and brutal, would be mercifully short.

•• ‑‑•‑•‑••

Tools and supplies rattled around in the aluminum hull of Lobster's beached boat as he dragged it from the lobby on a carpet runner, the makeshift conveyance leaving a breadcrumb trail of brown woolly clumps. The man and the craft passed the stagnant pool and journeyed to the seawall where his davit and winch awaited.

He stepped onto the seawall, retrieved a container of rendered fish oil from the jon boat, and commenced to grease the cable on the davit's spool — an exercise meant to ward off rust and to preserve the braid of wire for which there was no replacement. He gazed across the wide sweep of sand scattered with SoBes, each searching for the stranded sea life that now grew scarce. As he leaned over the edge to spit, he espied the strange thing of pastel blue and white, partly uncovered, a hand-dug trench on one side. Beside it was a champagne bucket and several fish, abandoned. He saw one set of footprints coming — none going. He saw the trail of slime heading to the distant sea and shook his head, knowing.

Lobster tightened the heavy bolts at the davit's footing and swung the crane's arm seaward. He unwound a generous length of cable from his winch until its hooks rested on the sand below, then rappelled down the sheer face of the barnacled barrier. He serpentined his hardware in and around any accessible purchase of the part-buried wood, metal, and fiberglass thing that did not belong — through rungs of a ladder, the base of a bench, and the thick support from which the entire assembly derived its strength. He surveyed the immediacy for assistance but found none; his brethren bereft of empathy and engrossed in their scavengings. With the champagne bucket and a sense of urgency at what would, in accordance with his maritime observations, no doubt soon occur, he freed the perimeter of the odd structure enough to attempt retrieval.

He mounted the seawall. With one eye on his prize and the other on the beach ephemeral, he worked the hand crank with haste. The structure was exhumed with a sucking sound and the stench of sulfur and rot. The crane arm strained against the weight, testing the bolts that held it to its foundation. He hoisted the find over the lip of the seawall, then righted it to take a closer look. Its light hues of yellow and pink and blue and green were weathered but its essence was preserved from decay and destruction by its entombment. A boxy shelter atop a tall stand. The steps led to a seat in the shaded cubby. "Some kinda perch," said Lobster to himself as he tested the integrity of its fasteners and joins. He climbed the ladder, wiped the bench with a rag, and seated himself — a king on his throne. His subjects dotted the beach, bent as birds searching for their supper.

There among them was the selkie. And he wondered if she had brought with her fair winds or foul.

•• ••••••••

Gen had migrated away from the disagreeable crowd to the low islands of sand jutting from the reflections of the clouds above, where an occasional fish still floundered in the shallow pools. The SoBes had not dared to venture to this extremity, save for one intrepid forager, a frail, misshapen man. In this sodden desert, these two unpersons could separately finish their common chore while avoiding animosities.

The weave of straw came to the attention of the man. It was delicate but intact, and when the SoBe lifted it from the sand, he discovered it to be a wide-brimmed hat sporting a tricolored band. A novel find, and well-suited to the midday sun. He shook it off and popped it onto his head. A whoosh of wings — something swooped upon him, gleaming outstretched talons nearly snatching the hat. "Hey!"

Gen looked up. She saw the straw Tula atop the SoBe's head and the white, blue, and red of the band. A thing strangely familiar among the unfamiliar. Her brow furrowed and her mouth opened, recognizing the floppy regalia, yet, in her shock, unable to recall the monicker of her avuncular friend.

Hoyl swooped in again, this time knocking the headgear to the sand. A breeze carried it seaward, tumbling end over end.

The SoBe went chasing after, but within a few strides, he and the headwear encountered the first wavelets signaling the return of Poseidon. The next curls fully engulfed the banded straw chapeau in foam, and the man, considering the consequences, headed sprightly back to shore, leaving his fish and his find behind.

Gen watched the sea where the hat had absconded below the waves. "Edison."

··–—●··

The gulls ceased their bickering. At once, a tectonic silence. Lobster rose inside the colorful cubby, doffed his cap, shaded his eyes, and squinted oceanward. On the horizon, a froth of white clashed with the seabed. He formed his hands around his mouth and yelled, "Run!!"

Gen looked up from her task toward the voice and then to the incoming surf — at once mesmerized by its uniformity, stretching from an extreme of compass points perfectly parallel to the shoreline.

The white froth turned coffee brown. It approached the near-shore muck. It gained in height. A hiss grew to a roar. The SoBes scrambled back to safety above any reasonable mark of high water.

Gen realized she was alone. The signal of impending doom rushed past her ankles, thrusting her forward against the drag of the mud sucking at her soles. She broke into a sprint. She struggled to stay upright, the water now to her waist, its inertia carrying her toward an unhappy collision with the panoply of knife-edged mollusks on the seawall. She reached vainly for the seawall's concrete cap — too late — she braced for impact.

An accommodating hand lifted Gen onto the platform as the ocean engulfed all that it had recently relinquished. She looked into the eyes of her deliverer. It was Kafka.

He steadied her, tenderly holding her. "Anyone who cares about you has to realize that you need a little looking after. Nothing else really matters." Kafka peered up at the bridal suite balcony. Gen followed his gaze. Luddy stood, hands on the rail as if in judgement, momentarily joined by Taffy. The boy gently turned the girl's chin toward him. "Don't concern yourself about anybody. Just do what you think is right." He pulled her to him and held her close, her head on his shoulder.

"Oh, Kafka." She sighed.

"You are both the quiet and confusion of my heart." He looked up again at the sovereigns on their veranda. Taffy spoke into Luddy's ear, then the two retreated into their suite.

Gen espied the grumpy fisher at the far end of his seawall, now hooking his recovered boat to his davit. Feeling her stare, Lobster glared back. He sized up the pair's chemistry, then turned away. Beside him, his new pastel perch. Gen knew exactly what it was. A lifeguard stand. Just like in her videos.

•• •—•• •

Beyond the world of the young lovers, the sea roiled, frustrated perhaps that she had not taken the scavengers to her depths. The hotel groaned at the final assault, here and there shedding bits of itself with a splash, exposing arteries of rusted rebar. Across the canal, the two remaining walls of another resort dominoed into the waves, leaving tombstone slabs above the waterline — a portent for the ruins still bleaching in the sun. The waters heaved, then settled to their natural repose.

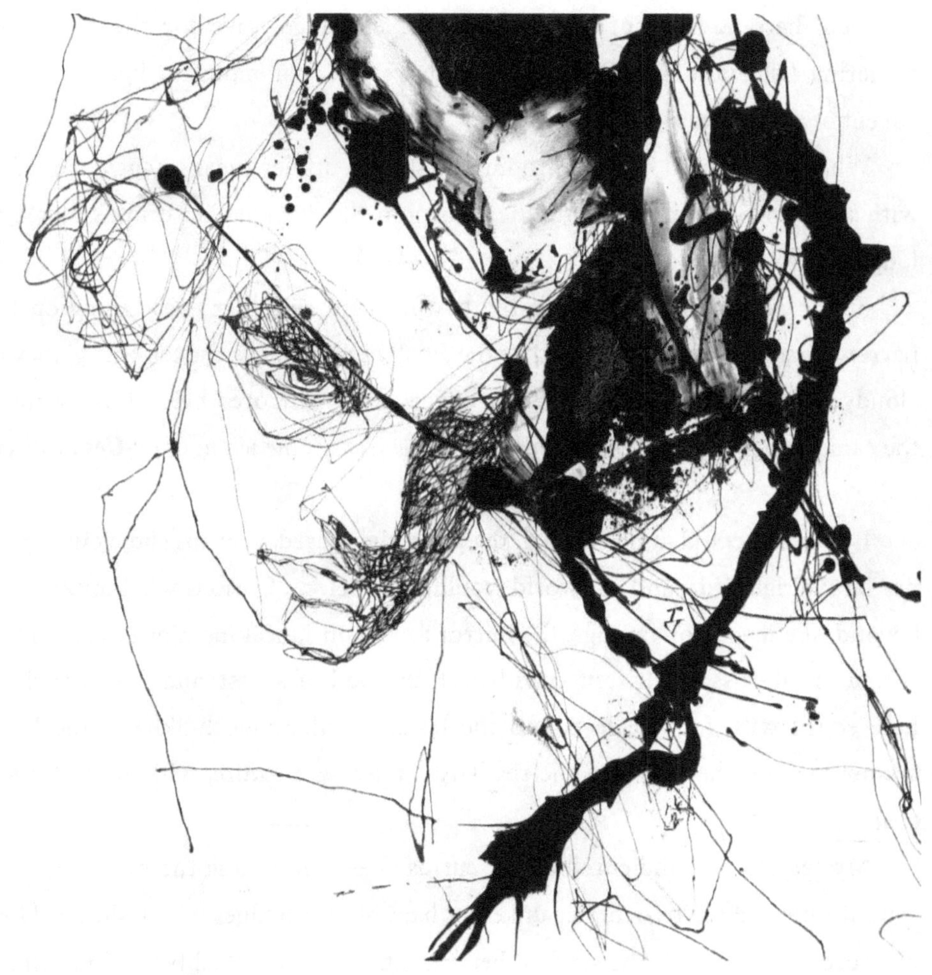

BOOK IX:

At One With the Vast Sky

The tides were uncomplicated, feeling no malice or beneficence. They had taken and given, the SoBes both injured and rewarded. The tribe had developed a language and lore around these events — more to cope than to understand.

Gen, herself, had not lost in the tidal exchange, save for the misery of gathering fish with the rabble. Her heart was, in that moment, light with the advent of a long-dreamt desire.

When she entered her hotel room, she slipped off her sneaks, soggy and laden with sand, and carried them into the bathroom. She wiggled her crinkly toes, grit lodged between.

She tossed the footwear into the two-handled sink, her eyes falling on the narrow mirror above. Illuminated by the small high window, the looking glass was cloudy, soft as gauze, a sort of bright, silvery mist. Mirrored behind her, a room the same as her own, but reversed. *This whole place is the wrong way. Upside down. Inside out.*

If only she could jump through the glass, she mused, perhaps she would come out on the right side, and her world would be as before. Curious what mystery lay beyond, she tugged on its edge, the mirror arcing on squeaking hinges, revealing a rusted metal caisson christened with scat, the wad of a nest, and a bent shelf. A hole edged with fur led deep into the building's decaying bulkhead, the hotel seeming to breathe with organic regularity, a living creature, with all under her auspices.

Mystery solved, and cured of her curiosity — Gen swung the mirrored door shut. It reflected the frizz of her unkempt hair, black smudges where she'd rubbed her nose and forehead. She smelled her armpit. Grimaced. Well beyond needing a shower. She was a tinge embarrassed the boy had encountered her in her sullied state. He had not seemed to mind, though. Perhaps it did not matter.

She rinsed out her footwear in the basin, sandy water circling the drain, as she contemplated a spot where she could lay the shoes to dry.

At home, her soggy moccasins customarily basked in the sunlight of her broad windowsill. Here, the narrow ledge might offer just enough space, she thought, once she retired her plush friend to her bed. Her feet crunched on the rotted rug as she crossed the room, stretching the canvas shoes open.

The ledge was bare. Her fluffy companion had gone missing. "Coral!" Gen stomped her foot and threw her shoes on the floor. Suddenly, she pictured the intriguing young man coming into her room at that very moment — her anger now seeming to her petty and childish. Tears conjured, then dried. She put the wet shoes in the sill's waning sunlight.

She weighed her loss against her gain. Perhaps this was the exchange that the spirits of the sea expected her to make.

9.2

An enormous housefly tickled the mound of scraps formed from things that once sported fins and gills and suckers. Balancing on the edge of the plate of offal was an ancient kitchen knife, the bloody blade worn to the merest suggestion of purpose.

The SoBes had finished their noisy orgy of filleting, having eaten the best flesh raw, the remnants of their culinary creations now in oversized pots, stewing over embers of driftwood logs that fueled the commandeered commercial kitchen stove. A layer of wood smoke found its line of demarcation and hung in the air at a singular stratum, convenient to any nostril. Gen waved the cloud away from her face, silent eddies dancing across the room.

They seemed not to like her. The way she spoke. Her form. Her color. She did not care for them, either. Their manner. Their odor. Their pallor: beneath a relentless sunburn, a pinkish gray that reminded her of newborns and death.

She had learned to wait for the insufferable chefs to vacate the kitchen before she started her own preparations. Until they returned, she had the cutting board to herself. No bumping or shoving or disparaging stares. Importantly, the room would have had time to clear of the stink from sweat and filthy clothes.

The hands of the girl were adept at many tasks: writing, drawing, handling the fragile equipment in her mother's lab, deftly thrusting through a banana plant trunk without injury. Her hands had been gaining competency with complex technical systems under the tutelage of her electromechanical father. Those same hands had recently acquired the skill of plucking live fish from shallow pools. Now, her hands set about mastering another skill: the cleaving of heads and tails, and evisceration, while suppressing revulsion.

She slapped the first silver carcass on the cutting board. A pair of saucer eyes bore witness from the tall glass case. The lifeless squid in the cooler awaited the same fate. Perhaps with their alien acuity, the eyes would have looked on with curiosity and condemnation — had their owner not, a few days earlier, taken the bait.

The peaked lights flickered with the hotel's fickle power as she worked a knife down the length of her fish, separating flesh from bone, and when she was satisfied, she set the pinkish slab to the side and plucked another specimen from her dented bucket. This odious toil and conscripted congeniality were for the benefit of Marina and Coral — her "charges," as Lobster put it. To her, it seemed pure spite that the SoBes foisted this chore upon her.

Just above the stainless steel prep table, Coral's head hovered, supervising the preparation. "Wait. You gotta get those. See? There and there," said Coral, pointing to white ribbons wriggling in the flesh.

"Yuck," said Gen, prodding one with the tip of her knife, her face contorted in disgust. "What are they?"

"Worms. You gotta get 'em out. If you don't, they go inside your tummy and grow up and a whole bunch of them come out your... you know." The little girl motioned southward and giggled.

Gen raised an eyebrow, not sure if Coral was just telling a story, but she didn't want to risk it. She deftly flipped the parasites from the flesh with the knifepoint. She examined the fillet with near-paranoid vigilance. She rinsed it and sliced it into appealing geometries, which she then arranged on a plate with considerable care atop a bed of dried seaweed. Coral's stomach growled as she followed the activity from the table's edge. As soon as Gen turned to wipe her hands on her ragged towel, the waif snuck a square and stuffed it into her mouth.

Gen brushed her hair from her forehead with her wrist, careful not to touch her face. She sniffed the towel. It reeked. She rinsed her hands in the sink and wiped them on her own shorts. "Take this plate to your mother."

Coral took the plate and turned to go.

"One more thing," said Gen. "I want my doll back."

"Didn't take it."

"You did. From my room."

"Did not!"

"Stop lying."

"You're not my friend! I hate you."

Coral pushed the platter back on the table and disappeared through the kitchen's double door. It swung closed, leaving Gen alone with the prepared fish and the pile of scales and guts buzzing with flies.

•·—·—●·•

Gen carried the plate of food — weightier in its obligation than its contents — down the dim hallway, past doors shut against the day's end. She found Marina's room number, remembering that it ended in thirty-nine, the maid's age, a fact that Coral had indiscreetly let slip.

Gen knocked. She turned the handle, and the door yielded. The setting sun lit the room blood-red. The lodging was worn like her own, though a bit larger, with two mattresses on metal frames. Marina lay curled up on one bed just beyond the reach of the sun's waning beams. She was still in her blood-stained housekeeper's uniform, staring from doleful eyes into an abyss. "Marina?" said Gen.

The woman emanated an anguished groan, mouth slack.

"I brought you some food." Gen laid the meager meal on the nightstand. Even in the shadows, she could see the maid's sunken cheeks and the skin hanging from her bones. She surmised Marina suffered not only from shock, but from malnutrition. Gen regarded the monochromatic meal — no fruit, no greens — and she sighed. These environs would not yield a more varied diet.

She heard the click of the bathroom door latch. "Coral?"

Gen cast her gaze about the shambles. Clothes and found trinkets languished on every surface of the newly neglected space, the maid having kept tidy all quarters but her own. A fishing rod stood idle in a corner next to Reef's hard-won boots; his well-used cast net hung from a nail. The scope of the cleaning task stunted her brief impulse to alleviate the cluttered sorrow.

Gen fluffed Marina's pillow. The widow, trapped in her own dark thoughts, breathed a sorrowful sigh and turned her face to the wall.

The chore was as unrewarding as it was unpleasant. If the widow did not recover her senses soon, the obligation to the pair would be without end. "Coral…?" Gen said as she turned to go. "Don't forget to lock the door, okay?" Gen closed the door behind her. She waited. Then she heard the lock bolt find home.

9.3

The gray dawn crept into Gen's room. She rose, yawning and stretching, her belly still heavy from the questionable and limited diet afforded on this perplexing archipelago. She dragged herself to the window; the pane, opaque with dew, cried dirty tears down the wall. This would be another day filled with the thankless preparation of sustenance for the widow, mingled with servile capitulation to the tribe. *So much for making friends.*

She cleared the mist with her palm. A speck of green caught her eye. A plant had burst to life from the dirt-encrusted sill just outside her window, its delicate tubular stem crowned in a cloud of fluffy seeds ready to parachute on the breeze. She identified it as *Taraxacum officinale*, the common dandelion — edible from root to flower — once so plentiful it was considered a pest to be eliminated. Edison kept a planter box overflowing with the weed. The leaves were bitter but palatable and provided another source of minerals and vitamins. Gen's affinity for the plant was more elemental. The bright yellow of the blossom, she remembered, made her happy.

Edison had told her that plants needed just four things: sun, air, water, and soil. And she would rather eat flowers than rancid fish. Keeping her eye on the ephemeral phenomenon, she tugged at the window frame. *Gotta get it before the wind picks up.* The window, still sealed by years of paint, would not yield.

••——•••

Gen crossed the hall to the vacant guest suite. A rag of curtain billowed from the opening that once had been a sliding door. She could see now that an entire corner of the room had fallen away. She slipped through the breach with care, onto the broken balcony. Much of the railing was missing. A bit of concrete crunched underfoot. Her toe caught on a chunk and sent it flying. It caromed off the lower terraces, and after a moment, splashed into the canal below. The drop would inspire second thoughts in most; she dived from such heights every day at Eos and had no such qualms. She surveyed the ledge that wrapped around the exterior. Sections had crumbled, but, she calculated, enough remained for her excursion, and Gen stepped into the sky.

Wind whistled around a cornice and blew through her hair. Her fingertips found their tentative purchase on the structure's skin, digits penetrating the imperfections in the surface, and she shuffled along the narrow projection on the balls of her feet. She made her way around a second corner and to the region of her own room. Pressing her nails into a fissure in the concrete, she inched toward the little plant — so alone in the hostility of this place; so much like her. A loose pilaster crumbled to the waters far below — her eyes followed it down. A splash. Attracted by the perturbations in the water, a dark form patrolled the swirling canal between the hotel and the adjacent rubble. *Don't fall. Not now.* Her toehold came to an inconvenient end, her prize on the far side of the sill. She stretched tendon and muscle until her fingertips felt underneath the jagged leaves. Then she delicately tugged the dandelion's thin root from its mooring.

STATUS: SECTOR LOST 01:09:003;06 (See Technical Notes)

The rooftop patio terrace, oft occupied with the daily pursuits of the SoBes, was presently silent, save for the sounds of water and the cry of the occasional gull echoing in the crumbling canyon. On the tiled plateau just above the waterline, neat mats of seaweed lay in varied stages of desiccation. Cast nets baked on the vestiges of an awning's aluminum frame. Beside a parapet, improvised spears and gigs and other contrivances for scavenging awaited the collective pangs of hunger. Reclining where the SoBes had left it, the columnar castaway idol gazed idly skyward.

Among the offscourings below the patio terrace, Gen stood waist deep in the canal atop the cement riprap blocks that helped hold the hotel's submerged walls upright. She dredged a bucket of muck from the shallows exposed by the regular ebb of the tide. She walked it up to a disused recess in the building's façade she had corralled with chunks of spalled concrete. She nudged a stray chunk into place with her toe. The fishing nets, draped to dry, screened her space from prying eyes, offering some semblance of solitude. Alone in her work, she was content.

Though the plot was modest by any standard of gardening — a mere two arm's lengths on a side — it would suffice. She emptied the mud onto a bed of rotting seaweed in the center of the makeshift planter box and knelt beside it. She kneaded the constituents into a unified mass. After a while, she appraised her labors and, dissatisfied with the proportions, gathered another armful of algae from the tidewrack and placed it on the pile. She merged the black sludge and sargassum with her hands until the mélange became uniform in texture. Her arms were dirtied to the elbows, her eyes teary from the gaseous byproducts of decay. She tilled the newborn soil into fine furrows with a finger. Then she looked with affection at the prize she had plucked from her sill. It waited patiently in a cup, its sphere of snowy seeds primed for their time in the sun.

Coral made faces at Gen through the glass of the double door. She pretended not to see, and the waif darted back into the gloom of the hotel.

Gen held the dandelion to her lips and blew its aerial fruits onto the fresh bed. She transplanted the hopeful donor among its daughters and blessed the patch with rainwater from a nearby bowl. She caressed the soil to ensure that each seed would adhere, then covered the furrows. *Perfect. Nature will do the rest.* A jab — she drew her hands from the humus and looked. A crimson gash in her palm. Scarlet streaks on the black earth led to jagged rebar jutting from a concrete chunk. She pressed her thumb into the dripping wound as she watched her blood soak into the soil. A shadow moved across her cultivations. She squinted into the sunset to see Hoyl — the mechanized bird soaring on the day's last thermal.

A door swung wide as SoBes filed out onto the patio. Ten in all. All men. Gen made herself small in the corner, veiled behind the drying cast nets.

The men positioned themselves on either side of the massive totem whose length had bisected their dominion. They tilted the idol to vertical. It rocked into place. They lingered, tentative in their reverence, unmetrical utterings emerging from their mouths, the syllables indiscernible. Their repertoire of improvised incantations spent, they stood awkwardly mute for a moment, then retreated from the platform. All was silent. Gen was again alone.

She parted the fishers' nets to get a look. The glistening shell eyes of the towering Mo'ai glared down. She startled. The imperious totem was taller than she would have guessed, its shadow a sundial signaling the coming of another long and sultry night. At the idol's stucco feet, she saw a silver platter containing a single fish. *An offering?*

The idol eclipsed the setting sun. The eyes grew red, the mouth, cruel. Gen stood, rattled but defiant. The wind intensified, howling along the riprap. It intoned on the iron rebar that reached its rusting fingers from the seawall. The tide reversed and gurgled over the rubble that was once a city. In this shrinking world, there were two in opposition: the idol and the sixteen-year-old girl.

9.4

The noonday sun beat down on the shoulders of a scrawny man in tattered pants. He retrieved a cast net from the metal drying rack, inspected the mesh, and with practiced panache, gathered it together, tucked the bundle under his arm, and clambered down to the waterline. Two women organized a tangle of wet seaweed across the patio tile with particular care, conveying to the task an unearned importance. A man threw a baited line into the canal, hopeful.

A mother, her hand on her little boy's shoulder, approached the towering faux-stone Mo'ai. She whispered in the child's ear and pointed to the base of the totem. He crept forward and placed a small conch shell among an accrual of fish and fowl and trinkets of local significance. The boy looked up into the terrible eyes of the idol. He darted back to his mother and clamped onto her leg, and the pair, without ceremony, scurried to the aegis of the hotel.

Her elbows resting on the remnant of the vacant suite's balcony rail, Gen followed the bustle below her on the patio terrace. It was a painting with no frame. The people, simple. Their tasks, unremarkable. The scene, pastoral. Their daily routine suggested to her the familiar toil of Edison's colleagues tending the majestic bamboo stands, a ritual with which, she had thought until recently, they were content. She wished she had not learned of the darkness in their hearts, and their disdain for her genetic father.

Her consolation was that here at Deco, the SoBes were leaving her to herself. Still, she wondered why these strangers harbored some secret scorn for her, as well.

A golden glow emanated from the farthest corner of the edifice, a singular spot of vivid color against the muted panorama. Her garden patch boasted a crowded mass of blossoms. A wreath of stout green leaves ringed the festive display. Her verdant plot seemed to have bloomed with exceptional swiftness. She had sampled a few of the leaves herself; they were as fresh and crisp as she remembered, a respite from the swill that was, here, considered food. She would include some in the widow's diet to help her regain her strength and her forfeited reason.

9.5

As on each day of her new life, dawn crept into Gen's window, bringing anew the realization of her stranding in this strange and depleted land. Today, though, she sat up and gazed at her reflection in the sliver of dresser mirror and saw herself almost smile. This would be the first harvest of her golden bounty. There would be little time to reap before the intolerable humidity overtook the expanse, and so she moved with newfound energy as she prepared for her day.

•• −•−•−●•• •

Gen opened the door to the tiled terrace, her dented pail spilling over with tap water. The SoBes stopped their labors for a moment to glare at the girl, then returned to their work.

The shadow of a passing bird drew Gen's eyes to the clouds. Edison's winged machine was tracing a twitchy pattern in the sky, as if its solid state mind could not overcome an inherent illogic. It reminded her of the dance that bees do when warning of danger. *I see why Uncle Edison said it wasn't finished.*

Still enthused despite the chilly reception, she leapt over a heap of drying seaweed, moving toward a far corner of the patio terrace, leaving behind half the water in a trail of drips. She pushed aside the fishing nets hanging from the awning frame, toting her bucket to her private plot.

It was gone. A smear of soil crossed the tiled surface as if a great hand had swept the entire garden away. The pail handle slipped from her fingers and thumped on the tile, the water splashing at her feet. The SoBes turned to see.

Gen rushed to the crumbling castellation and looked over the ledge where the terrace met the canal. Remnants of the flowers and leaves lay brown and wilted at the tidewrack, her edging stones tossed over and strewn across the bank of riprap that braced the hotel wall.

Her eyes scoured the empty spot where the golden tribute to her efforts had once reached for the sun. A collage of footprints in the mud — some large, some small, some with shoes, some without — evinced the perpetrators of her garden's destruction. Gen's jaw clenched. Her hands formed into fists.

•• —•—◉•• •

Boom. Boom. Boom. Boom. Lobster ceased his tale spinning mid-embellishment, his eyes on the ripples in the water pitcher atop Luddy's serving cart.

Luddy felt the rhythmic percussions through his desktop. "Odd."

Lobster poked his head out of the bridal suite. Doors opened along the hallway, and their bedraggled occupants peered out, faces a mix of fear and ire.

•• —•—◉•• •

Boom. Boom. Boom. Boom. Venting her unbridled anger, Gen punched the hotel wall over and over. Her thundering blows shuddered the steel superstructure. Her knuckles left craters in its stucco skin. Boom. Boom. Boom. Boom. Several SoBes shrank away. Others dropped their tools and ran inside.

Tremors traveled from the hotel pediment through Kafka's fingertips and to the base of his brain. Peeking over the edge, he discreetly observed the girl's percussive display. On a lower tier, a shadow elongated. A female form, familiar in its stealth, approached the patio. The youth retreated to the immutability of his windmills and water tower and dilapidated domain.

It had made the consort's stomach churn and her slumber roil. It had threatened her position, her comfort, her safety. It had evaporated whatever fleeting joy she had. The festering sore was a vestal rival, and she was hunting for the pit in its perfection. Indulging her new avocation, Taffy had trailed the bucket-toting teen down to the patio terrace, now echoing with rhythmic thuds.

With a devilish smirk, Taffy peered from around a corner. Pounding the wall was the pugilistic girl, each blow exerting a terrifying power. Taffy stopped short. She bent and drew from her ankle sheath a thin blade, its sharpened sliver glinting in the sun. She felt a pressure wave — a flying object hurtling a mere hair's width over her head. She froze. One bronze wingtip grazed a gash along the wall beside her, white dust in its wake. She glimpsed the mechanical bird as it soared skyward.

Hoyl measured wind speed and humidity, then error-corrected, banked, and recalculated the optimal course for interception. Its crystal eyes scanned in infrared and across its other measurable spectra for the target and its vulnerabilities. It flapped its wings to gain velocity, then went into a ferocious dive. Just as it reached the coordinates thus calculated and micro-adjusted in real time for temperature variations near the surface, Taffy was gone.

Boom. Boom. Boom. Boom. The tempestuous teenager felt a tug on the hem of her top. Gen spun around, her two bloodied fists poised for a fight.

It was Coral. The six-year-old flinched and stepped back. Struggled to get the words out. "Luddy says… um… come see him."

9.6

The door of the bridal suite was open, and Gen could see its single occupant: a man neatly dressed in white, ensconced behind his intricately carved wooden desk. He was thin, and she surmised he was tall — taller, it seemed, than most of the inhabitants of the hotel. He sat, hands folded, motionless — no indication that breath entered or exited his lungs. The sun streamed in, framing him in a wedge of brilliance. She had met him — or more accurately, sensed his presence — on that first day, directing others from the shadows. The aged carpet scrunched under the girl's feet as she crossed into the suite at an oblique angle, avoiding his gaze. "I remember you," said Gen, curtly.

"Please come in," said the man. "I am called Luddy."

"I know."

Luddy sat stoic, unmoved and unmoving, Gen reflected in the lenses of his mirrored sunglasses, her image bisected by the conspicuous crack in one lens.

"You created quite a disturbance," he said. His head followed her progress as she moved toward the window planter.

"So? I didn't hurt anybody," said Gen. The plants were green and plump, and perfectly placed for the best sun. She touched a leaf and found it firm and cool. One succulent looked familiar. *I had one like that in my room.* Her posture was stiff like the stakes that held the plants aloft, steeled against inquiry or further reproach.

"And did you think to ask permission of anyone before you set about your task?" said Luddy, coolly.

"Nobody was using that spot."

"You may have provoked them, if only by your industry."

"Provoked…? How would you feel if somebody killed all of *your* plants? I made that garden, and I watered it, and took care of it, and it was blooming. And somebody — a bunch of people — just ruined the whole thing!" Gen felt her voice rising out of her control.

"What would you have me do, and what would that accomplish now?" said Luddy, unaffected by her outburst.

Gen was disarmed by the man's evenness. "Find out who did it and make them… make them… I don't know." She sighed.

He shook his head. "The SoBes are prone to their jealousies. Their lives are hard. New things are a threat, and the unexpected terrifies them. But do not underestimate them. You are always in a certain amount of danger as long as you live here among them."

"Well, I don't care about this rotten old place, anyway. I'm going to find the big city where I can make real friends and look up at the skyscrapers and ride around in cars."

Luddy contemplated the girl's ambitions, and whether he should disabuse her of them. "As you say. I want to help you, Gen. But you need to govern yourself. Let me explain. Everyone here keeps Lobster at a distance. Do you know why?"

"Because he smells?"

"He's big, disagreeable, physically powerful, and you simply never know what he is about to do. They're all afraid of him, Gen, and they don't like him much, either."

"Well, I know *I* don't like him. Wait. Did he wreck my garden?"

Luddy allowed the unreasoned accusation to linger, unanswered.

"He's the one who dragged me here in the first place," she said.

"Perhaps I can persuade Lobster to ferry you back to where the two of you first met."

The girl's mouth opened at the affront, but found no retort.

Luddy continued. "As adults, we don't grant ourselves the luxury of exploding every time things don't go our way. None of us can help what happens to us, but we are in full charge of how we react to it. My point is, if you allow yourself to wallow in petty resentments, you will become just like the people you resent. If you want to have allies here, Gen, or anywhere else you can imagine, for that matter, you need to take command of your emotions. Didn't your parents teach you this?"

"Back home, everybody was always nice to me, even when I was upset," she said, tears welling in her eyes.

Luddy waited for her wave of emotion to pass. "Have you always been strong?"

"What do you mean?"

"It seems you are stronger and faster than most."

"I dunno. I guess I've always been the same."

"Even as a child?"

"Maybe. I don't really remember."

"You don't remember being a child?" Luddy was incredulous.

"Not really. That stuff gets foggy as you grow up, I think."

Luddy rose, turned his back on the girl, and moved to the stained glass window, a kaleidoscope of color cast upon the canvas of his white suit. "Did you ever consider that your parents were afraid of you? That the SoBes are afraid of you?"

Gen's brow furrowed. "Afraid of me? That's crazy."

"Perhaps."

Her knee trembled as she stared at the man's back. In these times, her mother would have poured the nectar of reassurance. *He's unbearable. Just like my so-called father.* She huffed. *How long till this is over?*

She wandered to the farthest geography of the suite, and to the A-frame of sun-bleached wood looking out to the sea: a wooden easel like her mother's, the one upon which perched a depiction of a lemur in a stand of bamboo. This canvas, though, faced away, too timid to reveal its virtuosity. Gen leaned in for a look. It was an impasto of an open boat with a man and a woman aboard. Excepting the woman's long white dress and bonnet, the painting was awash in color. The composition was of a quality uncommon to the imaginings of this place. The brushstrokes of a master in the making. A palette protruded from the easel drawer — on it, a rainbow of paint perfectly petrified, a brush locked in dried oils like an ancient beast in tar.

"Are you an artist?" asked Gen.

On this, the man was silent. He cleared his throat, then returned to his desk. "Please. Sit."

The girl plopped onto the pink chair across from Luddy's desk and folded her arms, burying her raw, grazed knuckles under her elbows.

On a credenza beyond his desk, a panel of round dials glowed a dim orange from their mahogany box. Alongside was a desktop public address microphone. A meter twitched rhythmically. Atop another box, a flat shiny black disk, spinning. A small arm near the center of the disk lifted. For a moment, the meter stopped. The arm arced to the outer edge of the disk, then set down. The meter came alive again at the command of the undulations dictated by the disk.

With the momentary silence of the building's ambient drone, Gen guessed this mechanism was the source of the insipid music that pervaded the building. An orchestral made easy for the listener. A soothing and unchallenging song, now annoying through repetition. A tune that should not be played over and over, but was.

Luddy explained to her that the player and its public address system predated the SoBes. He conjectured that it might have existed since the time the hotel was originally built. He assured her that the music, regardless of its quality, seemed to keep the SoBes somewhat tranquil — at least while they were within the walls of the building.

"Do you like this music, Gen?"

Her mind flashed on the boot heel of Dr. Rhodes, grinding Edison's player to dust, silencing the delicate symphony. "Dunno. I guess it's okay. Maybe if it wasn't played again and again. Uh… how do you know my name?"

"You were mentioned in this journal," said Luddy, motioning to the loosely bound collection splayed open on his desk.

Suddenly, she recognized the water-damaged pages. "Hey! That's my mother's. Give it back."

"You won't mind if I peruse it for a while. It is rare that new reading material comes into our possession here. You understand."

Gen rose to snatch it.

Luddy covered the journal with his hand. "Please. A few more days."

She had found the tome disquieting and inscrutable anyway, and deduced that the man might be more amenable if she agreed. "Okay. Just for a few more days," she said. "Can I please go now?"

"Your parents. How old are they?"

"I don't know."

"Older than me?"

"I guess."

"Did they find what they were looking for?"

She shrugged. Luddy sat silent.

"I don't know," she said. She stood and turned to the door.

"Wait."

Gen paused but didn't turn back, anticipating a parting rebuke.

"This plant you were growing. Is it edible?"

"Dandelions? Of course,"she said over her shoulder.

"How long do they typically take to grow?"

"Um. I don't know. Maybe two weeks. Maybe a little more."

"I see. And yours flowered in…?"

"Four days," Gen said, impatient.

"You have what used to be called a green thumb."

"Well, maybe a red one. I cut myself mixing the soil."

"I see."

Gen shut the suite's faded pink door behind her.

And after a moment, Luddy twisted a knob on the PA system. Monochromatic music infiltrated the suite from a disintegrating speaker. He closed the journal and pushed it to a corner of his tidy desk. He held his head in his hands. A tear fell onto his blotter.

•• •••••• ••

Gen pressed the elevator button as she had seen done. If Luddy would not help her receive reparations, she would at least have the satisfaction of using the man's mechanized transport now rumbling skyward from deep in its well. The mechanism groaned and clattered to a stop. The door slid open to three SoBes amid the malodor of death, the floor and walls still blood-streaked from the battle with the rainbow-eyed monster. They cowered at the sight of her. The door closed, shutting her out. Mortified, she ran for the stairs.

•• •—•••••

She slammed her door. Flipped the deadbolt. Her thoughts rolled like billiard balls that could not find a pocket. She paced the floor, then kicked the dirty pillow she'd dislodged from the vent, stirring a cloud of dusty karma. She sat on the bed, then flopped on her back and read the peeling ceiling. She stretched out her arms and pondered her swollen hands and tortured knuckles. She was disheartened that she had done more damage to herself this time than she realized, although her skin had already commenced its healing task. There would be no quick resolution for the problem at hand, though.

She had gone to see Luddy expecting his pledge to mediate on her behalf. His words were brief. Not clarifying. Not comforting. The man had seemed interested only in scolding her for a justified bout of temper, while the rotten bullies were allowed to escape culpability. *He's wrong about me!* She would never be like those mean, ignorant SoBes, and she didn't deserve their wrath.

She bolted from the bed and banged her fists on the dresser. *It's not fair!* She kicked the bottom drawer. She looked up at her reflection — shocked by an angry, torqued version of her face. *I'm not like them! Not at all!* She kicked the drawer again, harder. The drawer front flopped to the floor, broken, the glass jar with the yellowed paper tinkling to her feet. She snatched it up, twisted the rusted lid, and poured the brass key into her palm. Two handwritten capital letters crowded its round paper fob: an "A" and a "Q."

9.7

Her fingers felt along the imperfections in the fresco, rode the waves and undulations, and probed the pits in the painted plaster. She searched for the curve of a small circle hidden in the design — a strategically selected position within the art of the subject's bow, which concealed the lock beneath, occult from mischief and the profane. Her fingernails found purchase on the plug's periphery. Gen gently pried the chalky puck from its niche. She cupped it with care in one palm. She retrieved the key from her pocket, pressed it into the jagged receiver, and twisted until it conceded.

The clack of the retreating lock resounded in the wall, as if the vessel floating on the pastel river had woken from slumber. Fissures formed in the plaster painting, straight and true, and rose to beyond the height of a man and down to the floor. A narrow cleft crossed at right angles, and the architecture revealed itself in a cloud of white powder. It was a door, concealed behind lime and sand and pigment, in prescient fear of discovery — the artist and era, unknown.

She worked her fingers into the seam and forced the door open. She pulled against the vacuum of the space behind it, chalky chips and dust sprinkling her hair. She peered inside.

It was dark. A void of indeterminable dimension. She looked over her shoulder and, assured of privacy, tugged on the door until a wedge of light penetrated the abyss. Illuminated was a chamber of unexpected extent. Before her was the subject of the idealized wall mural come to life. On its massive wooden cradle rested an old dhow, the open-decked boat the length of five men. Christened in hand-painted capital letters on its rust-brown hull: *AFRICAN QUEEN*.

A half-dozen tarnished metal posts about waist high ringed the craft, united by the rotted remains of magenta-colored velveteen tubes. Some clung by corroded brass hooks, others so decayed they had fallen to the carpet.

Atop the frontmost stanchion, clear rectangular panels sandwiched a varicolored paper sign bearing a photographic depiction of the whimsical boat and its pair of passengers — a crisp color rendering of the same black-and-white image in the jar. Below the sign, a transparent, open box proffered a stack of trifold sheets. She took one out and flinched — beneath, empty sockets stared back from a tiny skull, an unknown squatter reduced to bones amid a clump of nesting materials. She opened the folded missive flat. One side depicted the same photo and bold letters touting an event, "Annual SoBe Film Festival," to be held in

"The Deco District." The obverse told the history of the craft and listed a timetable of activities in and around the hotel.

Gen circled the dhow, a coarser version of the glorified portrayal. She lifted herself over the gunwale and climbed inside. She recalled the vivid images of a pleasure boat projected within her simulated beach, her electro-generated friends frolicking alongside. And there was the derelict watercraft that she had discovered, suspended aloft in the trees at Eos. She had never been aboard a real watercraft until the day she was dragged unceremoniously onto Lobster's smelly little skiff. This example beneath her feet looked visibly aged — older than any object in all of her experience, and of a strange construct. An iron barrel in the boat's center sported gauges and valves and a smoke stack evoking the malign "pot-bellied stove" in her mother's lab. She surmised that the people in the boat might have used it for warmth or cooking. Upon a closer look, it reminded her of Edison's contraptions, and she speculated that the stove-like apparatus might have provided some form of propulsion, although its mechanics were a mystery. The ancient deck planks creaked with every cautious step of her explorations. It smelled from toil and untold seasons and neglect. This boat seemed built by another civilization, for a purpose she could not decipher. She reclined on the craft's side bench and pondered the puzzle.

In the forever night of the room, light emanated from thousands of tiny pinholes in the ceiling. *Stars.* Just like when she would lie on the synthetic thatch of her home, mulling her tomorrows and musing about a past that seemed ever out of her reach. On those nights, she would ponder the universe, and the incalculable calculations that could describe its character and composition. Tangents, orbits, trajectories, velocities — those, too, were just beyond her grasp. Still, Gen hoped the infinite orchestrations derived some order from the cosmic chaos. *There had to be a purpose.* In those moments, she was a minuscule part of the macrocosmos, at one with the vast sky — a feeling that had always melted her troubles and given her joy. Now, as she lay cradled inside the strange craft beneath the false starscape, she felt her equanimity drain away. The pocked ceiling, its span dictated by the room's perimeters, felt finite and small and cheap. Suddenly, she seemed to herself very small, and not at all comforted. She closed her eyes and the quiet of the forgotten room summoned a peace she had not realized she missed. *I must be the first person in here for ages.*

Tapping — like pebbles on a windowpane. She opened her eyes. She looked around, but no windows were apparent. The sound was sequential. Intentional. She disembarked the boat and, in the gloom, made her way around the perimeter in search of the source. It had originated overhead. She listened.

A tall aluminum ladder leaned against the wall in a lonely corner. Gen climbed to the top rungs and listened again. She tapped the ceiling. Another sequence of tapping followed in answer to her overture. She couldn't be sure, but now that she was closer, she could see that the ceiling was originally a skylight that spanned much of the space. In some rethinking of that space, someone had coated the glass, and now the decaying material flecked off in tiny pinhole chips. Her fingernails found an edge and peeled away a corner of the skylight's coating. Two large and perfected raptor eyes stared back through the dusty reinforced glass. She gasped. *Hoyl!* She teetered, holding onto the ladder's topmost rung. The ladder wobbled, fortunately coming to rest still in the vertical. Then she tore away another small section of the coating.

Hoyl spread its bronze wings and flew off, leaving Gen with a new perspective on her private refuge: the room, illuminated by a bright cone of sunlight.

Just as Egyptian tombs sealed for millennia revealed illustrations in vibrant tones, so, too, did this secret room, now alive with a rainbow of happy color. Banana yellows and soft blueberry blues mingled with strawberries and oranges brighter than their namesake fruits. A tattered sign welcoming all to the SoBe Film Festival hung from a rafter. Presently, Gen could make out the room's true dimensions. It was rectangular, its height approaching two stories, its length just adequate to accommodate the boat stem to stern. She dismounted and left the ladder in the corner.

Gen noticed a countertop that took up the wall opposite, cordoned off by a roll-down gate all akimbo, with a whimsical sign in faded pastels that read: "Ice Skate All Summer!" As she approached, the floor flexed with each step. She pressed the ball of her sneaker into the carpeted surface of the strangely vast room. The floor was hollow. A corner of the rotted carpet was torn back, the brittle plywood plank beneath it sitting ajar. She lifted the plank and saw a maze of tubes that snaked beneath the floor. Her mind sifted through the snow of lessons that had once danced inside her video-glasses and on her 3-D wall at home: a vague recollection of something called ice skating, with special boots and a cold surface made of crystalized water — and people young and old gliding and spinning. She had seen ice before, but only in the glaciers clinging to the sides of Mother's intolerably cold sub-zero lab freezer. The apparatus underfoot didn't quite fit the paradigm. No icy surface and no water — only the narrow piping meandering through its hidden space. Nevertheless, the design was intentional. She supposed the matrix was the mechanism by which the water froze solid.

A row of rusted cabinets stood sentinel behind the counter, along with rotting wood racks. Gen saw a shadow in one of the rack's cubby-holes. Inside: a pair of high-topped shoes with metal blades that ran their length heel-to-toe, the uppers of which were fast turning to dust. The storage cabinets were locked or rusted shut, but the side of one was so oxidized that she could peel its entire flank away like paper. A dozen plastic containers of paint were stacked inside. Some had been opened and were dried solid. Others had their seals intact. Some colors matched the hues of the walls and the hanging sign. She felt around on the cabinet's shelves, and her hand fell upon a paintbrush the width of her palm, with a wooden handle, the bristles stiff from a cursory cleaning.

Rude plumbing noises reverberated overhead, startling Gen out of her moment of discovery. She would not want to be caught where she didn't belong, especially by Lobster or someone as crude and dangerous as he. Still, it seemed to her that no one had been in this room for a very long time, so perhaps her secret adventure would remain so. Another loud noise from the cast iron pipes propelled her toward the exit.

Gen nudged the door open a sliver. Occupying the mezzanine was a single boy, fishing. She waited. Soon the youngster grew bored, retrieved his line from the depths of the deluged lobby, and departed.

She slipped out, then locked the heavy door. She blended the plaster seams with her fingertip to disguise evidence of the opening. She wedged the knot of plaster back over the lock and burnished the edge with her thumb. The fissures defining her breach were imperceptible. With her sneaks, she rubbed the dust and crumbs into the carpet to deter discovery. Then she stood back to inspect her handiwork: the fresco of the rickety dhow, a survivor amongst the ruins, the intrepid couple piloting her on the river of eternity.

And Gen's heart filled with longing.

9.8

Gen tapped her writing instrument on her lip as she contemplated the poetical work in progress in her personal notebook, the line straight and neat, the rhythm and verse pleasing enough. Filled with imaginings of the strange, magical room she had discovered, she was bent on capturing a dark but intriguing world that centered on an ancient sea craft, and the felicitous gathering place of young and old, gliding on bladed shoes upon a pond miraculously frozen and contained as if nature itself had been tamed. As she sat cross-legged on her little bed in her tiny servant's quarters, she worked her pen across the bottom of the page.

I found a key inside a jar,

A message, too, inside.

It led me to a secret door,

An enchanted room to find.

The treasure within a ship there was,

And set sail my ready mind.

I gaze upon the midnight sky,

Upon a star I asked it why,

And dreamt of friends,

And crystal towers,

And friends gliding by the hours.

Gen's brow furrowed. *This stinks.* In her rush to capture the moment, the sparkle had faded. This poem, she feared, was no better than those she had penned before. The discovery of the last intact room in the last standing hotel in all of

Deco was sheer felicity; the unique treasure behind the door deserved to be memorialized. The meticulously disguised exhibition hall was merely a museum of the world she had hoped to find. Her heart grew heavy with the realization that she was too late. By eons, she had missed the skating crowds and the admirers of the odd old boat. She slipped the pen in its holder and lay back to peruse the ceiling.

She was still unsettled at the destruction of her garden plot, and the tall man's refusal to redress her grievance. The unresolved matter crowned a heap of unhappiness: the disappearance of her stuffed toy; the pillow jammed in her room vent; the confiscation of her mother's journal; the disgusting fish and the feeding chores; Reef's violent death; the taunting waifs; her failed attempt at boat-jacking; Lobster's fishing net; the storm at Eos; the grueling, pointless circular trek; her parents' many lies.

And she had not seen the young man in several days.

Unresolved disappointment was a new emotion for Gen. She really disliked being told she couldn't have something or that she'd disobeyed a rule, and she had dreaded her parents' calm and clinical explanations of priorities and consequences — along with the work of convincing them of her stance. Now, she wished she could have that kind of civilized, manageable conversation and feel some semblance of vindication.

Whenever Gen would dream of meeting new people, she had not once considered that anyone could dislike her.

•• ─•──●•• •

The building slowly came alive. Stale air whistled between the cracks in the walls and teased the curled leaves of paint that dangled dead from the ceilings. The whole of the hotel groaned a greeting to the new and dreamless day. Mumbles of voices and sounds of lavatories resonated in the concrete and steel.

A rude burp erupted from her commode, rousing Gen with a start, her notebook of aspirational verse still resting upon her breast. She slipped on her shoes. She twisted the handles on the little sink and waited until the rust cleared before rinsing the sleep from her eyes.

The pipes buzzed between the walls. Sounds of hydraulic despair. She paused and listened. Would she be swallowed whole, digested in the dyspeptic belly of a great and flatulent beast? Raised and sharp voices echoed from below her window, fueling her growing unease. *Something's happening.*

She crossed the hall into the derelict room and treaded carefully out to the balcony. Below, a delta of dark liquid spread across the patio terrace, infiltrating even the onetime province of her secret garden. The klatch of SoBes gaped at the spreading black stain as it encircled the stucco feet of their imposing idol and spilled over the edge into the canal.

••⋯•━•••

Burbling black fountains erupted from the kitchen's floor drains. Toilets backed up in the hotel rooms. Sinks and tubs filled with dark and viscous liquid. The entire building, from bottom to top, saturated with a chorus of disgust.

••⋯•━•••

A cacophony of tinny voices vibrated up through the brass speaking horn into the bridal suite with panicked protestations. Luddy rose from his chair and leaned toward the horn, uttering assurances of an immediate response, then turned to Taffy. "We have a problem to solve, and with haste."

She sighed and laid Gen's journal face down atop Luddy's desk.

"I'm interested in a particular book," said Luddy. "On architecture. There is a reference to a city on the other side of the globe, since lost to the sea."

Taffy moved to the shelves of the decrepit library.

"Do you see the one I mean?" he said.

She caressed the broken spines and read off a few titles. He stopped her at the remembered title and she plucked the book from the shelf.

"Look in the index for Gatolo. G-a-t-o-l-o," said Luddy.

Her fingers followed the index, and then deftly danced over the pages, arriving finally on a reference. "Here you go. Gatolo. Venetian for 'drain channel.'"

"Continue."

Taffy read to him from the tome, detailing the ways of that more ancient, watery world. She described their drawings of crude wastewater tunnels running from each home directly into the adjacent canal — the commode's outside accomplice, the literal end of the line.

Luddy reclined, his feet on his desk, as his mind absorbed the engineering descriptions and anecdotes about the Gatolo belching alimentary contributions at low tide. "Perfect," he said. "Get Lobster."

Although Luddy's prescription struck Lobster and the other SoBes as both peculiar and ambitious, the noise and stench and lack of better ideas of their own motivated them to try it. A few men gathered pipes from the extras stashed on the roof beside the water tower and, by rope and net, let them down to the water's edge.

Two men clambered down to the building's waterline, and after some discussion and rough estimation based on Luddy's instructions, picked a spot for their planned breach. Wielding pieces of rebar, they punched a hole through the wall near the waterline where Lobster believed the main drain leading from the hotel's blackwater pipes had been blocked by some unknown obstruction. They jiggered the salvaged pipe sections through the building's fresh wound. Hardware was connected as prescribed, bound tight with rope and rags, and covered with chunks of loose concrete to hold their improvisation of plumbing against confiscation by the waves. This amendment Lobster signaled to the top floor, nodding to Taffy, who waited on the balcony.

Upon Luddy's cue, the sink in each room was left running. Showers were set to maximum flow. In unison, toilets were flushed. Hydrostatic pressure built to a rumbling crescendo of thousands of gallons of water anxious to find its most natural level.

A dark trickle emitted into the canal from the makeshift repair. The narrow stream, in Gen's estimation, was as black as the hearts of the people of this mound of architectural and human waste. She started to climb down for a better look, then stopped. *I bet if they could, they'd toss me in just for fun.* She crouched where she was, on a broad ledge — closer but safely out of sight and reach of the rabble attending the proceedings.

As she watched from her safe perch, Gen felt a deep rumble in the hotel's substrata. With a hollow groan, the narrow stream of dark fluid ceased. One SoBe bent to look into the maw of the makeshift sewer pipe, but another fortuitously pulled him back — just as an object shot out, cannon-like. A splash. The SoBe men at the waterline scrambled onto the terrace, hooting and guffawing at the startling blast and the spreading inky stain. The putridity of the unleashed effluent melded with the sea rot, the admixture a most wicked bouquet.

With his scoop net, Lobster landed the sodden culprit and waved it at Taffy, presiding from the penthouse balcony rail. Then he released it into the sea.

To her horror, Gen recognized the "clog" as her missing toy lemur: bobbing, impuissant, and as filthy as the foul water. She retched.

• • - • — • • •

While the SoBes jubilated over their solved collective dilemma and began filtering back inside, Gen slipped past them to the waterline. She plucked the last remembrance of her childhood from the fetid froth. She carried the plush companion to a less contaminated region of the canal where she bathed it like a baby, only her shock at this defilement forestalling her tears.

From the highest balcony, Taffy's lips curled in a wicked, crooked smile.

• • - • — • • •

A light brown swirl circled the sink's drain as Gen wrung the effluent from her cherished doll. *Why would somebody do this? Just to be mean?* She scrunched her nose; though bathed twice more in her sink, the stuffed toy's malodor remained. She raised its fuzzy ear to her lips and whispered. "Maybe you'll smell better when you're dry."

She placed the soggy toy on her windowsill, button eyes again searching for a faraway shore. A small cup ring marred the corner of the sill where the sickly aloe vera plant's clay pot had resided. *I wonder what happened to it.*

9.9

Gen had managed to wash herself in her tiny bathroom, attending her curly locks with her broad comb, expunging the fishy aroma from her hands. Her daily obligation to the woman and child fulfilled, her thoughts turned again to the young man on the roof and their tender, if brief, encounters. Her senses seemed to heighten, colors brightened, and she lost herself in a fairytale dream, overflowing with excitement and warmth.

•• ••◆•• ••

The door of the stair house closed behind Gen with a solid click, and she realized she had not chocked it. She found herself in the searing whiteness of the forever summer. "Kafka?"

The hotel's roof was black with tar in its various incarnations; here and there, a shiny obsidian bubble of resin presented as a tumor on its sun-baked skin. Gen prodded one welt with a strip of scrap metal. Petrified in its undignified deformation, it would scarcely yield. A river of the inky resin had meandered along a modest valley in the roof. Briefly revived of its ossification by the midday sun, it had memorialized the urgent strides of a fellow biped across its dark surface. Footprints. A pair — similar in size, dissimilar in tread and wear. *His.*

She called across the expanse from faux castellation to crenellation, "Kafka?" Silence, save for the rhythmic squeaks of the windmills and the call of a starving gull.

Gen could just see something beyond, blending with the cacophony of formations and elevations: a structure that was hardly a structure which, due to its occlusion by the maze of conduits and mechanicals, she had not noticed in her previous forays to the rooftop. The incongruous shed cowered behind a pile of random shapes that, had she been able to decipher them, would have emerged as construction equipment, roofing repair supplies, and maintenance refuse. The only objects familiar were a broom and a ladder. A younger vintage and lesser artfulness than the hotel proper, the shed's walls were an amalgam of wood slats and rusting corrugated metal panels, the slanted roof bolstered by a weave of driftwood topped with palm thatch.

She shielded her eyes from the glare and called again. "Hello? Kafka? Where are you?"

A hand clutched her elbow from behind. A voice, its tone a giddy collision of paranoia and cordiality, inquired after the purpose of her visit.

"Oh!" said Gen, turning to Kafka. "You scared me."

He softened his grip and took her hand. At her buoyant smile, he opined his felicity that she had returned to see him. Kafka walked her toward the shed and opened its door, gesturing for her to ingress. "The best thing about my burrow is the quiet. Of course, that is deceptive. At any moment the quiet may be shattered and then it will all be over. However, for the time being, the quiet is with me."

Gen peered into the dark and cluttered den. She could make out what seemed to be a narrow cot made of strips of wood and rags draped on a bent metal frame — nominally superior to sleeping on the floor. A lamp table pillaged from a hotel room abutted a chest of drawers, with only the memory of what it once was offering any resistance to collapse. Clothing in piles. An unoccupied hornet's nest suspended from its stalk. A Christmas snow globe dry as the desert. Half of a skateboard. Things of little meaning excepting to the resident of this hovel, all pocked with bird droppings.

She looked around. "You live here?"

The youth acknowledged as much, without a word.

"Why don't you stay in one of the hotel rooms?"

"Isolation is a way to know ourselves."

"I like it." She set foot in his sanctum. "It feels like you."

Kafka followed, unsure of the meaning of the girl's reply.

Gen's eyes lit up. Atop the dresser, in a vein of sunlight, was a dandelion plant in a glass jar half-filled with water. Kafka quickly pointed out that he had saved it for her should she want to grow the garden again. She stammered, so enamored that she couldn't bring herself to ask how he was able to save this single specimen.

Turning her attention to the hornet's nest, she prodded it with a fingertip. It relented with a slight crunch. "It's nothing. Like paper."

He indicated that she would be wise not to apply the same test to a real hive with active occupants, as the killers are both cruel and relentless.

Gen sniffed it. It smelled of death. She scrunched her nose. "Yuck! Why do you keep it?"

Kafka replied that he liked the absoluteness of it; there were no grays, only black and white, life or death. Inside was friend; outside, foe. Simplicity. The boy whispered conspiratorially that he had something more amazing to show her. He moved several of his junk possessions away from the dresser and opened the only still-intact drawer to reveal his incunabula. These were books, he proclaimed excitedly.

She had seen old books in Edison's library — artifacts of fragile construct, to be treasured and handled delicately. She had a few favorites on her own shelf. The set before her now, though, lay in a state of neglect bordering on abuse. Black with mold and sprouting mushrooms — comfortable in their dark and secreted space. Dog-eared, water-stained, and torn. A few stray pages in a neat pile on top. Among the printed works of fiction, a softcover manual on heating and air conditioning repair. A half-dozen identical copies of a hardback volume titled, *HOLY BIBLE Placed by THE GIDEONS*. And a nearly complete box set of works by a single author, a Bohemian novelist who fused the elements of realism and the fantastic, well-worn from repeated reading. Vestiges of a different time; of knowledge, civilization, persuasion, and utility. Gen stifled a sneeze.

"The kind of books we need are ones that act upon us like a tragedy. That make us suffer like the death of the one we love. That put us on the verge of suicide, lost in a forest far from human habitation," the boy said.

For a moment, Kafka's words rang familiar. "You've read all these?" she asked, tilting her eyes to the spine of the repair manual.

He equivocated, then after some hesitation, affirmed that he had substantially skimmed each volume. He took a book from the drawer and opened it to a page without conscious decision. He pointed to the print and explained to her that each group of symbols was a word, and that in order to read, one simply interpreted the combination of those words to discover the story. He could teach her this magical art if she was patient and willing to learn.

"I can read," said Gen. "Can't everyone?"

A subdued smile broke across his face. He urged her not to be embarrassed, as most people lacked the skill.

"But…" *I should have just let him teach me.* Her mind searched for something else that she could ask of the boy. She pulled her notebook from her pocket and slipped out her found missive recovered from the beverage container. "Maybe you can help me with this." She unfolded the paper. "I want to find this place. Do you know where it is?"

Kafka took the note in hand, angling it to catch a ray of light intruding from a cleft in the wall. He read aloud, halting, sounding out some words, racing past the more familiar. He huffed and shook his head, assuring her that whatever the place was, it was not located anywhere near Deco.

"Biscayne Elementary School? Are you sure?" asked Gen, a little disappointed. She reached for the paper.

Kafka pulled it back, suddenly recalling that there might just be such a location, and he promised to look into it on her behalf. He folded the note into eighths and dropped it into a blackened can atop the lamp table. Then he took her hand and interlaced it with his own, and brought his gaze to hers.

Gen started to retract her hand, picturing the self-inflicted damage to her knuckles, but relaxed at the sight of her already healed wounds. The boy caressed the soft olive skin of the back of her hand with his long, pale fingers, and inquired as to her home; her tribe.

She felt compelled to pour every secret of her soul into his dark eyes. After all, if he was to be her boyfriend, they should become better acquainted. She confided that she was raised on a farm; no, actually an island; her best friend is an ancient inventor of birds; that her mother is a scientist; and that her father is a robot. At this last bit of information, Kafka burst into cascades of hysterical belly laughter.

When he had calmed down, he proposed that her assertions were impossible; he knew nothing of science, and there was no such thing as a robot.

"No, I'm serious," said Gen. *Maybe that did sound a little strange.*

The youth seemed to suddenly recall an urgent matter that he had been setting about before her arrival on the roof and begged her indulgence to let him depart. The gallantry in his manner so impressed Gen that she volunteered to leave him to his important work with haste so as not to interfere further. He ushered her out of the miserable shack and across the tar to the stair house. Producing a key like Marina's, he opened the door for her departure. She glided into the dim landing as if on air.

The door shut, and Kafka scampered away to the edge of the rooftop, loosening his rope belt. He had just reached the castellation when the amber stream commenced.

That night, Gen would dream of a galloping black stallion, wild of mane and shimmering of coat.

9.10

"Lobster tells me that the repair seems to be holding." Luddy slipped the dusty tome back into the only slot available on his teeming shelf. "He claims the cause of the clog was an item belonging to our guest."

"She's trouble," said Taffy.

"Is she?"

Luddy returned to his high backed chair. He clasped his hands on his desk, ready to unweave the next revelatory web.

Taffy parked herself on the edge of Luddy's desk, then put her hand atop his, her painted visage reflected in his mirrored shades. "You know she throws fits and scares people. And everybody's complaining she's not doing her share."

"I was under the impression that she had taken on Marina and her child."

Taffy leaned into the stoic's ear and lowered her voice to a sultry whisper. "She spends most of her time with *him*."

Luddy sighed. "Perhaps she could do more to contribute. It would ease certain concerns."

Taffy thought for a moment, and a subversive smile curled her crimson lips. "Gotta be lots of good stuff still in that clinic. She could go in there, you know, like Jetty used to. Find us stuff."

"To my recollection, Jetty vowed never to go back in."

"There could be medicine, or whatever."

Luddy leaned back, fingers interlaced behind his head. "Jetty will be missed. You attended his bon voyage?"

"They always think it isn't going to happen, and then—"

"You may spare me the specifics."

Luddy was silent, an opening for Taffy to press her proposal.

"I could get Jetty's catch bag from his room," she offered.

Luddy remained with his own pondering. "Is she with the boy now?"

Taffy looked skyward, toward the tin hovel and its resident misfit. "How should I know? I don't follow her everywhere."

9.11

As was her habit after the morning's vile ritual of food preparation, Gen had returned to the broken balcony of the abandoned suite across the hall from her little room. She looked out over the shattered stubs of once regal edifices and structures of lesser prominence that treaded water in the canal, stretching to the northernmost horizon. Sunken rooftops, and walls etched away by time and the sea, white with salt and guano — a graveyard as forlorn as the one she had discovered during the nightmare circumnavigation of Eos. There was a calmness about it all, the ruin silent as it contemplated its own illusion of eternity. She leaned over, elbows on the remnant of railing, watching from her high perch as the SoBes set about their daily chores on and around the patio terrace.

The balcony bounced with added weight. Startled, Gen turned, teetered on the jagged edge, then recovered, cat-like. "You scared me."

"Did I?" said Taffy through a saccharine smile. She glanced over the rail at the busy SoBes. "Nobody likes you. Did you know that?"

"That's what *he* said." Gen's brow furrowed, recalling the uncomfortable conversation with Luddy.

"Who said?"

"Your father."

"He's not my father," said Taffy with a smirk.

"Oh…" Flustered by the revelation, Gen turned back to the rail.

Taffy grabbed her elbow. "Wouldn't you like to get along with everybody? So they'd quit complaining?"

Gen spun to face her. "Who's complaining? What did they say about me?"

Taffy shook her head. "I don't wanna make trouble for anybody. Enough to know some things were said." Taffy turned away and bit her lip. "Luddy thought if you just did something to prove yourself, something special, maybe they'd leave you alone."

"What is it? What do I need to do?"

"There!" said Taffy, pointing down several stories below the ragged balcony to a submerged storefront, its ulcered façade peeking above the surface of the canal. Streamers of rust delineated where a sign of uncertain vintage had once proudly purveyed the merchant's wares, where the ghosts of two letters could be discerned: "Rx."

"It's simple. See that building down there? That's the clinic. Just go look around at the shelves and pick up whatever is good and bring it back. Stuff that Luddy might like. Medical supplies. You know, to help out little Coral and her mother. Tools, if you see any. And anything interesting or unusual… or shiny. Shiny is good," added Taffy. She touched an earring.

"You mean… inside?" said Gen.

"Here. You can have my bag." Taffy pulled Jetty's net fishing bag from her shoulder and held it out to Gen with a big grin.

Gen hesitated.

"You could even go tomorrow." Taffy's smile faded with the thumps of Lobster's boots across the derelict room's floor.

"These parts be treacherous," Lobster said, looking at Gen. "Thought I oughta keep an eye on you." He glared at Taffy.

Taffy leered at the mariner. "I'm not doing anything."

A shadow drew Gen's attention upward. Kafka was peering over a crumbling rampart. Her heart skipped. *He's still interested in me!* Gazing up at the boy, Gen snatched the bag from Taffy. "Okay. I'll go."

The banister squeaked as Gen mounted it and dived off, graceful as a swan.

Lobster grabbed for her — missed. He looked over at the rippling waters and the girl hurtling toward them. "Taffy! What did you do!?"

Gen pierced the surface cleanly.

"What needed to be done." Taffy smirked. "What an idiot." She slunk past him and retreated into the depths of her crumbling castle.

Lobster looked up at the eccentric youth straddling the rooftop crenellation. Kafka's wild eyes locked on the fisher and the fisher glared back, their stony stares burning like the sun. Lobster produced a clear signal with a single vulgar digit; then he marched inside.

The projectile swept from behind with a rush of air and grazed Kafka's ear. Blood fountained from his left lobe. He recoiled, a hand clamping the wound, then he cockroached beneath the clutter of the rooftop.

Hoyl continued its flight down to the concentric waves informing Gen's point of entry, a bit of blood still clinging to one metallic talon.

9.12

Gen's eyes adjusted to the salt and the glare. The canal bottom was a patchwork of white sand and dark mystery, and everywhere danced an aurora of sunlight. There were dunes of dross unidentifiable, and seaweed outcrops waving as wheat in the wind. Familiar as a swim in her own pond at Eos, in this excursion she was accompanied by clouds of algae and a few curious fish. She could always hold her breath comfortably for many minutes at a stretch, and this capacity had afforded her much enjoyment during her frequent splashes back home. For a moment, she felt as free as in those remembered escapes from the uncountable oppressions of her parents.

Here and there, slabs of concrete jutted from the seabed. And here and there, the clashing of the current cleared sundry deposits exposing a flat, dark surface, replete with ceramic buttons and fragments of yellow running in the straightest lines. *A street?*

The clarity of the water was tolerable and, after a few strokes, the remnants of some earlier time beckoned her. Before her lay the bones of a civilization, battered by the elements, bleached and twisted, rendered to sand and rust. Gen saw an anthropomorphic shape under a blanket of sand. She waved a layer of silt away. A barnacled store mannequin stared back at her with faded eyes, its necklace encrusted in coral. She had read about Pompeii and Herculaneum and how the volcano Vesuvius had preserved things great and small under her sultry bosom of pumice. She imagined the snow of incandescent rock, relentless and silent, blanketing all; those ancient towns frozen in their last moments. The residents — their hopes and dreams and corporeal selves long gone after millennia — reduced to agonized human-shaped gaps in the cementitious earth. She wondered if she would encounter the same ghosts during her sub-marine skullduggery.

She swam under a lengthy rusted pole bent at its base. A lion's mane of slime covered its entire length to a receptacle containing globes of red and yellow, the last one broken and now home to a possessive crab. It waved a claw in warning as Gen paddled past. Resolving from beyond an algal bloom were rectangular geometries representing, she hoped, the submerged storefronts she sought. Below, their remains were in a better state of preservation than those above. Berms of coral sand piled against doorways, offering a bastion against the tide, and convenient nesting spots for burrowing things unseen. Huge plate glass windows, some intact, all coated with greens and browns, reminded her of a laboratory petri dish upturned on its side. Beyond that point was darkness. A dimension where monuments of some yesterday stood sentry. Totems of sea squirts and barnacles clung to once-terrestrial constructs, and towers of bivalves hung empty as if screaming into the void.

She swam to the closest of the spaces. It was distinguished by a recessed golden door hanging from a single hinge and held from sinking to the seafloor by an ambitious colony of sponges. Glassed-in platforms that she interpreted as display areas bordered the entry on both sides. Large capital letters, fallen from the façade, littered the entryway. Five that she could see. An "I," a "U," a "G," and two "Cs." Gen puzzled at what they might have spelled; regardless, they were not the "R" and "X" of the clinic that Taffy told her to explore. A broken mannequin leaned against a wall, attired in a coat of rags and stinging sea anemones. An invisible thread reeled in a small fish as two tentacled predators of the same polyp family fought over the catch. Disgusted, she pushed off.

Her lungs began to burn, and she curved herself upward, breaking the surface of the broad canal. She took a breath of the salty air and wiped her eyes. The hotel was eclipsed by the rising sun, its corona obscuring all definition beyond the merest suggestion of architecture. Gen could not see the crumbling balcony of the derelict room, nor Taffy or Lobster. She could not quite detect Kafka on his rooftop castle — though she was sure he was there, simply obscured by the radiance. She waved to show the boy that she was okay.

A glint drew her gaze upward. Hoyl circled her, soaring on its glass and silicon wings. She was strangely comforted by its presence. The electric owl spiraled up a column of rising air and vanished into the brightness.

She filled her lungs and dived below. Fingers of the burning sun pierced the shallows, reflecting and refracting in the brine, emanating as from a cathedral's stained glass pane. Her eyes again acclimated to the light and the shadows. Those things below the waterline shielded by the green-blue Poseidon, she thought, revealed what once was and the people who once were. As she swam back to the sunken storefronts, she felt the tug of the capricious current, only now considering whether the tides could hinder her search. Seeing a concrete walkway, she followed it until it dove under the sand.

A large mound rested parallel to the walkway's trajectory. Its shape suggested a wheeled vehicle. She had seen such things in her lessons — shiny conveyances moving at breathtaking speeds. This static specimen was barnacled, forlorn sponges poking from the rusting wheel wells. A school of small fry navigated its shell. The driver's window was open, while a side window sported a perfectly round hole the diameter of her thumb.

A grouper more than half the girl's mass approached, trailed by a retinue of tiny fish. It seemed merely curious; she put her hand on its flank and stroked its side. A ray of sunlight glinted off something inside the vehicle. *That's shiny. I'd better take a look.* As the inquisitive grouper studied her, she swam through the car window and pulled herself inside. She looked around the cabin. A pair of seats divided by controls. A steering mechanism recalling the one in the plane at Eos. Waving away the sand, she discovered the shine belonged to a small, rectangular object, two stylized letters engraved on its side. Folded neatly and wedged inside were remnants of a few peculiar slips of paper. *Some kind of flat clip.* She could just make out an ornate numeral "100" on a corner of the paper, which disintegrated by the time Gen realized that this must have been what her history lessons called "money." *At least it qualifies as shiny. No point leaving it.* She put it in the net catch bag.

She looked behind her, brushing aside blades of seaweed — delighted to see a bit of metal just under a pile of cloth. *Another one?* She lifted the rotted cloth. Underneath — a human skull! It bore a dental grill of gold that once flamboyantly adorned the upper teeth of the back seat's occupant. A hole in the skull corresponded to the perfect opening in the car's side window. She stifled a gasp, bubbles jetting from her nostrils. She shot to the surface.

The girl panted, more out of shock than shortness of breath. She checked for the net bag — gone! *So stupid! I shouldn't have been fooling around in there.* She filled her lungs and dived back to the barnacled wreck. The bag hadn't drifted far; it lay on the seabed next to the car. She swam down and grabbed it. *I'll stick to the clinic.* Gen pushed off toward the storefronts, a pair of eyes stalking her from beneath the undercarriage.

Her destination was just across the broad walkway from the automobile, an outline of the sought-after letters clearly defined above its entrance. The net bag strapped on her shoulder, she swam toward it. Like the others, its windows were broken, the door yanked off its hinges. A shard of glass hung from the frame like a guillotine. She carefully breached the hazard and entered with a few kicks.

Murkiness left the walls undefined, and it was difficult to orient herself, but she paddled on.

•• •—•—•• ••

From the undercarriage of the car emerged a hunter, the seed of dark nightmares. Eyes flashed with wily intelligence. The human-sized head sported a maw of jagged fangs overhanging its jaws. The eel was albino-white, longer than the encrusted vehicle, and had the girth of a man's thigh. It ribboned along, insolent of its cavalier dentition, two pudgy protuberances extending from its lower mandible, flaccid and testicular — the whole composition at once obscene and fearsome. An array of faint lights fired sequentially down its flanks, electrical clicks synchronizing to the flashes. It turned to the meddlesome grouper. A barrage of clicks — the grouper was shocked senseless, its limp body swarmed by a school of tiny fish whose fast work would leave mostly bones. The eel, though, had more ambitious prey in mind. It undulated toward the submerged clinic.

•• •—•—•• ••

Gen paddled toward the back of the building, passing several rows of tipped and upturned shelves encrusted with oceanic flora. All empty. She recalled a history lesson showing city people doing something they called "shopping," where they gathered the supplies they required from a central "store" — instead of simply making them. It crossed Gen's mind that people must have needed a great many things in those days. *How sad.*

The light from the canal had dropped off, and Gen was unable to discern top from bottom, as if alone in the vastness of a starless cosmos — the only illumination a greenish glow ahead. She swam toward it. Shock! She froze — her teeth buzzed — jolts of electricity coursing through her. Then she turned. An eel! Terrified, she kicked it away, her shoe flying into the murky gloom. She swam hard toward the emerald beacon, leaving the sea monster in a swirl of silt.

She spotted the source of the illumination. Inside the doorway of a large storage closet waited an immense angler fish, an ambush predator in its element. A fleshy stalk stood erect from its nose, dangling a lantern of chemical light the size of a softball, designed to beckon the overcurious and the unwise. It opened its maw, its lantern illuminating its cavernous gullet. She paddled past. She felt another electrical pulse and turned. Nothing. Turned the other way. The eel! Jaw agape, exposing ragged fangs. It lunged at her, then stopped short, as if coming to the end of its tether. Its tail caught in the angler's massive jaws, the eel clicked away with defensive electrical pulses, shocking the girl repeatedly. The angler's light shorted, intermittent, strobing, but it was enough for her to glimpse a set of stairs.

Fast running out of breath, she sped up the steps and got her head above water. She inhaled the musty air, blinking the stinging salt away as she emerged onto a floor entirely above the waterline. Daylight streamed from a ragged gap in the ceiling.

File drawers and cabinets lined a wall. Two desks along the opposite wall seemed frozen in time, their electronics dark. *It's like Mother's workspace.* A back corner was charred black from the long-extinguished fire that spurred the room's frightened occupants to flee, never to return. She sighed. *Like the fire I started.*

She tried drawers and doors in a row of storage — locked or stubbornly stuck shut. A last cabinet door yielded, its shelves jumbled with empty cartons for tongue depressors, lancets, gauze, ointments, and hypodermic needles. She swept the empties aside, exposing a stethoscope and a blood pressure cuff, which she put in her net bag, leaving behind a few medical implements she could not identify. A porcelain mortar and pestle set reminded her of the ones her mother used, so she added it to her growing collection. Among the spent medication bottles, she found a handful that seemed to be full and intact, their labels faded and nearly unreadable. She bagged them, unsure whether any would be useful. There remained a single medicine bottle with a saffron label marked "Sevoflurane." She checked the lid — unopened. She stowed the medication in her bag, then turned her attention to the desks.

On the larger desk were two stacks of pamphlets. She picked one up. It was a message about some type of disease called "Methuselah Syndrome," with warnings about counterfeit cures followed by a list of same and ending with a disclaimer of the list's exhaustiveness. It cautioned the reader that there was, in fact, no legitimate cure, and that the best course was to stay healthy as long as possible and to have end-of-life plans in place.

The pamphlets in the companion stack listed suggestions for how the reader might have a calm, intelligent, sensitive discussion with those persons with whom the reader disagreed about empirically provable facts versus popular deceptions. Its obverse diagramed defensive hand-to-hand combat maneuvers, should the discussion degrade. She collected one of each missive.

The desk drawer was ajar. She jiggled it open. A plastic zippered bag held a half-dozen identical pens emblazoned with a "Collins Clinic" logo and the "Rx" symbol. She grabbed the bag, fitting the pamphlets inside and sealing it. Beneath it was a small music player, just like Edison's device. *Maybe I'll keep this for myself.* She found another bag, empty, and sealed the player in. She touched a key on the long-idle computer keyboard, lifting the dust from the letter "G." *How silly of me to try it.*

She turned to the other desk, where a girlish bag of pastel pink, blue, and yellow lay open on top. She peeked inside. A pink bikini. A shrunken bottle of goo that paradoxically promised suntanned skin along with protection from the sun's rays. A pair of pink thong sandals whose rubber soles had curled from heat and age. A rolled-up terry cloth towel, dusted in white sand, moth-eaten and rotten. And a small pink box with "Smokin' Babe" printed on the lid in glittery cursive script.

Gen set aside the decayed towel and shriveled bottle. She opened the box. A small, floral-patterned tube, a reservoir at one end. A yellowed plastic jar glittered in dried leaf crumbs. A thin packet artfully labeled "rolling papers." And a pink clear plastic cylinder with a metal collar and gear mechanism atop. The cylinder seemed to have liquid in it; she held it to her ear and shook it. She re-packed and sealed the box. As she returned it to the beach tote, she espied in the bottom a small cloth pouch. Inside, mirrored aviator sunglasses. She tried them on. If they were video-enabled like her glasses at home, then they must be broken, she thought, but she placed them back in the tote. Luddy's glasses were cracked, and he might appreciate a new pair.

She rolled up the beach tote, exhausting the air, zipped it, and stuffed it in the net bag. Then she stopped at the top of the staircase and scanned the room. It had been scavenged before, and there was little else left to be had. She descended the stairs, back into the silted water of the clinic, taking a deep breath before submerging.

She proceeded cautiously in the darkness, eyes stinging from salt. Suddenly, the angler's light flashed on. Now, she witnessed the giant fish gulping down the last few feet of the eel as it backed into its dim storage closet domain.

Without warning, the eviscerated remains of the savaged grouper smacked Gen in the face. A confetti of fish scales rained in the void. Flustered, she pushed the corpse aside. Her lost shoe floated in the swirling waters. She slipped it on as she made her way out of the shop and to the surface.

9.13

The aquatic adventurer burst from the water, holding up her net bag, laden with found treasures. Gen gulped the fresh air. "I did it!" She wiped her eyes.

From a rubble pile at the edge of the hotel, two waifs looked her way, looked at each other, then returned to their fishing.

She searched for her audience. The balcony where she had left Lobster and Taffy was still, save for the scrap of curtain undulating in the breeze. She scanned the rooftop castellations. No sign of the young man. She sighed, crestfallen.

She paddled her way to the patio terrace. The SoBes had retired from their morning chores, nets and seaweed laid out to dry. The Mo'ai had been amply rewarded for its imagined blessings and contributions. The sewage stench had abated, supplanted by the stink of rotting fin and feather at the idol's feet. The buzz of flies competed with the susurration of the surf. Her once-golden garden corner had been swept and backfilled with sargassum mats. The stucco wall still bore the bloodied cavitations of her wrath, a reminder of the unhappy episode and her new obligation to prove herself. *Nobody here. Good.* She entered the hotel through the glass door, the net bag strapped on one shoulder.

She crossed through the commercial kitchen where a few knife-readied SoBes crowded around the main work table, eager to divide up their day's bounty. She wondered if their enthusiasm for the meal included gratitude to the catch or the catcher, or if all praise now flowed to the indolent idol. Hungry eyes tracked a misshapen fish being produced from the cooler, its skin pocked by louse-like parasites. A cook flopped the afflicted fish onto the table, and a large crustaceous parasite popped from its mouth, clacked across the table, then dropped to the floor. With a chuckle, he speared it with his knife and flipped it into a pot boiling atop the stove.

As she passed through the mezzanine, she glanced at the fresco. *Nobody's bothered it. My secret room is safe.* Down a hallway, she could see the usual open doorways. At this hour, the SoBes would leave their doors ajar for air circulation — availing them, too, of the crackling drone of the piped-in music that saturated the public spaces. Most had grown accustomed to the repetitious scratches of the instrumental tune. Some believed it to be part of the mechanics of the aged building; to most, it was merely a calming white noise.

At the steel doors, she pressed the call button, and with some consternation, the grumbling machine admitted her. The SoBes had expunged the evidence of tragedy as best they could — the flesh and blood of man and beast. She selected the topmost button as the metal maw slid shut. The vertical chariot lurched, groaned, and shuddered, then relented and ascended. Her clothes and bag dripping on the moldering floor, she pondered her unsatisfying return. No one had witnessed her achievement. *Maybe I took too long. Like on my birthday.*

Voices drifted through the wedged-open door of the bridal suite. The confabulation caromed down the hall, tapering to indiscernible thrums in Gen's ears. *Just get this over with. Try to be friendly.*

Gen knocked. The voices stopped. She convened her courage and slid in. "I'm back! I found a bunch of stuff."

Taffy sprung from the pink chair, one eyebrow akimbo. She furtively overturned the journal onto the corner of Luddy's desk.

"Gen. Come in." Luddy rose from his chair and leaned into the speaking tube. "Hold the room service for now. I will tell you when I am ready." He turned, bracing himself on his high-back. "You 'found a bunch of stuff,' did you?"

"Taffy said to—"

"Gen agreed to do a little scavenging for us, Luddy."

"Down in that clinic," Gen said. She tugged at the seat of her clammy shorts.

"The clinic. Very well," said Luddy, seating himself.

Taffy put her hand out to intercept the bag. "Give it over—"

"Gen, please lay out each item on my desk," interrupted Luddy. He interlaced his fingers and set his elbows atop the blotter. "One at a time. And tell me about each. How you found it. What you think makes it valuable."

Gen's brow furrowed at the further demand. *This is going to take forever.* She reached into the bag. Her hand fell upon the metal clip and she held it up. "When I found this, there was paper sticking out that had numbers on it. It isn't from the clinic, though. There was this cabin with wheels sitting on the bottom. A car, I guess. An automobile. I've only seen them in videos. I picked this just because it's —"

"Shiny," said Taffy, snatching the bauble from Gen's fingers. "Gold."

Gen paused, taken aback.

"Continue," said Luddy.

"It looked like somebody died inside there, so I got out."

"Then he won't be needing it," said Taffy, angling the money clip to the light.

"Let us take a full measure of the haul, and then I will decide who receives each item," said Luddy, his palm up. Taffy reluctantly relinquished her prize. Luddy's fingertips sought its dimensions, the bit of mush pinched inside, the faint texture of the carved initials. "Do you know what money was, Gen?"

Gen nodded.

Luddy held silent, then continued. "Instead of the customary trading and barter, people would trade this paper — this money — for food, shelter, even labor. They would collect it and later use it in trade. Perhaps the owner of this shiny gold thing had considerable amounts of money, hence the need for a holder."

He set it aside on his desk next to the overturned journal. "What else have we?" Luddy placed his hand atop the golden clip just ahead of Taffy's.

"I grabbed a few medical things," said Gen. She pulled her next find from the net bag and laid it out on the desk. "This is a stethoscope. My mother has one."

Luddy slid his fingers across his desk, coming to rest on the object, then crawling along its dimensions and textures, working his way from the eartips down the crazed rubber tubing to the disk-shaped chestpiece. Taffy hovered, almost parental, at Luddy's shoulder, her hand reaching out, then keeping to itself. Luddy detected her temptation and waved her away.

Gen remembered Luddy's request for description. "You can listen to a person's heartbeat… or their lungs. I mean, you could, if it wasn't falling apart."

"As you say, not in good stead, but yes, I believe you are correct," said Luddy.

As soon as he moved the stethoscope aside, Gen laid out the blood pressure cuff. "This thing is for measuring your blood pressure. You put the cuff around a person's arm, then squeeze this bulb here, and then you read the pressure on the gauge." She watched him take in its shriveled shape, carefully examining it, end to end.

"The pressure of your blood? What for?" said Taffy, impatient.

"Dunno. My mother takes mine all the time," said Gen.

"Anything else?" asked Luddy.

Gen plunged her hand back into the bag. "This is a mortar and pestle." She put the porcelain set before him. "My mother has a few of these, too."

Luddy perused the bowl and tool as he described and demonstrated their use to Gen, who concurred, having watched her mother mix her medicinal potions. Taffy flopped into the pink chair, crossed her legs, and rocked her foot.

"Continue," said Luddy."Okay. There was some medicine. Most of the stuff I saw was already opened, so you can't use those, but I found some where the lids were still sealed." She moved the mortar and pestle to Luddy's pile, and set out the half-dozen medication bottles of varied size and shape.

Taffy's eyes latched onto a vial with a bright yellow label. She rose, snatched it up, and scrutinized it. "Sevvv… um… S-e-v-o-f-l-u-r-a-n-e. Inhalation anesthetic."

"Sevoflurane. Anesthetic," Luddy said. "That puts people to sleep. Perhaps they kept such balms on hand to ease the distress at the end," he mused. "And what of the other medicines?"

Gen read off the layman's terms on each label as best she could from the faint print: insulin, cough suppressant, antibiotic, sedative, antipsychotic.

"Good work," said Luddy charitably. "Any more?"

Gen next opened a zipped plastic bag and let the six ballpoint pens roll from her palm onto the desk. "Pens. For writing. On the side it says 'Collins Clinic.' See the 'Rx' symbol? Just like the clinic sign."

Luddy took the measure of the batch of writing instruments. He selected one and removed the cap, stroked the tip on his index finger, then rubbed his finger and thumb together. He sighed heavily from an unspoken despair.

The tall man turned his head slightly toward Taffy. "We shall determine if we can make use of them."

Gen withdrew the two pamphlets from the plastic bag and held them out to him. "I found stacks of these on one of the desks."

Taffy intercepted one of the missives. "I'll read it." She peeled it open: "Methuselah Myths. Warning. Be aware of counterfeit cures for 'Methuselah Syndrome.' You may have encountered publi-casts or meta-blasts — whatever that is — claiming that do-it-yourself or privately vended cures are available, blah, blah, blah, there is no legitimate remedy."

Luddy sat up a little in his chair. "Methuselah Syndrome. Yes, that must have been what it was called."

Taffy continued, "The following is a list of purported and scientifically discredited cures. This list is not exhaustive. Pffft. This makes no sense. Pop-stoppers, Skin-nu, Collagene-X, Deworm-A-Horse—"

A heavy clop of boots halted Taffy's recitation. It was Lobster.

"Horse? What's a horse?" said Lobster. He gave a nod to Gen, his face a swirl of disbelief and relief.

Taffy clucked her tongue at him and slapped the paper on the desk, then took the second handout. "I hope this one's more interesting." Taffy read aloud: "Talking facts with loved ones. Hoping to have a calm, intelligent, sensitive discussion about Methuselah facts with a loved one? This pamphlet offers suggested talking points, blah, blah. What is this stuff?" She turned the sheet over. Diagrams of defensive hand-to-hand combat maneuvers. She laughed out loud.

Gen sighed at Taffy's mocking reaction.

"That is sufficient, Taffy. Continue, Gen," said Luddy.

She had nearly run out of treasure. She hesitated, then pulled the beach tote from the bag. *This is embarrassing. The bikini's in here. They'll see.*

"Whatcha got in there?" Taffy said. "Hope it's better than this stuff."

"Well, there's this." Gen reached into the colorful tote and produced the small pink box, "Smokin' Babe" scribed on the top. "There's all kinds of stuff in it," she said, opening the clamshell case and laying it flat atop the desk. Taffy and Lobster exchanged a glance and leaned in.

"Thank you, Gen." Luddy fingered the little containers and implements, coming up with the translucent pink cylinder. "A cigarette lighter. This made fire, Gen." He stroked the flint with his thumb — first sparks, then a flame. "We've come across a few of these before. I keep them here, away from the children." He let go of the button and placed the lighter in his top drawer.

Taffy picked up the plastic jar from the kit and opened it. A few tiny seeds fell into her palm. "Dirt." She let them drop to the carpet, then tossed the container back in the box. Her eyes brightened at the festive tube; she palmed it and tucked it in her top. She caught Lobster's leer and stuck out her tongue.

Luddy set the kit aside. "Is that everything?"

"Oh, almost forgot." Gen took out the little pouch. "These are for you, Luddy." Gen placed it on his desk. "Sunglasses."

"For me?" Luddy gingerly touched the pouch, then picked it up for a tactile exploration. He slid out the mirrored shades and felt along the wire frames.

"To replace your broken ones. Try them on," Gen suggested.

"He doesn't need—" blurted Taffy.

Luddy waved Taffy off. "Perhaps later, Gen, but thank you for your consideration." He set the glasses atop the journal, separate from the other prizes. "Anything more?"

"That's all, I guess," replied Gen.

"That bag's not empty!" said Taffy. She snatched the tote from the girl and upended it over the desk, giving it a shake. Out tumbled the pink bikini and matching flip flops.

Taffy's eyes widened as she grabbed the bikini top. "What's this?"

"It's a bikini. You wear it. To the beach," said Gen, her cheeks burning.

Taffy held the tiny triangles of cloth to her ample bosom. Lobster looked away, clearing his throat.

Taffy tossed it on the floor. "Looks like you mostly picked things for yourself."

Gen rescued the beachwear, tucking the embarrassing articles back in the colorful tote, slipping the strap over her shoulder.

Luddy drummed his fingers on his blotter. "Are we finished?"

"I guess so," said Gen. She set the net catch bag atop the desk — an item inside clinked on the wooden surface. "Oh, yeah." She took out the final find — the pocket music player — unwrapping it from its plastic bag. "This little box plays music. Uncle Edison had one."

"Edison? Like the ancient inventor?" Luddy mused.

"Well, he's not *that* old," Gen replied.

Taffy snatched the device. She held it to her ear and shook it. "Nothin'." Then she tossed it on the desk.

Gen picked up the player, flipped out the tiny handle, and started cranking. Her brow knotted. *This better work.* She pressed a button, and the diminutive machine came to life. To her relief, the strings and horns of a long-ago orchestra introduced a vocalist, Enrico Caruso, intoning in a phonogenic voice: manly, powerful, yet sweet and lyrical and in some language unfamiliar. The audio fidelity from the Lilliputian player was crisp and clear and surprisingly loud, while the tenor's voice was of heavenly origin.

Luddy leaned in. Taffy's congenital smirk faded from her face. Lobster's jaw went slack.

••·•—●·•

A dozen SoBes crowded the table in the commercial kitchen, knives competing to rend the carcass of an unfortunate fish. At least as many more had thronged the hotel cookhouse, trailing out the swinging door to receive a handoff from a relative or take their turn at the cutting board.

The music player's dulcet intonations found their way through the speaking tube and down to the kitchen, loud and crisp enough to pause the SoBes' carnivorous reverie. The carving stopped. The chewing slowed. They listened, soon teary-eyed and then sobbing at the profoundly moving performance.

·· ·· ··

The chorus of sobs found its way back up the speaking tube into the bridal suite where Luddy was now reclining, feet on his desk, rapt at the recital. Taffy looked at Luddy and saw in him a man captivated by the girl's music — led astray by a temptress.

Gratified that the music had stirred up the SoBes in the kitchen — and amused at Taffy's distress over Luddy — and with equal parts saltwater and anarchy in his veins, Lobster moved the player next to Luddy's public address mic, and pushed the seldom used announcement button.

·· ·· ··

The sweet music permeated the hotel's speakers with a clarity that filled the SoBes' distracted and weary ears. All stopped. Several put their heads outside their doors to partake of the auditory spectacle. Throughout the hotel, all were rapt. At the emotional refrain, a wave of wonder and weeping overcame them. On some primal level, they recognized the beauty of what had been — and the sorrow of what had been lost.

·· ·· ··

With Taffy, Lobster, and Luddy mesmerized by the music, Gen slipped out of the suite, tote over her shoulder, leaving the three to their myths and memories and regrets. She lingered at the stair door, exhausted by the ordeal, the public address speaker on the water-stained ceiling crooning of art and love and yearning amid the sobbing of the SoBes.

"Evil is whatever distracts." The youth's voice echoed in the void, the words swirling from the darkness. Somewhere above. Out of reach as the divine.

Gen called into the misty concrete shaft, "Kafka?"

Unseen, the boy answered in a revelation. That she had not been expected to survive her adventure. And that her errand was one engineered to assure her destruction. "Evil knows of the Good, but the Good do not know of the Evil."

Gen slumped to the floor, cold betrayal resounding in her heart.

••–•—••••

The silken opera in the unknown tongue seeped into the decaying domain. Doors closed, damming the flood of tears.

The day passed like any other, indifferent to the people and their tribulations. And when the hotel disappeared into the evening's shadows, no one bothered to turn on their lights.

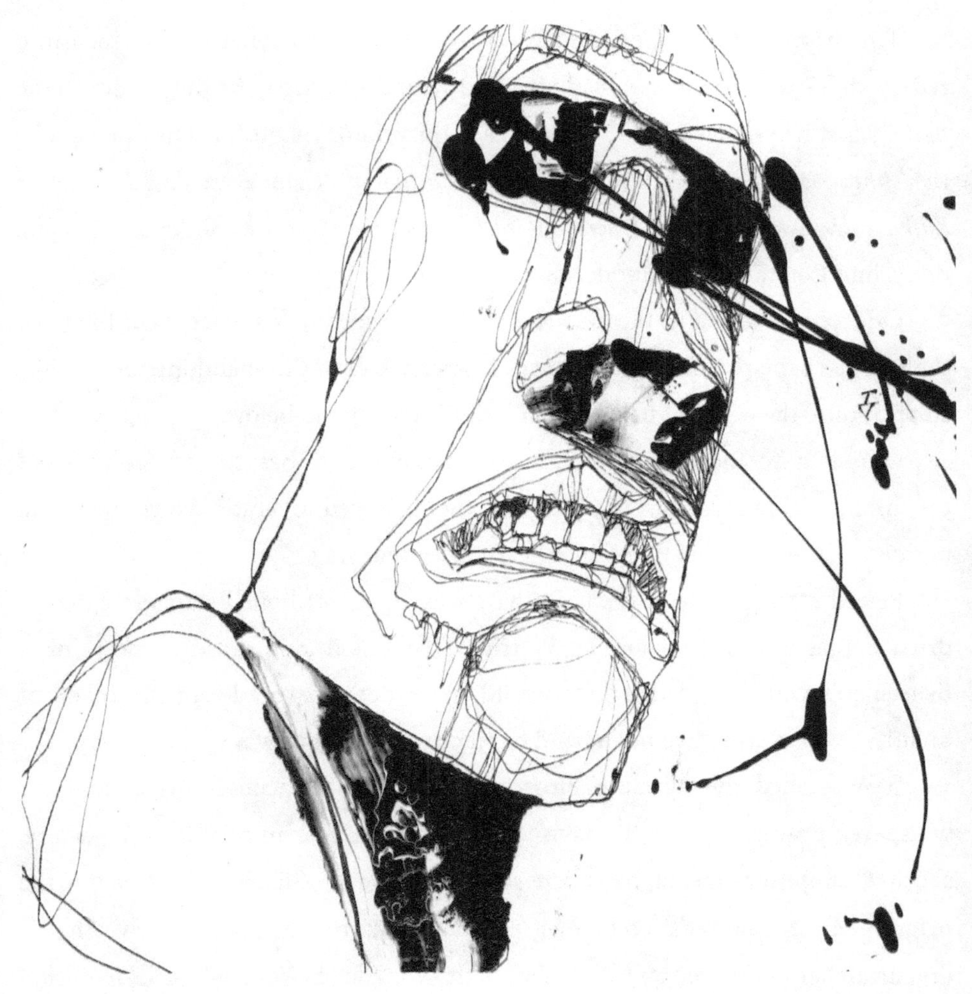

BOOK X:

A Threat So Unspeakable

The stoic idol cleaved the rays of dawn cast across the patio terrace. A pile of rotting fish, found baubles, buzzing flies, and rats ringed the faux stone feet of the Mo'ai — its shell eyes vacuous and unseeing, its head caked with an icing of guano, a fresh seaweed crown placed atop.

The morning found Gen already awake, fitful sleep having transformed into red-eyed despair. The nausea had returned with the new day, as the parties to the plot against her whirled in her weary head. Taffy. Luddy. Lobster. The SoBes. *Why won't they leave me alone? I've been feeding Marina and Coral every day! No wonder Kafka stays away from the others. At least he told me the truth.* She heaved again, dryly, into the stained commode. *I'm such a fool.*

Odd vocalizations in the distance broke the morning's silence. Gen followed the source of the peculiar discordance across the hall to the abandoned room. She stepped onto the decrepit balcony and looked to the patio below.

Oblivious to the olfactory offense, a handful of SoBes circled the pungent totem, mimicking as best they could the honeyed operatic voice that had permeated the walls and filled their hearts with yearning.

Placed atop the pile at the idol's base was a plate of boiled clams in a bed of dried sargassum, still steaming. A tribe that could not spare a meal for a fisherman's widow and daughter would spare nothing to adulate the token of divinity. A child stretched out a hand to pluck a morsel, but was swatted away.

Gen recalled the hyacinth blossoms, the curls of incense smoke, and the whispered prayers her mother lavished on the lapis altar in her lab — a gesture, she had supposed, meant to solicit scientific success. She had not known the magnitude of Mother's credulous spirituality until she saw the weathered dreamcatcher in the tree on the ancient path. Nor had she realized the desperation that drove Mother and the others to Eos.

Now, as she surveyed the SoBes, Gen sighed at the purposeless revelry squandered on the graven image — a thing disremembered on their shores by the rhythms of the tides. The tribe seemed to believe that the medley of wood, wire, stucco, and hype had journeyed from afar to sweeten their fortunes, to banish calamity, and to free them from their sufferings. To unlock its treasures, though, the totem had to be plied with treasure of their own. That by presenting offerings, they would somehow make the inevitable less so. That by surrendering their will to the Mo'ai, it would manifest the providence they themselves could not.

The deities born of humanity's fears and limitations in its shared prehistory had long blown away on the winds of broken promises. To Gen, the reverence paid to the totem was curious and confounding. She had no impulse comparable. Her mother's deference to smoky shrines had not saved her father, nor tamed the skies at Eos.

As she leaned over the balcony rail, her lemur pendant brushed her chin. She touched it. *Was Mother's world as hostile as this?* Watching the gaunt guests fawn over their fetish, Gen was overcome with pity. In a domain where any change could lead to misfortune, they were not so much wrathful toward her as they were afraid of the unknown.

Struggling to survive in their harsh environs, the SoBes harbored an instinctive nostalgia for a more predictable and kinder world. The impulse was there all along, Gen decided, and only by the arrival of the totem was their latent mysticism sparked. And she recognized that the tribe's weakness, now exposed, could be the reason their society had stalled.

She mused that these people, nevertheless, had weathered the same ebbs and flows their entire lives, and the lives before theirs were no different. Like her mother's own deeper concerns that Gen only now began to fathom, had the SoBes some terror looming that she had not yet witnessed? A threat so unspeakable that they yearned for a divine hand to hold it back?

10.2

Upon rousing from profound slumber, the teen reflected on recent events. In the crisp lens of daylight, she recast her misjudgment of the personal trial. That she had detractors was certain. In question, now, was the architect of her attempted annihilation. Luddy seemed to have all but forgotten about the garden incident, and Lobster would want her to shoulder the burden of Marina and Coral. She had yet to reconcile with Taffy.

If Gen were to have a place among the SoBes, she would need Taffy to desist from her antagonizations, and for that, she needed the tall man in her court. Her earlier petition for redress from the stony leader wrought only an unsparing reprimand about her own indiscipline and an unflattering comparison to the crass angler. Although the prospect filled her with dread, her liberation lay in petitioning the man in the gilded suite.

She recalled a time when her parents had forbidden her some trivial request. Uncle Edison stepped in and persuaded them to relent — what he called a "parley." Someone must speak for her.

STATUS: SECTOR DAMAGED 01:10:002:01 (See Technical Notes)

As at every sundown, the sea breeze had shifted. Windmill generators oscillated on their squeaky axes, seeking the strongest channels of salted air to charge their aged batteries. The water tower dripped steadily onto a mossy can tipped on its side. A few bird carcasses decorated the roof, feathers fluttering away in the wind. The boy was there, looking out over the depleted domain. He stood perfected in the warm rays, and Gen hesitated to approach, lest she spoil the canvas.

Kafka's gaze remained fixed on the orange horizon, and he spoke: "Last night I dreamed about you. I can barely remember the details of what happened. All I know is that we merged into one another. I was you and you were me. Somehow you finally caught fire."

The youth was some other being, she mused, and considered that she might be falling in love. Gen queried Kafka of the crimson nick on his ear, but he dismissed it as trivial. She told him of her distress and asked him to arrange for her to have a word with Luddy outside of Taffy's influence. To this he was agreeable and directed her to come to the bridal suite when the Moon was rising in the east. And there, as the evening drifted in as a tide, among the ruins and the desolation, she rose on her toes and kissed him on his scruffy cheek.

•• ••••••

The door to the suite was open. The room was quiet and gray, lit only by the full Moon, its edges faded to infinity. Luddy stood at the stained glass window, a soft rainbow corona radiating from the contours of his white suit, the multicolored glass splashing a cathedral of subtle color. Gen knocked softly.

"Enter," said Luddy.

Kafka was sitting in the pink chair, silent. She touched his hand as she crossed the room. She sensed that negotiations had concluded before she arrived and that her singular contribution would be to receive the verdict. She stole a glance into the bath; the curvaceous consort was abundantly absent. Reassured, Gen joined Luddy in the prism of the leaded glass pane. The mirrored sunglasses she had salvaged from the clinic reflected the tableau from atop his aquiline nose. She smiled.

Gen looked back to Kafka, but he gestured her to proceed. Bolstered by the boy's presence, she poured out her concerns and suspicions to the tall man. With cool cordiality Luddy conceded that it was the nature of the SoBes to provoke one another on occasion, as was the essence of people beset by scarcity. He assured her that Taffy was, nevertheless, benign.

STATUS: SECTOR LOST 01:10:002:05 (See Technical Notes)

With the awkward matter settled and tension abated, Kafka joined Gen and Luddy in the rays of the radiant palette, the trio gazing at the romantic spectacle.

For Gen, the colorful art glass had, on that first day, loomed almost as overbearing as the gaudy suite's occupant — the day the coarse fisher had plopped her netted body on the pink chair to be interrogated by the white-suited man. On the day she had confronted Luddy about the defiling of her garden, her eyes had only skimmed the window's design. She had scarcely considered it when she'd returned with the treasures from the submerged store.

Now, as with each time she was near the youth, her senses heightened, painting anew the details of what was before her. A newlywed couple frozen in a forever kiss beneath a bough of green crystal palms. The translucent lunar disc dominating a cyan sky, its artfully rendered reflection dancing on the ocean waves. With a few differences, the imagery reminded her afresh of the beach scene in her home tanning suite at Eos.

Tonight, in the gentle moonglow that penetrated the colored panes, the visage of young love inspired her to brush against Kafka's forearm. He took her hand in his.

They stood before the idealized nuptials, a kaleidoscope of colors reflecting upon their faces — the majesty of the sister planet lensed through art and the ages.

"A kind of dream," she said, turning to the boy.

"Please — consider me a dream," Kafka replied without taking his eyes from the webwork of lead and glass.

"The hour is late," said Luddy brusquely.

Kafka let Gen's hand drop.

Gen glanced up at Luddy, his brow now furrowed and his jaw clenched. Then she turned to Kafka, whose eyes were fixed beyond the moonlit pane, she supposed, to his own thoughts. She returned to the serene scene that had enraptured her, but the sweet moment was lost.

From the shadows behind the canvas on the easel, Taffy peered out. The dim gray light drained her vampish allure. An impulse rose in her throat to shout something spiteful, but a curious phenomenon froze her solid. Unlike the two men, a faint glow emanated solely from the girl; her skin shone a color not among the many-hued panes of the glass mosaic. She blinked hard, unable to banish the illusion. Gen was fluorescing in the filtered moonlight. Taffy's mouth opened but made no sound, and she retreated into the darkness.

10.3

The kitchen doors swung out to emit Gen and her usual plate of fish for Marina and Coral; on this day, she moved with renewed purpose. *I'll get this delivered. Then maybe I'll go up to the roof to see him.*

As she crossed the mezzanine, she stole a glance toward the fresco. The seams were intact — her private sanctuary undisturbed. Balancing the plate on her palm, she bypassed the stairwell in favor of the steel doors, then pressed the "up" button and waited. Recent days had been without event due, no doubt, to Kafka's parley and Luddy's influence. She would soon see little Coral again, and she smiled.

Warm droplets pinged the crown of her head and drizzled down her back. Titters from above drew her gaze to a pack of feral children peeing over a walkway rail. "Hey!" said Gen, the plate and its contents exploding on the carpet as she darted into the stairwell in pursuit. The giggling gaggle took off running.

She tracked them up a staircase, then down another, their inborn maps of the building keeping them a few paces ahead of her. She had lost her sense of direction by the time she caught sight of the herd of wild scamps slipping behind carved wood double doors.

She sped to the elaborate entrance and peered in. Silence. The youngsters had vanished into the shadows and recesses — consumed, it seemed, by the room. As her eyes adjusted to the gloom, she could see the shattered skeletons of tables and chairs scattered across the fusty emptiness. A chandelier splayed in a heap on the floor. An audio console, smashed, wires blooming from its insides. A single sunbeam slicing from some source uncertain, a few pugnacious photons tussling with the dust in the stale air.

Gen's brow furrowed. As with the realm of the ancient dhow, she had missed the moment to experience this place as it was meant to be. All of Deco seemed a ruined shadow of the big city of her dreams.

The rays betrayed a tall, crimson velvet curtain spanning a raised platform. *Those brats. They're in the curtains!* She made her way toward the platform, a carpet of moist debris scrunching under each careful footfall. The raised area was about as high as her waist. She had seen such things in her mother's nanobooks. *A stage.* Where inventive people would don costumery and pretend to be other people who maybe never were. The room, she surmised, was once a plush auditorium large enough to hold more guests than there were palms at Eos.

At the front of the stage were a half-dozen piles of rags and several pairs of men's and women's shoes. The sensuous serpentine of heavy red fabric came alive, undulating rhythmically.

She bent to look beneath the drapery hem. Six pairs of adult-sized naked feet stood toe to toe, male and female — a fold of pulsating curtain the intermediary, sheathing their bodies from chance direct contact — together, but separate in their ecstasy. A chorus of beastly moans and grunts. The once-lavish fabric, an unwitting participant in the onanistic intimacy, dust billowing from its rotten ruddy skin.

Gen turned away, mouth agape, a jumble of horrified confusion. The wedge of light flickered. She followed the dusty sunbeam to its source: a crack that spanned floor to ceiling, open to the outside. She peered through. An eye looked back at her — she shrieked!

The grunting halted. Six heads emerged from the velvet folds, along with flashes of bare arms, legs, and chests. Six pairs of eyes silently stared at the unintentional voyeur. She recognized a few of them. *Worshipers of the Mo'ai.*

She stumbled on a chair in her panicked flight from the bacchanal.

10.4

A column of sunlight pierced the cathedral of dust. It illuminated the brochure stand, its announcement of the festival long forgotten, and a decayed bladed boot lying lonely beneath. Reclining on the starboard side bench of the *African Queen*, Gen contemplated the imperfections in the ceiling and the play of light within the cavernous room. She lifted herself on an elbow and looked toward the door, affirming that she had shut it completely, lest she be discovered in her private and somber oasis. She pillowed her head with clasped hands, studying the starscape of pinholes in the dark-filmed skylight. She saw the pillar of noontide beaming from the wedge she had rent in the tinted coating.

Gen's anguished mind replayed a cannonade of insults: the young males micturating upon her from the upper terrace; the inscrutable carnality of the undulating curtains; and her garden of golden flowers, wiped from the Earth. She would push these torments aside, only to have them intrude again to inflame her psyche. Her heart latched onto a brilliant, if fanciful, notion: sailing the whimsical vessel back to Eos.

She tried to imagine herself in the open ocean in the old barque. *I wonder how long it would take.* She would need to stow food and water. Perhaps she could fit it with a sail, as she had seen in her history videos, or fashion an oar from a palm frond — although the effectuation of either seemed elusive. She turned her attention to the strange iron cylinder amidships. She opened a hatch, put her hand in, and withdrew a palmful of ashes. Uncertain how or whether the crucible could be enlisted to propel the craft, at least it might serve for cooking. *I'll need driftwood.*

Eos was out there, she knew, and surely it wasn't far. The fishers were in a much smaller boat than this one. She recalled Lobster had said the "compass" of her deliverance was southeast. It meant nothing at the time. But now, considering the sameness of the sea — such knowledge would help her confer with sun and star on her trek. *Yes, it could work. I could try.*

Perhaps to preserve the fragile courage she was enjoying in that moment, she remained purposefully oblivious to the practicalities of the task: moving the landlocked craft to the water; compelling it across tempestuous seas; and facing what aftermath awaited at Eos.

Home. She had almost forgotten the sound of the word. *I could sleep in my own bed. Run through the forest. Swim in my pond. Read forbidden books from Edison's shelves. But what about Kafka? I'll ask him to come along and help me. Yes, I might just do it.*

Her anxieties abated, she closed her eyes and nodded off.

The *African Queen* rocked gently on the glassy sea. Gen lay on the bench, the sunshine warm on her skin. She always loved the sun and it seemed to have an affection for her, as well. She listened to the soft, rhythmic lapping of the water on the hull, and the flapping of their makeshift sail draped from the mast. Kafka placed a piece of driftwood into the furnace compartment and shut the hot metal hatch with a rag. He smiled at her, his face smudged with ash. He bent down and kissed her, then sat at the stern, taking to the tiller.

On the horizon, a pristine skyline beckoned white and glistening, and Gen's heart soared. A living metropolis whose glass spires stretched upward, piercing the tallest clouds. She could almost see its happy denizens in high windows, waving. She took her place beside the boy, and the pair piloted the boat steadily toward the crystal vision. The tiller jerked violently as a gust spun the little craft away from their destination. Rain pelted their skin and pinged the hull. They fought the wind and the waves, but could not correct course. The city faded into the mists. Gen reached out, as if she could pull it back into view.

A scraping sound heralded an impact with a sandy shore. The boat stopped short, tossing Gen to the deck. She stood up and scanned her surrounds. On the beach was the seaplane she'd discovered on her odyssey around Eos. "We're here, Kafka. My home!" She turned to the stern. On the bench, only the boy's bone-dry snow globe, his souvenir hornet's nest, and a mildewed book, titled *The Man Who Disappeared*. "Kafka?"

Scattered across the beach sand were the memprints from her discarded album. She picked one up. It was an image of Dr. van Hauk proudly stepping onto a pontoon of his plane. She saw her green knapsack upshore near the sawgrass, the furry black and white lemur doll poking from the top. She reached for it. The toy came alive and scampered into the forest canopy.

She started up a path, and soon she was in the dense woods. A few short steps and she was at her home. It was as she remembered; picture perfect. Not a thatch out of place. The front door opened with a swish. Gen called into the dark. "Mother?"

She walked through the house and into the lab. The furnace was burning, and a chill ran through her. Her mother's journal was open on a desk. She read the page:

The individual genome recordings were encapsulated in micro chambers, each the size of a pea, 144 in all.

She called out again. "Mother…?" She felt the puka shells of her choker and started to count the dozen-dozen pure white charms backward, with increasingly frantic enumerations.

A blur of bamboo rows sped beneath Gen's feet as she held tight on her zip-line, flying above Eos, her floral sun wrap whipping in the wind. Her countdown ended just as she set down atop the high cliff above the pond she'd swum countless times.

She dived in, enveloped in a nimbus of bubbles. She glided with a school of small fish, moving ever downward. The curtain of fry disbursed — the lake bottom, a desert of human skeletons, an identical puka choker around each neck. Her sisters! She screamed.

All at once, Gen was lying in her childhood bed, in her own room.

Her mother leaned over her, watching with an uncharacteristic look of concern. "Gen? Wake up, honey."

Gen's eyes snapped open. "Mother, it's you!"

"Yes, darling."

The bedroom door swished open to admit her father — the real, flesh and blood man, Dr. Lee van Hauk, in his customary white lab coat. She felt as though she had always known him this way.

He moved to her bedside. "She seems all right now."

Edison leaned into Gen's open bedroom window, joined by two of his fellows, Dr. Laurel and Dr. Rhodes, both in lab smocks. All smiles.

"You got quite a bump on your head. We thought for a minute you might leave us," said Mother.

Edison and his assistants glanced at one another.

Gen raised up on her elbow. "But I did leave you. That's just the trouble. And I wanted to come back for days and days." She looked into each of their faces, stroking her plush lemur toy.

"You just had a bad dream," said Mother.

"No, it wasn't a dream," Gen insisted. "It was a real place. And there were people there just like you, Mother, Father. And Edison and the others, too."

"Oh," nodded Edison, doffing a discordant fisher's cap and feigning seriousness as Laurel and Rhodes chuckled.

"But you couldn't have been, could you?" said Gen.

Mother shook her head and smiled. "Oh, we dream lots of silly things when we—"

"No, Mother, it was real. It was the big city, but not at all like I thought it would be. And some of it wasn't very nice. All I kept saying was I want to go home. And now I'm home."

The adults laughed at the teen's insistence.

"Don't you believe me?" Gen said.

"Of course we believe you, Gen," said Father.

She smiled broadly, looking at each of them. "Anyway, I'm home! And this is my room, and you're all here. And I'm never leaving, ever, ever again, because I love you all."

Laurel said wistfully, "I kind of liked it a little bit better when there were cities and… and we could have real parties. Things like that."

"That was before he effed everything up and took the world with him," said Rhodes, throwing an angry glance at Gen's father. "She's an aberration, that's all I'm saying." Rhodes pointed at him. "Maker of monsters!"

Hoyl, wearing a tiny straw Tula, lit upon Edison's shoulder. Gen could see its steel talons digging in, crimson stains forming on Edison's floral shirt.

Where Father had stood, Lee II now presented a birthday cake, the rotating Ferris wheel of tissue samples fluorescing among the lit candles, his holographic face in smile mode. "Happy birthday, Gen."

"Understand that you are destined for greater things," said her mother.

Beyond her window, the palms bowed to changing winds.

"Storm coming," said Edison.

The cake burst into flames.

A brilliant flash and a great crack of thunder snatched Gen back from her dream.

She sat up with a start, heart booming, chest heaving. Branched lightning filled the skylight, briefly bathing the *African Queen* in electric blue. She tried to get her bearings. In the flashes, she saw the tiller; the rotting bow; the black, ash-filled cylinder; and the ragged banner above, welcoming attendees to the long-ago event. Another great blue bolt exposed the gaping defects in the hull.

She knew she had not gone home. She knew that the boat could not sail — not without extensive repair. And she knew, too, that she had reawakened into her nightmare.

10.5

STATUS: SECTOR LOST 01:10:005:01 (See Technical Notes)

The serving plate emptied and her responsibility fulfilled, Gen left the widow and child, and started down the hall, dirty dishware in hand. She sighed. The burden had become what she had most feared — thankless and unceasing. But by disappearing into the rhythm of the hotel, it seemed she could remain invisible to the wrathful SoBes.

Behind her, the door latch clicked open, and light footsteps caught up with her. A tiny hand took hers.

"Wanna see something?" said Coral, trotting to keep up with the teen's longer strides. She lowered her voice. "My secret place."

Gen's brow furrowed, hoping the girl had not discovered her littoral retreat and its once-frozen sea. The dirty plate brushed her leg, and she frowned at the greasy smear.

"Leave it there." Coral pointed to one of the stacks of tarnished serving trays habitually left in the halls outside the guest rooms.

With a guilty smile, Gen furtively abandoned the platter without breaking stride.

"C'mon!" Coral took off running — Gen followed. The youngster led the teen through a zig-zag of service corridors and wall breaches, down into the core of the labyrinthine structure.

Coral stopped short, latching onto the brass post of a luggage cart sitting idle in an alcove. "Push me." She climbed aboard.

Now Gen recognized the long corridor, with its downward slope and niter encrusted walls — thankfully, nowhere near her vaulted hideaway. She shoved and the bell cart began to roll, picking up speed — she hopped aboard and pushed off. The cart fishtailed down the incline, wheels clattering, the pair giggling, loose strands of Coral's braids fluttering. Momentum carried them past the low point and upslope, slowing down.

"Okay, stop. Stop!" said Coral with a laugh. "Here."

Gen dragged her heel, and they came to rest at a tangled tree of exposed pipes. Hints of red and white paint flecked from the maze of corroded conduit, which once fed the fire suppression system that veined the ceilings of each room and hall. Coral dismounted at a nondescript door, one of a pair set into a discreet recess, only the silhouettes of their former signage remaining: one figure with long hair and one with short. She shot Gen a conspiratorial smile and turned the knob.

Light glowed softly through the high glass block window. Tucked between the pipes and a service elevator, the tiny powder room was unanticipatedly feminine, with pinks and greens predominating a picturesque and perfected world in peeled and faded wallpaper. It had perhaps been a toilette élégante in its time. A dilapidated metal partition corralled the single commode, its door missing. Empty shelves and a broken garment rack occupied the back — a staff uniform bunched below, its soft blue peeking from a patina of black must. Gen imagined this place was exclusive to the female help, who'd primp and become acceptable before coming under the critical eye of paying guests.

The girls' reflections animated a fissured, full-length mirror, the silver eroding from its edges forming a dark halo organic in its encroachment. A corner shard, lost to the ages, exposed a bit of flowered wallpaper behind, more vivid than the rest of the wall.

"Here." Coral reached into a narrow fissure in the floor and withdrew rusted scissors too big for her diminutive digits. She slapped them into Gen's hand.

"Make mine like yours," said Coral, probing her coiled pigtails. "The boys are pulling on them."

"I read somewhere… I mean, I think they do that to get attention," said Gen, recounting the borrowed personal experience she had been fed. She considered Coral's fine hair, the care that had gone into the intricate knots beneath the frizz, and the likelihood that the girl's mother had not attended to it for some days.

"Why?" asked the youngster.

"Why what?" said Gen, already lost in the planning and engineering of the task unfamiliar.

"Why do boys do that?"

Gen thought. "I don't know. I guess they're different." She wiped the blades on a dusty rag draped on a shelf. She let Coral's braids down. They were longer than Gen expected. "Are you sure?"

Coral nodded. "Same as you."

Gen took the measure of her own coiffe, exhaled, then grasped a braid and sawed it off, the blades recalcitrant. She placed the severed section in Coral's hand for safekeeping — a token of youth's innocence. She proceeded, improvising the cut, as crude as it was, offering the other braid for the child to tend.

After some time, the barbering ceased, and Gen examined her handiwork, satisfied with the results. "All finished."

"I wanna see." Coral spun around to face the mirror. "It's nice." She turned her head from side to side, beaming as she admired Gen's artfulness.

The pair stood together, scrutinizing themselves in their reflections. Similar in many ways save for height and hue. Both shared bobbed locks and slim, girlish physiques. Coral's fine features portended an uncommon beauty in some future presently unimagined by either.

"You gots teaters," said Coral. "When am I gonna get teaters?"

Gen considered. The SoBe children seemed to her slow-growing — undersized and unchanged in the time since her arrival. She actually could not remember her own physical evolution. Most of those touchstones that she thought of as her memories were imparted to her via the vidy-lenses and audy-fones, and the soft yet persistent incantations that emanated from her whisper-pillow in the night.

Gen's reflection barely fit in the frame, tall as she was. The vibrant section of wallpaper exposed by the broken-off corner supplanted part of her pretty face. A garden of hibiscus flowers, lush palms, and a stand of bamboo sprouted from her head, birthing a paradise lost.

"What do I do with 'em?" asked Coral, holding the braids out to her.

"Don't you want to keep them?"

"No, you can have 'em."

"We'll each take one." Gen chose a coil and slipped it into a pocket. Her fingertip touched the brass key. At the proper time, Gen mused, she would show her young friend her own secret room and the ancient craft that bore her youthful dreams.

"Now, you," said Coral. "Wait right here, okay?"

"Okay." Gen smiled.

Coral stashed her braid inside her skirt pocket and disappeared, the door closing softly after her.

Gen occupied herself with looking at the recurring design of the pretty wallpaper. She pondered how people must have lived when the hotel was still a hotel, and how this moment here with Coral seemed so perfectly normal. Two girls engaged in some girlish grooming.

•• ••••• ••

Gen had begun to think the child had simply abandoned her there when the familiar elfin footfalls approached.

Momentarily Coral entered, a rolled cloth in hand. "Mommy's asleep."

"What's that?"

"I'm gonna make you a skin picture." Coral unfurled the roll. Inside, her mother's well-used, handmade tattoo tools: a vessel of pigment and a few stick-like implements, one with a sharp point.

Gen hesitated, but then, remembering the marks she'd seen on others, offered her wrist to the little girl.

"No. The ankle. It's prettier."

Gen sat on the commode and held out her leg. "What is it going to be?"

The child knelt down at Gen's feet. "A surprise."

Coral began her work, tapping an image from her young mind into Gen's flesh. With pigment and punctures, Coral inked the simplest of designs. The needle stung, and Gen gasped a few times, but did her best to be patient.

"You bleed funny." Coral shrugged and wiped away the excess ink. Then she rocked back, sitting on her heels. "Okay. All done."

Gen turned her ankle to see. It was a pair of shallow double arches, one larger than the other.

"Seagulls," said Coral.

"Pretty."

"The littler one is me," Coral said, beaming. She reassembled the tattoo kit, placing the implements side by side in the cloth, and then rolling it up. "Are you gonna marry the boy on the roof?"

Gen sat up straight. "What made you say that?"

Coral shrugged. "He's crazy. Mommy said."

10.6

A skewed rectangle of morning's light shone onto the hallway wall opposite Marina's room. The door was open, Coral peeking from behind the jamb.

Gen entered with a two-handled serving tray, two silver domes, one larger than the other, promising a banquet for widow and child. "How is your mother?"

"Okay."

Gen lowered the tray to Coral. "Under the big cover."

Coral removed the unwieldy silver dome with both hands. Underneath was the plush lemur — missing a button eye, a bald patch on its torso where the faux fur had worn to the canvas. Coral beamed.

"It's yours now," said Gen.

Coral took the stuffed doll and held it tight. She scrunched her nose.

"Sorry. I washed it the best I could," said Gen.

"It smells like Lobster," said Coral, and they shared a laugh.

Marina lay curled womblike on the bed, eyes open and unblinking.

Gen set the tray on the nightstand nearest the woman and uncovered the meager and unappetizing portions. "That's all I could find today."

Marina struggled to rise, and Gen helped her sit up at the bed's edge. She looked at Gen and nodded faintly. The sunlight kissed Marina's face, betraying wrinkles beyond her years.

"You made my hair good, too." Coral fingered her freshly bobbed locks with one hand and picked at the spartan plate with the other.

Gen's smile faded as she felt something sticky coating her palm.

"She's got the sores," said Coral.

"Sores?" Gen wiped her hand on her shorts.

"One on her arm and one on her neck."

Gen checked. Marina's forearm bore an oozing canyon, a second open lesion below an ear. "How long has she had these?"

"I dunno. Maybe these many days." Coral held up three tiny digits.

Marina began to weep.

Gen realized her gaze had fixed on her late mate's idle fishing gear and empty boots. "Coral. Get some water for your mother."

The little girl ran into the bathroom. Gen heard the twist of the rusted faucet. She edged the plate closer, then placed a fork between Marina's slack fingers. "I'll try to get more tomorrow."

A familiar floral scent. Gen paused; the aroma of her own perfume wafted into the room. She had scarcely given the ornate little vial a thought since Eos, and now her nostrils filled with remembrances of her childhood home. Following the fragrant trail to the hall, she called back to Coral, "Remember to lock the door."

Gen crossed the threshold. From behind, a moist rag trapped her nose and mouth. She tried to scream — tried to breathe — but the fumes were overwhelming. Not her perfume; something else. Sickly sweet. She tried to break free but her arms and legs would not cooperate. Her knees buckled.

In her anesthetic haze, Gen saw something drop to the floor. A treasure she had salvaged from the submerged clinic — the distinctive medicine bottle, caution yellow. It rolled to a stop: Sevoflurane.

As Gen faded, a woman's voice drifted on the ether. "She won't be any more trouble."

BOOK XI:

You Are Here

A throb rose from nihility until Gen's own pulse hammered her awake. Her eyelids fluttered open to obsidian darkness. She was alone in the void. Her vision acclimated and soon the vista revealed itself as a vast collision of nebulas, galaxies, and distant suns, clear and sparkling and conspicuously constrained within the steepest of canyons. She tried to sit up, but her limbs were leaden, and she crumpled supine, again face to face with the crowded star field. A distinctive, winged contour traversed the expanse, punching a hole in the night. The girl called the name of her avian familiar, and then quickly faded into her medicated oblivion.

On the first day, Gen awakened with the dawn, her bed a ragged park bench backed by a trellis of dead vines. She found herself among the remnants of a forest valley, once as prolific as any she had wandered. A yellowed tapestry of ivy climbed along the twin walls of the great canyon. The broad wilted leaves of palms hung flaccid from their trunks, too exhausted to reach skyward. Beneath those scattered palms, a desiccated carpet of weeds and dry flowers. A solitary deciduous tree, barren of foliage save for a lonely branch, a single withered fruit drooping. A stand of bamboo, every culm yellow and lifeless, the shriveled blossoms of their mass flowering a suicide note to the Earth. It seemed to Gen that she must be dreaming.

She rose and walked an overgrown path, the leaf litter crunching underfoot. She quickly fatigued and was compelled to return to the bench to rest. She would remain at the place in the forest where she had awakened so she could be found with expediency when they returned for her.

On the second day, Gen again roused at daybreak, the solsticed sun in ascent between the walls of the once verdant chasm. No one had come to collect her. She scanned her environs for plant life that would offer sustenance. All was brown, the leaves crisp and dry.

She sat on the bench and puzzled at her familiar, yet unfamiliar, surrounds. The string lights that festooned the parklike forest and roped up its palm trunks had been bereft of power for unknown ages — the gorge illuminated only while Helios galloped across the heavens. The vine-draped canyon walls struck her as uniform and steep — unlikely a natural formation. She moved closer and pulled at the dried, meandering tendrils of a well-established creeper. The curtain of leaves fell away, and when the litter settled, she saw a platform and rail evincing a balcony, one among columns and rows of them, the opposing side of the canyon a mirror image. A hotel with many rooms stacked one atop another, positioned so each suite partook in the former greenery.

She contemplated the confounding geography of the Deco hotel — around every corner a new room or passage or stair. The structure seemed larger inside than outside, with myriad massive, yet hidden, chambers. She certainly had not seen this part of Deco before. Now, she doubted the SoBes had ferried her to this forest after all, her circumstance more likely due to a somnambulant stroll. A wave of vertigo forced her back to the bench. She lay down and closed her eyes to the garden and the honeycomb of empty rooms.

The dappled sun faded to gray, and droplets began to fall on her. The sprinkle became a steady shower that fell across her body. She opened her mouth and drank the rainwater in, beads shining silver on her flesh.

Behind her decaying divan, beyond the trellis braided with withered vines, just out of sight, lay another bench nearly back-to-back with hers. Its occupant also rested recumbent, bones bleached, clothed in weathered rags, the cranium crushed by a hostile hand.

11.2

A boy pressed his ear to a hotel room door whose number ended in 39. The odors of the hall melded with his own, and in that sense, at least, he was invisible. Beyond that door resided the flotsam of the unfortunate fisherman Reef, and uncertainty. The voices inside rose in a drumbeat exchange that seeped into the hallway.

The young eavesdropper sneezed, and the door swung open abruptly, emitting Lobster, his grizzled face afire. The man glimpsed the inquisitive brat speeding into the gloom. Marina sat on the edge of her bed, red pleading eyes watching as Coral peered out.

Lobster put a hand on the little girl's chest and ushered her back inside. The door latched shut behind him, his heavy boots thumping down the bleak corridor.

On the third day, Gen rose renewed. An opaque mist enveloped the forest. She could not see more than a few paces in any direction, heightening her sense of isolation. Days had passed since she had awakened in this strange place. It had been even longer since she had last seen her capricious paramour. Something dire, something unimaginable, could have happened to him. And she wondered about little Coral, too.

•• ——••• ••

Gen navigated a pastiche of staircases, working her way upward, hoping to get a bearing. Some stairs curved, some ran straight, and none were the same length or angle or direction. Some presented doors locked or rusted shut.

A narrow flight led her inside a many-windowed chamber in the shape of a crescent, most of the panes fractured as if by a great hand. A pair of chairs with high backs and armrests were fixed in the center before a console housing dials, levers, joysticks, toggles, dozens of screens in various dimensions, and a wheel. The configuration seemed to her a rendition of the wrecked seaplane at Eos, though on a massive scale — an aircraft of impossible magnitude.

She had awakened in a forest. She had unveiled an abandoned wing of the SoBes' hotel. She had discovered the helm of a mighty aircraft. In truth, this place was all of these — a dominion that encompassed a multitude of realms. She leaned out of a window to look for wings or propellers, but the tenacious fog occluded an answer. She elected to go back to her point of origin to puzzle out her discoveries and to stay close to the forest, should someone return for her, after all.

She retraced the Escher-work stairways with their arbitrary intersections and blind alleys. She realized she must have missed her level only after she found herself on a broad outdoor platform with a metal and wood rail that vanished into the opacity. Its infinite length was interrupted by a gate leading to rudimentary steel stairs that descended into a mystery of mist. A fat, torus-shaped object hung from a rack below the wooden guardrail, faded orange with four dingy white stripes. She pondered its purpose. The letters that once marked the plump ring had weathered to illegibility, save for a single letter "Y" obscured by algae. She wiped it with her hand, exposing three more. "City." She brightened.

During her childhood explorations of the idle guest facilities at Eos, she had discovered paths with rails of metal, wood, or even thick ropes, which all led inexorably to the disused dining facility. Now, she formulated a simple plan. She would follow the railing to the nearest junction with the old hotel, continuing to listen in case someone called for her. Choosing her direction by fiat, Gen's left hand tickled the handrail, dodging splinters as she progressed.

•• ••—◆••

Overhead, pairs of long, curved metal arms dangled rusty cables, each set labeled in even numbers. The strange apparatuses seemed mightier versions of the crane that Lobster employed to hoist his battered vessel and the disentombed pastel kiosk.

Gen continued following the path's hazy endlessness and, after a time, a feeling lodged in her stomach that she had chosen the least expeditious direction. She looked back. She could just see the orange of the ring staining the fog.

She pressed forward, palm gliding along the weathered balustrade. Within a few dozen strides, the railing rose into a wild serpentine. The walkway's planks transformed to braids of coal, a jagged black void impeding her progress. She marshaled her faculties to gather the totality of what lay before her. A ferocious blaze had long ago ravaged the structure, leaving a chasm of metal warped into obscene organic shapes, which dived and climbed and vanished in the mist. Residue of smoke and char ringed the gap.

She would not be deterred from her expedition. A steel stairway leading below the wreckage remained mostly intact. Dauntless, she hopped down to the landing, a metallic clang resonating through the chasm. Her footfalls echoed off ancient iron as she descended the twisted stair. Something soft and crunchy brushed against her hair. A hive the size of a beach ball hung pendulously from above, humming with life. A cloud of paper wasps emerged to assert their sovereignty. She leapt from the landing into a pit of darkness. All around were intimations of agonized beams bent by heat.

She felt her way along until she reached a cavernous space, water over her ankles. Pinholes of origins unknown afforded a few rays of light, revealing stalactites of rust suspended from pipes overhead. The inverted pinnacles played a sonnet of drips into an infinite pool stained wine-dark, the steel structure dissolving into eternity.

In the dimness of the waterlogged chamber, a faint blue glow beckoned from beyond an open metal door. She entered the room. It was free from the direct effect of fire and lined on one side with once-ornate shelving now rotten to a wraith of carved wood. It bled smuts of moist fibers mingled with flecks of varnish. Silken threads smothered the surface in a dense matrix, tendrils of white reaching out to the few virgin territories remaining.

She moved closer. The threads were glowing. She traced the webwork across the length of the case, to its origin. A bulbous, multi-lobed tumor of bioluminescent fungus, the mass of three pineapples, clung to a cleft in a cabinet, sequestering its qualities uncommon. She thought it bright enough to read by. She prodded the luminescent lobes with her finger. They felt as firm as any garden vegetable, each emitting a different color — from softest blues and greens to red-pinks to primrose yellow. The fruiting body gave off an aroma of earth and nuts and flowers. An olfactory memory flashed: a meal her mother had prepared with fresh fungi harvested from the forest.

Gen's stomach grumbled. She plucked a bit of the glowing clump and took a delicate bite, then slowly chewed, enjoying the pleasant texture and umami. She took another bite, and another, her face bathed in the rainbow. She broke off more pieces from the luminous bouquet and slipped as many as she could into her pockets. Thinking she might introduce this protein source to the SoBes' diet, she made a mental map of its location.

She sensed movement. The whole of the structure creaked and shifted. The metal door clanged shut, locking her in. Something dripped on her head. In the subtle radiance of the luciferin fungus, she saw the rusted ceiling, perforated and paper thin. Gen climbed atop a table and tore at the wound until its circumference matched her body, then pulled herself through to the level above.

The darkness hampered navigation, but she continued to another flight of stairs and emerged on the other side of the burned-out chasm. Relieved to see the daylight, she oriented herself to the rail, again keeping it to her left.

Moving along the walkway, she idly peered inside a few of the windows, most of the rooms merely black caverns. Slivers of ambient light offered occasional hints of a civility lost to time. She reached into a pocket, retrieved another glowing chunk of fungus, and popped it into her mouth.

••·─●·•

A halo traced the edges of her hand, and for a moment, the sky tasted like prickly pear. Gen's vision narrowed to a single plank of the walkway, one end curving upward. Her perception sharpened to the wood grain of its curled corner, just beyond her left shoe. She raised and lowered her toes, a squeak resounding from a rusted screw with strange clarity and amplitude. A wave of queasiness swept through her, and she stopped. Painful contortions snatched her belly, doubling her over. Promptly, suddenly, violently — she disgorged her entire morning's consumption onto the path. She lay on the walk, curling around her distress, groaning, and clutching her abdomen.

After a few harrowing moments, the biliousness passed and now her body felt relaxed; she smiled. She rose and resumed her trek — although it seemed gravity had magnified, her limbs pleasantly leaden.

Gen detected a minute shift in each of her senses — subtle but perceptible. Sights, sounds, smells, and textures grew more vivid and more unreliable at the same time. Curiosity evolved into anxiety as she puzzled at these sensations. It had been days since her groggy awakening in the forest, and just as long without food, and she supposed that this was why she felt so peculiar.

The mist seemed to toy with her vision. Grays and whites took on hues of blue and pink, and her shoes shone the colors of a verdant flower patch. Even her bland blouse had taken on a shimmering rose. The foggy, far horizon drew in toward her body, and she focused on each plank and the rail as their sharpness intensified. She accepted this newfound visual sense. Decided to explore it.

She followed the rail's dictate, assenting to the uncanny uncertainty of her perceptible rightward arc. Objects around her seemed to contain patterns within patterns. The rail bore iridescent, snakelike scales as colors shifted toward magenta. A subtle rhythmic thump rose in her ears like the waves beating Lobster's jon boat. She turned her head left, right, up, down — playfully conducting the rhythm as it magnified to a symphony of cadence. A hungry gull cawed for her to pay heed to her ankle, where she witnessed the two avian arches take flight from her flesh. She laughed joyously. The railing continued to curve, though she was sure she could straighten it simply by wishing it so.

The persistent pulses aligned with the breaths of the undulating platform as it chameleon'd from hue to intense hue, and she knew that there was no distance nor difference between her cells and the molecules of the walkway, the rail, and the mist. Beneath her feet, green bamboo strips lay flat, bobbing as if afloat, sunbeams prisming between. She dived through the bamboo stalks into the clear waters of her pond at Eos, then surfaced to drink a test tube of Edison's bamboo liquor, now sweet like mango nectar.

Under her hand, the serpentine rail curled into the steering wheel of a bowrider sport boat, *The Beagle*, suspended in the mangroves at Eos. Wings sprouted from its gunwales, and it glided skyward, taking her high above a bloom of skyscrapers surrounded by a glistening sea, beckoning to the teen with dazzling colors and the felicitations of friends. The buildings tumbled outward into the vast ocean, and a black, angry, swirling chasm formed in the center. Traversing the wall of the deepening whirlpool: her stuffed toy lemur; memprints scattered from the album; her parents' intrusive drone; the lab incinerator, breathing fire; the oozing white sap of the caustic apple tree; a killer leopard seal gnashing its teeth; a patch of yellow dandelions filling the periphery of her vision; the Mo'ai trailing its rotted offerings; Luddy removing his sunglasses, gazing at her from Hoyl's electric crystal eyes; and the youth from the rooftop — all vanishing into the whorl. The maelstrom deepened until it exposed the sand, where rested the bones of her unfortunate sisters. Then, as suddenly as it had started, the violent vortex collapsed onto itself until the water was glass-smooth and at peace.

Her footfalls became intentional and reverent as she followed the perfected boxy geometries of the posts below the sinuous handrail. Inside each, the books from her shelf multiplied alongside Kafka's mildewed tomes, ethereal light emanating from between the volumes. She peered through into the fractal of libraries upon libraries. She yearned to offer a name to each geometry, but the words seemed unpronounceable, and she left the task to some greater spirit. Now, she scribed her own tale, beginning within her pocket notebook, the ink giddily running off the page and onto the walls of the Deco hotel until she had chronicled every story in the cosmos.

Her fingers gently curled around her lapis pendant, and she became the selfsame dark Delphic stone venerated in her mother's shrine. Mother placed a sweet hyacinth blossom at her opalescent feet, Gen awash in love and adoration and acceptance. In the glow of Mother's beaming face gathered those Gen had known at Eos: Edison, her father, the other scientists; all smiles. Gone was her anger at their secrets and deceptions, supplanted by the profound grief that she had forbidden herself, until now. Joining the joyous gathering were the mesmeric youth, the orphan and widow, the sultry consort, the gruff fisher, the tall man, and the bedeviled guests of the inundated hotel — all in a brilliant oneness with the boundless universe. She was part of them, and they, her — enveloped in a chrysalis of equanimity, warmth, and belonging.

The mosaic pixelated into sparkling droplets, which sublimated into the wood-topped metal rail, the planked path, and the persistent fog. Suddenly overwhelmed with anxiety and self-doubt, Gen wondered if she truly was, as they said, a defective being — if her own flawed actions and attitudes and failures had triggered the tragedies that had befallen those she cared for. She crumpled onto the wooden walkway and wept uncontrollably. When the storm of emotion had passed, the teen rose from her hands and knees, reuniting with the handrail. As she resumed her journey, the sensation of the barrier's arcing abated. The candy colors of the relentless fog had muted, but seeing beyond the rail remained futile. She found herself inexplicably hungry for a slice of pineapple cake. Though emotionally exhausted, she came to know a sense of peace and even forgiveness from those she had wronged.

The intense hues had returned to the whites and grays she had perceived at the start of her trek. The railing and walkway straight before her, she regarded her monochromatic surrounds, the muted tones of her shoes, and her pale top. With the sorrow and conflict now wrung from her, she felt more at peace in that moment than on the blissful morning of her sixteenth birthday.

•·-•—•·•

Gen had been traveling with the vivid apparitions for a time and distance unknown. At its end, the experience — at turns breathtaking and traumatic — left her with a warmth for all humankind; a feeling of unity that she vowed to nurture. She continued forward, enthused to rejoin the SoBes, confident that she would soon be swaddled in felicity.

The smooth curves and lines and elevations of this wing of the hotel seemed to echo the grand style of the main building, though on an ambitious scale that she could not fathom. Above her head, another series of ragged cables swung from their curved pipes — enumerated in odd numbers, contrary to the first set. Like the others, no boats hung there awaiting favorable seas. She thought of the little jon boat swaying in the breeze, and her vain attempt to wrest it into the sea. She surmised that there must have been a great many SoBe fishermen once, Lobster possibly the last of his kind.

She realized only now that, for all of its nutritional promise, the fungus had proven to be a variety that induced vivid and sometimes frightening fantasies, and thus it was risky fare to break her fast. As with the little apples of death, no caring soul would be at her side with elixirs to absolve her sins of capricious curiosity.

She plucked the remaining pieces from her pockets, still glowing soft greens and pinks and blues, and flung the noxious chunks past the rail and into the fog.

Several paces ahead, a smudge of piquant orange overcame the mist. As she approached, the orange resolved into a ring beside a gate. She thought it a sibling to those she had seen at the outset of her travels. That this structure might have repeated features did not surprise her, given the multiple sets of curved pipes she had passed beneath.

The fog had thinned to patches, and she looked over the rail at the jot of water now visible far below. The discarded fungus bits twitched on the surface as piscine mouths nibbled at their edges in a swirl of rubbery lips and fins, reminiscent of when Mother tossed crumbs to the koi in her personal pond, the creatures eagerly accepting the free meal.

The delicacy grew scarce. Dorsals sliced the surface, twisting and turning erratically — a confused frenzy of fin and gill, flashing silver. In another moment, they were belly up, motionless. *Oh, no. Did I kill them?*

Her eyes fell to the metal stair, leading up from the waves, then up to the gate where she stood, next to the orange ring. She saw her handprint where she had earlier wiped the letters clean. She was perplexed. The gate, the ring, the stairs — familiar, she realized, not because they were twins to the ones she had left behind, but because they were one and the same. She had returned to her point of embarkation.

Gen cast her gaze to the vista newly unveiled, the smiling sun having defeated the moody mist. The faded pink rectangles of the Deco hotel rose lonely on their scrap of sand, rubble trailing either side for miles. Between her and the domain of the SoBes lay the expanse of the great bay. For all her travels, she was now impossibly far away.

She bounded up the exterior stairways back to the behemoth pilot house, then climbed atop its roof. At the pinnacle of the edifice was a huge, whimsical, winged, smoke-stained funnel, faded letters proclaiming: "City On The Seas." Then she gazed across the bay toward Deco — she could see no bridge — no connection to the hotel.

She turned to the opposing vista. A dozen mammoth half-sunken structures dotted the waters, like skyscrapers laid upon their sides sans the right angles of terrestrial architecture. Their smooth lines evoked the aged dhow, Lobster's fishing boat, or the stranded pleasure craft that sailed the mangrove canopy at Eos. Some were upturned with keel and props exposed, others tipped to reveal myriad layers bereft of tenancy. A graveyard of shipwrecks.

She recalled a silly story Edison had told her. Three blind men touched an elephant — the first man proclaiming it was a tree; the second, a snake; the third, a rope. She had been exploring her surroundings piece by piece, but now she comprehended the whole. The confounding maze she thought a forest or hotel or aircraft was none of those things — nor was it the city. She was on an enormous ship — marooned on the only wreck that had come to rest upright on the silted floor of the bay.

Then a greater truth washed over her. Just as she had not appreciated her special place among the people of Eos, she had misjudged the magnitude of her difficulties with the SoBes. And they had delivered her to her exile.

She screamed fury into the azure sky, her vocalization dying forsaken on the impassive breeze.

11.4

"Subject was expected to progress at the pre-designed, accelerated rate. See chart above. Physical development to date has exceeded the timeline by 2.24 X." The woman paused her reading, scanning the dense cursive and block printed entries, hand-drawn charts and tables, and barely legible, miniaturized margin notes. "Subject has exited pre... pre-pube?"

"Prepubescence," said Luddy.

"I know, it just sounds funny," Taffy continued. "However, mental and emotional development lag..." A fingertip grazed her tongue, and then flipped the rippled page of the now dried journal as she reclined against the edge of Luddy's desk.

"Where was I?" She found her place among the crowded scribbles. "Lag the original pre-designed rate by 1.45 X. Recommend enhancing enrichment to include positive examples of males and females within the putative age range in common social situations. This addition to the curriculum will stimulate subject to assimilate essential social signals in order to realign emotional development with physical, mitigating negative maturity scores." A giggle escaped the woman's lips. "So, this mean she's stupid or something? Can I take a break?"

"Please do. Mark your place." He put his feet atop his desk.

Taffy dog-eared the page. As she started to flip the journal closed, a clump of pages parted. A sparkle registered in some primal region of her brain. Her eyes twinkled, a covetous grin curling a corner of her mouth. She set the open diary on the desk, then turned toward the window, holding up her find: a finely crafted silver earring, its design an owl and a dreamcatcher with tiny feathers. She admired its delicate workmanship, allowing the light to dance across its intricacies. "Pretty." She slipped the unearthed treasure into her pierced earlobe.

"Let me see."

"It's nothing. An earring. Stuck inside that grubby book," she said, leaning toward him and jingling the bauble.

Luddy took it between his thumb and index finger and gently felt its fine contours. "Put it back."

Taffy clucked, irritated. "You always gotta spoil things. It don't belong to nobody."

"It was obviously a bookmark. A reminder for a passage of particular importance. I want to know what is on that page," he said.

She hissed. "I won't lose your place." She folded the corner of the page.

"Please continue. On that bookmarked page."

She frowned.

"Please," he said.

She picked up the journal. "All right. Let's see." She skimmed the notations, took a breath, and read aloud. "Results finalized. Sample confirms previous data regarding the full cessation of PANoptosis—"

A knock announced the intrusion of Lobster's greasy head, his burly form trailing him through the open doorway. He scanned the suite, dismayed, as if failing to find a lost item among the room's appointments. "Uh... everybody's sayin' there's scarce fishin' onshore," said Lobster, improvising, the comment having only just come to him.

"And you thought I should be informed of this condition," said Luddy.

"Be shippin' out again, come dawn."

"No need to apprise me of your plans. I assume you have procured a new shipmate."

"Ha. Don't need no ballast," said the mariner.

"Before you embark, check on the new drain channel. I am told there is a minor obstruction. Nothing you cannot handle alone."

Lobster groaned. He swung open the door for his exit, but froze — a matter digging at him like a stone in a shoe. "Have ya…? Nothin'."

"You have an issue to discuss?" said Luddy.

"Since you ask. Seems the selkie be shirkin'. Ain't fed the widow and child, last few days. The waif's been snatchin' bites off me plate."

"Is that so?" Luddy inquired.

Taffy caught Lobster's eye, slowly shaking her head. Lobster's brow furrowed at the warning. "Yep. Well, suppose the minnow'll turn up."

"No doubt," said Luddy. "When you see Gen, tell her I wish to speak with her."

"That I'll do," said Lobster, his eyes locked on Taffy. "Fine trinket. Scratch that up on the beach, did ya?" With a satisfied smirk, he closed the door after himself.

"Sample confirms previous data regarding the full cessation of PANoptosis in the subject Bambuseae. See? I marked your 'passage of particular importance,'" she snipped, fingering the finery at her lobe.

Luddy sighed. "If you really want it, you may keep it. For now."

11.5

At dawn on the next day, Gen rested her hands on the wood-trimmed gate in the rail that held the inscrutable orange ring. She looked over the side to the steps that rose steep and silver-gray from the foamy bay waters sloshing against the hull. She imagined some faceless unknown — one of the vulgar SoBes, perhaps — slogging up those stairs with her insensate body flung unceremoniously over his shoulder. Trekking across the abandoned decks of the rusting wreck. Descending to the vined and terraced canyon. Abandoning her on the bench, a tithe to Poseidon.

She supposed that at night, if the mists were merciful, she would see the glimmer of evening lights in the pink hotel, its façade softly aglow, pensive and brooding. The singular sign of life in this lifeless landscape. The beacon would remain warm and welcoming until the customary hour. Then, the bank of batteries in the roof's weathered turret would jealously conserve their power and commit the skyline to the night.

The boy would be there. Perhaps he was even now wondering what had become of her. He would not know where to look. She closed her eyes against the brilliant sun and touched her lapis pendant, nursing her ache with the balm of her mother's tales of shooting stars and destiny. She projected her longing across the expanse of the bay, willing her heart to him and listening deep inside herself for his answer. Her wish glided to the crenated rooftop and into his modest home — finding only dust and Mother's wispy gnosis. She opened her eyes.

She waved her arms at the distant spire. Then she realized that her opposition, too, might observe this display, and maybe even delight in her plight. She abandoned her pressing prayer for rescue.

She turned her attention to a mountain of furniture twice her height, bridging the gap between two towering sections of the ship. Tables and chairs were stacked dense as a hedgerow, legs locked, seats and backs entwined — a barrier to keep something in, or to keep something out. She saw an item familiar, buried deep in the stack, shaded from an eternity in the rain and the sun. She commenced to extricate it from the mass. She tugged. The avalanche of outdoor accessories cascaded over her. She emerged, satisfied with her brilliant success. Her prize was intact: a chaise lounge chair much like the one she had on her sim-beach at home, with cobalt blue slats, the armrests and ratchet hinges in perfect working order.

She dragged the lounge close to the rail's gate, sat on its end, and craned her neck to peer again at the watery vista. The view limited, she pulled the chair closer still. *When they come back for me, they'll come up this way. If they come back.*

In all the time she had suffered the company of the SoBes, survival had upended her dreams. Her priorities had narrowed to obtaining food and shelter, while shielding herself from the adversarial horde. Of the tribe, only one had seemed to be of her kind: the boy who called himself Kafka.

It came to her that the bursts of brilliance that punctuated the rhythm of the youth's speech were quotations of a single author whose collected works she had seen in his abode. What bound her to him, and him to her, she realized, was an affinity for those words, hailed from his memory in perfected pulses. And the words had charted a course to her heart.

Words. During her experience with the enlightening fungus, she had written in her notebook. She reflected on the moments of dazzling clarity; the cosmos had opened to her, and in the oneness, all knowledge was hers. These secrets she had penned, lest they be lost to eternity. She opened the pad. There was her unfinished poem on meeting friends — still disappointing, its simplistic themes embarrassing. The next: a rhyme about the secret room's brass key, attenuated into the uninspired. She paged past, seeking the pristine prose she had composed.

Her cosmic inspiration had flowed thusly: partial words devolving into random scribbles and half-doodles and trailing off into meaningless scratches. Pages of them. She groaned, and flipped through the literary carnage until she found a clean sheet, then placed her pen on the page.

I did not know what loneliness was,

Until I had someone to miss.

A pleasant smile,

A gentle touch,

And oh, the softest kiss.

She read it through, rolling the writing instrument between her fingers. *Better than the others. Maybe with practice.*

She waited. In the blue lounge. With the backrest that she could adjust ever so. And she waited. She studied the skyline and its ragged remnants doomed to be reclaimed by the sea. And while she waited, she watched the night embrace her would-be beau's abode across the bay — his humble shack with its musty books and misremembered souvenirs. Her eyelids grew heavy and soon she was asleep.

••—•—◆•••

The warm emotions she had embraced during her Delphian trek around the shipwreck had burned off in the blue-crisp daylight of her reality. The truth pierced her heart and opened a chasm of despair. A pain unfamiliar washed over her in waves that seemed to radiate from her core to the tips of her fingers and toes, forcing a sigh, and great torrents of tears. It was a sorrow like no other; a complicated grief for those gone from her, and a yearning for those same shoulders to sop her weeping. She tried to grasp for a center, a point of stability, but found none. The ache subsided suddenly. And then the cycle began anew, the void opening and consuming her with its blackness even as the sun arced skyward.

The tsunami of tumult had advanced and receded. Gen regained a measure of composure, the calm feeling new and empty and odd. *I am all alone now.* Practicalities crested and swept across her mind: food and water, a safe place to sleep, what to do with her days — and how to end her exile.

She was confident that she could wrest sustenance from the forest in the valley of the vines. With the panoply of rooms, she had her choice of locations to lay her head.

Gen puzzled through expectations of extrication, now proving unrealistic. She might have to save herself, which prompted the question of a suitable destination. The hotel would be a respite from the stark and lonely derelict. Yet, she thought any return to the SoBes' domain would be strictly a way station on her voyage to her true home.

For the time being, she would explore the wreck, caution a new priority. In this locale sans windmills and solar panels, she would limit her explorations of the cavernous interior to the daytime and, perhaps, the brightest phases of the Moon.

•·-·—●·•

The afternoon stretched into evening. Then evening ushered an inky night, and the notion of ever more nights spent on the shipwreck spurred her desire to depart this purgatory. She peeked over the rail to plot a potential swim across the watery expanse. There were no islands between the ship and Deco, no place to rest once she started. She guessed the swim would take an entire day — longer if the wind tussled with the waters. She descended the stairs to the half-sunken, algae-coated platform where the steps met the inland sea, to assure herself of the reasonableness of her assumptions. Presently the surface was as glass. She could leave now, but in the night, without landmarks, she would surely lose her way. *In the morning, though...*

As she visualized her crossing, the platform rose and fell, struck by a rolling wave. She grasped the rail. The waters surged again with menace and intent. Something massive moving fast in the depths. Hunting. Determined in its pursuit. She watched as the water roiled in a dance of life and death.

Suddenly, the black surface calmed. She recalled the pugilistic seals on the coral outcrop at Eos, and the beast that beheaded the fisherman. The bay harbored vicious creatures. Of this, Gen no longer had doubt. A swim back to Deco would be perilous.

She knew, too, that should she get there, the same intrigues would remain. Negotiating a delicate peace with the SoBes had not prevented her stranding. She would need a substantive plan to deal with the vindictive denizens of Deco, and time to provision for her exodus to Eos.

There rose from the bay a plume of diamond scales, which once adorned some great and unfortunate fish. They sparkled silver in the moonlight, and then sank, occulted beneath bloody waters.

11.6

At midday, Gen returned to the garden to search among the leaf litter for a living thing she might cultivate, like she had done with the dandelion. A fleck of yellow. Excited, she knelt and brushed away the debris, revealing a synthetic bottle cap stamped with a faded glyph of three green arrows in an endless chase. She sighed; not a flower. She placed it where she found it. With her fingers, she raked the leaves, still hoping to discover a seedling. Not a single prospect poked its head above the depleted soil, a layer of crystal glistening on its surface. She tasted it — salty.

Her stomach gnawed and twisted, a sensation more acute whenever she left the sunny top deck. She had seen the ringtails eat bark and dead wood during seasons of want, and following their custom, she plucked a handful of parched leaves from a shrub, folded them into her mouth, and chewed. They were bitter, and the desiccated shards proved hard to swallow. The crumbs coated her tongue and the inside of her cheeks, and absorbed what small sum of saliva she had available. She grasped her throat and coughed a plume of brown dust.

Gen scanned for any vessel that might have captured rain — a pot, a bowl, a glass. Nothing. She caught sight of an ancient strip of canvas awning clinging to a broken frame; pregnant, she hoped, with the weight of rainwater. She ran to it, then punched the belly of the bulge. Water disgorged onto her face and into her mouth and over her body. She gulped it down, gagging, trying to catch her breath, spitting masticated leaves. She pumped the canvas, draining the adventitious reservoir until the last drips found her lips.

She wiped her mouth and opened her eyes, grateful for the respite. She would not attempt another nosh on the foliage unless she could find something green. The breeze stiffened, and her ears perked up at a sound rising. It appeared to come from everywhere at once — a haunting moan that recalled the wind rushing through the bamboo stands of Eos. Her gaze turned skyward to a thin cord cleaving the clouds in two.

STATUS: SECTOR DAMAGED 01:11:006;04 (See Technical Notes)

Gen clasped the galvanized steel cable, squelching the vibration. She released it, and the mournful tone resumed. Her eyes followed the line a great distance across the deep chasm to a twin platform on the far side. *A zip-line. Just like back home.*

Clinging to the line was a weather-worn t-bar. No electric motor, the mechanism was gravity driven. She worked it off of the cable and examined its pulleys; the wheels had rusted solid. She tossed it aside. Under the faded metal awning of the elevated platform, she discovered cabinets holding an assortment of equipment: helmets, straps, tethers, and spare t-bar handles. She took another t-bar from a peg and checked the pulley; it seemed sound enough, relatively free of corrosion. She smiled. This would be a fun way to occupy her days, and a shortcut for traversing the great length of the ship.

As she was about to install the new t-bar trolley, a closer look at the wire rope revealed frayed and rusted strands. The rain-drenched and desperate faces of Edison and the other scientists suddenly crowded her psyche. The line, snapping in the storm. She squeezed her eyes shut tight, then opened them again. She set the good t-bar on the platform, beneath the awning. *Better not.*

On either side of the zip-line deck, elevated walkways led to the mouths of massive, faded orange tubes. She looked over the rail at the twisting flumes culminating far below in the rectangle of a pool half-filled with murky water.

At the mouth of one of the cylindrical structures, she found a sign that read: "Waterslide Like A Pro!" It depicted a man, arms folded and ankles crossed to illustrate the optimum pose for transiting the tube, alongside seemingly unnecessary safety procedures and a recommendation to follow instructions from "Your Fun Zone Attendant." *Fun zone?*

She laid down inside one of the strange tubes and crossed her arms and legs, bracing for swift movement — but she stayed put. She sighed, then scooted forward, sliding half her length, the dry surface tugging her skin. Several nozzles ringed the tube. *It needs water.* She climbed out.

From her high vantage on the waterslide platform, she could see tucked off to the side a wall parallel to the canyon's balconies, dotted with colorful protrusions. The bumps seemed to her to be spaced just right for climbing — an entertaining access route to the guest rooms and the main deck far below. She balanced atop the rail and launched herself, catching a bump in one hand, then securing the other hand, and then her feet. She pulled her body tight to the wall and exhaled. Awkward, to be certain, but she knew she could master it. She lowered herself about a body length, moving from purchase to purchase with pleasing ease.

A shimmering geometric reflection projected onto the wall next to her. She released one hand and pivoted out to scan for its source. Across the garden, sunlight glinted gem-like from a large, round feature among the gray flora, most of its surface overcome by dead vines. The sparkle winked at her. Noting the location of the spherical shape, she aimed to explore it when she reached the main deck. She reassessed the balconies she'd seen from above. *I can get to the rooms from here.*

She spidered horizontally across the rock face toward the suites, and when she'd reached the last of the handholds, she lemur-leapt onto the rail of the closest balcony and climbed in. She tugged at the sliding door — locked. Her brow furrowed. Below her, a shred of curtain waved a beckoning hand from beyond an open slider. She eased herself down and slipped inside.

The door opposite was ajar, the breeze breathing through a stateroom as ornate as Luddy's bridal suite, although smaller, most of the space absorbed by the overlarge bed, unmade since the moment its occupants had risen in some long-ago hurry. A desk. A fanciful lamp. A video screen, controller beside. A dresser, drawers emptied. A small blue valise spilled on the floor, nondescript pastel clothes in a heap. Two other suitcases lay open on the bed, sloppily stuffed — the larger a foul-weather gray and the junior-sized, a vivid pink. A kerchief draped across the pink case, its whimsical design a pair of seagulls in flight. Gen's mind flashed to the marks on her ankle and the little girl. She stashed the scarf in a pocket.

She peered into a narrow opening. Blank eyes, blood-red lips. She gasped. A shriveled human head stared back from the quartz counter, a mass of blonde hair atop. A fleeting movement startled her again — only her reflection. She stepped inside the bathroom. Merely a mannequin, she decided, like the one in the canal storefront, though missing trunk and appendages. Gen felt the blond strands, then slipped the wig off the head and onto her own, the aged cap's elastic crackling in her ears. Tucking her short, curly locks underneath, she stood beyond the doorway to catch the best light. She giggled at the stranger in the mirror. She studied the bangs that hid her brow and the straight, shoulder-length tresses, flaxen against her dark skin. She beamed. *I look just like Mother.* She peeled off the hairpiece and carefully returned it to the polystyrene scalp of its owner. She glanced at her reflected image one last time to toss her raven curls.

Off the counter rolled a glittery cylinder. She caught it and slipped off its ruby cover. She dabbed the waxy crimson contents with her pinkie. *Make-up. Like the girls in my lessons. The ones with boyfriends.* She capped the tube and parked it on the cluttered countertop next to the conceited head.

Stepping back onto the balcony, Gen turned for a last look inside the opulent suite. She fleetingly entertained an enchanted future where she and her young man would take up residence in such a place — as the monarchs of this city on the seas. She sighed. *What if I never see him again?*

She looked at the wall she had climbed, but the glistening beam had faded.

••·-•—◼•••

Lowering herself to the main deck, Gen released her grip on the bumpy façade, landing on her feet inside a small corral on what once had been a padded surface. She leapt over the fence, heeding her urge to investigate the source of the reflection that called to her from the high wall.

At the margin of the forest, she stepped up onto what she thought was a platform, but she slipped and tumbled on her behind, the leafy coating a lubricant against the slick surface. She sat up. She brushed away its concealment with the knife-edge of her hand. The dark, smooth thing was interred to a depth just sufficient to occult it from all but the most scrupulous of acuities. It lay like a ghost beneath the desiccated soil, its angular form and high relief the only inkling of its place of slumber. It was heavy, Gen surmised, as it had settled nearly flush with the earth of the lifeless landscaping.

The base was attached to remnants of black cables curving down into a conduit that snaked below the nearby deck's surface. Her fingers attained purchase, and she tilted the monumental sarsen vertical. It registered solidly in its long-forgotten niche in the deck, leaf litter raining. The glassy slab was the width of her arms outstretched and twice her height — black as the petrified pitch that oozed from the roof of the Deco hotel.

Gen stood before the monolith. Its featureless plane coveted the light, a rectangle glistening obsidian-smooth. It loomed sharp-edged and ebony, despotic in its dimensions. Its apex cleaved a new horizon from the afternoon sun. She shielded her eyes for a better look. It was without markings, save for a raised inscription in a fanciful font: "YOU ARE HERE by Tycho MediaMaps Out-Of-Home Displays." She peered at its other side, hoping for instructions or controls. The obverse was the twin of the front, slick, mute, and mysterious. It seemed to her an indifferent void — like her mother's computer screens when the equipment was powered down for the night — the strange totem's divinity having terminated with the loss of electrical power on the vessel. If it were conceived to enlighten, its wisdom was lost to the ages now, as were the mechanisms of its animation and the wonders that it had borrowed from the remote sparks of mankind's collected cloud.

Another idol, Gen thought. Lifeless and dull as the stucco Mo'ai balanced on the patio at Deco, with its rotten fish and buzzing flies. For all its capacity to contain the knowledge of the world, now, the most this silicon mind could muster was the girl's own reflection in the smooth ebon.

She left the lonely slab to its amnesias and made her way toward the hemispheric feature that had shimmered from within the garden.

•·–•—•··

A dome of geodesic simplicity protruded from the leaf littered deck, its shallow arc perhaps intended to discourage a careless stroll atop its surface. A rail encircled its extent, considerable at about five paces across. By virtue of its prodigious organic cover, it had been spared ruination, the densely entwined vines deterring detection. She could make out a design through the leafless tendrils: a jewel of glass and color somewhere between art nouveau and bad taste, each facet contributing to the telling of a myth. Crystal porpoises rode rolling waves as twin seahorses pulled a golden chariot, its driver the sea king in his element, trident raised, loins bare. Gen flashed fleetingly on the boy bathing in the water tower — not quite sure why. She drew close, wiped a pane, and looked inside. Her eyes went wide.

Below, a man was reclining in an armchair, his black shoes ensconced on an ottoman, a thick tome open in his lap. He was dressed in white bedecked with filigree of gold, his face concealed beneath the black brim of a white cap.

I'm not alone! Gen banged on the glass. A small pane popped from its frame and tumbled to the carpeted floor far below, some distance behind the armchair. She called through the breach. "Hello? Hello!"

The man ignored the intrusion, engrossed in his pastime.

She rose and took stock of her position, reckoning that the room with the reader was two levels below. A service door nearby beckoned. She rushed through and descended into the darkness.

••—•—◆••

Gen emerged from the utility stairwell, greeted by blackness and sounds of drips and metal panels twisting toward repose. She felt a disconcerting slosh of water and sand sifting beneath the battered keel. Regretting her own natural impulsiveness, she moved by touch in the sultry belowdecks, a dank wall her only guide in the Stygian gloom.

Ahead, a glow, faint as the first stirrings of the cosmos. She homed in on the iridescent diorama — the singular space illuminated in the void. Her hand fell upon a handle, and she entered a room that conformed to the circular geometry of its skylight oculus. The pantheon of warm woods and brass and marble blurred as the girl rushed to her fellow guest. Finally, a friend; a confidante; a commiserator in their alienation.

"My name is Gen. I'm so happy you're here," she said, approaching the seated man in the white cap from behind. She placed a palm on his shoulder. "I don't mean to scare you."

His mildewed book fell to the floor, blackened pages fluttering like ash. His ivory digits rattled limp, and his captain's cap slid off along with most of his hair. Bones of pure white, still delicately balanced in their former human form, sat stoic in the comfortable chair, tattered dress uniform adorned with brass buttons and shoulder stripes, signifying something to someone long gone. His empty orbits stared at his lap, oblivious to the expatriation of his tome to the carpet, the skull lost in thoughts lost forever.

Gen stumbled backward, horrified.

Gen had breached a tomb and disturbed its denizen's rest. She spun away from the grizzly display, her eyes landing on the wayward pane from the oculus. "I'm sorry. I'm sorry. I'm sorry."

Her mind groped for an answer. *Did he die all alone?*

The shock crested and finally eased. She lifted her eyes. She was surrounded by shelves, from marbled floor to domed ceiling. Books and more books. In the open. Behind glass. Row upon row. Packed tidily on end, spines out. A wooden ladder to the upper stacks.

It all seemed untouched, still offering its luxurious, albeit dusty, appointments. Gold-leafed chairs huddled around ornately carved tables. The perimeter featured glassed-in cases with thick pillars at their corners in an exaggerated Corinthian pattern, the tops of the wood cabinets bordered by prominent dentils — a design inspired by Greek architecture, seasoned with whimsical flair. A yellowed depiction of the Trojan War danced across one wall: men with their swords and shields clashing, a giant horse at the gates of a walled city.

A larger-than-life statue dominated an alcove: the Greek god of seas and storms and earthquakes and horses, rendered as a muscular, bearded man with the curled torso of a fish, his trident poised to thrust home its pointed prongs. Above, carved into a slab of simulated marble, "Poseidon's Library."

A library. Gen's mother had spoken of the vaunted edifices devoted to holding the world's knowledge, though not covetously. Their wealth could be had by all who so desired. Mother would pause with a lament that went unexpanded, sighing that those gilded times were "before." As Gen stood among the stacks, she began to understand.

She turned again to the man whose solitary studies had been so permanently interrupted. His uniform bore a name tag: "Capt. Thomas Andrews." She focused her attention to his subject of interest — the tome that had kept him rapt until the moment of his expiration. She reached to retrieve his book from the floor. The binding gave way, hundreds of loose pages raining in a damp pile. One even-numbered page remained in her hand, its title in the top margin: *Mutiny on the Bounty*. Her brows knitted above sorrowful eyes. The fallen apart man, with his fallen apart book, on the fallen apart ship, in a fallen apart world. She let the final fragment flutter to the floor.

Next to the man's upholstered perch, a table presented a medley of material. She supposed that, anticipating plenty of time for perusal, he had pulled a number of intriguing titles for consumption. Gen bent so that the bindings were at eye level: *Silent Spring, The Revenge of Gaia, Moby-Dick, Ulysses*, and a hardcover of a play, *Inherit the Wind*. A glass with a mineral ring near its base sat atop a thick binder, embossed: *Electronics & Navigation*. An amber-tinted plastic container, half the height of the glass, lay tipped over, empty, label faded, a white cap beside marked with a familiar "Rx." The eclectic amalgam of objects, publications, and opportunity seemed to tell a story, but Gen could not make sense of the puzzle.

There was nothing further that could be gleaned from the reader. She was again alone — but not alone. Books encircled her, their pages booming softly with the silent voices of authors long dust. The collection in her room at Eos was limited to a few classics preserved by her parents as art or remembrance. She had taken pleasure in the feel of the plant fibers pressed to diaphanous sheets; the smell of ink and the musky perfume of the past. She had gorged on the stories and the poetry, though she could not always comprehend their significance. Now, in this vast cache of words, she desired something from the stacks for herself — some narrative or verse to balm her troubles and pass the time. After all, she was stranded on this island of iron and had no scheduled visit from friend or foe, nor practical itinerary for personal travel.

Her mother had forbidden her to touch the dog-eared scientific volumes in the lab for fear the girl might ruin the ancient bindings — printed and glued and bound, some stitched with thread. Indeed, in the wood and bronze cases, Gen could see these books were of another established tradition — words meant to be held and interpreted, not sequestered, or projected onto the retina. She approached a stack labeled with a little brass plaque, "A–C," finding herself among works of fiction arranged by author. She cocked her head to read a spine: *Fahrenheit 451*. Mother had held back this title, promising it to Gen when she was further along in her lessons. She grasped the book. It crumbled in her hand. She sighed.

Sagging under the weight and the damp, a wooden rack nearby displayed publications similarly stooped; once colorful pages coated now in mildew. Bold letters across one slick cover read: *FAMILY OFFICE MATCH*. She turned a clump of petrified pages to the photograph of a trim, athletic man, lines around his eyes and mouth, with wild red hair, stiffly posed as if his future lay in some distant star. Tall palms bordered an incongruous industrial edifice; beyond, the rectilinear shape of crisp, glass-smooth aqua; farther still, a green blanket rolling into infinity. Beneath the photo, an article. *Maybe that's a city building. And a swimming pool.* Intrigued, she read on.

The Immortalization of Cade

Part 2 of the 3-part series "To Live Long, First Prosper"

by Rue Gizmo

In Part 1, I explored the Telomerians, the elite longevity society of mega-billionaires experimenting on their own bodies in the pursuit of death-reversing optimization, and the team of doctors and scientists aiding that goal. Part 2 dives into the extreme health regimen of Cade Dicks, a member and evangelist of the quantified-self movement, AnalyMetrics.

I am waiting, close to an hour now, patient as an oak, at a round patio table for two. An oversized umbrella cantilevers against midday rays, which reflect from the marbled pool deck to scorch me from below, just for spite. It is now two o'clock. But for luminaries such as Cade Dicks, time is whatever he wants it to be.

The mega-mansion (he calls it his "cottage," though it would hardly qualify) stands gray and insolent of its tropical surrounds, a sleek and cryptic cube of recent construct, seemingly extruded up all at once from the earth. Like its owner, a mass that creates its own gravity.

He resides in the ground-zero of longevity, the suburban private island of UZALAZU, its name a compu-conjured palindrome. Orbiting most days are fast friends, bankers, and believers. But not today. Today it's only me, recording a Q and A with one of the world's singular extremes. And then it strikes me: this estate, swaddled by a private 9-hole golf course, and that again moated by the bay, was a bunker.

A sunbeam catches twin gold-clad doors ornamented in gears, wheels, and levers recalling a bank vault. They part with symmetrized precision as practiced servants tug on each great panel, the grand gates twice their height. The fortress disgorges my host, self-described healthionaire Cade Dicks, his blue-white smile beaming pearls from the horizon. Accompanied by two assistants, he advances, and I instinctively stand to greet him. He is dressed eclectically in candy-colored orthotic slippers, snug elastic licorice shorts, and a bio-measurement vest beneath an unbuttoned hyacinth aloha shirt.

Gen let the word "eclectically" roll around in her head. It found its way to her tongue, which twisted with the word's unfamiliarity. Curious about its meaning, she bent the magazine over the back of a chair to hold her place and went to the stacks.

The dictionary was dank and the page corners crumbled as she sought the confounding word. She read aloud. "Eclectic. Adjective. Deriving ideas, style or taste from a broad and diverse range of sources. Eclectically. Adverb. Synonyms. Assorted, mixed, ragtag, motley, indiscriminate, varied." *Oh. Maybe his clothes didn't go together.*

Satisfied, she fitted the rotted tome back into its entombment, and returned to her glossy page and her exploration of this unknown land. She continued:

He is shorter than I had imagined, and lithe, his muscles and veins on full display. He's rumored to be in his 50s, but looks every bit of 49. I find myself a little stirred, but mostly awed by the presence of the founder of gaming giant ToobStar, who poured his fortunes from Moon and Mars mining investments into his newly minted non-fungible hemp-inspired currency, Doobieum.

The assistants dissolved away—in their place, a silver beverage cart bearing a cocktail shaker sweating in the humid air, a champagne coupe beside. It's a bit early for cocktails, but I'm prepared to oblige for interview's sake. I actually lick my lips.

Dicks holds the strainer top with a finger as he pours from the shaker into the coupe. He sips. "Breakfast, lunch, and dinner," he says. When I ask if I can try it, his brow furrows. "It's every nutrient the body, or at least my body, needs, in the correct proportions, as determined daily by Dr. Fixx." Fixx is Romeo Billings Effix, a once board-certified nutri-masseur; the man who daily probes and studies every part, that is, *absolutely* every part, of Dicks. "And it takes building up a tolerance. If you had even a drop, your body would suffer a cytokine storm, and you'd probably succumb to anaphylaxis." He downs the elixir in one long, guttural gulp. Illuminated circuitry warps through his glass, changing in time to his pulse. I realize I'm seeing an OLED implanted into the epithelium of his pale forearm just deep enough to escape necrosis — the tick-tocking quantification of self.

The rigors that Dicks puts his body through are what physicians call "extra-medical": techniques that have no data to back them up, and for which research presents ethical concerns. He concedes he has been derided by the conventional medical community and the public for his radical regimen, but then dismisses the objections as "expected and fine."

I want to get into the philosophy that brings him to his next endeavor. I nod toward the garish pool, a sparkling sinkhole in Greek Revival glaring through the lens of too much money. An inscription undulates on its bottom. With a boyish grin, he explains his mantra, "Ordinatio vetat innovatio." I open my mouth to recount it in English, but he beats me to it: "Regulation inhibits innovation."

He gestures for me to sit at the poolside table, then takes the other chair. Casting his gaze to a bright future, he expounds the virtues of aggressive research into cures for a litany of maladies and morbidities; such cures, when perfected, to be offered to the masses. No more illness. No more death. Only the wealthiest can afford to conduct this research. Only these elites dare to experiment on their own bodies in the service of science. As with any hawker, his delivery is perfected, absent the social bumbling common to his ilk, and at a gallop that vaults over the inconvenient.

Yearning, he says, for a life liberated from human contact, Dicks and his fellow Telomerians are forming a new nation-state-at-sea to be free from restraints on their experiments. He and his fellow travelers will undergo a panoply of far more aggressive procedures aboard ship, orchestrated by his and other medical advisors. I inquire about the safety of the numerous unproven regimens to which he subjects his body. "True progress often comes at a price." A buzz and a blink emanate from his ghoulishly embedded device. The interview is over. "You can watch us launch," he says.

Moving fast as if to outrun discrepancies, Dicks takes my elbow and walks me to the circle drive, where awaits a cyber-limo, deep-space-black. A servant averts her eyes as she raises the gull-wing passenger door. Dicks slides into the seat, pulling me in after him.

"We're frustrated by the petty big government regs that block our efforts to explore all avenues to curing death," says Dicks. Hence the Telomerians' pursuit of their own sovereign state, with plans to develop, "sensible regulation around gerotherapeutics, human genetic augmentation, where our lab can work undisturbed—" He stops himself and I panic, unsure if he is having a medical issue, but he continues, "And of course, there are other needful things one can do with a sovereign country."

The cyber-limo whirs to rest on the rough-hewn planks of a commercial shipping dock, in the imposing shadow of the *Seas the Day*, a 3,000-guest pleasure cruise vessel purchased, gently used, by the Telomerians, bound for the open ocean. "It's all ours. Well, not entirely. Not yet. We're obliged in the purchase agreement to honor the existing reservations of some tour group, film fanatics playing dress-up, but only for the first leg of our journey. Lawyers. Am I right? We've been assured they will keep to themselves."

The chauffeur flips up the door for Dicks, who hops out. I follow. He tells me he is the last of the group to board, the ship's engines idling in anticipation of his arrival. "We have *The Day* nearly to ourselves, so let the experiments begin." Dicks grins. "As I always say, the question isn't who is going to let me; it's who is going to stop me." I acknowledge the quote, often attributed to Ayn Rand. "Who?" he says, then he plops into a waiting wheelchair that whisks him up the gangway into the depths of the behemoth before I can say, "bon voyage."

With a whoosh, the cyber-limo is gone. I will need to purchase a ride with one of the pedi-cabs at the far end of the dock. Time enough for that. I watch a flock of longshoremen hustle *The Day* from its berth; a Herculean task. The next time I see Dicks, if he grants the interview, he will be Methuselah.

The tugs nudge the floating city out to sea. The glistening cruise ship ghosts into the half-light. I had come to the interview doubting their claims. I am wondering now whether they will return with an answer that saves all of us from the inevitability of death. I hope so.

On that irresolute note, the article ended. She turned the fragile page, but the promised Part 3 was not forthcoming. Gen placed the gazette back where she'd found it. From another slick cover, a bright red-orange image seared her eyes: a prolific pyre feasting on printed works, papery ash butterflying before giddy minions in matched red caps. The inferno roared godlike, their Mo'ai, hungry eyes a-flicker. Above the flames and rising cinders, a headline, "Science: Are We Rid of It At Last?"

Gen considered Mother's words; why they had fled to Eos. Mobs; burned clinics; murder. If the rabble had found them—

More to escape the disturbing thought than to find anything specific, Gen retreated to the fiction stacks — this time "W–Z." Her fingertip traced along the colorful spines and elaborate titles, landing on a humble hardback, *The Time*

Machine. She slipped it from the shelf, the adjacent book tipping into the gap. *Machines. Edison would probably like this.*

The library went gray, and a sudden chill rippled goosebumps across her skin. A cloud occluded the skylight — or was it the progenitor of night? She could not be sure. In any event, her reading light had abandoned her. Two heavy, ornate wood doors stood sentry, guarding the treasures within. She pushed them open. The hinges squealed in protest, then relented, and Gen dissolved, with H. G. Wells, into the darkness.

Gen looked west, aligning her lounge with the sunset to wring the waning rays of the day upon her reading. With the pages thus sufficiently illuminated to peruse without strain, she flipped open the book. As was her habit, she would skim the first page, and the last, wading into the narrative as a tourist with half a map — intrigued by a journey that could take her anywhere. At the story's inception, a sentence stood alone:

"Can a cube that does not last for any time at all, have a real existence?"
And then these words rang out at the conclusion:

"…and saw in the growing pile of civilization only a foolish heaping that
must inevitably fall back upon and destroy its makers in the end."
Gen could not gather where these concepts might lead, but was up for the expedition, for she had time enough at last. She lowered the backrest of the chaise to the perfect angle and flipped back to the beginning:

"The Time Traveler (for so it will be convenient to speak of him) was
expounding a recondite matter to us."
She rolled "recondite" around in her head, and after failing to make a connection between the abstruse word and anything in her experience, she made a mental note to revisit the library to consult with the dictionary. She read on.

The story and its artful archaic language calmed her, and soon Morpheus intruded on the geometries of the Fourth Dimension and the lively debate among familiars. Gen's eyelids fluttered, and she blinked hard, battling the god of sleep for the riches within the pages.

The breeze stiffened, and she considered inclemency, but the sky was clear and without hint of threat. She continued with the adventure:

"Now I want you to clearly understand that this lever, being pressed over, sends the machine gliding into the future, and this other reverses the motion."

Gen recognized that she, too, was a time traveler of sorts — transported in an instant from the age of science and civility to the inverse.

She heard, rising from the sounds of the ship and the sea, the tones of a woodwind. A melody with coherence and intent. She smiled as drowsiness overtook her, amused that her mind would attempt to fool her again. Her eyes closed. The book collapsed on her chest, open to the page where the scale model of the time traveler's machine vanished "as an eddy of faintly glittering brass and ivory." Her breathing became regular and soon she was in a deep sleep.

The chorus of woodwinds resonated in the bones of the rotting boat, the notes clear and incontrovertibly melodic, drifting over the barren deck in the sticky-warm twilight.

•• ⸺••

A fickle early morning breeze grazed the port side, toying with Gen's locks as she dozed on the lounge chair, the book still face down on her lap. The girl roused to the soft tones she'd heard the night before, now more distinct. She sat up, listening to the tune: high, low, softer, louder, a meandering melancholy melody from a source unseen. She could not quite determine if it was singing or whistling or a music player or even a public address system like Luddy's. *Not the zip-line cable, for sure.*

She dog-eared the page, closed the book, and slipped it beneath the lounge, safe should a shower come. Her mind sped through speculations. Perhaps the ship had another resident after all, or a SoBe had finally arrived to bring her back to Deco. She needed to find him... or her... or them. She stood still, homing in on the direction of the faint but pervasive sound. It echoed from within the inky recesses. She descended the exterior stairs, then moved inboard. Navigating a dim concourse, she continued, each footfall deliberate and gentle and silent to avail herself of every note, optimism waxing with each step.

•• ••—●••

She crept several more paces toward the hint of light beyond a heavy metal door, which lay open to the landing of a set of stairs once used by passengers and crew alike. The lyrical sounds beckoned ever louder, the stairsteps illuminated by a distant promise. "Hello?"

As she descended, the intonations came to resemble an amateur orchestration of wood instruments joined by a faint, eccentric beat. She smiled a little as she rehearsed aloud Edison's lesson on proper greetings, her steps ringing down the metal stairs. As the flight reached a switchback, she recalled his more recent reflection on the prospect of her having to strike someone someday. She stopped. *What if...?*

She made herself smaller and pressed forward, careful now to silence her movements, checking left and right at each step. The foot of the stairs in sight, she leaned down, peeking around a wall to spy on the intruder below.

A cavernous space lay before her, at its far end a broad platform open like a great garage. Scattered holes of varied dimension along the rusted hull sunbeamed to the floor. The oxidized openings sang, their tune rising and falling at the caprice of the wind, the whimsical drumbeat merely the languid taps of a chain against a pole. A grotto of sound and light, devoid of life. She approached the sound holes and covered a rusty gap with her palm, then another, changing the pitch, chuckling softly, having a bit of fun with the ad hoc instrument. Then she sighed. *Still alone.*

Though she had no name for it, she had found the ship's tender garage, where small craft once launched from a massive hatch so that adventurous guests could egress to the open water for sport, or embark to ports of call.

She surveyed the space, much of it undecipherable. Oceanic debris had washed in and out, tendrils of sand and seaweed dried in place, cluttering the floor. An enormous cradle stood empty, some large vessel having absconded out of the broad opening. A rubbery boot mounted on a thin, smooth plank reclined on a heap of puffy orange vests. Racks for small craft, vacant, restraints hanging like snakes. A rope lay in a neat coil on the deck among the dross. She picked it up and looked it over — substantial and sound, free of damage by the elements. She set it aside, supposing she might take it with her.

A lick of sun danced off something silvery. The girl nudged it with a toe, then pulled up the strange-looking object — long, tubular, and slim, with a handle on one end, a sharp point opposite, and a hand-cranked reel of line mounted underneath. She took it by the handle, and her forefinger fell upon a small lever.

A thwack! Gen gasped — the projectile shot across the room, the line squealing out behind. The pointed bolt stuck into a clump of something soft. She began reeling in the line as she walked the speargun toward its unintended victim. She pulled the barbed spear out of its target, some sort of rubbery cloth.

The material lay bunched up against an interior wall, shoved there by an assertive storm wave. She dragged it out to the middle of the floor, stretched it flat, cleared some debris, and stood back to survey its entirety. A small inflatable boat, its pontoon chambers airless. Printed on the soft material was a wheel with the twelve symbols of an ancient myth. Solid support panels ran across its flat bottom. Two oars and a foot pump lay nearby. The craft's rubbery sides had three fill nozzles: one for the port chamber, one for the bow, and one starboard.

A wonderful idea formed in her mind: inflate the craft and paddle away from this lonely metal hulk, gliding atop the water, safe from the aggressive sea creatures. *Yes. I think I can do it!* Like the girl from the old fairytale whose gem-laden slippers held similar magic, she had discovered that the power to go back home was within her grasp. She could finally escape the ship and return to the hotel. Perhaps she could also find out who banished her, and why. Suddenly, the thought of dealing with the SoBes left her dispirited. She considered bypassing Deco altogether and sailing straight home to Eos. *But what about him?*

•• ⋅–◀••

Through the fortuity of the ship's musical interlude calling her belowdecks, Gen had uncovered an unexpected solution to her isolation: a small craft that, with some effort, could ferry her safely wherever she chose to go. She longed to see Kafka again. And the youth could accompany her back to her home. If he wanted to go with her. She hoped so. Of all the SoBe adults, he alone had bothered to befriend her, and given his isolated perch atop the hotel, surely he had no more love for living among them than did she. They would sail by the sun and the stars. Regardless of any storm damage she might find at Eos, they would rebuild it — together.

Her plan had one obvious hole: the finger-sized puncture in the craft's port tube. She sighed. The bellows in her mother's lab, Gen recalled, required a perfect seal. Mother had fussed over the tiniest breaches, securing them with patches and glue she had developed for the purpose. If the inflatable boat could not hold air, it would be useless. She needed to devise some kind of repair to the damage she'd done.

Gen noticed a small rubbery square adhered to the flattened pontoon. *Maybe there's more of that.* She felt along the port-side chamber and discovered a flap. Inside was a kit containing two swatches of the same rubber patch material, a pumice stone, adhesive in a tube, and a printed sheet extolling the kit's merits and usage. Per the directions, she abraded the edges of the hole, worked a dab of liquified glue out of the nearly solid container, and secured the patch to the perforation. The final step entailed a waiting period. Lacking a timer, she counted backward at an impatient pace.

Her countdown complete, she tested the repair; despite her haste, it felt pleasingly secure. After some puzzling over the hose valves, she was able to connect the little bellows to the port pontoon. She worked the foot pump. As the long chamber slowly expanded, her spirits buoyed. *I'll be home soon.*

The inflation was slow going, the soft chamber expanding almost imperceptibly with each pulse of air. She squeezed the pontoon — encouragingly firm. She kept pumping until it grew full and taut and its constitution became resolute. Satisfied, she stopped and disengaged the pump nozzle, careful not to let the valve exhale.

She moved to its twin on the starboard side, attached the hose, and worked the inflator. The chamber flexed but did not rise. She pumped faster. Air wheezed out somewhere unseen. She examined the pontoon's surface, spotting another hole about the size of the one she had just patched. She speculated that the spear might have caught both chambers, but realized such an accident was unlikely. It was an old puncture, perhaps the reason that the craft had been abandoned. *Good thing I have another patch.*

Exhausting the dregs of the adhesive on the last swatch, she sealed the hole. *This better work.* She allowed it to cure, giving it a bit more time than her first repair. Again, she took up the inflation chore. The starboard pontoon flexed with each blast of air but remained flat. She examined her handiwork: perfect. She pumped harder, the pontoon hissing breaths. Hands on her hips, she stopped, frustrated, eyeing the stubbornly flat chamber. She lifted it, rolling it back until she could see its underside. Spanning the starboard and bow chambers: an arc of serrated teeth marks from a creature unidentifiable, the gash wider than the length of her forearm.

All that work. She groaned. The pump flew from her hand and thudded into the wall. She kicked the raft and tore it into rubbery pieces. Flustered by her own outburst, she slumped to the floor, her head in her hands. A tantrum would bring her no closer to freedom. No closer to home. *I'm never getting out of here.*

11.8

Portholes shone starboard, the eventide curtaining the forever sea. Mangroves bridged domains of air and water, and the world's weary eyes grew heavy.

Gen returned to what had become her outpost, the speargun slung on one shoulder, the coil of rope on the other, then she dropped the two finds at the foot of the lounge. She stood beside the port-side gate and the orange ring, gazing across the great bay to the hotel gleaming red in the sunset. The glassy surface beckoned. It still seemed to the girl a mere day's swim; maybe half that again, should the wind be to her disadvantage. She watched the ship's shadow lengthen as she contemplated all the impossibilities of her predicament and her aquatic adversary, unseen. How big was it? How fast? Could she outswim it? She would need to get a look at the beast. Bring it to the surface. Meet eye to eye.

The speargun would not do, its construct best suited for reeling in small fish. She did have that stout rope. But what for bait? An idea came to her — clear, colorful, and kaleidoscopic.

An hour passed before Gen emerged from the bowels of the boat, carrying a sheet of rubber scavenged from the deflated inflatable, the gray skin bulging, its astrological logo sheathing the toxic cargo secured therein. She laid the bundle on the deck. Unwrapped it with care to avert shamanic influence through her fingertips. The twilight glow of nature's ingenuity beamed upon her face, green and blue and caution yellow. Grotesque in form — the fruiting body, a contortion of flesh torn from its moist and secret space deep in the hull. A hunk of the hallucinogenic fungus, as long as her arm.

She tied one end of the rope around the waist of the tumorous growth, the other to the rail, hoping she had enough slack to reach the water. She tossed the baited line over the edge. A splash confirmed success. She looked overboard. She blinked, and the bait was gone. The water surface bulged. The line went taut. In another second the rail ripped from the deck, section by section, steel stretched to breaking, zippering toward the stern. The rope snapped — whip-cracking close to Gen's head. She flinched. Covered her eyes. Then she unfurled herself to look. The sea had calmed, the surface now satin.

11.9

Through the scattered fog, Kafka perceived the whistle: low and mournful and not intended to be heard as much as sensed. The vibrations meandered between the molecules of the encroaching dawn, an implication of sound, as if the lazy rendition was all that was required to convey the holistic character and intent of the renderer.

The youth raised his spyglass to the north. There was little to say which was sea or sky, but he saw what he meant to see, and whatever philosophies dictated Kafka's progression through this world propelled him to fling open the door of his miserable shack.

Gen's green knapsack lay empty on Kafka's cot, its guts arranged neatly on a smoothed portion of the disheveled blanket in a pattern that defied interpretation. The pink beach tote lay in a disregarded wad on the far corner of the bunk. Not simply a collection of the contents of the bags, the items posed in a peculiar geometry: a perfect rectangle in a grid arrangement, five across by three down, the categories not discerned by casual observation and possibly unknown even to the architect of the collage.

A tin of peppermint tooth powder; a partially dissolved soap in the form of a clam; a cast metal object reminiscent of the hotel; a toothbrush fashioned from a hard reed, its bristles pointed toward a wide-toothed comb; moccasins, aligned heel-to-toe, soles up; a coiled braid of flaxen hair, parenthesized by the pair of curled pink flip-flops; a sports brassiere stretched flat across the width of the cot; a pair of shorts inside out; a tee shirt, formed so its dimensions matched the shorts; and triangles of the pink bikini top, straps noodled off the cot's sides, the bottoms fitted between the two skimpy cups. He stared at his composition as if gaining some meaning from the order, count, color, size, shape, or perhaps texture of these novel possessions.

The doleful whistle penetrated the rickety walls. He turned, listening, then swept the artifacts into the knapsack. One item remained, uncategorized: a memprint that had broken free of a family album, depicting a girl in the lap of a silver-haired man in a flowered shirt, the elder reading to the younger from a thick tome, the pair beaming. Kafka placed the image gently, reverently, atop the edge of his dresser, among the mementos of things long forgotten.

Gen's sack slung over his shoulder, he took flight, slamming the door shut — the picture blown to the dusty floor.

•• •—◖•••

The tide had ebbed, exposing the wreckage of man's monuments to himself, concrete chunks relegated to bastions against the ocean's wrath. The jon boat bobbed in the shallows, laden with gear and supplies. Up to his knees in sea snot, Lobster labored to remove debris that the waves had washed into the hotel's makeshift sewer. In solving the previous crisis of sanitation, his repair inadvertently created new obligations that only he would oblige. An unpleasant task for an even more unpleasant man. His callused hands cleared the constrictions, and the pungent tributary again meandered mercifully to the sea.

A thump. Lobster turned. Behind him lay a fish, seemingly fallen from the sky, deep punctures along its flank. Hoyl circled back, swept past the fisher and peeped — then vanished into the gray dawn.

That same moment, Kafka arced from the terrace to a rubble berm across a narrow inlet, the girl's emerald knapsack in tow.

Lobster craned his neck, but could espy the young rebel no more. His curiosity piqued, he climbed to a better vantage. The mists of the early morning remained opaque, but the gruff mariner could discern the contours of a small boat with a white sail — on a heading due west into the bay.

11.10

The morning's mist had lifted, along with Gen's spirits, as she eagerly scanned the waters; no sign of the beast she'd baited in the bay, and beyond the gangway gate, smooth seas. Though she'd been denied a look at it, with luck, the effects of the fungus were enough to quell its malevolence. This would be her opportunity for escape. *I should get my stuff.*

The girl had few possessions; most, she supposed, still on her dresser at Deco. She checked a shorts pocket, the little waterproof notebook tucked safely inside. In another was the brass key; she hoped the tomb had kept its secrets. The time-travel novel had been fascinating; she had planned to complete it, and many more. She snatched the book from the lounge chair and wedged it into the waist of her shorts. *No way to keep it dry.* She sighed. She fleetingly considered staying until she had finished it, then wondered if the man in the library had made himself that same bargain.

··–•–•··

Among the fiction stacks, Gen found the gap that had contained her chosen volume, and slipped it home. Her hand hovered, then recovered the tome, turning at random to "Chapter VI, The Sunset of Mankind." Her eyes landed on a passage:

I thought of the physical slightness of the people, their lack of intelligence, and those big abundant ruins, and it strengthened my belief in a perfect conquest of Nature. For after the battle comes Quiet. Humanity had been strong, energetic, and intelligent, and had used all its abundant vitality to alter the conditions under which it lived. And now came the reaction of the altered conditions.

She closed the book gently, safekeeping the prognostication, and slid it back into the shelf. *How could he know?*

"Goodbye, Captain Thomas Andrews," she said softly to the bones in the upholstered chair, the sibilance of her voice and her soft footfalls expanding in the domed temple.

•• ••—•—•• ••

Gen stood upon the floating platform at the base of the gangway, algae carpeting its grated metal planks in bright green. She gazed across the great bay toward her destination. *Better leave now so I can get there before dark.* From this low vantage, she could see only the top of the hotel. Once underway, her view of the building would be intermittent as she bobbed between the waves. *I'll just swim straight ahead.*

Before her, the surface changed as if the bay had taken a breath. The water parted, a great beast breaching, sending a swell in all directions. The platform bucked wildly. She grabbed the handrail, her shoes sliding on the slime.

From the deep rose a monster of nightmares. Twenty paces from head to tail. Fins sharp as razors and an evil maw agape with dagger rows of fangs, flesh from some earlier meal still dangling. It breached like a righting iceberg, bloated belly breaking the surface in a slow roll.

It was dead. She surmised it had expired shortly after she introduced the fungal mass to the leviathan's gullet. Perhaps its altered state left it unable to respire, and she regretted the unintended cruelty. With the threat removed, at least she could continue her planned swim to Deco.

A creature emerged from a gill slit, surprised by its own surfacing. Its body gray as rotting flesh, bigger than a human child, barbed along its length so as to preclude extraction by its victim. It was without eyes; in their place, bulbous sensory organs pulsed obscenely. Its maw opened like petals of a ghastly flower, exposing concentric rings of triangular teeth. As quickly as it had appeared, it drove its head into the carcass and burrowed until it vanished inside. The white belly of the monster ripped open, revealing a writhing mass, an orgy of sightless creatures hollowing it from within.

Stirred by the frenzy and the rot, the waters around her swarmed with the scavengers. She could feel their meaty bodies impacting the platform in their rabid pursuit of the carrion.

Eyes wide at the horror, Gen backed up the gangway stair, all the way to the gate.

11.11

The hotel stood companionless against the gray-white sky, indifferent to its decline. Within, iron bones and concrete caissons fought back the sea. It could feel the parasites crawling under its skin, roaming through its bowels like worms in an old dog. It seemed to know the names of each of those who had overstayed his welcome. It was tired of their pettiness and their arguments, and resented their complaints and the paucity of their dreams. It considered, in imperial silence, letting its guard down — just once — to invite the waves and the tide to transport the disinvited to their reward.

Now, the hotel could feel the drumbeat of a dozen of the interloper's feet. They swarmed from the rooms and the halls and from every floor. Stumbling, crashing over furniture and idled fishing tackle — the sounds of pursuit, punctuated by the soul-twisting screams of a little girl.

Coral emerged from the mezzanine onto the terrace, the lemur doll clenched tight, eyes wide with terror. A column of children spilled from the same fissure, wilded by the scent of the hunt. The pack advanced past the racks of fishing nets and dried seaweed, the older boys and girls taking strides twice the span of Coral's. Quickly the edge of the almost submerged platform came into view, as hounds and fox found themselves in the shadow of the giant Mo'ai.

"Gimme!" said their leader, a twelve-year-old in tatters and bare feet, a serrated tooth from some outsized benthic beast dangling from his rope belt.

"No!" said Coral, tears washing narrow rivulets down each dirty cheek. She squeezed the plush toy tighter.

Two girls seized Coral by the shoulders. She struggled, a throng of feral children closing in all around.

The twelve-year-old reached to his belt line. A flash of white, and his tooth dagger was at Coral's throat. "Gimme!!"

Coral felt her fight drain, and she loosened her grip. A filthy hand yanked the doll away, and Coral collapsed in a ball of despair. The bully held the prize high as the others closed the circle around him and the pompous stucco god. Bellies worm-distended, they animated scrawny arms and legs in idiot gyrations, a tide of wordless rhythms rising from their gullets.

Coral screamed again and reached out. "My dolly!"

An adult appeared in a window above, and the woman's eyes met those of the young felon. The boy realized the potential for punishment and manufactured a moment for a graceful exit. "You want it? Go get it," he said, mashing the plush toy into the mass of putrefied offerings at the totem's feet, flies scattering.

The horde followed their leader back into the hotel, laughing and jumping in celebration of this most recent conquest, leaving Coral to rescue her doll from its throne of seaweed and fetid fish.

Coral wiped her tears. She stood, dusted her elbows and shins, and smoothed her faded dress. She put her hands on her hips and stared, defiant, at the totem with its shell eyes and soulless grin. "I want my dolly."

Coral reached into the rotting refuse of the altar to retrieve the prized plaything. A cloud of flies rose in protest, landing briefly on her arms and her face, before alighting again on the stinking sacrifices at the idol's faux-stone feet.

She shepherded her button-eyed friend to the terrace edge, dipped it in the water, and groomed the filth from the plush prosimian's frayed fur — a tender baptism by the hands of a child.

There was a splash in the distance, and Coral ceased her ministrations, looking toward the disturbance. Nothing, except a ripple propagating up the canal, curiously crossways to the currents, begotten neither by fin nor flipper. The girl appraised her work, smelled the lemur's stuffed head, scrunched her nose, and headed back inside.

Wavelets broke on the rubble berm that secured the hotel's margins from the relentless sea. Whispers warped in the mists, moist with malevolence.

BOOK XII:

A Storm, He Said, Was Coming

A zephyr softened the late day heat and played with a lock of Gen's hair. She had taken to guarding the gate, as she thought of it, positioning her lounge chair near the gangway egress, the speargun by her side should any beast of the sea trespass into her realm.

In the diminishing daylight, Gen continued the vaunted H. G. Wells novel, having retrieved the moldering title from Poseidon's Library. A soggy appellation for the home of brittle print matter, she mused. Still, if she ever saw Kafka again, she would tell him of the ample literary cache; perhaps she would tell Luddy, as well.

She sat up to surveil her watery domain. With no intruders in sight, she took up reading where she had left off. A half-dozen additional works awaited her in a tidy stack beside the lounge chair, shielded from the elements by another swatch of the inflatable raft. She had little else to do except absorb the sun's nourishing rays, which lifted her spirits and staved off her hunger.

Thumps and clangs rattled the ship's hull, snapping Gen's reverie. Rhythmic percussion moved up the gangway steps. She silently traded the book for the speargun. She aimed the weapon toward the gate, adrenaline coursing with each heartbeat. A glimpse of a crop of deranged dark hair, whipped by an up-drafting breeze. Flustered, she pulled the trigger — the spear whirred through the air, harpooning the life preserver with a thud.

The startled intruder uttered an explicative that Gen had never heard before. A hand shot up, dangling her truant knapsack, the footsteps still ascending. "I may have arrived late, but I'm here now."

She recognized the voice. "Kafka!" Exhilaration flooded her being. She tossed the spent speargun to the lounge and rushed to him.

The youth pulled her tight to his chest, and they embraced. Over the girl's shoulder, he scanned the surrounds like prey on hostile terrain: the weapon on the chair; the fortification fashioned from outdoor furnishings; a bulkhead door, ajar; and the sheer drop left by the destroyed rail.

He took her face in his hands and gazed into her hazel eyes, tendering felicitations of relief at her wholesome and radiant condition. Momentarily, he recalled his errand and offered her the green bag.

"My knapsack!" she said, snatching it from his hand, but genuinely pleased that the boy had thought to bring it. "Um, thanks."

He puzzled at her peculiar label for the item, but then nodded. As she opened her sack, he averted his gaze, taking in the sea.

Gen made a quick inventory: a change of clothes; girlish toiletries; the pewter souvenir; her beaded moccasins; the brassiere, which she concealed from the boy's view; and, curiously, the bikini and flip-flops she recalled leaving in the pink tote. She felt along the bottom for the perfume bottle, then stopped, recalling that it had long ago gone missing. Her hand fell upon Coral's sundered braid — she wondered if the little girl even remembered her, and she hoped the toy lemur was still in her care. There was something else not at hand, though. "It's not here," she said.

The boy inquired with innocence as to what she might have expected to find, then quickly asserted that he had encountered her bag on her dresser where she had left it.

"Mother's journal," said Gen. "Thick, lots of loose papers, with a band around it. Like a book, but handwritten."

The answer inspired relief in Kafka. He mused aloud that if her missing possession were any type of book, it most assuredly would have come to rest upon Luddy's desk.

"Yeah, I guess you're right. Luddy must still have it," said Gen. "Hey, how did you know where to find me?"

He professed to Gen his distress the moment he noted her absence, describing a desperate, top-to-bottom search of the hotel, where he quizzed one SoBe, then another, regarding her whereabouts. No one seemed to know — but, he continued, there was a rumor that she had left for the metal hotel in the bay. So he hurried to her side, remembering, gentleman that he was, to bring her bag.

"All I know is that I was trying to feed Marina and Coral, which they're making me do for some stupid reason, and somebody put a smelly rag over my face, and then I remember waking up inside this place. And I remember a woman's voice."

Kafka was silent for a moment, allowing the cloud of his secret thoughts to pass; then he concurred with her untidy understanding of the incident, but suggested that her view of events might be colored by her dislike of the SoBes.

"Those people are all so mean," she said. "Somebody put me here, and I'm going to find out who and why."

The boy disavowed possession of further details, and offered that no matter the reason, it was unimportant, now that they were together.

"Wait. How did you get here?" Gen ran to the rail and looked over. Tied to a cleat at the gangway platform, a sailboat bobbed and wrestled with the line in the gentle waves. Sky blue with a white sail and just enough room for two. Adorable, she thought. A broad smile overwhelmed her face. This was everything she desired — the two of them, together, without the awful tribe, on an island all their own. And if they wanted, they could even sail away to Eos.

12.2

Kafka studied the beaming girl, then took her again in his arms. His amorous lips devoured hers, his hand traveling down the arc of her back to her hip. Senses overloaded at this fleshly sensation, Gen swatted his paw away. Their lips parted. She stepped back. The youth smiled almost imperceptibly and moved closer, emboldened by her sparky rebuff.

Gen retreated again and took his roaming hand in hers. "There's so much I want you to see. Come on," she said, leading him toward a flight of stairs.

He followed, wincing, her grip so tight he thought he felt a bone crack.

STATUS: SECTOR DAMAGED 01:12:002;03 (See Technical Notes)

She showed him the captain's helm and the constellation of controls, explaining that they could admire the sea around them from that high vantage, as he often did from the rooftop of Deco.

She showed him the zip-line — just like she had back home, which they both could use to speed across the length of the great ship.

She showed him the grandest of the pools, suggesting it could be filled again for a swim, since the bay was rife with creatures that appeared to be particularly unfriendly.

She showed him a hallway with a selection of unmolested staterooms, any of which could be suitable for them to take up residence — one in particular with a balcony that surveyed the seas just like Luddy's expansive suite.

She showed him the vessel's forested park with its walkways and benches, a place that, with some effort, they could make green again.

She showed him the magnificent skylight, the clue to her discovery of the ship's library. She told him of its towers of books — a wealth of knowledge and endless stories to entertain them both — discreetly omitting mention of the deceased captain. With a gruff brevity, Kafka dismissed most works not written by his namesake, and then refused her offer of a tour.

Gen's shoulders slumped with the weight of her deepest wish — unexpressed, and not intuited by the boy. They stood atop the highest deck. He cast his gaze to the horizon, and she studied his profile. Her explorations with him had rekindled her appreciation for the structure, yet the boy's reaction to the ship's wonders seemed indifferent, his denigration of the library most disappointing.

She thought perhaps she was getting ahead of herself. *But why not.* She squared her shoulders and took a deep breath, exhaled, then smiled broadly. "Wouldn't it be perfect if we stayed here together? Just you and me."

Kafka spoke without looking at her. "There are times when I am convinced I am unfit for any human relationship."

"There's everything we need, right here. We just have to clean it up a little, that's all."

The boy scratched his thin beard and furrowed his brow, scanning for a robust counter. He inquired as to how she had managed her requirements for food and drink.

"I've been drinking rainwater. There's plenty enough. As for food, nothing really. But that's okay, because as long as I'm in the sunshine, I'm not hungry."

His brows soared to their highest arch, and Kafka forgot to breathe or blink. Belatedly, he let out a light laugh.

"At least think about it," said Gen.

His eyes fixed upon a shipwreck in the distance, belly up, the hull more hole and hollow. He advised that their bliss would be provisional, as her ship's own hull would rust, become unstable, and roll over. He knew this, he explained with great gravity, as his mother told the tale of just such an incident when she was a young girl. That some had tried it back then. Their ship had overturned and only she had survived, clinging to a raft of corpses. In any case, he opined, the structures were difficult to defend.

"Against what?" asked Gen.

On this, the youth was silent.

Gen's thoughts returned to that first day in the open ocean, lost and weak and alone, when the dreadful fishermen caught her — death all around. "When I, uh…" She stopped, realizing her story of survival would not offer empathy, but only affirm his dire view.

She stroked the peachy stubble of his cheek and touched one of the scars that extended from the corners of his mouth. "What happened?"

Kafka pulled away. "When you stand before me and look at me, what do you know of the grief in me and what do I know of yours?"

Gen wilted. She started to speak, then stopped. *I shouldn't have asked. Stupid of me.* She removed her gaze from him and refocused far at sea, not daring to try to discern which ship had wrecked his mother's life lest she dredge a secret best left sunken.

A moment hung between them — silent, heavy, and unwieldy, the barque of their bond run aground on a barren shore.

Kafka pointed toward the southeast where a large swath of the horizon had filled with black clouds. A storm, he said, was coming.

12.3

Atop the hotel roof, the cooling air called the blades southeast. The smallest windmills turned their fanned heads in unison. The largest of them answered, its rusting bearings relenting to the current coming fast off the sea. Blades blurred into a frenzy, struggling to consume the gusts. Lights brightened for a moment before ancient resistors and rheostats redirected excess electrons through cables to batteries housed in the stuccoed castle keep of the mechanicals. Blackness overtook the afternoon, and lightning played silently among billowing clouds.

Here and there, large droplets thumped the rooftop's patchwork of tar and rubber. The surface of the water tower's stores rippled with the random impacts. Patters struck the east balcony of the penthouse suite. And below, the gods of the air and the sea spat in the eye of the faux stone Mo'ai.

•·-—•··

Luddy rested his elbows on his desk, hands clasped, his index fingers to his lips, while Taffy lounged, catlike, on the heart-shaped bed, languidly turning a page in Gen's mother's journal, the dreamcatcher earring dangling from her plump lobe. "Process number such and such, etcetera, has an effect not dissimilar to reversing many diseases in which telomeres are shortened, such as pulmonary fibrosis, now a fully curable condition."

Taffy flicked the page with her finger. "There's that word again. Telomeres?"

"Ah. Recall when we were discussing DNA, the stuff that determines what you are? They're an aspect of your DNA. I think whatever they were studying had to do with lengthening lifespan," said Luddy. "It appears that these people had solved the problem."

"These people. You mean science people?"

"Scientists. Yes. Perhaps despite themselves."

"If you say so." Taffy yawned.

"Carry on." Luddy stood, taking up the crystal carafe from its home on the cart. He swirled the pitcher to judge the measure of it as he moved toward his window garden.

Taffy paged ahead in the journal, scanning, then stopping short as she tripped over an abbreviation. "What is a 'k-W'?"

"How is it used?" He drizzled precious drinking water onto his pampered succulents.

She found her place again. "Subject physical development exemplary. Exhibits dynamic readings in excess of seventeen kW, sustained, up from twelve in the thirty-day period prior."

Luddy paused, head at a slight incline as if to refill a long-emptied memory. "Kilowatt. It was a method of measuring power."

"Like the lights?"

"And work."

Taffy nodded, unsure. "Huh. What kinda work? Cooking?"

"More fundamental. For example, lifting or pulling."

"How much is this, um, kill-a-what?"

"About the power of six men like Lobster."

"All at once?"

"Yes. All at once."

She skimmed down the page, eyes darting back and forth until she frowned. "Luddy?"

"Yes."

"The thing they're talking about."

"Yes."

"It's a girl."

Luddy froze. Water spilled to the floor.

A boom that would have toppled Jericho resounded through the resort. Thunder rattled the windows — lamps flickered. Taffy gasped. A grinding crunch drew her attention to a fresh fissure in a wall. "We got a new crack."

•·-·—•·•

The idol surveyed a world it could not perceive. It felt nothing in its bones of rotting wood and wire and fiberglass. It remembered not its reign as a restaurant landmark — the grass skirts and pineapple drinks and hipsters and hangers-on. It saw not the offerings at its feet; heard not the songs of praise. It knew not of promises made in trade for health, revenge, or material things. It had not clemency for those who prostrated before it or abdicated responsibilities to it — nor judgement for the ones who had pledged faith before exploiting their fellow, their flock, or the earth. The idol looked out on all before it with its shell eyes and its long dull faux-stone face and it was indifferent.

The torrents beat the sea-snot canals to froth, the dense rain an ocean in the heavens. The gray curtain obscured the gray specters approaching. Carefully, quietly, they pulled their canoes of stretched skin and scattered markings onto the terrace; turned them over. Carefully, quietly, they concealed them with the seaweed the SoBes had diligently laid to dry. Carefully, they snatched the frayed fishing nets from their racks, dragging them behind. Quietly, they glided through the pounding roar with the deft of old assassins, steely tools at their waists glinting silver.

The invaders did not tremble at the feet of the Mo'ai; the true god, they were certain, was fat and golden and alive, the prompt provider of pain. They moved gray and silent, cloaked in the tempest. Probing the hotel's perimeters. Infiltrating its interiors. In this ocean, the gray things, with their gilded god, were the color of death.

12.4

Hoping to escape their awkward silence as much as the approaching weather, Gen and Kafka had retreated from the topmost deck. They found themselves in the garden, in the canyon of vines, the scallop arcs of the many balconies lending form to the amber stems and lifeless leaves. They stood under the naked canopy of a dead tree, the bark and branches sparkling with crystals of salt, a string light snaking up its trunk, a lone withered fruit dangling from the lowest limb.

Kafka twisted the wrinkled sphere from its brittle branch and studied it, perplexed by the once-ruby skin. He brought the corpse to his nose, grimaced at its vinegar scent, then tossed it to the dirt. "A fine setting for a fit of despair," it occurred to him, "if I were only standing here by accident instead of design."

Worried that she had been too forceful in proposing a future together, Gen grappled for a way to return to the sweetness of the boy's arrival. A smile crept over her face as she pointed to her bench. "Wait right here," she said with conspiratorial delight, as she disappeared up a stair. The youth nodded, unsure of her plans.

He paced, uneasy at the imposition — sat on the edge of the bench — and abruptly rose again and resumed his march. A tap on his shoulder spun him around. His eyes went wide, and he let out a surprisingly high-pitched howl, backing away until he thudded into a wall.

"Don't be afraid." Gen was adorned in the blonde wig she'd discovered, lips crimson, her slim body lost in the folds of a pastel frock that, on a more curvaceous frame, might have been fetching.

He slumped, cowering against the wall, pointing at her head.

"It's me, Kafka! It's me!" she said, slipping off the hairpiece and tossing it to the bench. "I found it in a room. It's for girls. To look pretty."

The boy heaved a sigh and rose to his feet. "My 'fear' is my substance, and probably the best part of me."

Suddenly, his gaze moved beyond her, his face twisted in puzzlement. Gen read Kafka's eyes, then turned to see the sky transformed raven-black, the blue ether upstaged by a ravenous monsoon obscuring the entire aft. The hiss of precipitation rose from the clear silence as the metallic cacophony marched from the stern of the great ship toward the bow — a roaring gray curtain consuming all before it.

Boom! A brilliant white bolt struck the fanciful winged funnel atop the aft deck.

Gen grabbed Kafka's hand, and they sprinted. In a moment, the torrent caught them — the stinging shower soaking the pair. They ducked under a sagging balcony, just as a river began to cascade over its side. It became a waterfall — a wall of silver. It bent the light into a halo, shutting out the world with a ring of mist and rainbows and the mesmeric melody of the relentless rain.

Kafka shielded Gen with his body, his sinewed hands braced on the wall behind her. The rain-soaked gossamer garment clung to Gen's form, her curves emerging from the moistened fabric. He slid his hands to her waist. She put her palms on his chest. She could feel his warmth. New; intoxicating. She trembled — so close to the young man, gazing into his eyes.

Kafka touched the tip of his nose to hers. "I've felt abandoned without your closeness. It's all I ever dream of. The only thing." His lips met hers.

Still uncertain of what came next, Gen pulled away. He kissed her again. This time, her lips rewarded him eagerly.

12.5

The pelting downpour pummeled the penthouse roof in a relentless roar, conquering the quiet of the bridal suite. Luddy stood at a window, a fingernail tracing a narrow fissure, the ferocious rain weeping through the imperfection.

Journal in hand, Taffy had parked against the desk, crossed her legs, and leaned back, a palm bracing against languor and apathy. She took a breath to continue, then sighed. "I don't understand this stuff. Doesn't everybody come from the mother's stomach?"

Lost in thought, Luddy located the leak in the pane. He rubbed a drop of the encroaching rainwater between his fingertips.

Taffy turned the open journal face-down on his desk. "I'll read it later," she shouted over the din. "There's too much noise, anyway." She slipped the perfume bottle from her brassiere, and dabbed a bit on her person here and there, where she had known the male of the species to roam. She set the vial on the desktop with a tiny clink.

From the brass speaking tube came a shrill cry: "Bocas! They're here!" A sickening scream erupted from the horn.

Luddy turned to Taffy. "Quickly! The house current!"

She dashed to the mechanical clutter behind Luddy's desk and flipped an oversized wall switch marked "HOUSE." Just as the bulbs went ember black, she rushed to his side. "Let's go," she said, tugging at Luddy's hand.

Lightning spasmed through the suite, illuminating the panic. He peeled her off and stepped back. "Save yourself."

"Luddy! No!"

"Shh. I would slow you down."

"But..." Taffy hesitated.

"Quickly. Go," he whispered.

•·--·—●·•

Taffy felt along the wall and out into the hallway, closing the suite's door softly behind her. She was alone in the inky corridor. Her fingers inched across the tatters of wallpaper to the doorframe of the stairwell. She wedged herself through it in the smallest of increments, lest a squeaking hinge or footfall betray her position. Above, a broken roof hatch flapped in the gale; blue-white shards stabbed through the opening. Eyes wide, breaths shallow, she waited on the landing, listening.

•·--·—●·•

Vigilant, quick, silent, a SoBe man crept across the expanse of the darkened auditorium toward the labyrinth of halls and stairs, and safe hiding. Lightning flickered through a wall fissure newly sprouted from the hotel's infirm foundation. An arm — lanky, pale — swept out of an open doorway, covering the man's mouth, whisking him into the shadows.

The man cried out — a hard, sickening thump stifled his protestations.

•·--·—●·•

Coral's twelve-year-old tormenter and two of his minions, all whimpering and tear-soaked, huddled in the blackness behind a battered wall. The smallest peered through a hole at the flecks of movement and mayhem beyond. The leader shoved him aside, eyes claiming the vantage.

A fishing net cast over their backs — they struggled against the braided nylon, wrapping themselves into a piteous, screaming ball.

•·--·—●·•

The wire sped around two wrists, quick and tight and brutal. A leather braid bound arms at the elbows, a hand freshly amputated. Men and women and children, captive, ceded to fate; dragged by crude bindings. Cadaver gray things slipped between shadows as anguished cries cleaved the dark.

•·--·—●·•

Folded in the wad of her blanket, a SoBe woman sheltered on her bed, as still as her quivering limbs would allow. Hairs stood erect on the nape of her neck. She moved a corner of the bedcover, just enough to make sure the door was closed. It was not. The glint of steel hovered mid-air forever — until forever ended.

12.6

"Wait," Gen said in Kafka's ear as she slipped his arms from her waist. With a shy smile, she peeled the soaked frock from her body and tossed it aside. Her damp top chronicled her nubile shape.

A corner of his mouth turned up, and he took her in his arms again and pulled her close and pressed his lips to hers.

She closed her eyes, relishing the warmth of his kiss, promising herself not to rebuff him again. Her mind was a whirl. *He does like me. He wants me to be with him forever and ever. This is really happening!*

Carefully, quietly, his hand cupped a soft curve; she flinched, wondering if she should allow it, but resisted retreat. Carefully, quietly, the youth's fingers freed the fastener on Gen's waistband, and moved past it.

His brow suddenly furrowed, surprised and confused by his unproductive expedition. He broke off the kiss. Frowning in frustration, he ceased his interrogation of her anatomy and withdrew his hand.

The stunned girl tried to read his eyes. "What? Did I do something wrong…?"

Fighting the urge to accuse her of deceit, Kafka stammered, scrambling to conjure a palliative excuse.

A face thrust in from the cascade — pale and clownish, saliva dripping from cheeks slit ear-to-ear, its Glasgow smile baring rotten teeth chiseled to points.

Gen gasped and froze, her mind overloaded with terror.

The thing glared from lidless red eyes. It stepped forward on gray spindly legs jutting from faded tartan plaid shorts, a filth-encrusted polo shirt draped on its starved frame. The creature raised its silvery weapon in translucent hands, bony arms high.

Kafka pushed Gen hard through the waterfall into the stinging torrent, shouting for her to run.

She stumbled, then sprinted away. She looked over her shoulder. "Kafka?" The balcony groaned and shuddered under the cataract draining from the upper decks. "Kafka!" She started back for the boy. Two more intruders! Her shoes skidded on the rain-slicked planks. She turned again and ran across the deck, the pair of bipedal beasts in pursuit.

As Gen sped away, another grinning devil stepped into her path, its slender silver shillelagh held high. She veered. It swung and missed, then gave chase. *The climbing wall!* She hurdled the corral and launched herself onto the colorful holds and ascended. The fiend started up the wall, the others of its ilk disappearing into the complications of the building.

A clang of metal on metal. Gen glanced back — the intruder's silvered staff reverberating on the deck far below. Surprised at the forfeiture of its weapon at that great height, her pursuer clung close to the rock face. She locked eyes with the thing — human, yet not. Freed of the implement, it scrambled after her with resolve.

She looked up: a dead end. Nowhere to go. To one side: the railing of an upper deck at an impossible distance. She leapt across the chasm, a hand latching onto a slippery rail post. With conviction, the creature followed, bisecting the air in an arc, soaring half the required span before gravity intervened. It clawed at the air, stupefied by its own miscalculation. As Gen scrambled over the rail, a horrible thud. She peered at the pale body crumpled on the lower deck, a crimson pool spreading.

Before she could process the pity welling in her, another of its kind crested the top of the stairs. She ducked behind a cabinet under the shelter of an awning. It was familiar: the cache of equipment for the zip-line.

She was soaking wet, shaking with cold; she thought she might be in shock. She quieted her breathing and listened. No more frantic patter of pursuers' feet.

They seemed to her both malnourished and mal-intended. She had seen no living things like these, the only analog in her studies, a holographic image that had dodged her mother's diligent editing: a subject of autopsy.

She wondered what they wanted with her. She pondered the feral swine at Eos — her trespass on their territory and her narrow escape from their tusks. She considered that the ship might be the domain of these barbaric bipeds, who only now detected the two human strangers. It would account for the inexplicable noises and the deck furniture fortress. She needed to explain her presence, that she had no intention of taking what was theirs. *But how?*

Beyond the cabinet, the deck panels creaked. Gen held her inhalations so as not to draw the gray brute to her rusted refuge.

The creature was upon her, weapon high — a cleaver. She raised her arm to block its arc, and the blade sliced off her fourth and fifth fingers at her first knuckle. Tumbling onto the launch platform, she grabbed the first thing in reach: the t-bar handle she had left behind. She slammed the monster with it. The maniac staggered backward; its cleaver went flying. Shaking, she fit the trolley on the questionable cable. The marauder came at her. She turned in a flash, knifing her hand through its chest. Eyes wide, it slumped to the platform.

Gen looked at her hands, one missing digits, the other bloody up to the elbow — she moaned. Thumping footfalls echoed. Something ghostly moved in the rain. She gripped the t-bar and pushed off into the storm.

Thunder shot fear through her bones as the pulley wheels squealed along the ancient cable. The downpour punished her skin. Between the rainwater and the blood, the handles proved slick; she tightened her thumbs over her fingertips. Mid-flight, she espied an intruder, tracking her from the deck below. *How many are there?* Blinking away the raindrops, she struggled to keep tabs on it. Just as she closed in on her destination, she looked up — yet another creature mounting the landing pad, a metal rod held high. She squeezed her eyes shut, cocked her leg, and kicked — her heel landing solidly on its gullet. It dropped the weapon and grabbed its throat, choking, gurgling, staggering, then folding over a rail. Foam oozed from its garish grin.

Gen's feet touched the rotted rubber of the landing platform, and she let go of the trolley handles. She looked at the crumpled thing. "Oh, no... I didn't mean to..."

Clutching her wounded hand, she ran.

Occult in the complexities of the superstructure, another awaited. From its vantage above the promenade, the thing observed the girl — injured prey. Patient and cunning, the predator judged distance and speed, and plotted Gen's trajectory to the likely point of interception. Blade clamped between its sharpened teeth for safekeeping, it crept as a phantom into position. It narrowed its focus to the quarry below, fast approaching.

It could not perceive the silent flap of wings — only the pinch of metal talons that lofted it from its unrighteous perch. The creature arced out over the sea and within a moment of realizing its new and unfortunate circumstance, the ravenous waters frothed red and it was gone.

Gen soon found herself traversing tufts of sun-bleached green plastic turf sprouting from the smooth surface. Scale models of structures, familiar to her only from her studies, congregated in nonsensical orientation. She was in pain. She crouched behind a tower — flecks of faded black and white stripes spiraled around its tapered cylinder, the fresnel beacon at its apex, fractured.

She unfurled her damaged hand. A shuddering gasp escaped her: a grotesque vacancy where two delicate digits had been. She remembered the scarf in her back pocket and wrapped the bleeding stumps tight to staunch the flow and clamp the pain.

Struggling for air in the ocean of raindrops, she looked around. She was alone in a forest of minified architecture and outsized animals. Fanciful faded representations of a windmill, a barn, a monstrous fish, and castles of sand. A man-sized snail with a broad smile and storybook eyes. A wooden sailing rig helmed by a peg-legged pirate, patch over an eye. A great bird roosting on a nest, atop a single oversized egg. A robed woman on a pedestal, one arm cradling a tablet, the other lofting a torch, a crown of seven rays upon her head. Gen looked into her weary eyes and tried to recall the meaning, but couldn't.

Narrow ramps led to and from and under and through the fabrications, each with a small hole at its furthermost point. She stood amongst the fantastical menagerie, blood still dripping from the rain-soaked memento. She held her wounded fist above her head, hoping to ease the throbbing. Something underfoot. A thin metal shaft with a grip at one end and a cudgel at the end opposite, resting inside a jagged-edged porcelain bowl. She turned it over with her toe. A human skull stared back from long vacant sockets. A delta of bleached bones, their pattern made random by a succession of scavengers. A soul-searing scream reached up from her throat but retreated, drained of spirit.

From between the sheets of sky drumming the deck, a specter emerged — gray and insane and moving fast, blade high. It flung the weapon toward Gen, catching the robed lady at the neck with a clean decapitation, the blade pinwheeling overboard. The liberated head bounced on its crown.

Gen fled, the thing in pursuit. She sped past the waterslide, its orange mouth devouring the deluge. She stopped. Felt the surface of the flume, now slick. Scanned the faded instructions beside. She jumped in, lay on her back per the illustration, and vanished — ferried by gravity and the rain. The marauder dived in head first, slaloming, graceless, gray body slamming against the tube.

The elements had crazed the aged chute with cracks. Banking the curves, Gen glimpsed a hole eager to swallow her, part of the river escaping past its keen edge. Instinct splayed her arms and legs — she straddled the hazard and continued her winding ride. Close behind, the pursuer sailed headfirst across the gap, the far rim catching its middle, cleaving it at the waist. Its bottom half plummeted to the pool. Its top half surfed the thrilling twists and turns of the bloody stream, life spilling out.

Gen splashed into the sludge of the shallow landing pool, tumbled, and came to rest facing the exit spout, legs splayed like a rag doll. Eddies of silt and rodent carcasses swirled about her. She spat and wiped her face.

Another splash — the intruder's top half planed into the water, slosh-landing between her legs, its gray face frozen in a horrible Cheshire grin. The torso bobbed — a fishing float in a shallow ichor sea. Gen shrieked, then rolled over the lip of the pool onto her back. Deep breaths and sobs. She tightened the blood-stained scarf around her throbbing hand. The angry sky twisted and roiled. She closed her eyes, letting the rain wash away the fear.

A gurgling growl. She opened her eyes.

An ashen brute trained its wild lidless eyes on Gen's cranium, wielding a long tubular cudgel overhead. She braced for the inevitable.

A tingle flowed through her body. The marauder's matted hair lifted in urchin spikes, obeying some electrostatic field. A blazing white bolt and a boom. Her ears buzzed. She blinked away the flash-blindness. The assassin dropped to the deck, hair singed, skin blistered and smoldering, its feet adhered to the surface, blown off above the ankles.

Shaken, the girl stood. Steam curled from her clothes. Jagged scorch tracks on her arms and legs mimicked the electric dance of the sky.

Colors and sounds melded, recalling her unworldly experience with the luminescent fungus. Lobster and Edison, Luddy and her living father, wrapped around, twisted, entwined. Edison casting a fishing net. Luddy crashing a seaplane. The fire in her mother's lab. Her bed at Eos floating in the library of the great ship, books aflame. Her parents' angry words echoing down a Deco hotel hallway. Memories juxtaposed with dreams in curious combinations.

The stench of burned flesh yanked her from her illusions.

At her feet lay the scorched corpse. She marshaled her scattered thoughts, then remembered to breathe, inhaling great gulps. The throbbing of the butchered hand crescendoed, the stumps now naked, cauterized by the current. Beyond, the scarf lay in a puddle. She wrung it out and dressed her wounds. The amputations remained a gruesome sight, she realized, and she wondered if Kafka would think her unappealing.

Gen stood above the horror. She had vanquished the alabaster adversaries. Their blood ran anemic in rose-colored rivulets.

Across the expanse she could see a slope of rubble; a balcony, collapsed. The place where the youth had romanced her behind the cascade. "Kafka!"

12.7

Footfalls thundered up the old hotel's top floor hallway, doors opening and slamming shut. Luddy's fingers searched the desktop for the perfume bottle. He pitched it hard against a wall. The vial shattered, the exotic sweetness pervading the suite.

The penthouse door banged open. Butcher's blade at the ready, the gray and skeletal thing explored the space with a tracker's skill, snorting sharply at the foreign fruity fragrance. Between a corner and his beloved bookcase, Luddy stood stock-still, breaths undetectable, his habitual rigidity an asset in this assault. Random flashes crossed the creature's fearsome visage, mirrored in the lenses perched atop Luddy's aquiline nose. The intruder detected no movement. No sound. No scent of living flesh. It grunted and retreated to the hall.

•• ••—•• ••

Coral put her ear to their hotel room door. Determined strides thumped up the corridor. She peeked out — gray shadows moving in the dark. She shut their door and locked the deadbolt. "C'mon, Mommy. We gotta hide."

She took Marina's hand, coaxed her off the bed into the bath, and latched the door behind them. Braced against the pastel tub, Coral held fast to her mother, cradling the near catatonic. The child heard the bedroom door rent from its hinges. Terrifying screams, moans and sounds of struggle bled in from the hallway. She shivered as the spartan furnishings crashed against the walls. For a fleeting moment, silence laid heavy, and Coral exhaled. Then a window shattered.

Jolted, Marina snapped from her torpor, her face now contorted with fear. Her eyes darted around the tiny bathroom, searching for an escape. Marina fixed on a humble rectangle of light. She grabbed her little girl, holding Coral up to the jalousie. "Try to get out."

The girl peered between the glass slats and looked down. A long sheer drop to the sea. "I can't, Mommy. I can't."

Marina espied the ceiling vent and lifted her little girl onto her shoulders. "Pull, little one. Pull."

The girl's tiny fingers locked onto the vent grill. It clattered to the tile floor. Coral scrambled up inside the duct. She peered over the lip. "C'mon, Mommy."

The doorknob twisted slowly — testing.

"Go!" whispered Marina.

Coral crawled away, the plush lemur falling from her little hands into Marina's, the tiny bell on its collar tinkling.

343

The bathroom door burst open. A hellish thing entered, drenched in the stench of death. The gray-faced ghost towered over the cowering woman. Marina collapsed against the commode, holding the doll tight, weeping. A lightning flash revealed the oozing sores dotting her arms and neck. The fiend sniffed her, then growled. In the staccato flashes, it scanned the room with red, lidless eyes. Its cadaverous foot brushed the displaced register that lay on the floor. Then it looked up to the opening where Coral had left behind a trail of tears.

•• ••—••••

Silent flashes of lightning sliced through shadows. Heavy blades hacked flesh and cracked bones. Faces concealed in tight and secret spaces. Faces revealed in luckless moments. Grisly sounds: the severing of sinews, the shattering of teeth.

Scarlet portraits of lives brought to their most horrible end.

•• ••—••••

Fragments of an unholy procession flickered on a wall. Thunder crashed. A pair of pale marauders lumbered down a hallway, hauling two insensible SoBes, heads bloodied, artlessly ensnared in their own fishing net. Dragged by the bindings around his ankles, a SoBe made a pitiful attempt to escape, clawing up bits of rotten carpet with his bound hands. Another invader followed, a vermillion delta meandering down his torso, a limp youth draped over each shoulder.

•• ••—••••

The squeaking wheels of the luggage cart, laden with crimson cargo, squeezed the moisture from the ragged rugs and crackled over shards of glass. Moans of the injured and the dying reverberated in the once-splendid rooms and long halls. Four SoBes, hands and legs bound, lay lengthwise across the tubular rolling conveyance. One hung upside down from the cart's bag hook by his bloodied ankles, tongue lolling in agony. The wicked wraiths ushered their spoils along a row of ornate, arched portals that once led to the sauna, the exercise room, and the business center.

The hotel terrace door opened to the bellowing storm, then closed behind the brass hearse — a recessional of the suffering and the dead.

••-•—•••

Rain pelted the terrace and the faux stone idol. It pinged the metal frames where the SoBes hung their fishing nets — where once were draped bright canvases that shaded happy guests from a southern sun. Skin boats were flipped upright and slid back onto the choppy canal. Wavelets drummed the crafts' taut hides. Canoes thus queued, the bloody booty was loaded with care — no more weight fore than aft, nor port to starboard. Atop a heap, a single SoBe struggled against his restraints but soon drained of energy and hope, whimpered, then went silent.

••-•—•••

The drumbeat of battle ceased, the hotel now host to the wails of those who remained. The tempest, cover for the incursion, had tempered its ferocity. Taffy stood in the shadows of the stairwell, motionless, stifling sobs. The lull in the storm offered her some solace; she momentarily considered that the danger must have passed and that she should rejoin Luddy.

A thing determined and malevolent drew her into the blackness before she could scream.

••-•—•••

Tears streamed down Coral's cheeks as she crawled through the maze of ducts. She felt her way along decades of dust and hair balls and desiccated rodents to a right-angle turn, its terminus a vent dimly lit from beyond. She strained to see through. Looking back: red eyes bulging from a devil's face. The grate burst open. Ashen arms grasped for the girl.

The child's soul-shredding shriek echoed in every margin of the aged edifice.

The clouds had drained their ire. The deluge had spent itself; the pounding reduced to mist. The ship had gone silent save for the trickles of rainwater navigating their way to the sea.

Gen gathered her flagging energies and ran toward the wreckage that was the balcony. Furious caws and a black-purple fluttering turned her attention to the base of the rock wall. A murder of crows had converged on the broken body of her fallen pursuer, the mass writhing like flies. She shuddered with revulsion.

She reached the landslide of shattered concrete and twisted steel. She peered into the pile, searching for some sign, some movement, a tuft of his dark mane — dreading a glimpse that would confirm the worst. A pair of bloody feet and battered footwear protruded from the heartbreaking collage, streaked in delicate brooklets by the subsiding rain. "Kafka!" Frantic, she set to burrowing her beloved from beneath the tons of rubble, flinging away ragged blocks twice her weight, her tears streaming over the catastrophe. "I'll get you out!"

She mustered her strength, hefting a massive slab of reinforced concrete. She tossed it aside. Beneath, a bloodied cranium crushed flat. "Oh, no!" She turned away. Then she dared to turn back. A gray elbow. Tartan shorts. Not Kafka. Simultaneously repulsed and relieved, she scanned the steaming deck for the boy.

Gen rounded a corner and entered a covered passage, coming upon algae-laden tracks trailing in from the rain-washed gangway. *Is this where those things came from?* She followed the footprints, stepping over an upended bench and through a smattering of shards from a concrete planter. Beside a bulkhead door lay a familiar form, prone on the deck — the youth, insensible.

She eased him onto his side. His shirt was torn, his forehead sporting an oozing scuff. Gen took his face in her hands and stroked his cheek. "Kafka...?" She saw his chest rise in response. "It's me. Are you all right?"

His eyelids fluttered, then unsealed. He touched the abrasion on his forehead, then examined the moist red of his fingertips. He blinked and looked up at her.

"It's over," she said, tears welling. "They're all... they're... dead."

Kafka's brow arched. "It is always questionable to intervene decisively under odd circumstances."

She asked him what he knew of the attackers. The youth replied simply that they were called Bocas. He insisted the ship was indefensible, as he had emphatically argued before, and that they should not remain aboard.

As he sat up, he caught sight of the scarf swaddling her severed digits, lending form to her injury, a ruby stain across the moist fabric. Kafka inquired as to the cause and condition.

"It's nothing," said Gen, cradling the injured hand. "They'll grow back."

And for the first time, the boy was sans riposte.

He grabbed the wheel of the bulkhead door as if to pull himself up. She lifted him to his feet. He startled at the ease with which she maneuvered his mass. He leaned against the door, legs uncooperative in his support. His pitiful posture signaled to her his infirmity.

"I have an idea," said Gen. Her footfalls receded into the advancing twilight.

The youth waited apprehensively in the dim and empty and silent breezeway. The first twinkles of stars appeared on the horizon. He crumpled and sat with his back to the door.

The rumble of small wheels announced Gen's return with the deep blue chaise lounge. "Here. Let me help you."

She ushered the boy to the recliner and laid him upon it. Intuiting the angle most comfortable, she adjusted the backrest, the hinge ratchets clicking solidly their accord. "How's that?"

Kafka absorbed her ministrations without protest. Then Gen lifted the foot of the blue lounge, tilting it back onto its little wheels. Surprised, he gripped the armrests tight.

She pulled the lounge behind her, wheels squeaking. "You're right. Let's leave this ship and get back to the hotel." The rig and its reluctant rider sloshed across the ship's decaying deck on a heading due west, where the orange ring, the gate, and the gangway beckoned.

STATUS: SECTOR LOST 01:12:008;14 (See Technical Notes)

The girl looked over the remaining rail and down the algae-stained gangway. There waited the elfin sailboat in the softest blue, tied to the floating platform, white sheets lain across her diminutive deck. Ten paces out and partially submerged, an overturned canoe bobbed in the still waters of the bay, a frayed rope trailing. Waning light revealed a patchwork of familiar two-dimensional grids inked in its translucent hide.

The lack of signs of recent habitation within the steel hulk and its lonely rooms — along with the pale creatures' revealed mode of travel — dispelled her misapprehensions about the strangers, and confirmed they were not indigenous to the once-buoyant city. The silence bespoke their consummate expulsion from the grand and decomposing paradise. She guilted herself for the trespassers' demise and their undignified disposal under black quilts of ravenous crows.

Feeling the boy's eyes surveying her, Gen turned away and tightened the dressing on her injuries. She wondered aloud how the invaders chose their moment to assail her inelegant sanctum, and why they neglected to safeguard their sole means of passage against the impending inclemency.

Kafka was sitting on the edge of the lounge chair, fingertips calibrating the abrasion on this forehead. He offered no theory other than the Bocas' haste: that in the ferment, they must have simply failed to make fast their canoe. He had no thoughts on their motivations, speculating that they might have followed his craft unseen as he raced to her side through the morning mist.

Gen pressed him on the origins of the invaders.

Rubbing the back of his neck, he wove intricate and inscrutable patterns in the viscid air, reluctantly elucidating that the Boca clan resided in the north.

The girl's curiosity piqued, she posited he might be referring to a place she called "the city," a congregation of towering structures and crowds of people at work and at play. The boy professed no knowledge of realms such as she described. He knew little of how the Bocas lived, yet was insistent nothing lay beyond their abode. That was where the world ended.

Gen puzzled over his definitive proclamation — not the first, but the oddest.

She lamented the condition of the creatures and wondered aloud why anyone would contort himself into such an awful beast.

The Bocas, the boy relayed, were descended from the high and the mighty. They had, over time, shed superficialities in favor of survival and immediate sustenance. For this, other qualities were required. The clan pivoted to the practices of marauders — which may have always been at their essence.

The sky had cleared, and the first crystal twinkles appeared in the approaching infinity. The curtain of rain had drawn back on some stage far away, and the strum of the storm upon the magnificent caisson had long ceased. Drips and dribbles tumbled down the rusting façades to visit the deck briefly before continuing their boundless journey.

Waters reached outward pond-smooth to the distant hotel and its artful angles. Upon the lodging's windows, the sparking embers of the waning day melded heaven and earth. The sun and the moon danced for the attentions of Gaia's liquid essence, and the tide abided.

From the south came a soft illumination that divided the bay from the darkening horizon. It resolved into a broad river of the cheeriest blue-green, wending into the gray waters with a radiance to buoy spirits and inspire passion. The glowing river advanced through and around the sister derelicts, their promises of fun, adventure, and romance muted now and forever.

Schools of fish fled the stream's leading edge, overwhelming the surface in arcs and chevrons and excited loops. The air perceptibly warmed and became still. The bulge of fluorescent water embraced the great ship, painting its entirety in shimmering delight. It tickled the hull with aquamarine, and it flowed around and beyond the shoal upon which the vessel was beached, and soon the breadth of the bay was aglow.

"It's beautiful," said Gen. "Come and see."

Kafka rose from the lounge. The pair leaned on the rail, eyes cast over the illuminated waters. If not for the terrifying events of that day, Gen would have thought it romantic. She asked if he knew what caused the breathtaking glow. He told her it came from a place that once made power without the wind, and that had succumbed to the waves long before anyone could recall. Now, the ghost of it set the water aflame.

He turned to her, and she to him. He placed his hands on her face. Something about him — his wild hair, the cut of his jaw, the cryptic knowing behind his eyes. Something about her — her mystery, her smooth symmetry, her quiet power, her transcendent perfection.

"You are so vulnerably haunting. Your eeriness is terrifyingly irresistible," he said.

They pressed together, no atom of space between. And the boy with the wild hair and cryptic knowing and fetishistic footwear opined that they should stay there forever.

Gen looked beyond the youth's shoulder and out across the bay infused with the palliative glow of strange particles and prospects of love. She saw the foundering canoe. She saw its mooring rope trailing, a short length still attached to a cleat, cut with haste. She saw the floating platform covered with emerald slime. She tipped her gaze to the great ship's deck, where an accretion of green tread marks grayed in the waning light — the tracks in accord with the discrepant stamp of the boy's mismatched soles.

Their forms parted and Kafka leaned in; she turned away, his kiss landing on her cheek, his hand trailing her arm down to the fingertips as she left him at the rail.

Gen stretched open the maw of her knapsack, fishing out her moccasins, the spare clothes, the bikini and sandals from the flooded clinic, her toiletries, and Coral's hair braid. Missing: one bottle of perfume (child-size) and one scientist's journal (well-worn).

Neatly stacked, the books borrowed from the ship's library waited patiently with their shipwrecks and prophets and poets and ancient heroes and robots dreaming and tomes aflame and invaders from dead planets and travelers through time and love unrequited. She was glad she had covered them with a swatch of the inflatable boat. It protected them from the burning rays and the drowning rain — with the unplanned benefit of concealing them from the grinning marauders. And now she wanted them in their best condition if she were to share them with Luddy. She slipped the largest volumes into the sack with care. She began to add the remainder by size and by mass so that each would be safe in transport.

The boy, jealous at her redirected attentions and curious as to her intent, fired a romantic salvo. "You are full of cloudy subtleties, and I'm willing to spend a lifetime figuring them out."

The girl paused her task to confirm that her notebook was on her person. She felt another pocket for the tarnished brass key and fished it out, shielding it in her palm from the boy's view. She ruminated on the secret room and phantom boat that ferried her on romantic dreams and under sparkling constellations to Eos, and into the warm embrace of family and old friends. A trip she hoped the two of them might venture. How foolish it all seemed now.

"I'm going back," said Gen. She pocketed the key and began to repack her personal items around the books to best secure each tome from abrasion.

Noting the urgency of her movements, he moaned that there was no pressing need to return to the Deco hotel.

The knapsack was plump with cargo, yet one small paperback remained in hand; an extra piece after a completed jigsaw. Gen glanced up at him. "You were right. This ship is indefensible. It isn't safe here."

To that, the boy had a visceral reply. He grabbed Gen by the shoulders and lifted her to him, lips ravenous as in those moments beneath the balcony's silver cascade. The book slipped from her hand. When he finally relented, she opened her eyes.

He said, "It was not my intention to make you suffer, yet I have done so."

A pop echoed across the expanse.

"What was that?" she asked, as a trail of smoke arced in the distance.

Kafka shrugged and shook his head, speculating that Luddy might have fired a flare in error. The youth asserted that the tall man was not adept with mechanical things, and it was only by happenstance that he had not already burned the hotel to its foundation. Then the boy seemed to brighten, suggesting they stay the night; he would be willing to remain a few days just to be together.

Gen retrieved the paperback she had dropped to the deck. Her lapis pendant flopped against her chin. It was the first time she had thought of it since the boy had come up the gangway of the great ship. She felt its precise contours and recalled her mother's strange words: that they had tried to mend the world. Her destiny, they had told her, was in the necklace — that the details were revealed in handwritten notes between the worn covers of Mother's journal, and that she would understand when she was older. Having seen this depleted land, it seemed her parents' efforts had failed.

She mulled his offer to remain with her, frustrated by his equivocation. "You were the one who said we ought to go back."

Something about him darkened. A change in his countenance like a cloud before the sun. The youth attested that he had made no such suggestion and that she lacked the insight to interpret his meaning and intent, a flaw that bode ill for her future. He reminded her that Luddy had possession of the journal and her secrets — as did Taffy, in all likelihood. She was different, he said of Gen, and the SoBes detested the unfamiliar.

She wondered if he was right, and that she had been exiled simply because she was not like them. She was stung by the intrusion into her mother's writings and regretted not snatching them back from Luddy. Her thoughts clouded with what could have been unearthed from it. Things about her. Things even she did not know. If ever there was proof that she was a threat to the trepid tribe, the journal would be ample damnation.

Gen retreated to the chaise lounge and sat down to load the last book into her knapsack. What Luddy might do if she returned was uncertain, but she knew that the truth about her past and her future was not to be found here on this ship. That truth lay in the notes written in her mother's hand, resting upon a desk, atop a decaying building, across a vast and treacherous bay.

Another pop. An orange comet sailed skyward, a smoke trail arcing unmistakably from the Deco hotel's penthouse balcony.

Gen detected defeat in the youth's eyes as if a secret lay bare. "It's them, isn't it?"

The boy's brow furrowed, and he said that nothing could be done; that her request was unreasonable; that if they set sail for the hotel, it would take much time to get there.

She redoubled her effort to fit the final volume into the top of the overflowing pack — the collected works of an author long dead: *Metamorphosis and Other Stories*.

Watching her struggle, Kafka spoke. "A book is a pickax for the icebound sea within us."

It could not be known what the boy thought, or if he thought deeply, or at all. This she knew. That his overtures rang familiar had given Gen little pause. She had read the same brooding stanzas in her own books at Eos, and she surmised the youth must have had meager fodder for discourse in encounters romantic. Still, she had appreciated the creativity in his repurposing of the author's words; she yearned to apply such inventiveness to her fledgling poetry.

Now reappraising his merits, she found he bore none that she had, of late, discovered in his namesake: a man known by contemporaries for sincerity, absolute truthfulness, and precise conscientiousness. Rather, the boy was coarse, equivocating, cavalier, obtuse — a hardened shell, enigmatic in its core. There was little resemblance, she supposed, aside from his spare stature and disagreeable accommodations. The name and cadence borrowed sans the spirit, the youth's genius diverged, too, from that of the long-suffering scribe — being relegated to the recitation of appropriated writings strategically placed for maximum manipulation.

Gen turned the book on edge and tried to work it in, hoping to take advantage of some unseen asymmetry in the scant space in the sack.

Playing de Neuvillette to the author's de Bergerac, the handsome youth had wooed her with the words of another; words he could nary understand. He had twisted the sensitive and gifted writings of the scribe into tools of contempt, made vulgar for having left his lips. Worse, it was not from ignorance but from a black hole for a heart, and his libretto now rang hollow as music manufactured by a cold machine. And the slime on his shoes confessed that it was he who severed the canoe from its mooring.

No matter the angle or approach, the remaining book would not submit to inclusion. Gen sighed and sat on her heels. Her wish to take it was out of sentiment, she realized, having consumed every word during her banishment to this island of steel. She wrapped it in the rubbery piece of the inflatable raft and laid it to rest beneath the blue chaise. She pulled the knapsack's drawstring tight and secured the flap.

Gen's eyes fell to her ankle and the inky arches of the two seagulls in flight.

12.9

Knapsack on her shoulder, speargun in hand, Gen sped down the gangway stairs, her footsteps ringing the metal treads. Kafka's enchanting craft awaited: molded of fiberglass and plastic and a mere four paces long — a child-sized vessel more suited for play than serious seafaring. She looked up the steps at the boy hovering at the gate. "I'll come back for you."

Kafka glanced at the Boca canoe, now farther adrift. Beyond retrieval. He warned sternly that she had no experience with sailing a boat.

A pop from across the bay sent another orange projectile skyward.

"I can figure it out." She tossed her belongings into the sky-blue hull, climbed into the wobbling and bobbing craft, and sat down, then took an oar and dipped it. The mooring line tugged taut; she began unwinding its hold on the cleat.

Eyes wide with alarm, the youth hurdled over the gangway gate and bounded down the stairs two by two. Amid the metallic clatter of his footsteps, Kafka warned it would take hours to reach the hotel. She could help no one. She would die in the attempt, along with the rest — all for people who hated her.

Finally free, the little craft edged away from the platform. The boy leapt the growing gap, landing next to the tiller, the tiny vessel close to capsizing. Gen clutched the gunwale. She moved just fore of the mast as the youth folded his lanky limbs into the pilot's position of the single-handed sailing dinghy.

••-•—•••

They embarked across the luminescent bay. The boy used an oar to align their ark with an agreeable breeze, then he hoisted the modest sail. With some hesitation, the canvas billowed white and full and soon the dinghy languidly advanced toward its terminus — the old hotel, fading pink and gray with the day's end.

Gen looked back at the place of her exile: the once-floating island, the size, it seemed, of the entirety of Eos. The great vessel slept on the bed of the bay, an eternity from favored ports of call and following seas. The queen of empty promise waited stately and patient on her brackish throne for karma and rust to roll her over.

Reclining against the gunwale, she contemplated the sky, then the waves rippling silver as Selene broke full over the bay. Gen studied the boy as he finessed tiller and sheet, ferrying them across the inland sea, his hair tossing in the wind.

Rainwater sloshed into Gen's shoes. She hoisted her knapsack to the higher ground of her lap. The craft rocked, rolling a small cup against her toe, a string tethering it to the gunwale. She began to bail, guarding the sack on her knees, preserving the bindings and the pages of lives and experiences and wisdom and what-ifs that had lent her solace and guidance in the days of her banishment. The books would add to the body of knowledge that Luddy conserved in his garish suite atop this world.

Another volley of signal flares illuminated the night. Beautiful in their own way, she thought. Had it not been for the loneliness of her expatriation and the recent savagery, this tableau would be idyllic. The gentle waters, the Moon, even the sparkling arcs over the hotel — and most of all, the young man who propelled them across their private sea, whose mind and motives were once a delicious, opaque mystery to her.

She turned her gaze to the dome of stars. The constellations presented to her the boundless possibilities, and she began to contemplate the consequential course that humanity had charted upon them. From a book in the ship's library, she recalled the terse words of an ancient sage: "Choice, not chance, determines your destiny." The peoples of the world had made that choice and had not chosen well. They had reduced themselves to the savages of their prehistory. They had squandered the bounty forged by their antecedents: the limiting of suffering. And they shared, now, only in limitless suffering.

The shape of an owl stenciled the twinkling tapestry above, and Gen sensed that Edison and her family at Eos were still, in some unknown way, watching over her. She traced the pearlescent beads of her necklace with a fingertip, pondering what destiny lay before her, her bedraggled hosts, and the little girl she would call her friend.

In a few days, Gen would embark on a bold venture that would change the course of her future and the fate of the world. In time, she would study the writings of her forebears, distill the aspirations and desperations that sparked her creation, and come to recognize the glory and the tragedy of her existence. And after thirty-four revolutions of the dead planet around its star, she would hold the hand of the one she cared for most, until the once tiny hand that had inked twin birds — one larger, one smaller — slipped away.

·· ·—·—●·· ·

And in time Gen would float in the sea with the ghosts of old philosophies and with the endless pain and toil that yielded less than nothing in the long shadow of selfishness and ego and the coveting of things minor in major ways; and the thing that had come down from the trees in that distant dawn multiplied and spread and laid waste to the thin skin of decay that mirrored to them art and love; and the many could not or would not see that great wave rushing toward shrinking shores; and those who could see the coming change could do nothing against the rush of time and the water and the fire and the wind that swept the dying surface of the earth; and another thousand years or a thousand-thousand would pass before the islands of their rubble hives would be drowned and the water would rise ever slower until the poles again froze and land emerged washed clean of the living breathing toxins that had changed it without consideration for what had to be; and the earth patient and earnest in its endeavors and in its own time restored to a degree at least the faded memory of what had been before; and at this moment the girl of the forest and the waters and the creatures and the soil floated asleep on the great sea and dreamt of the upright stands of bamboo and their inviolable pact to bloom and die together and rise from the earth again stronger and to rise into the light once again to undo the mistakes that could be undone.

The dainty dinghy changed tack, and the sail flapped. Gen roused from somnolence. The sheet filled with wind in the boy's adept hands, and he centered the tiller, the bow pointing to the jagged mosaic signaling their journey's end.

Then Kafka remarked, somewhat offhandedly, that the Bocas were cannibals.

She would not hear him; she did not want to hear. For now, she was contented. The warm breeze. The water glowing the softest aquamarine. Comets crossing orange in the night. The velvet surface bulging here and there with the rhythm of life. The little sailboat gliding across the bay. The beguiling boy at the rudder. Lulled by the lap of wavelets against the thin plastic hull, Gen closed her eyes to hold onto the dream, if only for a moment longer.

Postscript

"If seas rise 20 feet over the next 2,000 years, our children and their descendants may find ways to adapt. But if seas rise 20 feet or more over the next 100 to 200 years — which is our current trajectory — the outlook is grim. [...] Warmer temperatures following the previous ice age caused disintegration of one polar ice sector after another, causing seas to rise in pulses of three to 30 feet per century. Today, accelerating ice melts in Greenland and Antarctica are almost certainly the beginning of a new pulse of rapid sea level rise."[1]

- Harold R. Wanless, PhD, Professor and Chair of Geology,

University of Miami

---

[1]. Wanless, Harold R. "Sea Levels Are Going to Rise by at Least 20ft. We Can Do Something about It." *The Guardian*, 13 Apr. 2021.

Afterword

The joy in the dusty toil of archeology and paleontology is in finding bits of things, filling in the gaps with likely truths, and supposing what the whole thing was most likely like. The cave and rock wall art of our prehistory is a whisper from our hairy and loping progenitors, a story of their days on this earth. Such narratives, fading inscrutable with the passage of many dozens of millennia, are left for the imaginations of the various doctorates from which to dream a plausible tale.

So it is with ancient documents, texts and letters. Original religious writings may dwell in decaying scrolls until discovered, or reduced to ash by zealots doing what zealots do. With unrealized literary works, perhaps an author was taken by the reaper at a moment inconvenient to his publisher's deadline; such inspirations may sequester in a jumble of notes until tossed into the hearth by heirs, or sorted and edited into an assembly worthy of a reader's time.

Restoration is sometimes a matter of literary forensics: analyzing existing fragments and synthesizing new material to resonate with the same brightness as the original author, if carried through to fruition. One might consider what may have been in Dante Alighieri's secreted space the night before he died; an unfinished poem to his beloved Beatrice, perhaps. Beethoven's 10th symphony remained a pile of jots and scribbles until musicologists and computer scientists transposed his essence into code and bridged the space between the notes to extrapolate the composer's likely attack, if not the zeitgeist of his time.

With degraded texts and art, such as that revealed from our deciphered cube, the toil lies not so much in synthesis, but in discovering the meaning of those works and restoring their former glory. The publication you hold in your hands is the fruit of just such labor.

A note on the restoration:

During a bucket-list excursion to the majestic New York Public Library main branch, I found, quite by chance, the artifact: a holographic data cube of iridescent material with odd and deliberate markings. The artifact seemed casually slipped in the stacks, collapsed between the pages of a lonely mis-shelved and un-catalogued book of prose poetry. Admittedly, I am no technologist; in fact, I am behind the curve in all things digital. The cube was far beyond my personal ability to decipher, so I assembled a crew with the skills requisite: a moonlighter from a government cryptology lab, a retired physicist from CERN (a family friend), and a forensic linguist, to name a few.

Thus began a search for what was recorded inside and its meaning. The story that emerged is a reconstitution of the data extracted from the artifact, and the re-ordering of components that appeared out of sequence.

The narrative unfolded initially as a note of thanks from some unknown future; gratefulness for a teen girl's contribution to the mending of the world. So profound was the message that an eccentric personality of Silicon Valley fame fueled my team's continued efforts with an R&D grant.

Over 18 months of teasing the data from the quantum realm, the team extracted as much of the text as possible, given the artifact's ephemeral construct. What resulted was the tale of a young girl's remarkable odyssey, and the story of her fall through the nightmare looking glass of our shared destiny.

Some material was degraded during the process of conversion ("lossy" as the computer geeks say). The research team and I would like the reader to know that we made every effort to restore the narrative to its original meaning. A few creative liberties were taken in assembling the narrative, and I beg the reader's forgiveness.

Due to the nature of the data extraction and interpolation, the story features experimental elements. Irrespective of the narrative's technical genesis, BAMBOO is presented as fiction.

I would like to thank the scientists, linguists, and others who have contributed to the restoration of the text. Their names and university or government affiliations have been withheld by request, given the politics of the moment, and in consideration for the safety of their friends and family.

Clark Hilton, Los Angeles

Technical Notes

The artifact had much in common with ancient manuscripts. As with such texts, we wished to reconstruct the original narrative from extant corrupted versions. Just as with historical documents, this challenge is of cardinal importance to the humanities.

About data extraction from the artifact:

Among techniques for extracting data (including manual techniques), we used a proprietary variant of Expectation-Maximization (EM) to solve this problem. To perfect the story structure, we paired this approach with a comprehensive review by developmental book editors and a celebrated writer who has participated in motion pictures with an accumulated box office of over one billion US dollars. In a small number of cases, literary contributions (i.e., synthesis) bridged the gaps in the narrative lost to incomplete inscription or intermittent extraction. The team tasked former members of US government agencies in the fields of cryptology, astronomy, and astrophysics to confirm certain aspects of the cosmological key used to unlock the contents of the cube. With a little math, the key was located in the constellations as they would look at a particular longitude and latitude, approximately 1,024 years from the date of discovery. The details on this approach will be included in future editions of this manuscript, contingent upon clearance from the appropriate US government agencies. Our paper, "Quantum Interpolation of Data Extracted from Non-Dimensional Ephemera Utilizing Contemporary Narrative Constructs," is pending peer review.

In the span of the 18-month project, the quantum cube was analyzed with digital forensic methods, with the primary goal to reconstruct literary writing processes, analyze writing methods and strategies, and contextualize them within the parameters of contemporary forms of historical and literary restoration. The procedure was mostly successful albeit inevitably inexact, each pass introducing some errors into the text. Orthographic discontinuities were accommodated due to considerable drift from the modern standard.

The original "alphabet" was not found among the known living or dead languages. Some holographic stereometries resembled combinations of Arabic letters and Linear B, where the phoneme could be reproduced by projecting high-intensity coherent light through the symbol.

What followed was a restoration of the narrative, incorporating reconstructions and minimal new material. Sections identified in Exhibit Beta as "Lost" or "Damaged" define regions where extraction failed in toto or where the narrative could not be logically bridged within the time constraints imposed by the original research grant.

The forensic analysis produced deep reconstructions of writing methods and identified singular text processing strategies. This analysis traced processes stylistic, historical, archival, and provenience to help the research team assess intent and more closely match the original meaning. Anticipated holographic file formats were applied in this procedure (see US government agencies, above).

During the reconstruction, certain forensic features typically discarded during archival processing were recovered for reference, such as data anomalies embedded in document files and metadata granularity.

The quantum lattice proved markedly fragile in the contemporary setting and over time. Extracting the data was lossy, produced noisy text, and ultimately proved destructive to the recording media. It maintained a serviceable state of preservation with only a gradual degradation of extant material until suddenly sublimating to what appeared to be a boson-fermion plasma, precluding additional scans.

About sectors labeled "lost" or "damaged":

The names of sectors marked "lost" or "damaged" are artifice — constructs of our own. The reader should not infer, imbue, or attribute any meaning to the manner of the cataloging of the scans as they were not extant in the original data. The nomenclature references the positions, time/date, and success rate of each set of extractions. We have maintained the internal system of cataloging for our convenience only.

About AI-generated prose:

The story of Gen is not a work generated by artificial intelligence. To preserve the integrity of the narrative, 99.093% of the material was derived directly from the artifact, and the remaining 0.907% was restored manually via creative methods or interpolated from a private, cleared database of our own construct.

No part of the source or bridging material was manufactured using the publicly available AI-driven natural language processing tools. Common tools such as proximal policy optimization and generative pre-trained transformers have their place. Such tools were not applicable to our task of preserving the integrity of the extracted material.

About "artistic license" and Machine Learning (ML):

ML was the primary interpolative tool for the recording matrix sectors where the narrative was significantly intact but lacking clarity in dialogue or description. This toolset consisted of the team's Quantum Cognition Engine (QCE), working in parallel with the aforementioned EM algorithm, on a proprietary, schemaless database containing popular public domain works of drama, fiction, and religious texts from antiquity to the present.

Given the context of the narrative at a particular point in its progression, the algorithm sorted for the best match to the question, "What goes here now?" from the selection of all likely conversations, dialectics, sermons, and settings. Because the human story is shared and possesses few variations on a theme, this proved an elegant and expeditious means to an end.

The quantum cognition method of reproducing otherwise unavailable text ultimately introduced an eclectic and perhaps uneven tone but has proven superior to ad hoc dialogue writing for preserving the meaning of the passages. Any usage of material excerpted from existing works that are not in the public domain is intended as transformative, and the team apologizes for any error or omission. The recovered text is presented as the novel, "BAMBOO: A Post-Apocalyptic Odyssey," and serves as *Exhibit Beta*.

The following letter was the output of the initial data reconstructed from the cube's superficiality and was the motivating force in attaining the original research grant. See *Exhibit Alpha*.

Exhibit Alpha: "Gramercy from the Scions"

Greetings from a distant future!

We, your beneficiaries, send this message to you, our forebears, with gratitude from the time ahead. Whether by some quantum-manipulator in your own twilight, or equivalent near magic, the means by which this missive comes to you is of no concern. That our intent to send tidings is enough. That our blessing caused some harmonic, some ripple or vibration in the universe encapsulating our good will, is quite sufficient, as we have then repaid our great debt to you.

We cannot presume that the story of Gen was inspired by some real person, or if her travails were some amalgam of parables told from mouth to ear, embellished for color or cause. We can only say with certainty that we are here, and that we would not be, had Gen not been, in some form, physical or philosophical.

It is too late for you. Your time is lost to the ages, buried under layers of missteps and foible. Not all is lost. We, the heirs to all you have wrought, good, but mostly bad, find you yet still deserving of our most sincere appreciation. For it was you who destroyed the world. You provided us the paradigm of how not to be. You, by your imperfections, have also sent us the deliverer.

Know that we are content. We are happy and fulfilled. We observe. We seek understanding and knowledge and self-knowing. By our combined will, we sought to mend the world, and have. We followed your formula, though not precisely. We have turned it upside down. Inside out. Right to left. What you have done, we have undone. What you have hated, we now love. What you have coveted, we share, and with the ultimate in equity. We live in abundance, beyond reproach, and in a rare crisis engage all challenges with equanimity. We live our lives unafraid. We dance and laugh and make music, and create new realities as if the cosmos were clay in our hands.

In the fog of our shared history, beneath the layers of faded memory, myth, and misrepresentations, there is one truth. One way to be. A single path to whatever perfection can be attained: to be kind to ourselves and to all things great and small.
We appreciate your infinite pain and your tears.
We appreciate your steadfastness in strife.
We respect your hope when there was no justification for hope.
We are your legacy.

With joy,
Your Scions

Acknowledgments

SPECIAL THANKS:

To our editor, Shaun Duke, PhD English, Professor of Digital Rhetoric and Writing, for helping us tease the narrative from the ether. Dr. Duke is an active participant in the science fiction and fantasy community, and four-time Hugo Award finalist for his podcast dedicated to examining the literary, cinematic, and cultural world of science fiction, fantasy, and horror.

To Edward Saxon, Oscar® winner, Professor of Cinematic Arts, University of Southern California, tibi gratias pro inspirante.

To Derek Murphy, PhD, story magician and creativity alchemist, for sharing his expansive knowledge of narrative architecture.

WITH MANY THANKS:

To our literary agent for seeing the possibilities.

To our publishers for their vision and agility.

To the scientists who contributed their brilliance and their weekends.

To the mystery financier, who shall remain mysterious.

To the university for the lab space and the many kilowatts of power.

To that other munificent PhD for telling us what goes where and why.

To our intrepid attorneys for their magnanimous and clement reckoning.

To friends for their tolerance.

To Homer for the map.

To that visitor to 7 Eccles Street.

To the New York City Public Library and libraries everywhere.

To the reader, in hopes of your amaranthine kindness.

To Gen for mending the world. We hope we got your story mostly right.

NOTES:

I owe a debt of inspiration to Kahlil Gibran, author of *The Prophet* (1923), for the cadence of the gravelly dialectic at sea.

Passages were energized by James Joyce's *Ulysses* (1920), passim; notably, a bit of seafaring business expressed as Platonic dialog, and the omniscient, augury passage in the story's resolution.

A bottle of aqua vitae to Robert Louis Stevenson and his House of Shaws, which inspirited Gen's treacherous climb.

Much joy and felicitude to Felicia Fairhope, author of *2 Weeks 2 Utopia*, who translated the public domain works and letters of Franz Kafka from their original Praguean German into idiomatic English, and who would accept but a single rose for her linguistic toils.

A note of acknowledgement to the historic figures surrounding the ill-fated *H.M.S. Titanic* for the archetype of the stoic captain of the *City on the Seas.*

A tip of the hat to Herman Melville, author of *Moby Dick* (1851), for his themes of obsession and Gen's recollections of having the story read to her by her putative father.

Gen's reading encounters were enriched by excerpts from the 1895 novel, *The Time Machine,* by H. G. Wells, an early exemplar in the realm of eschatological expression.

I am indebted to Rod Serling and his fabled TV series, *The Twilight Zone,* for a mother-daughter quarrel influenced by a fragment of the 1960 episode, "The Lateness of the Hour," and for the workshop commotion transformed from "It's a Good Life" (1961), teleplay by Rod Serling, based on the 1953 short story of the same name by American writer Jerome Bixby.

Deep background for scientific verisimilitude was inadvertently provided by countless vaunted journals and magazines and newspapers and no small number of frustrated professors, whose influences over the years are both greatly appreciated and too numerous to catalog.

A passage in Gen's metadream was inspired by a moment in the 1939 motion picture, *The Wizard of Oz* (story adapted for the screen by Noel Langley), a film in which the author's affable and lionized cousin played a starring role.

Architectural elements, particularly the old hotel, were conjured from the author's own memory of being kidnapped as a child, ensconced in an ancient resort hotel on a faraway shore, and allowed to run amok for an eternal summer — resulting in a basement-to-rooftop familiarity with all things "hospitality."

The aphorism, "Choice, not chance, determines your destiny," often attributed to Aristotle, is rendered from the philosopher's preeminent work, *Nicomachean Ethics,* c.350 B.C.E.

A Note on the Type:

Crimson, a serif font influenced by the vaunted Sabon typeface and others, appears throughout the body and major headings. The sturdy san-serif face **Alte DIN 1451 Mittlelschrift**, inspired by DIN, appears in headers & footers, section numbers, and the sector status indicators. The title is set in the futuristic display face, **BEBAS**. Occasional special fonts include Sexmith in the author's note to the reader, handwriting script **Comic Jens Free Pro** in Mother's journal, Helvetica Neue in Dr. York's transcript, the penmanship script *Imrans School* for the bottled missive, Web Serveroff in the Scions' gramercy, and **Typographer Gotisch** to cast the calligraphic curse.

About

The Author

Clark Hilton is a writing duality who, as prognosticator, marcom master, screen scribe, and business innovator, has garnered over 200 awards including 15 Tellys and an ACE nomination. As a technology entrepreneur, Hilton developed an intelligent, network-effects-driven infinite-sided SaaS platform that recombines underutilized IP into new business opportunities. Hilton is also a children's storybook author and writer of science-focused edutainment.

The author oscillates in the quantum realm between the swamps of Hollywood and the hellscapes of Florida. To learn more, visit ClarkHilton.com.

The Artist

The spirited depictions introducing each Book were created by fine artist and illustrator Csaba X. Kasik using original ink techniques, inspired by the design concepts of the author.

Kasik's work features pencil & ink drawing, painting, and experimental techniques and materials. To learn more, visit CsabaXKasik.com.

The Narrator

Chuck Brown grew up listening to the radio, and was fascinated, both with the music and the voices of the people who filled the spaces between the songs with entertaining and informative banter. He has been a voice on radio and television for many years.

He is a fan of audio books, and has hundreds in his personal library. He has found great delight in reading audio stories for children, as well. To learn more, visit ChuckBrownVoiceover.com.

Reading Group Discussion Questions

For a comprehensive study guide, see: ClarkHilton.com/bamboo-discussion

1. How is the protagonist like the average teen? How does she diverge?

2. Gen is told that it is her 16th birthday. How likely is it that this is her actual age? What clues in the narrative support your view?

3. What is the role of deception in the protagonist's life? How does deception disable her? Who withholds facts from her and why?

4. How does the story's epigraph foreshadow the protagonist's destiny?

5. What is the significance of books and libraries in the story? How does literature illuminate the protagonist's path? How does literacy (or illiteracy) inform the characters' worldviews and places in society?

6. The author claims to have extracted the narrative from an advanced technological artifact. How does the message of the holographic cube portend humanity's destiny? Can you name any other novels or true stories that were influenced by mysterious discoveries?

7. What is revealed to Gen about the world? About her family? About herself?

8. Many stories are influenced by ancient myths and folklore whose foundations lie in even older tales. Which mythologies do you recognize in this narrative?

9. The story's world reflects challenges from the environment. How do these influence the protagonist's personal journey?

10. The world of the story seemed to have experienced a catastrophe that was initiated by a convergence of events. What political and societal events precipitated them? What indicators point to this world as post-apocalyptic?

11. Several factors (environmental, social, political) appear to have contributed to an endemic disease - can you think of similar events in present society?

12. How is the writing style in *BAMBOO* more like poetry than narrative prose?

Reflections and New Findings

So that was the end of the story, it seemed. Our empathy for Gen, our affection for her, had grown with the painstaking transcription of her story into the form you now hold in your hands. She remains someone we'd want to know, and by the time we said our goodbyes, most all of the team secretly felt quite parental toward her. And I wondered what had become of Gen and the SoBes. We wished that life had resolved more amicably for Gen; that she had found the acceptance and love she craved; that her world had not gone to rubble.

Perhaps that wish sparked doubt in my mind whether, in our technocratic approach, we had faithfully and fully interpreted the text. Had the cube given us all that it could? And if we had been more cautious at the outset, could we have preserved more of the quantum cloud that bore the echoes of this girl's pain and anguish and perseverance in a world hostile to her very being? With the fermionic degradation of the holographic cube, the answer seemed hopelessly lost.

In the months that followed, I received a flood of items purported by their senders to be additional media of the same ilk as our holographic cube. To a one, they proved to be inert contemporary facsimiles of the original — some cleverly constructed, others merely plastic cubes containing 3-D links to valueless non-fungible tokens. I appreciated the ebullient marketing, as I myself had indulged in a bit of the same for this project. Nevertheless, I lost hope of encountering any new writings.

It was then that one of our team, who had returned to employment at a private R&D company, approached me with some news. He had by chance hit upon a new method of recovering the remaining sublimates. He proposed we re-expose a chamber we thought empty, where once resided the first exudates from the cube. Upon my accord, there was introduced a solid that superconducted at room temperature. As a bugle at reveille summons troops to rouse, a new condensate, rich with data, emerged literally from the ether. It had been there all along, simply out of phase with our comfortable continuum. We set out to recover what was expected to be a handful of lost sectors. To our delight, we had unlocked an entirely new volume – a continuing narrative that casts light on the questions that remain. We are evaluating now, and hope to have the material transcribed and collated within the next year. Our grant provided the means for the initial discovery and its translation. The team is in need of funding for this next stage, and details of the progress we've made and our crowdfunding initiative can be discovered on my web site, ClarkHilton.com. We thank our patrons and contributors and hope to have the next volume of Gen's epic story on bookstore shelves before too long.

More from Books Illuminated

If you've enjoyed this book, we hope you'll tell others, or write a review! We also invite you to subscribe to our newsletter to learn about *new releases* and join our affiliate program (where you earn a commission of sales you recommend) at BooksIlluminated.com.

Here are more books you'll enjoy from Books Illuminated, available from BooksIlluminated.com and wherever you buy books.

"2 Weeks 2 Utopia" by Felicia Fairhope

"The Odd Ms. Bodkins and the Big Crunch" by Brother Goose

The upcoming sequel to "BAMBOO" by Clark Hilton

Memorabilia & Collectibles

You can make the exclusive artwork featured in this novel yours on clothes, drinkware, framed art, and home goods. Black and white fine art ink originals by Csaba X. Kasik inspired by design concepts from the author, capturing themes and quotes from the story. Visit ClarkHilton.com/merch.

Qui librum de hac Bibliotheca surripit, mutet Serpentem in manu sua et dilaniet. Percutiatur Paralysi et omnibus membris eius uredine.

Languet in dolore, clamans ad Misericordiam, et non sit securus agoniae suae, donec defluat in dissolutionem. Vermes libri

rodant viscera sua in signo verme qui non moritur, et cum demum ad ultimum supplicium ierit, eum flamma inferni in aeternum et in aeternum consumat.

=Bibliothecarius Veteris Almanack, scriptum est iocus Anno Domini millesimo nongentesimo nono*

* For him that stealeth a Book from this Library, let it change to a Serpent in his hand and rend him. Let him be struck with Palsy, and all his Members blasted. Let him languish in Pain, crying aloud for Mercy and let there be no surcease to his Agony till he sink to Dissolution. Let Book-worms gnaw his Entrails in token of the Worm that dieth not, and when at last he goeth to his final Punishment let the Flames of Hell consume him for ever and aye.- The Old Librarian's Almanac 1774, written in jest, copyright 1909